THE SHUTTLE BROKE CLEAR . . .

. . . of the dust and hurtled into shockingly transparent air. Chekov's instincts had been right—they were only seconds away from contact with the surface.

Dust-swarmed inertial dampers struggled against the violent shifts in mass, but couldn't entirely save them from the impact. It came with a weird sluggishness, as if the ground had somehow oozed around their shields instead of crashing into them. Then silvery curtains of water geysered up over the windshield, and all view of this world was drowned. . . .

STAR TREK®

NEW EARTH

BOOK THREE OF SIX
ROUGH TRAILS

L.A. GRAF

NEW EARTH CONCEPT BY DIANE CAREY AND JOHN ORDOVER

POCKET BOOKS

New York London Toronto Sydney Singapore Belle Terre

This book is a work of fiction. Names, characters, places and incidents are products of the author's imagination or are used fictitiously. Any resemblance to actual events or locales or persons, living or dead, is entirely coincidental.

An *Original* Publication of POCKET BOOKS

POCKET BOOKS, a division of Simon & Schuster Inc.
1230 Avenue of the Americas, New York, NY 10020

ISBN: 0-671-03600-9

First Pocket Books printing July 2000

10 9 8 7 6 5 4 3 2 1

Printed in the U.S.A.

ROUGH TRAILS

Chapter One

"SHE'S AWAY!"

Without benefit of an antigrav, the crate tipped gracelessly over the lip of the shuttle's hatch and fell free. Chekov leaned to the extent of his safety cable and watched the container tumble toward the ocean of airborne dust below, wondering how much chance they had of it landing anywhere near the drop target. The high-pitched shriek of its sonic beacon was swallowed up so quickly by the howl of Llano Verde's winds that he suspected if it went too far astray, it would never be found again.

Behind him, Plottel's voice, muffled by a filtration mask already several wearings too old, intoned blandly, ". . . and three and two and one . . ."

The crate's parachute ripped into existence with a *whhuf!* Chekov could imagine but couldn't actually hear over the roar of the dust storm outside. Fluorescent orange billowed into violent bloom, snapping the crate out of reach of the maelstrom only briefly before relaxing back into its descent. Almost immediately, wind tipped the parachute sideways and began dragging the crate sharply lateral of its original drop path. Storm-blown dust and sand swarmed the crate, the lines, the 'chute like famished ants. Once the air sealed behind the drop, Chekov couldn't even tell where the supplies had torn their way through. Swallowed by this wounded and angry planet, just like the sonic beacon. Just like everything else.

"Heads up, C.C."

Kevin Baldwin didn't have to give a jerk on Chekov's safety line to get his attention, but he did it anyway. The sudden assault on Chekov's balance while hovering ten klicks above Belle Terre's surface launched his heart up into his throat. He grabbed at the sides of the hatch with both hands, but clenched his teeth before gasping aloud. That instinct let him preserve at least a modicum of dignity. Backing calmly away from the opening, he tried hard to ignore Baldwin's laughter as he disconnected the lifeline and shouldered out of its harness.

The hatch rolled shut with a grinding squeal that made Chekov's teeth hurt. Dust in the mechanism, sliding between the parts. Dust in everything—the air, the floor, his hair, his clothes. When Reddy, the shuttle's pilot, had promised they'd be above the ceiling of the dust storms, Chekov had assumed that meant they'd be flying in clear air. Instead, it meant Reddy kept the shuttle just high enough to avoid clogging the intakes on the atmospheric engines; Chekov, Baldwin, and Plottel could stand in the open hatch under the protection of goggles and filtration masks, but didn't have to wear the kevlar bodysuits required by stormgoers on the surface. Not much of a trade-off, considering he'd still have to buy a new set of clothes the minute he set foot in Eau Claire. Or, at least, he would if he wanted Uhura to be seen with him in public.

Swiping uselessly at the front of his trousers, Chekov finally settled for patting himself down to dislodge the uppermost layers of grime. "I never thought I'd hear myself say this." He stepped sideways out of his own dust cloud. "But there's too much olivium on this planet."

Plottel and Baldwin shucked their breath masks before the light above the hatch had even cycled from red to green. "Maybe." Plottel didn't smile as he crossed the cargo shuttle's deck to dig a battered canteen out of a locker. "But if it weren't for all that olivium, Starfleet wouldn't have stuck around, and we'd be deprived of the pleasure of your company on this little flight."

Chekov watched him fill his mouth with water, rinse and spit into a disposal pan, then pass the canteen on to Baldwin. "And if Starfleet weren't here, there'd be no one in-system with rations to spare for your emergency supply drops."

"If Starfleet weren't here—" Baldwin discharged a mouthful of water at Chekov's feet, creating an anemic slurry of mud, dust, and olivium. "—we wouldn't be in this mess to begin with."

Chekov nodded once, lips pursed, then went back to beating the planet out of his clothes.

This was an exchange they'd had, in various permutations, at least twenty times since the cargo shuttle kicked off from the orbital platform above Belle Terre. Chekov had given up pointing out that, while Starfleet's actions might have directly led to the gamma-ray burst that most everyone called the Burn, it was only because of Starfleet that the planet still existed at all. Allowing the Burn had actually been the best in a very short list of options. While it all but defoliated most of a hemisphere, the colonists had been ferried out of harm's way. When house-sized segments of Belle Terre's largest satellite slammed into the face of her smallest continent, there was no one there to kill, no homesteads to lay waste. The combined Starfleet and colony ships, led by the *Enterprise,* had salvaged half a planet and an entire colony from otherwise certain destruction.

And the colonists had yet to forgive them.

From the moment they left Earth's gravity well, the Belle Terre colonists had bristled with fierce independence. They made their own rules, picked their own battles, all but spat upon Starfleet's offers of help and personnel—even when that help saved them from the numerous disasters that had plagued the expedition practically from the word go. Even now, when extended dust storms threatened the small continent of Llano Verde with starvation, the *Enterprise*'s sacrifice of its own rations to assemble relief supply drops was accepted with palpable resentment. The fledgling colony had nothing to spare for its own members, but the *Enterprise*'s continued humanitarian support was interpreted as an implied criticism of Belle Terre's ability to take care of itself.

This flight to the surface was no different. The volume of olivium dust laced through Llano Verde's soil after the Quake Moon impacts made transporter travel there impossible, and Captain Kirk had issued a moratorium on Starfleet personnel hitching free rides on civilian-operated shuttles. Which put Chekov in a bit of a bind. He'd been left on the orbital platform three weeks ago when the *Enterprise* set out to patrol for pirate traffic, keep an eye out for the Kauld—aliens who had attacked the expedition—and search for the missing vessel *Rattlesnake.* Chekov was officially cut loose, on leave, grounded. Sometime in the next two or three months, the light courier *City of Pittsburgh* was due at Belle Terre to pick up Chekov, John Kyle, and two other *Enterprise* crewmen for reassignment to the newly commissioned science vessel *Reliant.* Until *City of Pittsburgh* arrived, Chekov, Kyle, and the others were expected to rest, relax, and comport themselves in a manner that wouldn't aggravate the Belle Terrans any more than was inevitable. In general, this translated into long stretches of profound boredom as far away from the colonists as possible. Chekov spent the time trying to get used to seeing himself with executive officer's bars on his shoulder and answering to the title "lieutenant commander." He hadn't felt so small and ill suited to a uniform since being named *Enterprise*'s chief of security two years before.

Which was why he was once again violating Kirk's prohibition to join Sulu and Uhura for dinner in Eau Claire, the continental capital of Llano Verde. The two had been stationed there with Montgomery Scott and Janice Rand for several weeks, cut off from chatty communiqués by Gamma Night and olivium-contaminated dust, not to mention swamped with work and colonial frustrations. Long months away from shipping out to his new assignment, Chekov was lonely, insecure, and painfully bored. Part of him feared he'd never make the kind of lifelong friends on the *Reliant* that he had on the *Enterprise;* another part half-hoped their reunions would somehow prove him too indispensable to let go. He would be allowed to serve under Kirk on board the *Enterprise* forever.

In reality, he knew all he would get out of the trip was a good dinner and a few precious hours of socializing before he returned to his restless and unrelaxed days on the orbital platform.

Chekov had made an end run around Kirk's moratorium by refusing to be shuttled surfaceward like so much cargo. He knew about the weekly runs to airdrop emergency supplies across Llano Verde. Showing up in the bay just before Orbital Shuttle Six kicked off, he offered to help the civilian laborers pitch the crates toward their assigned drop points in exchange for a shuttle ride down to Eau Claire. It wasn't just a chance to "pay" for passage, it was also a chance to be useful, sweat off some of his frustrations, and leave a positive impression on the colonials. Or so he'd thought. Vijay Reddy, the pilot, suggested that Chekov leave the heavy lifting to the laborers and ride up front with him. Not about to be coddled out of honestly paying his way, Chekov insisted on remaining in back to work alongside Baldwin and Plottel. Since neither of the laborers objected, Chekov assumed they were perfectly happy to have an extra set of hands.

By an hour into the flight, he'd figured out where he really stood. When he wasn't dragging a crate—without help—forward from the cargo hold, he was supposed to either lend his back to shoving the crates through the airlock, or sit out of the way on one of the armless benches welded into the bulkhead. His comments weren't welcome, and neither was his presence. They spoke to him only when forced to, and made no effort to censor their bitterness toward Starfleet when they talked between themselves. For his own part,

Chekov swallowed most of the angry comments that sprang to mind. Another hour or so and they'd be on the surface. He would part ways with them in Eau Claire, and contemplate Kirk's wisdom in recognizing from the outset that the colonists needed as much physical and emotional space as Starfleet could give them.

A little communications panel high on the bulkhead chirruped with incongruous cheer. Unlike communicators or even crystal-based radios, intercom systems based on hardwire connections still functioned perfectly despite all the olivium radiation Belle Terre could throw out. The wall speaker, however, buzzed from the weight of the dust coating its tympanum. "Dave, how many crates have we got left back there?"

Plottel touched the container on which he sat as though silently acknowledging it in his count, then craned his neck to check the deck behind him. "Three up front, another twelve in the hold."

"And who's scheduled to get most of them?"

Baldwin set down the canteen and reached out to steady the cargo manifest dangling near the hatch door, squinting at its dust-fuzzed display panel. "Four go to Desert Station. Everyone else gets two or three."

"Okay." Reddy paused, caught up in some piloting duty, and Chekov felt the subliminal shift in mass that meant they'd changed heading without slowing down. "Hold out one from the Desert Station drop. They'll have to make do with three."

"Sedlak isn't gonna like us changing the manifest like that," Baldwin warned.

Invoking the continental governor's name injected a startling level of annoyance into Reddy's voice. "Sedlak isn't here. We've got an extra drop on the list for the northeast side of Bull's Eye—a group of herders who got stranded by the storm."

"What the hell were they doing out on a day like this?" But Plottel was already scrubbing at his goggles to clear them, getting set for another round of labor.

"They went out three days ago, before the dust got so bad. The ranch they're attached to didn't get word down to Eau Claire until yesterday, and the spaceport wasn't able to punch through the dust to the orbital platform until just now. Otherwise, we could've just put additional shipments aboard." The speaker snapped, nearly drowning out Reddy's grumbling sigh. "Now we're going to have to shortchange somebody. It might as well be Desert Station."

Ironically, if a Starfleet officer had made the same suggestion, there would have followed ten minutes of defensive resistance before any action could occur. As it was, Baldwin and Plottel started untangling their safety harnesses while Chekov was still stealing a single swallow of water from Baldwin's abandoned canteen.

"Is there any way to contact Eau Claire?" Chekov asked as he scooped his own harness up off the filthy deck. He'd given Uhura the original arrival time, and didn't want to leave her pacing the spaceport, wondering what had become of him.

"Don't worry about Eau Claire—they're used to this." Plottel was either trying to reassure him, or head off any fretting before it began. "The spaceport won't even consider us late until we're three hours past our scheduled ETA."

Chekov repressed a sigh. "It wasn't the spaceport I was worried about," he said, but without much expectation of being listened to. "Is there any way to contact anyone on the planet?"

" 'Fraid not," Baldwin said, wrenching the hatch open on the sea of roiling dust outside. "Nothing gets through that dust out there, not unless it's falling through." His grin was wide enough to see around the edge of his dust mask as he gestured toward the open door. "Feel free to take the message down yourself, C.C., if you want to. We won't try to stop you."

And they might even help me on my way, Chekov thought, remembering Baldwin's previous push. He reached for the nearest lifeline and clipped it on a little more quickly than dignity allowed. Even the howl of Belle Terre's dust storm wasn't loud enough to drown out the resulting shout of mocking laughter.

"Uhura to Sulu. Come in, Sulu."

Uhura had said the phrase so often over the past five weeks that by now the words slid out of her mouth without the slightest effort—or attention—on her part. She pressed the correct transmission key on her experimental communications panel, paused for the appropriate time afterward to allow a reply to come through, but no longer really listened for an answer to her call because no answer had ever come. "Auditory feedback fatigue" had been the official term for it back at Starfleet Academy. Out here, on the nebulous fringes of known space, people just called it communications burnout. It was a condition most often seen in the crew of disabled ships who spent so long listening for an answer to their distress calls that they missed hearing it when it actually came.

"Uhura to Sulu. Come in, Sulu."

Uhura had recognized the syndrome in herself about two weeks ago and been horrified. Her entire career in Starfleet was based on her ability to listen. She knew she had a keener ear than many other communications officers, and she prided herself on her ability to thread out a signal buried in electromagnetic noise, or hear the barest scratch of a message through the resounding silence of subspace. Finding herself adrift in a numb haze of not listening, not even sure how many hours she had spent repeating the same six words without paying attention to them, had shaken her professional confidence right down to the bone. Could something as simple as futility really overcome all those years of training and experience?

"Uhura to Sulu." She fiddled with the gain on the transmitter to keep herself alert, watching the transmission histogram on her monitor spike into alarmed red then fade back to green as the computer compensated for the adjustment she'd made. The reception histogram, which was supposed to display the frequencies of Sulu's response to her hail, remained a dull, flat-lined gray, just as it had since the first day she started hailing him.

A burst of irritation momentarily clawed a hole through Uhura's boredom. There was absolutely no reason this experimental communications system shouldn't be working. The pall of olivium-contaminated dust that hung over the island subcontinent of Llano Verde during its long, dry winter was known to attenuate every known kind of subspace and electromagnetic transmission. But the dust had created a dense surface layer in the planet's stratified troposphere, permanently trapped beneath cleaner and colder air above it. The knife-sharp boundary between those air masses should have been able to amplify and reflect back any signal that managed to reach it—every computer model and Starfleet expert Uhura had consulted agreed on that. So while Janice Rand worked on augmenting the city's short-range communications using olivium's natural crystal resonance, Uhura had designed a long-distance communications system that relied simply on punching a strong signal up to the top of the dust layer and letting nature take care of the rest. All she had to do—in theory—was calibrate the system by noting which electromagnetic frequencies created the best reflections at different points on the subcontinent. With computers varying her output signal nanosecond by nanosecond as she spoke, and a special receiver carried in the experimental shuttle Scotty had designed and Sulu was test-flying around Llano Verde, the whole project should have taken about two days to complete.

In theory.

"Uhura to Sulu. Come in, Sulu."

"Commander Sulu's flight plan said he was going all the way to Mudlump today, down on the south coast," a familiar voice said from right behind her. "Could he really answer you from there even if he heard you?"

Uhura sighed and turned to face the stoop-shouldered man behind her. His green-hazel eyes were puffy, his thinning reddish hair badly needed a trim, and his colony uniform was rumpled and coffee-stained. He looked exactly like what he was: not a rugged settler, but one of Belle Terre's too few and too overworked technical experts, hired on long-term contracts to help the colony through its initial growing pains. Despite her own tribulations, Uhura managed to summon up a sympathetic smile. No one could fault the colony's initial strategic plan for not taking a planetary catastrophe like the Burn into account, but it didn't make life easier for continental government employees like Chief Technical Officer Neil Bartels.

"The transmitter I sent with him is automatically programed to reply on whatever frequency it just received." She accepted the steaming mug he held out for her, grateful for the bracing combination of Belle Terre spices and artificial caffeine concentrate. After several weeks of conferring over technical specifications and borrowing circuit-testing equipment, they'd fallen into the habit of sharing a cup of afternoon tea before the last and dullest stretch of the day. Uhura privately suspected that Bartels would have been even happier to spend his break discussing his numerous technical problems with Montgomery Scott, but the chief engineer had spent the last few weeks out at the spaceport as Sulu ran his shuttle through its paces. "Any reply from it should get bounced and amplified by the atmospheric boundary layer exactly the same way mine did on the way to him. That means it will arrive right back here."

Bartels lifted an eyebrow at her over his steaming mug of tea. "Even if his Bean is jumping really fast at the time?"

It was a measure of Uhura's stress level that the nickname the irreverent Llano Verde colonists had given Sulu and Scotty's antigravity vertical flight vessel could no longer spark even a flicker of amusement. "That's why I'm using a range of simulcast frequencies," she said, rubbing at the frown lines that seemed to have engraved themselves permanently into her forehead. "I tried to stuff in as much bandwidth as the system could handle without getting any negative interference on the carrier wave. I'm not sure it's really enough to compensate for Sulu's movement over an extended broadcast, but if he lets me reply every so often—"

"Assuming he ever hears you."

Uhura winced. The disadvantage of chatting with fellow technical specialists was their clear-eyed grasp of the crux of a problem. She knew exactly how to extrapolate reflectance angles to all parts of the subcontinent once she had a minimum set of established values, and she'd even figured out how to correct the system for daily meteorological variation of the boundary layer. But she still had no answer for the fundamental question of why Sulu had never, not even once, heard any of her experimental hails.

"Have you talked to the weather people lately?" she asked. It wasn't an attempt to change the subject, although Bartels's puzzled look told her he hadn't followed her train of thought. Llano Verde had gotten its name from its previously lush semitropical climate. At some point, those Burn-disrupted rains were going to return, washing the olivium dust out of the atmosphere for a while and making the need for Uhura and Rand's new communications systems much less urgent. "When are they predicting the dust season will end?"

The technical officer sighed and drained the rest of his tea. "Depends on who you ask," he said. "The computer modelers think we'll get spring monsoons in the next month or two, but the hydrologists keep saying they don't have the field data to support it." He ran a hand along the top of her console, brushing off dust and shaking his head ruefully. "I'm not sure how rumors spread so fast through the Outland without any real communications system, but I've already got half the continent begging me for flood-control dams while the other half is yelling for irrigation channels."

Uhura's tea suddenly tasted acrid on her tongue, as if her taste buds had just noticed how foreign those native spices were. She swallowed the last of it with difficulty. "I'm sorry. I know I should have had this system up and running for you weeks ago—"

"Hey." Bartels reached out to pat her arm in a half-gentle, half-awkward way that struck Uhura as oddly familiar. It took her a moment to realize that it was the same inept manner in which Chief Engineer Scott dealt with the human aspects of his job. "I wasn't blaming *you,* Commander. We weren't the ones who called up Starfleet and demanded an overnight fix for Llano Verde's transportation and communications systems. Governor Sedlak tried to tell Pardonnet that even Starfleet technology couldn't solve the mess the Quake Moon made of this continent, but he just wouldn't listen. And no one else has made any more progress than you—"

Uhura shook her head in disagreement. "Mr. Scott and Commander Sulu have the latest version of the Bean running almost full-time. All they have to do now is work out a navigation system that doesn't depend on making constant contact with the orbital platform—"

"Just like all you have to do is find the right frequency to bounce off that dust layer. It's like they say in the Outland—you've got to swallow a whole lot of dust before there's room in your throat for any water."

Uhura smiled at the colony technical officer, appreciative of both his support and the unique way he had phrased it. "I've never heard that saying before."

Bartels snorted. "That's because you don't have Outlanders tracking radioactive dirt into your office two or three times a day to tell you exactly how they think you should be doing your job." He swept up the empty mugs with a clatter, as if the mere thought of his constituents had flogged him back to work. "Come to think of it, don't bother to get that system of yours working any time soon," he advised her as he left. "I hate to think how many more irate citizens I'd hear from if they could just pick up a comm and call their complaints in."

When he first felt the deck jolt beneath him, Chekov was struggling to back his way out of the cargo hold while towing five hundred kilos of malfunctioning grav-sled. It strained to keep its belly even ten centimeters above the decking, and every irregularity reached up to trip it, knocking it off course and killing its momentum. He'd cursed and kicked his way through moving a dozen other crates in exactly the same way. While his patience decreased with every repetition of the battle, he wasn't about to complain. So when the deck thumped against the soles of his feet and made him stumble, Chekov wrote it off to the grav-sled bottoming out yet again, or Plottel and Baldwin indelicately rolling one of the crates in the forward compartment.

Then his sense of balance attenuated in a moment of free fall, and the liberated grav-sled slewed sideways like a drunken bear. Whatever official safety procedures he'd once learned for handling grav-sleds flashed out of existence as he danced aside to avoid being crushed against the remaining crates in the hold. When full weight returned an instant later, Chekov was already halfway up one of the access ladders with his feet pulled up out of the way. The sled slammed back down to the deck, and the wall of crates it had bumbled against teetered but refused to fall.

Plottel and Baldwin were nowhere to be seen in the forward hold. The hatch to the outside whistled dolefully, adding more dust to the mosaic already filling the shuttle floor. A flash of what he at first took to be ochre landscape rolled into view through the opening, followed by an equally dismal patch of khaki sky. Chekov hadn't thought they were close enough to the surface to see beneath the pervasive clouds. Then he realized it wasn't ground he saw but the eerily sharp demarcation between the "clear" airspace of safe shuttle passage and the roil of Llano Verde's dust storm. There was something odd about the orientation of that boundary, something that clashed with Chekov's own internal sense of balance. Either the edge of the dust storm had become vertical rather than horizontal, he thought, or Reddy was turning the shuttle in a banking turn so tight that centrifugal force had overcome the usual pull of gravity.

Keying the airlock closed on the jarring view, Chekov went forward to look for the rest of the crew in the cockpit.

"I tell you, there was nobody." Plottel's filtration mask hung from one hand while he combed the fingers of the other through his dust-caked hair. "We should have been right on top of them, and I couldn't see a soul."

Nodding in terse reassurance, Reddy waved everyone away from the back of his seat as he made delicate adjustments to the board. "Give me a minute to see if I can get back to our original coordinates."

Chekov leaned between Plottel and Baldwin, stealing a glance at the controls, then up at the viewscreen. It looked as if the shuttle was making a tight circle around their drop coordinates, but he could see that Reddy was actually keeping his helm at dead center. He wondered if they'd gotten caught up in some freakish dust-storm squall. "What's going on?"

"They're dead."

Plottel cuffed Baldwin across the top of his head. "Nobody's dead." But his own voice was too angry, his eyes too frightened to carry much conviction.

"What happened?" Chekov asked again, a bit more sternly this time.

No sharp comments about meddling Starfleet officers now. Reddy leaned aside slightly to open up Chekov's view of the panel, his hands never ceasing their rapid play on the controls. "The coordinates for those stranded herders put us inside the Bull's Eye crater, not on the outside rim like I thought. Most of the crater interior is water. I didn't want to waste the drop by putting the cargo in the lake . . ." His voice trailed off, and the shuttle gave another convulsive buck.

"So you went below the dust to get a visual on the ground?" Chekov asked incredulously.

"Yes." Reddy never took his eyes off the viewscreen. Chekov wasn't sure why, since dust now skated across it in waves so sheer and fast, they might have been plunging through a sea of gauzy curtains. He couldn't believe the pilot had really thought they'd have a chance of seeing people on the ground in this mess. "There was a clearing in the dust. I thought it looked big enough—"

"—for us to fly in and out of," Chekov finished. "But it wasn't."

"No," Reddy admitted. "And now we have to find it again."

Chekov frowned and helped himself to the copilot's

chair, trying to make sense of the readings flickering across that side of the control panel. The altitude sensor put them at five thousand meters up, while the ground detector insisted they were within skimming distance of the surface. One velocity indicator had them flying at a steady two hundred kilometers an hour, while its backup flashed the warning for stalling speed. Chekov glanced across at Reddy, his frown deepening.

"Olivium contamination," the pilot said before he could ask. "Bull's Eye is one of the Quake Moon's impact craters. Radiation levels are a thousand times greater there than on the rest of the planet."

Chekov heard Baldwin snort from behind his seat. "Yeah, that nuclear stuff will only kill you. It's the subspace crap that messes up the instruments."

"So the only way to relocate your clearing is by dead reckoning?" Chekov glanced up at the forward screen, set to full transparency now that external visual sensors were rendered useless by the olivium. It didn't make much difference. "We need to pull above the ceiling of the storm."

"What we need is to make sure those lost herders get their supplies!" Plottel fisted one hand on the back of Reddy's chair. "They're counting on us to keep them alive!"

Chekov unleashed all his frustration with the colonists in a single fierce glare. "We need to pull up! A downed shuttle and crew of dead people won't help those herders, or anyone else on this planet."

"We can't."

Chekov shot a startled look at Reddy. "What?"

The pilot's dark face was stiff with restrained panic. "We can't pull up. We're losing thrust."

Swallowing the sour taste of dread in his mouth,

Chekov stretched in front of Reddy to punch at the blast controls for the atmospheric engines. The gut-sinking surge in acceleration that should have followed the thruster fire never came. Instead, coarse juddering slammed through the shuttle's frame, and Chekov's adrenaline spiked along with the temperature gauge before he could slap off the engines.

"The intakes are clogged." He searched the console for some encouraging reading with growing alarm. All he saw was olivium-sparked incoherence. "Can we recalibrate our sensors?"

Reddy forced a quick reboot through the main shuttle computer, then shook his head stiffly. He looked almost too tense to breathe.

Chekov dug behind himself for the seat restraint, settling back to belt in. "We have to slow our descent." He didn't even turn to look back at Plottel and Baldwin. "Get back and strap down."

"Using what?" Baldwin wanted to know. He sounded near to tears.

Plottel made a calming little noise, and Chekov heard him tug the other man toward the cockpit doorway. "We've got the safety harnesses," Plottel said evenly. "Come on, Kev."

They passed out of hearing, and just that quickly out of Chekov's thoughts. The faint spasm of guilt following his silent dismissal didn't last long—his years in Starfleet had taught him not to tangle up his concentration with things outside his control. That meant Plottel and Baldwin, Sulu and Uhura, any chance of a career on board the still-distant *Reliant*—

Wind caromed against the shuttle with a sound like wild banshees. Chekov gripped the edge of the console, his stomach lurching up into his throat. "Inertial dampers are failing." It wasn't a guess.

"Everything's failing." Reddy fought to bring their nose up, might have been succeeding, all his efforts drowned in the pounding of wind and sand. "No attitude thrusters, no antigrav backup—"

Of course not. Not on a shuttle this battered by countless trips down through the dust storms of Belle Terre. Chekov tried again to boot up the sensor displays on the copilot's console, blowing a glitter of accumulated dust off the controls and wishing cargo shuttles had anything resembling a survivable glide ratio. The front windshield writhed with sun-stained browns and reds. Hints of horizon, flashes of what might be water. Not sure what inspired his sudden urgent certainty, Chekov reached over to grab Reddy's sleeve. "Raise shields."

The pilot spared him a single sideways glance. "We're not a starship. The only thing these shields are good for—"

"Raise shields!" Instinct, faster than thought. Without waiting for Reddy's understanding, he pushed the shield generator to maximum. They'd been falling stern-first, dragged down by the weight of engines and emergency supplies. Now their rear kicked upward, hard enough to throw them both forward into the dual panel, fast enough to make the shuttle echo with the groan of metal fatigue.

With an abruptness that made his gut clench, the shuttle broke clear of the dust and hurtled into shockingly transparent air. Chekov didn't have time to wonder if this was the same clearing that had first lured Reddy to the surface, because their trajectory was taking them straight down into it. And at the bottom, far too close, he saw the glitter of raw, reflected sunlight. His instincts had been right—they were only seconds away from contact with the surface.

Dust-swarmed inertial dampers struggled against the violent shifts in mass, but couldn't entirely save them from the impact. It came with a weird sluggishness, as if the ground had somehow oozed around their shields instead of crashing into them. Then silvery curtains of water geysered up over the windshield, and all view of this world was drowned.

Chapter Two

EVERY NEW WORLD is a new chance to learn. Uhura had first heard those words back at the Academy, from a venerable xenosociology professor who'd repeated them so often that mischievous cadets would mouth the words along with him when he wasn't looking. At the time, Uhura had thought it was a hackneyed teacher's phrase, perhaps a way to justify a life spent analyzing other people's field studies. But after she'd graduated, she'd found herself repeating the old xenosociologist's motto a surprising number of times. By now, more than ten years into her career as a Starfleet officer, it had become the lens through which she viewed every world she visited, whether safe or terrifying, fascinating or dull. When you were someplace no human had gone before, you couldn't help but learn something . . . and you couldn't ever consider an instant of your life wasted, even if you were repeating the same six words over and over for eight hours a day.

"Uhura to Sulu. Come in, Sulu."

Belle Terre was especially fascinating to Uhura, because it was a world just on the verge of becoming new, taking the first small steps that would allow the human race to blossom into yet another of the many unique cultures that had formed on colony worlds throughout the Alpha Quadrant. And of all the settlements on Belle Terre, from the carefully planned cities to the newly cleared pastures and windswept coasts, the Burned island continent of Llano Verde provided the most scope for studying human adaptation and survival. The settlers who came here had chosen to stake their claims in this most devastated sector of the colony. They were feisty, stubborn, and strong-willed, and as a result they had been especially swift to develop their own regional culture.

Idiomatic sayings and mocking nicknames for places, people, and things had sprouted up like weeds through the dust and the mud. Millefiore turned into Miles from Nowhere. Desert Station became Desperation. Ludlum dwindled ignominiously into Mudlump. The disrupted rivers and lakes created by the Burn had been given names like Bull's Eye, Useless Loop, and Splat. Even the continental capital of Eau Claire had been rechristened Big Muddy by its residents when tons of windblown dust made the waters of its central river dense and murky rather than clear. Outlanders referred to the capital by even less respectful nicknames, such as Au Contraire, We Don't Care, and So Unfair.

"Uhura to Sulu. Come in, Sulu."

The only good thing about communications burnout was that it gave Uhura plenty of time to mull over her observations of Llano Verde. One thing she had recently decided was that the level of citizen dissatisfaction in this part of Belle Terre seemed unusually high. Neil Bartels had enough sense of humor left to joke about it, but according to Sulu, the hostility of Outland settlers to their own continental government was growing stronger all the time. Some of that might be a reaction to the stress of living in conditions so hostile to human life, but it still didn't bode well for the long-term health of this fledgling democracy.

It was a measure of Sulu's concern, Uhura thought, that he had begun pressuring Scotty to declare their experimental transport vessel ready for service, despite its makeshift navigation system, so he could begin actually helping stranded colonists he saw on his flights, instead of just reporting them to the colony's overworked Emergency Services Division. Of course, if Captain Kirk couldn't convince Montgomery Scott to hurry in the middle of a pitched battle with Klingons, there wasn't much chance of Sulu speeding him up just because of a little radioactive dust and colonial unrest. The chief engineer insisted on making sure the Bean's antigrav engines really were completely dustproof, and that it had at least a crude semblance of its own internal navigations system, so it didn't have to depend on leaping up above the dust layer to find out where it was. Of course, that would have been easier for Scotty to do if Uhura had managed to get her signal reflectance system working a few weeks ago. . . .

"Uhura to Sulu," she said, her voice suddenly sharpened by frustration. "Come in, Sulu."

"Sulu here."

Uhura stared at her control board in sheer astonishment, barely able to believe she was really hearing that faded wisp of reply, even though she could see the tiny bluish tinge on the reception histogram. After a moment, she shook herself out of her daze of surprise, aware that she was acting exactly like those stranded crewmen whose disbelief kept them from replying to the first signs of rescue. Her fingers flew across the panel, locating the frequency that had come back most strongly on Sulu's side of the board and punching up its strength for her next transmission.

"Uhura to Sulu. Please give me your location and altitude."

This time, the pilot's response wasn't quite as faint, but its histogram told Uhura it still wasn't coming in as clearly as it should have. She tried adjusting the sensitivity of her receptors, but the computer had already tuned them to maximum levels. "I'm on the ground," Sulu said. "At the spaceport."

Uhura's first reaction was pure annoyance. After five weeks of system failure, the last thing she was in the mood for was Sulu's mischievous sense of humor at the end of a long day. But then she realized the pilot wasn't calling her on the normal hardwired landlines used for communications throughout the city. He was, for the very first time, successfully using the signal reflectance system installed in his experimental shuttle.

"How's your reception of my signal?"

"Lousy," Sulu said. "That dust-layer amplification thing doesn't seem to be working too well."

"No." Uhura sighed. The spaceport was where her signal transmission tower was located. Sulu should have had crystal-clear reception there, with a straight up-and-down vertical signal path. If her signal was barely reaching him now, no wonder she'd had so little luck contacting him in the outflung regions of Llano Verde.

"So, do I get treated to dessert tonight for having thought to check our reception at home base?" Sulu inquired cheerfully. Uhura began to reply, then caught sight of the time display on her board and frowned instead.

"What are you doing back so early?" she asked. "Did you have problems with the Bean?"

"No, it's fine." Sulu sounded amused. "I just figured I'd better quit early, or Chekov would talk you into going out to that same boring meat-and-potatoes restaurant we went to last time. Tell him it's real Belle Terre barbecue tonight, guanaco ribs with olivium sauce and all the trimmings."

"I can't do that, since he's not here." She wasn't sure whether to laugh at the absurdity of using her sophisticated communications system to discuss tonight's dinner menu, or to cry at the fact that it was probably all she *could* use it for. "He hasn't come in from the orbital platform yet."

"Yes, he has." Sulu's voice sounded as if it was fading, but Uhura didn't try to adjust the signal frequency again. She could hear the snapping sounds that meant the pilot was stripping off his flight safety gear. "The last time I popped up above the dust to check my coordinates with the orbital platform, Kyle was keeping their communications officer company. He told me Chekov's cargo flight had dropped off their screens an hour ago. Since I didn't see it at the spaceport, I figured they'd already unloaded their cargo and left again. Are you sure he's not waiting politely outside your lab for you to get finished?"

"I'll check." Uhura swung her chair around and

headed for the lab door, with an inexplicable sense of urgency nipping at her heels. There was no one out in the main hall of the technical center, but she hurried down to the entry desk and made sure the clerk hadn't let through any other Starfleet officers besides her and Rand. Then she ran back to her lab, but it was already too late. The bluish light had faded from Sulu's side of the board. The pilot had obviously not waited for her to get back before starting to make some inquiries of his own.

It was several long minutes before Uhura's landline buzzed. She grabbed it, not even bothering to identify herself. "Is he at the spaceport?"

"No, and he never was." Sulu's reply was as blunt as her question. The bridge crew of the *Enterprise* had weathered enough emergency situations to avoid wasting time with unnecessary words. "The cargo shuttle never landed here."

Uhura took a deep breath, feeling the ramifications of that statement seep ugly and cold into her bones. "Then when it dropped off the orbital platform's screens an hour ago—"

"—it was crashing," Sulu finished grimly.

Shields held the water at bay. Glossy cataracts rode the interface between energy and fluid, and the big shuttle drifted downward like a cargo cannister filled with rocks. Chekov switched atmosphere control over to manual while Reddy powered down the antimatter drive; even so, the pressurized sections of the shuttle pulsed uncomfortably hot by the time the ship bumped to rest in the mud. The shuttle groaned, then tilted distinctly starboard one more step. Too deep in the dust-churned lake for much surface light to penetrate,

Chekov couldn't tell if the water just beyond their shield barrier boiled. But he could feel the push of extra pressure against his inner ears, and heard Baldwin in the passenger compartment complain about the pain.

Like a hull breach in reverse. He wondered if the outside pressure was enough to crush the shuttle once the shields came down. They'd find out soon enough.

"How could . . ." Reddy swallowed audibly, pushing a little straighter in his chair as he stared out at the cloudy water. "How did you know we were over the water?"

Chekov's stomach had just rediscovered the fluttery void that followed adrenaline overdose. "I didn't," he admitted. "Not for sure. But if we weren't, the shields couldn't have saved us, so we didn't lose anything by trying." As it was, that shell of cohesive plasma had absorbed enough kinetic energy from their fluid impact to almost make up for failed inertial dampers. It was the only reason they weren't having this conversation in the afterlife. "See if you can raise the orbital platform on the radio. I think we're still beneath that clearing you saw in the dust." He was only a little surprised to find his hands shaking as he unhitched his seat restraint. "I'm going back to check on the others."

A splash of wet decking greeted him when he shouldered open the powerless door between cockpit and central compartment. Panic shot quick looks at airlock, frame seals, bulkheads before Chekov fully registered the split supply crate or its scattered contents. Plottel's canteen lay shattered under one corner of the ruined carton.

"Wow . . ." Baldwin looked around somewhat dazedly, but made no move to get up from the cargo floor bolt where he'd secured his harness. "That wasn't as bad as I expected."

Chekov took a deep breath to cleanse the alarm from his throat before picking his way through the mess. "Don't be so sure of that."

Plottel froze, looked up from unbuckling his harness. "What's wrong?" He didn't do as well as Chekov at hiding his apprehension. It showed clearly in the dilation of his pupils, the clenching of his hands. "Didn't you get the engines back on line?"

"We got the shields up." The seal around the cargo bay hatch was dry, and Chekov couldn't detect any temperature variance across the surface of the door. "They're keeping us pressurized, but I'm not sure for how long." He crossed to do a similar inspection on the airlock. "We're on the bottom of the lake."

Baldwin nearly choked. *"What?"*

Always the pragmatist, Plottel asked the more cogent—and answerable—question. "How deep?"

Chekov was forced to shrug as he turned to lean back against the airlock frame. "There's no way to tell. The bottom." He shrugged again, frustration growing. "I don't know where we went in."

"What do you mean on the bottom?" Baldwin's tie-off slammed taut when he tried to scramble indignantly upright. "How does a shuttle end up on the bottom of a lake?"

"It crashes, Mr. Baldwin." Chekov snapped him a glare, at the end of his patience with colonial ignorance and self-involvement. "It goes too low into olivium-contaminated dust, and it crashes in the middle of nowhere, where God himself will be lucky to find us." He pushed off from the bulkhead and stalked across to the shuttle's pathetically small equipment locker. "That's how."

Silence followed him for the first few steps. Then

Plottel's voice volunteered to his back, "Bull's Eye crater is about a hundred meters at its deepest point. I—" Hesitation filled with the sound of a safety harness clattering to the floor. "Do you think we went down that far?"

"If we did," Reddy answered from the cockpit doorway, "we're looking at an external pressure of about one hundred kilopascals." He addressed his information toward Chekov, tacitly accepting the command chain that was already forming. "Not enough to kill you in principle, but way more than you want to take on without some kind of diving gear."

"No luck contacting the surface?" It wasn't really a question.

"There may not be any olivium in the air above us, but there seems to be plenty in this water." Reddy made a sour face. "Our only hope is that Eau Claire thinks to look for us in the vicinity of our last drop."

"That's not our only hope." Chekov looked at the equipment locker again. "Just our best one."

Baldwin finished shucking his safety harness with a snort. "You've got some other bright idea?"

Chekov nodded slowly, still thinking, as he worked open the lock on the front of the cabinet.

"We've got a lot of leeway for rescue." Plottel sounded more like he was trying to convince himself than the others. He craned a desperately hopeful look at Reddy. "Life support's still working, right?" At Reddy's nod, he brightened artificially. "That means we've got air indefinitely. And there's enough food and water in the supply crates to last us for months."

"And we do what with our waste products in the meantime?" Baldwin wanted to know. He'd begun gathering up the supplies from the ruined crate, stacking them precariously in his arms for lack of anywhere else to put them. "I don't know about you, but I don't even want to live with a month's worth of my dirty clothes, much less anything else."

"We're not waiting here for a month." Chekov pulled the first two environmental suits out of the locker and let them fall on the floor behind him. He had to step over the broken parts of a field battery pack to reach the other two.

Reddy looked quizzically down at the jumbled suits, but didn't move to pick them up. "Commander, sitting tight might be our safest course. At least for now."

Chekov draped the last suit, sans helmet, over his shoulder to free up his hands for the atmosphere portables. "Mr. Baldwin's right." He passed Reddy an O_2 mixer, slid the rack of pressure governors ahead of him on the floor. "We don't have the waste management system to handle four people. And even if Eau Claire thinks to send a rescue team to our last scheduled position, what are the chances sensors will work well enough to locate us under water? How long will it take to search two hundred fifty thousand cubic meters of lake using only divers and line-of-sight? Will they even think it's worth doing?" He flipped the suit off his shoulder and shook it out to check the size. "I don't intend to wait and find out."

Plottel took the suit without seeming to realize it when Chekov thrust it toward him. "So we just bob to the surface? Do you have any idea what the waves are going to be like in this weather?"

Baldwin's objection was more to the point. "I can't swim."

"You don't have to." The first suit he picked up was a size too short for Baldwin. Chekov set it aside and sorted through the small pile for another. "They're called environmental suits because they encase you in a livable environment. Whether you're in vacuum or water, the suit doesn't care—it maintains a healthy pressure and gas mix regardless. And it's heavy enough to keep you weighted down for walking on the bottom." He passed a suit to Baldwin, but glanced at Plottel. "Even if there are waves."

"This is nuts," Plottel said.

"No—" Reddy scooped up the remaining suit, bobbing his head eagerly as he scanned for the matching helmet. "No, he's right. This is how they teach you EV work—by suiting you up in a water tank and letting you maneuver around." He shook open his suit with a grin. "Good idea, Commander Chekov."

They wouldn't know that for certain until they walked out on the surface.

Chekov kept an eye on Plottel's bleak expression as the colonist fumbled numbly with the seals down the front of the suit. "You *do* know how to use an environmental suit." He looked between Plottel and Baldwin for some hint of familiarity with the equipment. "Don't you?"

Baldwin paused with his suit hiked up to his waist, only one sleeve attached to the torso, and that backward. Behind him, Plottel fussed with his own gear through a blush dark enough to almost hide his expression. "They showed us a training vid before we set out for Belle Terre." Plottel spoke softly, not lifting his eyes. "It was for emergencies. We weren't supposed to ever need it."

No one was ever supposed to need it. "Well, this is your emergency." Chekov picked up two of the helmets and passed them across to Baldwin and Plottel. "First, we need to verify that your suits have all their parts. On the torso, you should have a locking ring for the helmet, and intact seams between the breastplate and the sleeves. . . ."

Sulu hated Gamma Night.

He was probably the only one in Llano Verde who cared about it. The rest of Belle Terre might complain about breaks in communications when the astronomical blackouts hit, but in Llano Verde, the constant swirl of olivium dust meant the colonists had no communications to lose. Most of them barely knew when Gamma Night fell, and the province's technical office was far too overworked to bother predicting it. That had often left Sulu in the vulnerable position of being several kilometers above the ground when the neutron star's shadow swept down, unable to contact the orbital station whose precise tracking sensors he depended on for navigations. The loss of geographic location wasn't so crucial, although it was exasperating to have to navigate back home by unreliable compass readings, or by following the Big Muddy River with all its meandering twists and turns. What really scared Sulu was altitude. When the dust was thick enough, the olivium in it disturbed all the altimeters and even threw off the safeguard proximity alarm. Since those were also the times when Sulu couldn't make visual contact with the ground, he was forced to hover safely in the stratosphere until the worst of the dust storm had passed or until Gamma Night ended. He'd spent one miserable night trying not to fall asleep at the antigrav controls, and had only been able to orient himself when he drifted out over the ocean and saw sunlight dancing on waves below. He was in no hurry to repeat that experience.

Now Gamma Night was threatening to fall again when he least wanted it to.

His normal ship's communicator—not the experimental one that sat silent as ever in the copilot's seat—chirped and began the standard greeting. "Belle Terre Orbital Platform to Vertical Flight Vessel A-Three. Come in, Vertical—"

Sulu stabbed at the override button to cut off the rest of that unnecessary hail. "Have you managed to triangulate the shuttle's last transmissions yet, Kyle?" he demanded, not caring if he offended the station's civilian communications officer. Lieutenant John Kyle was on interim leave from the *Enterprise* just like Chekov, but he could still pull Starfleet rank over the colony's regular staff in an emergency like this. And the first thing the former transporter chief had told him, when Sulu had brought the Bean up into the clear air of Belle Terre's upper troposphere to report the cargo shuttle missing, was that Gamma Night was due to arrive at the station at any moment. Unlike Llano Verde, the orbital platform cared enough to work through the complex quadratic equations that predicted when the swath of interference would hit.

"They've got it roughly centered on the central quadrant of Llano Verde, but they're having trouble getting any more specific than that." Kyle's British accent sounded much crisper than usual, which told Sulu just how rushed they were for time. "Apparently, the shuttle was flying through some fringes of dust when it last reported in, which distorted the usual subspace polarization. I did get a list of ground locations that were scheduled for cargo drops. Transmitting now."

Sulu toggled the voice/data buffer on his communications panel to make sure the subspace packet had been stored, blessing the *Enterprise*-trained officer's efficiency as he did so. If Kyle hadn't been there, the colony's station crew would probably still be asking him if he was sure the shuttle had really crashed. "Any luck contacting the *Enterprise?*"

"No. They were due to hit Gamma Night twelve hours before we did. They're pretty far out on the edge of the system—Captain Kirk was trying to lure some lurking vessels out of the cometary cloud to see if they were pirates or just passing aliens." He could hear Kyle take a quick replacement breath, then resume the brisk flow of information. "Given their position relative to ours, mutual blackout could last at least eighteen hours. Assuming immediate return after we reestablish contact, their ETA is at least three days, maybe four. Orders?"

Sulu wasted a few seconds sorting through his limited set of options. "Contact colony headquarters and report the missing shuttle as soon as your Gamma Night is over," he said. "I'll report in eighteen hours from now on the status of our search for survivors. If you don't hear from me then, contact the *Enterprise* and request an immediate return to Belle Terre." He paused to let Kyle acknowledge the orders, but his subspace communicator remained ominously silent. "Sulu to Orbital Platform. Come in, Kyle."

There was no reply.

Sulu clenched his teeth, trying not to give in to the pessimism that had dogged him ever since Captain Kirk had sent him down with Scotty, Uhura, and Rand on this frustrating planetary mission. It was hard not to feel that Belle Terre was a colony with a jinx on it. Bad enough that it had to endure the random silences of Gamma Night; even worse that it was so far away from the rest of the quadrant that it was effectively an orphan system. But to have suffered a planetary catastrophe like the Burn *and* to have become the newest target for all the galaxy's marauding bandits and power-hungry alien races seemed like more bad luck than any colony, no matter how well prepared or how dedicated, could withstand. And today that jinx had definitely turned personal. Of all the cargo runs that could have crashed over Llano Verde, why did it have to be the one Chekov was on, during the worst part of the dust season and in the midst of Gamma Night? And why did his request for Captain Kirk's assistance have to get cut off right before he could even be sure Kyle had heard it?

Sulu punched a quick sequence of commands into the Bean's antigrav thrusters. The little craft turned back toward the continental capital, dropping to a lower cruising altitude with the stomach-lurching speed only antigravs could create and control. The surface of Llano Verde's dust layer came into focus below him, billowing like a silent steel-gray sea. Sulu knew from experience how misleading that aqueous appearance was. He'd once taken the Bean down into a dust storm that looked like that and found himself whirled into a maelstrom of wind shears and cyclonic gusts. His quick stab at the antigravs—made almost before he'd consciously realized the danger he was in—had kicked his experimental vessel up out of the dust again, seconds before it would have been smashed to smithereens against the ground.

Sulu tried not to think about what could have happened if he'd been flying a larger, conventionally powered vessel, but his years of piloting experience couldn't be silenced that easily. He knew how fast a craft could drop in the wicked wind shears of Llano

Verde, and how badly sensors could malfunction here. He knew how little chance there'd be to survive with dust clogging the exhaust ports and olivium radiation crippling the inertial dampers. But the most bitter knowledge Sulu possessed was that there was absolutely no point in scanning the landscape for signs of shattered wreckage from Chekov's cargo shuttle.

Because nothing on the surface of Llano Verde could be seen beneath its dust.

Chapter Three

BY THE TIME they finally got the environmental suits assembled, Chekov could see that the crew of the orbital shuttle had settled into whatever ruts stress carved for them. Baldwin had moved into that place of easy calm belonging to men who've realized their survival is no longer in their own hands. It made him more pleasant to work with than he'd been during the less eventful leg of their flight—he hadn't cracked a single off-color joke, or invented any new, annoying nicknames for anyone—but it also made him more of a concern. Chekov knew from experience that people who had accepted death as an option often weren't as careful about their safety. That left everyone else in the party to worry about their safety for them—one more worry than many groups could survive.

In contrast, Plottel had grown so careful, so fearful of succumbing to some error or oversight which no one could foresee that it was all he could do to count the fingers on his gloves, and check and recheck each seam. Chekov pretended not to watch as Reddy patiently helped him into the suit almost the way a parent dresses a toddler. At least the pilot had defaulted to the kind of optimistic, caretaking mode Chekov could depend on to help rather than hinder the coming walk.

Chekov himself stepped through assembling his suit in grim silence, making a conscious effort not to snap at his companions for a slowness he knew was all in his head. Time always attenuated for him under stress. Minutes stretched to the breaking point, and everything from fumbling with a suit to small talk devoured precious seconds. He'd figured out some years ago that this internal time dissonance was his own perception, not reality, and he tried hard not to berate his teammates for failing to feel it, too. He couldn't always keep the irritation out of his voice, though. At least no one here felt the need to critique his social skills under duress, the way Sulu usually did.

While all of the environmental suits were technically fit for use, Chekov was glad he didn't have to trust any of them in hard vacuum. He finished verifying that the breathing apparatuses functioned at least well enough to keep anyone from suffocating, then divvied out the cheap O_2 mixers and gas exchangers according to suit user's height, weight, and experience. As the one among them with the most complete EV training, Chekov took the atmosphere unit with the greatest risk of failing. At least he had some hope of maintaining enough presence of mind to keep from drowning.

Suited up and fitted with breathers, they could barely squeeze far enough into the airlock to seal the door behind them. Chekov reached for Reddy's hand without speaking. They knew that the olivium suspended in the crater's water was going to make suit-to-suit transmission impossible, and, while everyone had been introduced to the concept of touching helmets to talk, Chekov had a feeling they'd do better relying on pantomime whenever possible. He closed Reddy's hand firmly around the back of Plottel's equipment belt, then took Plottel's hand and connected him likewise to Baldwin. Baldwin intuited the next step and took a grip on Chekov's belt before he'd even turned away from Plottel. *Pragmatic,* Chekov realized with a start. People convinced of their own demise became weirdly pragmatic. He gave Baldwin a curt thumbs-up, then turned to put his own hand on the airlock controls. He took a breath so deep, the CO_2 gauge on his respirator jumped just a little. It was finally time to go.

Water rushed the airlock in a glassy wall. Prepared as he was for the impact, the force of it still surprised Chekov. He staggered backward a step, felt Baldwin's grip on his belt let go, lost sight of the airlock's outer hatch in a tempest of mud and debris. Then, just as abruptly, the tug and swirl of fluid stilled, leaving him upright and suspended in a slow-motion universe. Compared with the dizzying lightness of microgravity, the suit's weight and the water's drag turned every movement into a leaden slog. It was like running through ever-thickening air in a nightmare. Like bugs struggling in amber.

They reassembled their human chain in a silence that somehow seemed even more isolated than before, then stepped one by one out into the morass.

It wasn't as dark as Chekov expected. Sediment hung suspended in lacy draperies over forests of shattered stone, all of it lit by a dim luminescence that twisted and fractured as the surface high above them danced. Each labored footstep puffed up silt the color of ink. It paused in a knee-high roil, talcum-smooth like Martian soil, painting a story of where they'd come from and where they were going.

Chekov chose a careful path among the boulders and stones. "Ejecta," the geologists in the *Enterprise*'s science labs had called it. Fragments of Belle Terre's surface rocks flung skyward when the Quake Moon slammed home, only to fall and make their own impact craters throughout the belly of Bull's Eye and its surrounding slopes. No plants here, no fish. A dead lake filled with muddy water so radioactive Chekov couldn't even bring himself to look directly at the reading on his heads-up display. He hoped fervently that the upward trend beneath his feet meant something—that they were headed for the surface, and shelter, and some way to contact civilization before breathing and drinking and wearing this place damaged their cell structure beyond any chance of repair. He didn't want to think about how many kilos of olivium-tainted dust would glue itself to their clothes if they had to shed their suits to heft themselves out of the water.

When he first felt the tug on the back of his suit, he assumed Baldwin had lost his footing somewhere beneath the curtain of mud they'd churned up with their passage. He slowed, putting out one hand to catch the rock in front of him, and hoped Baldwin could right himself without pulling everyone else down. The second tug was stronger, and the third turned into a fourth, fifth, and sixth in rapid succession. Damning the inflexibility of hard-shelled torsos, Chekov turned cumbersomely, groping for Baldwin's arm to stop the pulling as he did so.

He saw where Baldwin pointed before he'd even finished his turn. A dozen meters back the way they'd come, Plottel and Reddy huddled in a near embrace, surrounded by a swirl of mud, helmets touching. Plottel's movements, as jerky and animated as the water would allow, told Chekov almost as much as Reddy's still, calming posture. It occurred to him only now that he might have made sure before they left the shuttle that no one was claustrophobic, or pathologically afraid of water. Disengaging from Baldwin's grip as gently as possible, Chekov told him, "Stay here," while gesturing the same command with both hands. The words might not have carried across without a radio signal, but the expression apparently did. Baldwin nodded obediently and took a seat on the nearest flattened boulder. Chekov retraced his path down the incline, uncomfortably aware of how the veil of mud surrounding their small party billowed and thickened as he trudged his way back through it.

Reddy shuffled aside slightly as Chekov approached, creating just enough room for Chekov to fit his helmet into the discussion without letting go his grip on Plottel's shoulders. Their voices sounded thin and distant, blurred by the water the way they wouldn't have been by the purity of vacuum.

"I can't tell where it's coming from—" Plottel's eyes shone with fear, his breath so hot and rapid that he'd made mist on the inside of his faceplate. "—but there's a lot of it, and it's still coming—"

Reddy nodded calmly. "All right, don't panic—"

"Don't tell me not to panic!" Plottel wailed. He struck at Reddy's hands to dislodge them, but couldn't get enough momentum through the water to do much besides bump him ineffectually. "Whenever you tell me not to panic, I know it's even worse than I thought!"

Chekov interrupted before Plottel could work himself into hysterics. "What's wrong?"

"My suit's leaking." Plottel heaved a deep, shaking breath, then stated, more evenly, "I've got water in my suit."

Chekov's own heart hammered. This wasn't space, he reminded himself. A breached suit didn't necessarily mean anyone was going to die. "How long?" It was the only thing he could think to ask.

Plottel shook his head. "I dunno. Just a few minutes. I felt wet, on my one leg, and I thought I was imagining it because of all the water. But now it's higher, and that leg's real heavy." He lifted his right leg somewhat awkwardly and moved it around to demonstrate. "I can feel it sloshing in my boot."

"All right—" Chekov stopped himself just short of telling Plottel to stay calm and not to worry. "We're not too far from the surface," he lied. A little lie—he was pretty sure the surface was only a few dozen meters above them, and the upward trend of the lake bed had to be a good sign. "Can you stay with me and keep moving for just a little farther?"

"And if my suit fills up before we get out?" Behind the steam on his faceplate, his eyes looked wet and wide. "I don't want to drown!"

Chekov shouldered Reddy aside and placed himself so squarely in front of Plottel that he blocked all view of everything else. "I won't let you drown," he stated firmly. When Plottel slid his gaze away, Chekov took his helmet in both hands and gave it a little shake to bring them eye-to-eye again. "There are ways to share atmosphere between suits," he went on. Not that any of them would work with these suits, under these conditions. "If we have to, we'll tear the breathers out of the suits and buddy-breathe until we get to the surface." It would leave them both chilled and soaking, exposed to more radiation than Chekov cared to think about, but it would keep the water out of their lungs. Assuming they could do it at all. "I promise, I will not let you drown."

This time, Plottel's eyes never left Chekov's face when he nodded once, stiffly. "Okay." That kind of trust came with a terrible price.

Chekov returned the nod, then took hold of Plottel's wrist and angled himself to bump helmets briefly with Reddy. "Stay with Baldwin. Get him to the surface and find some kind of shelter." They didn't dare keep up their human chain from here—Chekov and Plottel had just become the damaged members that it was safest for the group as a whole to leave behind. "We'll be up right after you."

He hoped to God that wasn't another lie.

It had taken more time than Uhura had expected to track down Chief Engineer Montgomery Scott. It wasn't that he was done working for the day—Scotty was *never* done working. But now that he had the antigrav thrusters on the Bean nearly perfected, his troubleshooting skills were in high demand with Llano Verde's other technical specialists. Uhura began at the spaceport, checking in with the technicians who were designing a dust-repelling shield for the landing pad. They sent her to the cargo-loading area, where she was proudly shown the dustproof antigrav castors Scotty had designed for the baggage-handling carts before being redirected to the spaceport's power-distribution grid. From there, she had to take one of the new underground walkways across the city to Big Muddy's main power-generating station, where the magnetic antimatter containers had been reacting badly to olivium corrosion.

By then, it was almost dusk and she was starting to regret having run out from her lab without the protective cloak and sewn-in filtering scarf that Big Muddy residents called a dust muffler. She was also starting to fret over the amount of time the search had taken. She knew Sulu would be coming back to the spaceport as soon as he'd informed the orbital platform about the shuttle's disappearance. If he couldn't find her or Scotty, the pilot might decide to take the Bean right back out into the dust storm, to search whatever area the station had pinpointed as the site of the crash.

That was the frustration with a city limited to the use of hardwired landlines for communication. You couldn't just say someone's name into your communicator and let the computerized switching system locate them for you. Sulu would have to buzz the number for her lab, and although Uhura had left Janice Rand there to answer for her, Rand wouldn't know where Uhura's search for Scotty was going to take her, any more than Uhura currently did.

Where it did eventually take her was to a nondescript warehouse deep in Big Muddy's industrial sector, the only one with lights still on now that night had fallen. There were no underground walkways within the warehouse complex, and Uhura had to pull up her uniform collar to cover her nose and mouth as she hurried through the swirling dust. The acrid tang of Belle Terre crept into her throat. Uhura knew she couldn't really taste the trace levels of olivium in the blowing sediment, but just knowing it was there, emitting its transperiodic combination of subspace and hard radiation, usually made a phantom burning sensation slide down her throat when she swallowed. It was a measure of her urgency that she felt nothing but grit tonight as she coughed her way through the warehouse's dust-sealed doors.

"Krista, did you remember to make one of those pasta dishes vegetarian?" demanded a voice from behind a bank of equipment-laden shelving. "Greg says he's not eating guanaco sausage anymore."

Uhura followed the sound of the voice to a passageway jammed with coils of optical data cable and water pumps. At its end, an athletic young blond woman and a wiry dark-haired man huddled over what looked like a remote data-processing station, doing something with a laser welder. Knowing from experience how badly engineers tended to react to interruptions, Uhura waited for the hiss of the laser to fall silent before saying, "I'm looking for Commander Scott."

"Hey." The woman looked over her shoulder, eyes narrowing in unexpected annoyance. "We just got him here, after *weeks* of asking. You can't have him for at least—"

"She's Starfleet, Bev." The dark-haired man straightened, dusting metal fuzz off his gray-green uniform. "Commander Uhura, isn't it? Commander Scott's back in our data control room with Chief McElroy, trying to make some olivium-frizzed pressure transducers talk to our central processing system. Do you want me to get him for you?"

Uhura shook her head. Intellectually, she knew there was no sense interrupting Scotty's work, even as her stomach twisted with urgency. "I can talk to him there, if you'll show me the way. In the meantime, could one of you please call Tech Lab J9 and tell the person who answers what your landline number is here?" She could see the puzzlement in both their faces. "I'm expecting some urgent news about a shuttle crash."

"The cargo shuttle from the orbital station?" The blond woman leapt to her feet with an alacrity that reminded Uhura of a Starfleet cadet. "On my way."

The dark-haired man didn't say anything, but he led Uhura at a brisk pace down another cluttered passage, past digital map displays of river levels, wind conditions, and pressure fronts. They ended up at a tightly sealed airlock, where he paused to give her an apologetic look. "If you could just brush off the worst of the dust, Commander—"

"I know, to keep the computers from crashing." Uhura had already recognized one of Llano Verde's standard defenses for protecting sensitive data-processing systems against olivium contamination. She beat as much dust as she could off the thick material of her uniform, running her fingers through her hair and swiping off her dangling earrings for good measure. "This wouldn't happen to be the province's climate modeling center, would it?"

The young man snorted and sealed the airlock behind them. "Not a chance. You wouldn't see climate modelers working through their supper." Uhura watched a diaphanous veil of dust drift off her clothes and skin as the air vigorously cycled inside the cleaning chamber. "No, we're the hydrology and meteorology division—the idiots assigned to collect actual data on what the Burn is doing to Belle Terre's climate." A light went green above the inner airlock door, and he reached out to unlock it. "Which is a hell of a lot harder than staring into computerized crystal balls and making grand predictions."

Uhura followed him out into a room so thickly studded with data-processing stations that it looked almost like a starship's bridge. On the far side, all she could see of Scotty were his legs and feet sticking out from under one of those control panels. Based on the stream of technical instructions emerging in his rolling Scottish brogue, it sounded as if he had already found the source of their problem. A bearded man who must be Chief McElroy squatted beside him, looking a little overwhelmed by the help he was getting. Even from the airlock door, Uhura could see that his face was wind-callused and reddened by too much olivium exposure. Federation medical science could heal the DNA damage caused by olivium radiation, even weeks later, but it required daily treatments out in the field to keep your skin from reacting as if you'd soaked in too much ultraviolet.

"Dr. Anthony, you're just the person I needed," McElroy said, looking up in relief. "Do you and Weir have any spare P537 signal modulators?"

"Not lying around loose," the younger man said. "I'd have to yank them out of the extra hydrographical units."

"Then start yanking," said Montgomery Scott's muffled voice. "I'll need at least three of them to get this finicky data-stream receptor of yours to sort out transponder signals from olivium noise. It wouldn't hurt to throw a couple of J-channel buffers into line, too, so we don't clog its little silicon intake valves with too many water level measurements at once. And while you're at it, bring me some—"

"Commander Scott," Uhura interrupted. "There's been a problem with the shuttle."

Something clattered inside the control panel, accompanied by the sound of a ferocious Gaelic curse. A moment later, Scotty hauled himself out to stare at her in dismay. "It wasna the antigravs, was it?" he demanded. "I told the lad we needed to give them a weeklong shakedown under maximum dust conditions—"

Uhura shook her head. "I'm sorry, sir, I didn't mean the Bean. It's the cargo shuttle that was due to land here tonight. It fell off the orbital platform's tracking screens an hour too early, and hasn't been heard from since."

"Not the one Chekov was hitching a ride on?"

Uhura nodded. "We think it must have crashed somewhere in the Outland. Sulu took the Bean out again to see if the orbital station could pinpoint its last known position. He should be coming back any time now."

That made Scotty grunt in approval, but the other two men exchanged dubious looks. "Um—why do you want to find out where the shuttle was before it crashed?" Anthony asked politely and, Uhura thought, somewhat pointlessly.

"To send out a search and rescue party, of course."

"A continental search and rescue party?" Chief McElroy clarified. "Or a Starfleet landing party?"

"The *Enterprise* isn't parked in orbit above Belle Terre anymore," said Montgomery Scott. "She's busy chasing folks away from that stuffed olive you call a Quake Moon."

"Which means we'll have to request a rescue team from Emergency Services." Uhura glanced back and forth between the two scientists, sensing even stronger undercurrents of doubt surging between them. "What's wrong with that? The shuttle was an official colonial vessel."

McElroy sighed. "That's the problem, Commander.

You see, colony personnel are considered morally expendable, because they knew the risks they were taking when they decided to settle here."

He sounded as if he was quoting something, but Uhura couldn't imagine that any of Belle Terre's colony charters had included a statement like that. "*Morally* expendable?" she repeated, frowning. "What does that mean?"

"It means that our continental governor considers survival something you have to earn to stay in the colony's gene pool, not something you have an innate right to," Anthony said bitterly.

McElroy lifted a restraining hand toward his subordinate, although his lips had also tightened beneath his beard. "We were sent out here from colony headquarters to measure the effects of the Burn on microclimates as well as on the entire planet's weather," he told Uhura quietly. "That meant we had to spend months installing monitors all over Llano Verde, and hardwiring underground optical cable networks to connect them all. It was dangerous work, especially near the impact craters. They were brand-new back then, and real unstable. We lost two of our field technicians on Splat—" McElroy paused, a muscle jerking beneath his callused skin. "No matter how many times we asked for a rescue mission, all Governor Sedlak would say is that we should have known the risks we were taking, just like the settlers did."

"He *never* sent out a rescue team?" Scott demanded.

"Never. I must have sent a dozen messages back to colony headquarters, protesting Sedlak's hands-off policy, but all I ever got was boilerplate from Evan Pardonnet's office, saying that every province in Belle Terre had the right to choose its own destiny."

"We're not residents of this colony," Anthony said grimly. "Sedlak doesn't have the right to choose *our* destiny!"

McElroy sighed. "You know that, and I know that, but it doesn't cut any dust with Llano Verde's Emergency Services. They're always happiest when they've got an excuse to hunker down in their underground barracks and pretend they're too busy to actually rescue someone."

Uhura took a deep breath. She was starting to understand where the rising level of hostility among Outlanders was coming from. "I don't think a hands-off policy is going to work with a Starfleet officer involved," she said. "Our policy has always been to rescue lost crewmen unless it endangers too many other lives."

"And if we have to," Scotty added, "we'll take our Starfleet vertical flight vessel and go looking for the cargo shuttle ourselves."

That statement made McElroy's eyebrows jerk upward, but it was in surprise and admiration rather than scorn. "In that case, let's see if we can help you find it," he said, and waved Anthony to a nearby meteorological panel. "What time did the crash happen?"

Uhura backtracked through the past few hectic hours, trying to remember when Sulu had finally answered her hail. "Between fifteen hundred and sixteen hundred hours."

"Bring up the atmospheric pressure records for two hours on either side of that time slot, Greg." McElroy was tapping commands into another data station. "I'll filter them at maximum sensitivity for pressure variations two orders of magnitude or greater with a duration under ten seconds."

Scotty grunted his approval of that. "Explosion wave front," he told Uhura, when she slanted him a puzzled look. "A shuttle crash is about the only thing that would match those parameters."

He didn't say whether the crash that matched those parameters was one the crew could walk away from or be pulverized by. Uhura felt her shoulders lock up with tension as the data processors ran their filtering routines, not sure whether she should be hoping for a positive or negative result.

"Results coming up now." Anthony watched lines of intricate numbers pour down the screen in front of him like a greenish waterfall. Apparently he was familiar enough with their data-coding system to keep track of what it meant. "Data output by sector. Shorelines negative. Coastal plains negative. Fluvial valleys negative. Alluvial fans negative. Crater slopes negative." He glanced over his shoulder. "That's everything, Commander."

Uhura bit her lip, not sure whether that was good news or bad. "You're saying that none of your stations recorded a shuttle crash?"

"Not this afternoon." McElroy turned to face her, smiling. "We've got some holes in the system, of course, especially around the impact craters. But the chances of the cargo shuttle landing in one of those data holes by accident should be pretty low. I'd say your lost shuttle might just have managed to land itself intact."

"In which case, a search and rescue mission becomes an even higher priority." Uhura glanced over at Montgomery Scott and saw the way his tired shoulders had straightened under his wrinkled Starfleet coveralls, as if the mantle of Captain Kirk had fallen over him. She responded as automatically to that aura as if the captain himself were present. "Orders, Commander?"

"We'll head for the spaceport, and see what Mr. Sulu's managed to find out," Scott said crisply. "And then I think we'll pay a wee visit to the continental governor."

They almost made it to the surface.

Chekov couldn't see where the water met the land, of course. The gale-force winds that had battered their shuttle also thrashed the top layers of water, splashing it about like a playful lion. By the time they found themselves laboring up a slope of tumbled rock as steep as a flight of stairs, waves dragged against them from every direction, and churned-up mud rendered the water as opaque as black glass. Chekov's grip had migrated from Plottel's wrist to the handle on the front of his breastplate. He could only see the other man's face when their helmets touched, and then only in the dim amber light of his suit helmet's heads-up display. They'd progressed more and more slowly with every step taken, until Chekov felt as though he were dragging more of Plottel's weight than Plottel himself. When the colonist finally staggered to a stop, Chekov didn't try to urge him forward. He turned, clapped their helmets faceplate-to-faceplate, and saw the water lapping at Plottel's chin before either of them had a chance to say anything. They'd run out of time.

Despite his promises to find some way to share their atmosphere, Chekov couldn't imagine any way to rip out either breathing unit and manually carry it. Not quickly enough to prevent one or both of them from drowning in the process. Leaning backward in his suit to turn his gaze upward, he hoped the slurry of mud thrashing about above them really did indicate the pounding of the wind and the violence of open air.

"Listen to me . . ." He brought his faceplate back into alignment with Plottel's and began again. "You have to trust me."

Plottel had tipped his head as far back in his helmet as he could. His breathing was audible even across two thick panes of transparent aluminum. "All right."

"When I tell you to, take three deep, fast breaths, and hold the last one." Chekov put both hands on the breastplate's seal, his eyes locked with Plottel's. "We're just a few meters under the surface. Swim straight up." Although filled with dust, violent and wild, the air above them could theoretically be breathed. At least well enough to sustain them until a rescue party could yank them out, carry them back to the orbital platform, and treat them for olivium exposure. "Are you ready?"

Plottel nodded, eyes filled with tears.

Chekov took a deep breath of his own. "Now."

He counted breaths along with Plottel, waited to see the other man's lips press shut on the last one, then tore open the breastplate to breach Plottel's suit.

The flooding could only have taken seconds; it felt like hours. Plottel's face squeezed into a fist of discomfort as frigid lake water overran his helmet; then he fumbled the container off his head and kicked himself free of the suit Chekov had already yanked down around his hips. Chekov pushed the colonist upward, wanting to help but painfully aware that he was no longer a component in Plottel's survival. Leaving the suit where it had deflated, he turned back to the incline and continued on his own, no longer impeded in his climb to the surface.

He found no distinct interface between water and air.

Battering currents and sluicing mud somehow passed into pounding wind and the rattling roar of dust against his helmet. Both environments left him equally off-balance and blind. It wasn't until he'd clambered several body-lengths up the crater's side that he realized it was dust caking in the joints of his suit that slowed him, not the friction of storm-tossed water.

Rising up on his knees, he tried to search the rocky shore for some sign of the others. He thought he could see a clear glitter of sunlight dancing farther out on the water, but here on the shore blowing dust obliterated the world beyond a few meters, and the continual skreel of grit against his helmet rendered him as deaf as the olivium-poisoned water had. Chekov made an awkward circle on hands and knees. The lake's surface whipped and frothed with such fury that he had no hope of finding Plottel among the waves if the man hadn't already made it to shore. Chekov was just steeling himself to continue up the crater and hope for the best when a tear in the dusty curtain revealed a huddled form farther down the shoreline. It was too small and soft to be a boulder.

Dust caked Plottel's wet clothes and hair just as Chekov had feared it would, painting his still form in a glitter of sodden olivium. "Plottel?" Chekov wasn't sure if the sound would carry through the air. It exploded overloud inside his helmet, startling him with its realness. That Plottel couldn't hear him seemed impossible. He closed one heavily gloved hand around Plottel's shoulder and shook him sharply. "Plottel, get up! We have to find some cover!" *Please don't have drowned—I promised I wouldn't let you drown!*

But it wasn't water that darkened the front of Plottel's coverall or soaked the dust-stained rocks beneath him. Rearing back on his heels, Chekov dragged his hand across the stone and turned up a palm smeared with muddy red. He had only a moment in which to realize something far worse than drowning had ravaged Plottel's body; then a series of powerful hammer blows shattered his breastplate and sent him sprawling back down the slope into the water.

Chapter Four

LAKE WATER exploded into Chekov's suit, swarming the torso with cold and flooding his helmet until olivium-poisoned sediment stung his eyes. If he'd been breathing, he'd have gasped in a lungful on the first shock of impact. Instead, whatever force had shattered his breastplate and breached his suit had also stunned him half-senseless. He landed spread-eagled in a cloud of mud, and recovered the urge to breathe only an instant before the awareness that he was foundering more than a meter underwater.

With no breath to hold, he gritted his teeth against a compulsion to inhale and flailed to pop the helmet's latches. It tumbled free, disappearing downslope among the rocks and silt and darkness. There was no longer a torso seam to rupture—the breastplate had shattered into a dozen jagged pieces, taking all semblance of suit integrity with it. He struggled out of the gear as if it were a dead skin. Lungs burning, he kicked toward the surface, hoping the dust-choked air was more breathable than the water.

Wind tore at him the moment he broke surface. Blinding, searing, screaming wind that instantly clogged his uniform with dust and tore away the sound of his own coughing. He crawled forward on all fours, found the shore with both hands by the simple expedient of dragging himself from chill water to even more chilling air. Rocks towered higher than he remembered from his first exit, but Plottel's body was still visible when he rose up to squint beyond a curve of slanted stone.

Plottel's body, and the barrel of a weapon longer than his own arm.

Chekov threw himself to the side, grabbing the gun's barrel and pushing it the opposite way even as he used it to yank the stranger off balance. A sharp report, loud enough to echo down the crater despite the winds, kicked the barrel with considerable force and struck it suddenly, fearfully hot. Pain hissed across his palm. He released his grip involuntarily, catching the stranger's striped face scarf instead, and brought the man down with a fierce blow to the temple. Then they both dropped to the dust, the gun and its overhot barrel sandwiched between them.

Dust slid, slick as ice, over the sloping rocks. It carried them halfway back to the water, ramming them against a shoulder of welded granite and sending the weapon skittering down the bank ahead of them. Chekov heaved clear of the gunman, not liking their proximity, and rolled into a crouch with the upper slopes of Bull's Eye at his back. He didn't like the shroud of white noise spun by the dust storm, liked even less not knowing how many others might be with this gunman, or how many of them carried the same loud, destructive weapon. When the stranger climbed to his feet, turned partly away, Chekov tensed himself for anything. "What the hell are you doing?" He had to shout to be heard over the wind. "I'm from the *Enterprise!*"

The gunman answered by spinning and aiming a rather inexpert swing at Chekov's head.

He intercepted the blow without having to think about it, then returned a faster, more precise strike before taking the man's legs out at the knees. He knew it was a good hit—could tell by the jolt it sent all the way up to his shoulder, and by the heavy pulse of pain it drove through his already-burned palm—but he didn't expect it to take the man down altogether. After what felt like an eternity of waiting for the gunman to rise, Chekov dropped cautiously, awkwardly to one knee and reached to feel for a heartbeat through layers of dust-laden clothes.

The wind seemed suddenly alive again. Driven back temporarily by the adrenaline rush of combat, it slammed into the forefront of his awareness again, bringing with it all the dust and radiation he had hoped to avoid. Feeling suddenly shaky, Chekov ducked his head against his sleeve and willed his breathing to slow, his lungs to stop rebelling against the filthy air. The dust caking his clothes and hair would serve him almost as well as a cloaking device right now, buying him a few precious moments. He found the gunman's heartbeat beneath his hand, thought he would be relieved at the discovery. Instead, he horrified himself by hesitating over whether or not he should leave this man alive.

Despite Eau Claire's directives, there was no kevlar bodysuit protecting the gunman, only heavy cotton trousers, several layers of tunics, a coarsely woven green-and-orange striped face scarf with a sewn-in filter, a pair of plasma-welding goggles, and the finest link chain gloves Chekov had ever seen. What skin he could glimpse beneath goggles and scarf was as olivium-burned and dust-dry as any other colonist's, and the shoes on his feet were the same Federation issue Plottel and Baldwin and Reddy wore.

You can't just kill a colonist.

The *Enterprise* had made the long trek to Belle Terre to protect these people. Instead, the pioneers had been ravaged by dust storms, preyed upon by raiders, put on the defensive by other equally desperate colonists. God only knew what the man thought when he saw Plottel and Chekov.

Still, to murder an unprotected man on a lakeside just because he was unfamiliar . . . It went against everything the Federation—and Belle Terre—was meant to stand for.

So did killing an unconscious assailant just because you were horrified by what he had done. And leaving him for the storm to kill wasn't much better.

It proved harder than Chekov expected to roll the man into the lee of a boulder. Wind shoved at him with malicious abandon, and microscopic crystals of olivium lashed his hands and face with an unrelenting sting. He couldn't breathe deeply enough to drive off dizziness, couldn't see well enough to avoid stumbling over rocks so big they could break a man's leg. By the time the colonist had been safely tucked away from harm, Chekov's lungs felt tacky with dust, his mouth dry all the way down into his stomach. When his eyes slitted open, the wind sliced across them like razors and the dust sucked away tears of pain.

He couldn't find Plottel anymore, wasn't even sure how far down the shoreline he'd stumbled. This whirling, this sick dizziness that wrung out his insides like a dry rag, it wasn't just a lack of air. It was the horrible dryness of the Outland, the cell-destroying kiss of olivium, the incredible stupidity of surviving a shuttle crash, a hike through muddy water, only to die on the slopes of Bull's Eye because he tried to save a man who'd murdered one of his team. He went down hard, coughing, making things worse with each whooping intake of dust. Guilt clawed its way stubbornly above his rising panic—guilt over Plottel, over losing Reddy and Baldwin, over leaving Uhura and Sulu without even a clue where to look for his body. Then dust overwhelmed the last of his senses, and even panic was pushed down into darkness and smothered.

"We're wasting our time here," Sulu said. "Let's leave."

He made the suggestion more to fill the oppressive emptiness of the governor's office than because he had any hope of it being heeded. When it came to matters of civilian authority, Commander Scott believed in going by the book, even if that meant waiting an hour to get a ten-minute slice of a politician's time. And although Uhura and Rand had initially been as exasperated as Sulu that Governor Sedlak wouldn't meet with them until his evening meal was over, they'd since become so deeply absorbed in finding ways to solve Uhura's communications problem that he didn't think they even heard his plaintive remarks.

Sulu didn't have anything equally productive to occupy his time, so he'd spent most of the past hour counting the number of places he'd visited on the map of Llano Verde that spanned an entire wall of the governor's office. Most of the names on that map were no longer in use, Sulu noted, and some of them didn't even exist as settlements anymore. It made a stark contrast to the landing-site map he and Scotty had tacked up in their hangar at the spaceport, where all the official place-names of the Outland were scribbled over with one or more of the nicknames Sulu heard on his various journeys. Finding such deep apathy—or arrogance—in the office of the province's appointed leader didn't inspire much confidence in his leadership.

"We should have started looking for the shuttle right after I got back from the orbital station," Sulu said. "If we'd gotten out there early enough, we could have used thermal imaging to locate the crash site while it was still hot."

"According to the meteorologists, there wasn't a crash." Uhura used the tip of one finger to erase something on the data padd she and Rand were sharing, then tapped in another variable for the processor to test. "So there wouldn't have been anything out there to detect, even if we'd flown right over the shuttle."

"What if the meteorologists were wrong?"

"We still wouldn't have known where to start looking," Janice Rand pointed out. "And we couldn't have thermally imaged the whole subcontinent in the time it took the wreckage to cool."

"Not unless there'd been a rupture of the antimatter core," Montgomery Scott said dryly. "In which case, there'd be no one left alive to rescue."

Sulu drummed his fingers on the polished marble top of the governor's conference table. "We could have started by visiting the settlements that were scheduled for emergency food drops. We'd at least get a rough idea of where the shuttle went down by finding out where the shipments showed up and where they didn't."

The chief engineer snorted. "You're not going to find out anything by pounding on those settlers' doors in the middle of the night! From what I've heard, they'd be more likely to hit you over the head with a shovel than talk to you."

There wasn't much Sulu could say to that, since he was the one who'd first noticed the Outland settlers' hostility toward strangers. Fortunately, he was saved from needing to reply by Janice Rand. "*That* worked!" she said, tapping the data padd's small display excitedly to store the current value. "Now all we have to do is reprogram my olivium-enhanced signal detector for those scanning rates and integrate it into the transmission reflectance system. In a few hours, we might be able to contact the shuttle, or at least pick up its automatic distress signal."

Uhura nodded, folding the data padd closed with a sigh of relief. "While you do that, Janice, the rest of us can pack the Bean with as much food and medical supplies as it can hold."

"For the shuttle crew?" Sulu asked.

"For the colonists that the shuttle never got to." The worry and compassion in her voice made Sulu feel ashamed of his irritable mood. "Some of them must be starving, or the province would never have agreed to let us deliver emergency food supplies."

Sulu glanced around at the cold polished marble and etched glass of the governor's office, and felt annoyed all over again. "If this province had done its start-up a little more efficiently, maybe they wouldn't have needed emergency food supplies. Then Chekov wouldn't have gotten stranded to begin with!"

"What a remarkable discussion." The carefully measured cadence of that remark reminded Sulu instantly of Spock, although the voice that spoke was at least an octave deeper. Its rich timbre seemed at first to hint at warmth and humor, but one glance back at the speaker froze that impression stone-cold. The man standing in the doorway was tall and had the spare, cadaverous look of a lifelong academic. He also had one of the narrowest and most ascetic faces Sulu had ever seen, with slitted eyes as dark and unrevealing as those of a statue.

"Each of the individual statements is based on social values or emotional states rather than fact," the man continued. "Yet the progression of arguments is taken to be logically valid by all involved."

"Governor Sedlak." Scotty stood up from the table as the politician crossed the room, forcing his subordinates to do the same. "Commander Montgomery Scott of the *U.S.S. Enterprise*—"

"—currently attached to our Technical Service to improve transportation and communications," Marcus Sedlak finished. He took his seat without inviting them to join him, or seeming to notice the awkward hesitation before they did. "I am familiar with your mission, Commander, although I never approved of it. Given its remote probability of success, I find it an intolerable waste of technical expertise and time."

Scotty's face stiffened at that curt dismissal of his work, and Sulu half expected him to burst into an impassioned defense of his dustproof vertical flight vessel. But years of interaction with engineering professors had apparently taught him that it was futile to argue with academics.

"I'm not here to discuss my mission, Governor," the chief engineer said between his teeth. "I'm here to make a Priority One Starfleet request for assistance from your Emergency Services group. We've got a downed shuttle—"

"A missing shuttle," Sedlak corrected without the slightest compassion in his voice. "Currently only a few hours overdue." He lifted an eyebrow at Scott, a gesture far colder and more disparaging than Spock's version. "Most likely it has merely been delayed and will still arrive at the spaceport tonight."

Scotty's eyebrows beetled. "And it's equally likely, sir, that—"

"—the shuttle has crashed," Sedlak agreed. "In which case, there's a better than even chance that all crewmen aboard are already dead. In either case, a rescue mission is unnecessary." He favored them with what might have been supposed to be an understanding glance. To Sulu, it just looked supercilious. "I am aware that members of Starfleet tend to suffer intense emotional reactions to the loss of their social peers, but that's not a valid reason to risk the lives of more colony personnel during Llano Verde's dust season."

"It's my opinion, as a Starfleet officer, that any chance of the cargo shuttle landing with its crew alive is enough to justify a rescue mission," Scotty said stubbornly.

Sedlak inclined his head a minuscule amount. "Your opinion is duly noted, Commander. I believe that concludes our meeting."

Sulu could hear Uhura and Rand both take a startled breath in the silence that followed, but he kept his eyes fixed on Montgomery Scott. He could tell from the bunched muscles of the chief engineer's shoulders that he must have been clenching his fists beneath the table, but his voice sounded only a little gruffer than usual. It was the much stronger Scottish accent that betrayed the intense emotion he was feeling.

"It doesna *quite* conclude there, sir. I'm required by Starfleet Directive C-Sixteen to inform you that a Starfleet officer has been placed in danger on this colony. That gives me the right, under Federation Law, to disregard any orders from civilian authority that would impede my ability to rescue him."

The governor raised his eyebrows again, this time in an ironic look that seemed to mimic amusement. "I have issued no such orders, Commander, nor do I intend to. Please feel free to conduct whatever maneuvers you feel are necessary. I assume you will also inform Captain Kirk of the situation and request his assistance?"

"Correct." The long Scottish roll of *r*'s in that word sounded almost like a growl. "And I dinna think he'll be too happy to find out how you're running this province, Mr. Sedlak."

Sedlak's narrow face remained unmoved, only the tiniest glitter in his dark eyes telling Sulu he'd registered the implied threat. "Your captain's emotional state is of no concern to me, Commander Scott. When he arrives, all he will find is that I run this province in the most efficient manner possible. Any inadequacies are due to our suffering the brunt of the Quake Moon incident, an environmental catastrophe which I believe was caused by a certain James T. Kirk."

* * *

"Uhura to Orbital Shuttle Six. Come in, Orbital Shuttle Six."

She took her fingers off the transmission key, then glanced at Janice Rand. Since they'd hooked up only the transmission side of their integrated communications system so far, she wasn't expecting a reply, just a status report. The junior officer was staring intently at the various readouts they'd patched into the line. "Seeing any signal interference?" Uhura asked.

"Not on the main band." Rand clicked a dial through a range of frequency modulations, checking the readouts for each one. "Actually, it looks like we're getting minimal interference throughout the spectrum. I'd say our concatenation worked."

"Don't count on it yet." Uhura had spent too many useless hours at this control panel to believe in anything until it materialized. "How does the signal strength look on the short-range array?"

Rand swung around to check the bank of readouts behind her, wheeled in from her own lab down the hall and still trailing a few unattached cables. While Uhura had spent the past few weeks trying to hail Sulu, Janice Rand had cajoled a small army of smitten technicians and settlers into installing a hardwired detection array around Big Muddy, to test her olivium-enhanced communications system. Now that her system and Uhura's were calibrated to the same scanning rates, they could measure how strong Uhura's transmission signal output really was.

"That's strange," Rand said after a minute. "It's really attenuated near the spaceport, but it picks up strength farther away."

"Isn't that what your augmenter does?" Sulu's voice was muffled by the tall signal-processing unit, in whose shadow he was catnapping while he waited for them to complete their system integration. He'd finished loading supplies into the Bean an hour ago, and had been ordered to rest while Scotty tuned the antigrav thrusters and readied the vertical flight vessel for an extended mission. "Doesn't it make signals get stronger by bouncing them off the olivium dust?"

Janice Rand threw a stymied look over her shoulder at Uhura. No matter how many times they tried, they couldn't explain their two different methods of signal enhancement to anyone but fellow technical experts. "The signal's actually refracting through the olivium crystals rather than bouncing off them," Rand said. "Crawford's Law of Subspace Resonance says that a transperiodic element in a crystal lattice can amplify an electromagnetic signal when the subspace emission frequency equals wavelength times the Saunders Constant. Once Mr. Spock determined the range of Saunders values for olivium in its various crystal states, all I had to do was program my transmitter to concatenate those amplification wavelengths without creating any nodes of negative interferences."

"I knew that." His audible yawn made Sulu's words somewhat less convincing than they might have been. "So what's strange about the signal getting stronger as it travels away from the spaceport?"

"Nothing," Rand said. "What's odd is how weak it is right next to the spaceport. Our theoretical calculations of olivium interference didn't predict anything like that level of attenuation."

"No wonder I spent the last six weeks talking to myself," Uhura said ruefully. "Just because something works in theory doesn't mean it works in Llano Verde."

A figure paused in the lab doorway, anonymous

behind its dust muffler until a cheerful voice emerged. "Can I borrow that as my department's motto?" Neil Bartels unwrapped his filtration scarf with a glittering cloud of dust. "It's certainly more appropriate than 'Technology builds a brighter future for Llano Verde.' "

"How about 'A month late and a million excuses for not doing the work,' " Sulu said from behind the banks of equipment. "That's the version I hear most in the Outland."

Despite the light tone of his voice, Uhura knew the pilot well enough to know the comment wasn't made entirely in jest. His trips to the worst Burned areas of Llano Verde had made Sulu increasingly unsympathetic to anyone who worked in the relative safety and comfort of Big Muddy, no matter what technical or logistical problems they might have in getting their job done. She could tell from the quick downward tug of Bartels's eyebrows that Sulu's wisecrack hadn't gone over well, but then surprise washed away all other emotions on his face.

"Commander? I thought today's flight plan had you taking off at dawn for Splat." He took a step into the room, glancing around at the banks of extra equipment they had jammed in and cobbled together overnight. "What's the matter? Did something go wrong with the Bean?"

"No" was all Sulu said.

Uhura sighed and elaborated. "Rand and I are trying to combine our communications systems to jack up my signal strength, so we can contact the cargo shuttle."

"What cargo shuttle?" Bartels asked.

Uhura gave him a surprised look. "The one that our friend Commander Chekov was coming in on. It never made it to the spaceport last night." She saw the way his scruffy eyebrows shot toward his receding hairline. "You hadn't heard?"

The chief technical officer's disgusted headshake dislodged another shower of dust. "I'm supposed to be at the top level of administration in this province, and yet that—" He snapped his teeth shut on whatever he had been going to say, took a deep breath, then continued, "Governor Sedlak limits official communiqués to just the officials who need to deal with a problem. He says that's more efficient than a daily news update, because it doesn't distract the rest of us from our jobs."

Sulu rose from behind Rand's equipment bank, stretching and yawning. "You know, Sedlak's a lot more authoritarian than I expected from any governor on Belle Terre. Didn't you come here to get away from too much government control and regulation?"

"The settlers did," Bartels said. "But they're scattered across the Outland, out of reach. Most of the people in Big Muddy are contract employees like me, here for a few years just to help the colony get settled. We may not like how Sedlak runs the province, but we're being paid to get a job done, not to express our political opinions."

"In other words," Sulu said, "it's not your problem."

Neil Bartels grimaced. "Oh, it's our problem, all right. Every Outlander who comes in here mad about something makes it our problem! Do you think they believe us when we say we never heard about the tornado that killed their sheep, or the landslide that wiped out their town, or the militant isolationists shooting at them from over the hill?"

Uhura gave Sulu a reproving look. "Why don't you go see if Scotty needs any help with the Bean?"

The pilot snorted, not deceived in the slightest by her polite phrasing. "Yes, sir, Commander Uhura," he said, as if she were more than just a seniority step above him in the chain of command. "Call us on the landline if you get any response from the shuttle."

"Of course."

Neil Bartels stepped out of the doorway to make room for Sulu to leave, but came back in again as soon as the way was clear. "You're taking that experimental vessel out to look for the missing shuttle?" he asked worriedly. "Is that safe?"

"Not according to your governor," Uhura said wryly. "But since there's a Starfleet officer among the missing, he can't legally stop us."

The technical officer glanced from her to Rand, who'd spent the time since he'd entered connecting the last circuits on the signal-detection side of the system. "And you think you can actually find the shuttle by combining your two communications systems?"

"That's what we're hoping." A rainbow glow of lights sprang up across the detection control panel as Rand linked it to the lab's power supply. "Ready for a real test, Lieutenant?"

"Aye, sir." Rand scanned her detection panel, bumping all the sensitivity filters up to maximum reception. "Communications systems go."

Uhura depressed her transmission key and took a breath, preparing for another long haul of hailing. "Uhura to Orbital Shuttle Six," she said. "Come in, Orbital Shuttle Six."

"We heard you the first time," said an irritated voice from the detection panel, loud enough to make Bartels curse and Uhura and Rand both jump in their seats. "Where the hell have you been all this time?"

Chapter Five

"HEY, did you hear us that time?"

"We heard you." Only Uhura's long years on the bridge of the *Enterprise* enabled her voice to sound as calm as it did. Beneath that semblance of poise, her heart drummed hard with excitement. When she and Rand had first come up with the idea of combining their two very different communications systems, they'd considered all the possible technical problems and signal interferences they might encounter. What they hadn't been prepared for was the chance they would contact the downed shuttle on their very first try. "Don't worry, we're on our way to rescue you. Do you know where you are?"

"Do we know where we are?" This was a second voice, deeper and more sarcastic than the first. "We're in the middle of a dust blizzard, that's where we are! All our power's out and we're low on water and the *last* thing we expected was for this transmission-activated communicator to finally turn itself on."

Uhura frowned. Somehow, she'd thought the cargo shuttle's crew would sound a little more happy to be contacted so quickly after the crash. Perhaps they were feeling the effects of post-traumatic shock. "We'll try to triangulate on your signal, then. Just keep talking to us."

She motioned Rand to start the signal analyzer scanning through the concatenated frequencies it was receiving, sorting through the slight variations in distortion and polarization that they hoped would indicate the direction and distance of the signal source. Neil Bartels had disappeared a moment before, but he reappeared carrying what looked like a thin-film holographic map of Llano Verde. Since no further transmissions seemed to be coming from the shuttle crew, Uhura pressed her own transmission key again, praying they hadn't lost the signal.

"Uhura to Orbital Shuttle Six. How many survivors do you have out there?"

"Four," said the second voice. Uhura let out a deep breath of relief. According to the spaceport's manifest, the cargo shuttle had carried a crew of three plus its unofficial passenger. That meant all of them had survived the landing. She glanced over hopefully at Rand, but got a frustrated headshake in return. None of the responses they'd gotten so far had been long enough for her to track down the source of the signal.

"Can I speak to Commander Chekov?" Uhura asked, after another long pause. The former *Enterprise* security chief might be able to give her more useful information about the shuttle's landing site than the shocked civilian crew. Even if he couldn't, Uhura knew she could at least count on him to keep talking long enough for them to track the signal.

"No." That was the first voice again, sounding distinctly apprehensive now. "Um—how soon are you guys going to get here?"

"We can arrive within an hour, once we have your location." Uhura had an ominous thought, one that would account for both Chekov's inability to speak and the shuttle crew's frazzled demeanor. "Have you got a medical emergency?"

"Two of them," said the first voice, starting to shake. "Kinney broke her tooth last month and now Gabby's got a hot spot on her hind leg . . ." His shaking voice broke into a giggle for a moment, then steadied again. "Are you still there?"

Uhura blew out an exasperated breath. "Is this Orbital Shuttle Six?"

"Orbital Shuttle Six?" The deeper, more sardonic voice took over as the first speaker dissolved into helpless laughter. In the background, Uhura could hear a responsive chorus of canine yips and howls. "We thought you were calling Outland Station Six. Sorry about that."

Uhura's pent-up frustration boiled over before she could suppress it. "This isn't a joke!" she snapped into her communicator. "We've got an orbital shuttle missing and its crew unaccounted for—"

"And we've got a hundred hectares of farmland buried under radioactive dust!" Amusement and sarcasm had both faded from the unknown Outlander's voice. "The water we were supposed to irrigate our crops with has been stolen by a bunch of armed bandits, our automated farming equipment is useless because we can't communicate any instructions to it, and we're almost out of the emergency rations that were supposed to last us for a year. And every time we ask you people down in Au Contraire for help, all we hear is that the guanaco-herders on the other side of this damned impact crater are in worse shape than us, so we'll just have to wait. We don't even get to use this new olivium-proof communications system of yours, because you're saving it for your own damned emergencies!"

Uhura collected back her professional composure with some difficulty. "This communications system is experimental—this is the first time we've managed to use it successfully," she told him gently. "And whether you believe it or not, the government here in Eau Claire knows how bad it is out there. The cargo shuttle we lost was dropping off emergency rations to the worst areas of the Burn, to replace the ones the settlers have used up. You haven't gotten any of those?"

That got her a contemptuous snort. "The nearest settlement to us is run by a mayor who wouldn't give you a kick in the pants unless you paid for it. The only thing we'd get if we showed up in her town is a hard time."

Uhura glanced over at Bartels, who drew a finger across his throat suggestively. Rand's hand hovered over her board, ready to erase whatever tracking information she'd gathered. Instead of cutting the connection, however, Uhura left the frequency and signal strength unchanged, and tapped the transmission key down one more time.

"Outland Station Six, or whoever you are . . . tell me what you need in the way of supplies. We'll drop them off after we find the missing shuttle."

"Are you serious?" It was the first voice, no longer

giggling but still sounding a little shaky. "You're not just getting even with us, are you?"

"No." Uhura ignored Rand's lifted eyebrows and Bartels's warning look. "What do you need besides emergency rations?"

"Andrew's feeling the radiation pretty bad these days," said the deeper voice. "Bring us a better tissue regenerator if you can find one—and a lot more dog food."

"We'll do that," Uhura promised. "In the meantime, we'd appreciate it if you could spread the word about our missing cargo shuttle."

"No problem." Sarcastic again. "I'll be sure to tell all the dogs and chickens that I see. Outland Station Six, out."

Uhura cut the connection, then threw an inquiring look at Neil Bartels. "Is there really an Outland Station Six?"

"Not that I know of. There's no numbering system within individual Outland settlements yet, just the global plat numbers assigned by the colony's land distribution commission." Bartels glanced at the monitor where the tracking information was displayed, then unrolled his holographic map across Uhura's control panel. "Judging from that vector, I'd say it originated from one of the dryland farming claims on the alluvial fans around the Gory Mountains."

The chain of craggy peaks that stood in holographic relief under his hand was labeled Glory Mountains on the map, but Uhura didn't question Bartels's nomenclature. Like Sulu and Scotty, the chief technical officer kept track of the many nicknames settlers used in Llano Verde. "We can't get a more specific fix than that?" was all she asked.

Rand shook her head. "I couldn't get a distance estimate, sir. The polarization of their return signal was nearly isotropic."

"Probably smeared out from refracting through too many different crystal states of olivium," Bartels suggested helpfully. Unlike Sulu, he had understood from the beginning the different technical strategies Uhura and Rand had chosen for their communications systems. "From what he said about impact craters and herders, I'd guess he was on the eastern end of the Gory range, but I couldn't be more specific than that."

Uhura made a note of the frequency and refraction angle they'd used for that first transmission. "We'll try to contact them again once we've found the shuttle," she decided briskly. "In the meantime, Lieutenant Rand, I think we'd better add another amplifier unit to our polarization detector, so we can get a better distance estimate just in case we really do manage to contact the shuttle."

"Is there anything I can do to help?" Bartels asked.

"Not with that," Uhura said. "But do you think you could find a couple of hospital-grade tissue regenerators in the next hour? If the colonists need them for the radiation levels out there, we will, too. Oh, yes—and one hundred kilograms of dog food."

"One *hundred* kilos?" He gave her a startled look. "For just two dogs?"

"Two dogs at *that* homestead." Uhura smiled. If there was one thing Captain Kirk taught his officers, it was to take advantage of any opportunity that might help them carry out a mission. "Dog food wasn't included in any of the emergency rations the shuttle was dropping out there. And if Outland Station Six is a typical example, I think we can earn ourselves a lot of gratitude from the settlers by supplying it."

A distant roar pounded through him like a second heartbeat. Its power rattled the roof of the world, shattering what should have been silence into an endless white noise that hammered the dome of wind-washed sky. When thunder broke across the cacophony, it did so almost gently. A giant's hand, trembling the windows until the dream cracked open and reality spilled out across the dusty floor.

Chekov opened his eyes.

Dust glittered in the darkness on blade-thin bands of light, illuminating surreal hints of the room's interior without really giving anything away. Outside the metal walls, the planet moaned and raged at being cheated of the life she'd had before the Quake Moon had devoured her. It was the same cruelty he remembered from the Russian winters as a boy. Then, he would bundle deeper into the quilts and pillows of his bed to hide himself from the ravening cold. Now, the thin blanket under which he huddled was chill as well as damp, and he suspected nothing man-made could protect anyone from Belle Terre.

He struggled painfully upright. Every inch of his skin itched and burned, and his bones felt rusted together. While waking up at all was something of a pleasant surprise, he could have done without the headache or the desiccated mouth. He swung his legs over the edge of the bed, then paused, head in hands, to wait for equilibrium's return. The wind outside seemed to swirl the room in circles. He was vaguely aware of the heat in his burned right palm, and the deep, penetrating ache of his bruised sternum. For the moment, he couldn't recall how either got to be that way. Lifting his head slowly, he forced himself to focus on the items directly in front of him, and let that attention to detail draw the rest of his memory forward.

Brushed metal walls, stained by oxidation to a dull gray that had no name. A mirror, incongruously bright, and a packing crate upended beside a metal-frame bed to serve as a spartan nightstand. What little light penetrated the dimness bled through ill-fitting metal shutters a dozen feet away. A thin line of sand on the floor sketched the boundaries of that makeshift window. His uniform jacket, reduced by dust to a crusty oxide brown, lay draped across a second packing crate, this one nestled against the foot of the tiny bed on which he sat. A patch of dampness painted the jacket's outline on the thin, hand-stitched quilt underneath.

He wasn't sure what caught his attention first—the faint wisp of reflected brightness, or the intoxicating trace of scent. Whichever it was, he found the bowl of water on the nightstand without ever realizing he'd turned to look for it. It was lukewarm, stale from overzealous filtering, and so exquisite on his parched face and throat that it brought tears to his eyes. He didn't even swallow for the longest time, simply let the precious liquid sit in his mouth until the need to breathe forced him to pass it down. Somewhere during the third mouthful, it occurred to him that he had no proof this water was safe for touching, much less drinking. Luxuriating in its coolness as he rinsed the dust from his eyes and his sinuses, he realized that he didn't care.

Drowning the painful edge of his thirst abated the worst of his headache, although it did nothing for the rest of his aches and pains. It was a compromise

Chekov was willing to make for the moment. He rose somewhat carefully, one hand on the bed's metal headboard to stave off a rush of vertigo, and turned to find the doorway he knew must be nearby. He found it past the foot of the bed, pushed nearly closed without being latched. He knew even before he stepped away from the bed that the door led to a brief hallway, and the hallway to a larger central dome with a half-dozen other similar portals. Each of the modular prefab homesteads issued to Belle Terre colonists sported the same basic components and features; the only thing that differed was how the individual homesteader had them assembled.

This one was apparently a single-family dwelling. A jumble of pillows delineated a living space on one side of the central chamber, with evidence of computer consoles and entertainment units now long removed. A single long, grimy window let in precious little light above one of the empty console ports, and a crudely welded patch in the wall told where another window had once resided. Opposite these, a plastic table and six molded chairs clustered in a nook of metal cabinets; a reclamation tub and a gutted food-processing center punctuated one corner. Dave Plottel lay meticulously arranged on top of that little table.

Chekov crossed the darkened room gingerly, careful not to stumble over pillows or other abandoned pieces of someone else's life. An overhead light blossomed gently as he neared the kitchen. A living power source somewhere, then, with the usual complement of motion sensors and circadian controls. On the table underneath, Plottel seemed washed into curious relief, like a sculpture displayed in a museum. Chekov slowed, suddenly reluctant to immerse himself in the horrible details he knew were soon to follow. He closed one hand around Plottel's wrist and stood that way for a very long time.

If he hadn't been certain Plottel was dead at the lakeside, he had no doubt about it now. The man's skin was gray, his jaw slack, his eyes dulled by the omnipresent dust where they weren't completely closed. Barely a handful of blood darkened the breast of his coverall, and even that was so matted with sand and dirt that it almost disguised the neat little hole at its center, no bigger around than a human thumb.

Slipping one hand under Plottel's shoulder, the other beneath his hip, he rolled the body to expose the back and the tabletop underneath. The smear of rusty brown on the white plastic surface caught his attention first, but it was the fist-sized wound between Plottel's shoulder blades that held it longest. There wasn't enough blood left in the cadaver to do more than stain the table, but the tacky crust soiling the coverall from shoulders to waist spoke eloquently of hemorrhaging hours before. Nausea coiled like a sluggish snake in Chekov's stomach. His hand drifted absently to rub at his own aching breastbone.

He had Plottel's coveralls unfastened and pulled down over one shoulder when Baldwin asked drowsily from behind him, "What're you doing?"

Chekov glanced back over his shoulder only long enough to find Baldwin in another of the small, darkened doorways, looking as wind-battered and exhausted as Chekov felt. All the dust on his clothes was tawny and dry, sparkling ever so faintly in the kitchen's light.

Chekov turned back to the business of stripping Plottel's torso. "What do the colonists use for weapons in the Outland?"

"What?" Baldwin crossed the central chamber at a groggy shuffle, like a man just waking from not enough sleep. Or on the verge of succumbing to radiation exposure. "Phasers? Rocks? I don't know. The Burn killed every native animal on this side of the planet." He paused at Chekov's shoulder, blinking dully down at Plottel. "What have they . . . ?" He seemed to lose his train of thought for a moment, then took another step closer as his expression grew very still. "C.C. . . . Is that Dave?"

Chekov hesitated, not wanting to answer, knowing he couldn't just let the horrified question lie there. "Yes." It came out blunt and stiff, and much too insensitive. He wished he could take it back and start over.

"Well, he's not . . . I . . ." Baldwin tore his eyes away from the body to look pleadingly at Chekov. "He's gonna be okay?" It was a desperate question, one to which he must surely already know the answer. "He is, right?"

Feeling like a coward, Chekov broke eye contact and lifted Plottel's shoulders again. "He's dead, Mr. Baldwin." Then, because it was expected and not because he thought it would help, "I'm sorry."

"Why?" Baldwin asked, leaning forward to make Chekov face him again. "You didn't kill him, did you?" But his expression was angry, a bitter mixture of sarcasm and hurt. "You said everything was going to be okay—you promised you wouldn't let him drown. Reddy told me that," he added, smug in his awful knowledge. "He said you'd take care of him. *You* said you'd take care of all of us!"

"He didn't drown." *And everything isn't going to be*

okay—right now nothing about this situation is okay. This time when Chekov rolled the body, the absence of bloody clothing revealed every detail of the ugly wound in Plottel's back. Whether the sight of it shocked Baldwin into silence or he'd simply run out of momentum, Chekov couldn't tell. But he took advantage of the other man's silence to finish the examination he'd started before Baldwin entered the room. "Whoever killed him wasn't using a phaser. There's no cauterization along the edges of the wound." He didn't expect the details to mean anything to Baldwin, but it felt somehow important to help Baldwin understand what they were up against. Chekov fell silent himself for a moment, struggling to remember some pertinent detail of the rifle which had burned his hand on the lakeshore. He remembered the loudness of its report, and the shocking power with which something had slammed into the chest of his environmental suit and shattered it to pieces. That was good old-fashioned inertia—a mass accelerated to such a great velocity that it would impact any static object as though it weighed a ton. "It has to be a projectile weapon of some kind. Something the colonists put together for themselves." But what were they using for an accelerant? How had they figured out the ballistics of the projectile mass? He felt again the gut-wrenching kick of something all but invisible blasting apart his environmental suit, and wondered how he and Baldwin could hope to preserve themselves now that they didn't even wear that much protection.

Baldwin reached across in front of him with surprising tenderness, tugging Plottel's coverall back into place as neatly as he could without actually touching the body. Suddenly aware of his own bloody hands,

Chekov took a respectful step backward to give Baldwin access to his friend.

"Is there a bathroom?" he asked, very quietly. Years in security had taught him that there was really nothing he should be saying at a time like this, no matter how certain his heart was that there must be.

Not looking up from his simple ministrations, Baldwin merely pointed.

The bathroom was as small and spare as the bedroom, with nothing left but a still-active composting toilet and a discarded pile of cleaning rags. Enough to scrub the worst of the wet blood from his hands, but not enough to get the rusty details out of the creases. He did what he could, then stowed the dirty scraps behind the toilet where Baldwin wouldn't have to see them.

Back in the main dome, Baldwin had liberated the quilt from Chekov's bedroom and draped it across Plottel's body. It somehow made the death more personal now that the face was only a ghostly silhouette beneath the age-dimmed colors. Baldwin sat among the pillows on the other side of the chamber, his back to the kitchen, his face hidden in his own hands. Trying to grant him what little privacy he could, Chekov slipped quietly into the bedroom to retrieve his jacket, then took as long as he possibly could to shake the dust out of the fabric and shoulder it on.

Baldwin didn't look up when he finally reentered the chamber. "So, C.C. . . . Where are we?"

Chekov paused in fastening his shoulder strap, looking out the barely transparent window above the sitting area. What little he could see past the dirt was dimmed by the dust storm—a vast tract of dust and scrub leading toward an upward-slanting horizon that went nowhere. Turning away from the view, he finished arranging his jacket as he went to sit across from Baldwin. "I haven't the faintest idea."

"Then how did you find this place?"

"I didn't." Chekov returned Baldwin's startled look with a helpless spreading of his hands. "I thought you or Reddy knew of homesteads near Bull's Eye and . . ."

"And what?" Baldwin gave a sharp little laugh that didn't sound particularly amused. Chekov let him hold on to the anger, understanding that it sprang mostly from shock, and wasn't really aimed at him. "Dragged you here through the storm?" Baldwin went on, shoving to his feet in a spasm of frustration. "You think I'm too stupid to bring the environmental suits? Or smart enough to get us all past whatever killed Dave?"

"I don't think you're stupid." Chekov tried to drag him back to the practicalities. "Where is Reddy?"

Baldwin only stared at him. After an uncomfortably long silence, he said with some amazement, "You really don't know."

He didn't wait for Chekov to answer, just turned and walked into another of the dome's small doorways. Chekov rose to follow, his stomach churning again, his heart thumping painfully against the inside of his chest.

He knew Reddy was alive by his breathing, shallow and too rapid, alarmingly loud in the small room. But as he moved closer to the narrow bed, he also knew by the smell of blood and sour sweat that the pilot might not stay that way for long. He knelt, wishing for something more to do than lift the edge of the blankets and glance underneath at the damage. While the bandaging about Reddy's middle was neat and tightly wound, it was also sodden and warm to the touch.

Baldwin's voice was barely more than a whisper. "He didn't bring us anywhere, C.C."

"No," Chekov agreed grimly. He replaced the blankets, wincing in sympathy when Reddy murmured with pain. "But if he didn't, then who did?"

"Yeah . . ." Baldwin stirred uneasily behind him. "And are they still hanging around?"

"Crooked Creek?" Sulu had to stick his head out the opened side cockpit of the Bean, since the ship's internal communicator couldn't reach even as far as Scotty, working under the belly of their dust-scuffed metal beast. Although they were shielded from the worst of Big Muddy's dust by the spaceport hangar, enough olivium had filtered in through cracks to suspend a fine glitter in the air, and interfere with electromagnetic and subspace signals. "Mr. Scott, have you ever heard of an Outland settlement called Crooked Creek?"

"Don't think so, lad." Scott's gruff voice lifted to a shout to be heard over the rising whine of the right lateral antigrav generators he was tuning. "There's one called Up the Creek. Maybe Crooked Creek was its original name."

Sulu glanced down at the map and frowned. "I thought about that, but it doesn't make sense—Up the Creek's nearly six hundred kilometers away from the rest of the cargo drops they were scheduled to make."

Scotty picked up his engineering tricorder, yanking at the cables that he had to use for probing internal circuitry in lieu of remote sensors. "What about Useless Loop? It must have had some other name before that chunk of Quake Moon fell on it."

"True." Sulu scanned his much scribbled-on map

again, but couldn't find that nickname either. "Where *is* Useless Loop? I don't have it listed here."

"That's because we decided it was too risky to try to land there." The chief engineer plugged his cables into the left lateral generator, to test the antigravitational force being generated there. The only sensitive part of the Bean's propulsion system was the balance of its three antigravs. If one of them got tuned to deliver a stronger thrust than the others, the ship had trouble maintaining a horizon. "Bartels told us it sat right next to one of those big impact craters, where the olivium levels would mess up our instruments. Now, was it Humpty, Dumpty, or Splat?"

"What about Bull's Eye?" Sulu traced an imaginary line across the map, connecting the nine cargo drops that he'd managed to locate so far. The route passed directly over Llano Verde's largest impact scar. "That would put it in the right place. And the base map shows a crooked river draining off the northern slope of the crater."

"Does it show which of its loops turned into the useless one?"

"No. And if I have to scout around for it, I'll get thrown off the rest of my course." Just having a general idea of the town's location wasn't good enough for this trip—Sulu needed specific coordinates to program into the Bean's computer. With Gamma Night still blocking contact with the orbital platform, the only way he had to navigate was to keep rigorous track of map coordinates. That meant he had to laboriously preprogram their course using the Bean's digital map data bank and the list of settlements John Kyle had transmitted to him.

"Then leave it 'til the end of the flight," Scotty advised. "With any luck, it won't be the last place that got supplies dropped from the shuttle or the first place that didn't." He ran the rear antigrav thruster through its full power cycle, then cut the dull roar of the generator down to an idling hiss. "Don't forget, lad, Gamma Night will be over in another eight hours. You can check your position with the orbital platform after that."

Sulu opened his mouth to reply, but the echo of urgent footsteps off the metallic hangar walls suggested that the rest of their crew had finally arrived. He hurriedly deleted his incomplete entry for Crooked Creek and merged the remaining segments into a complete course plan. "So, did the J-channel buffers work?" he heard Scotty ask outside the Bean.

"Dear God, we hope not," said an unfamiliar voice. "Mr. Scott, please tell us that what we're looking at is just a malfunction in our data line."

Sulu looked up from his navigations panel, his attention caught not so much by the odd words as the ominous tone they were uttered in. He glanced through his open cockpit window to see three figures in gray-green government dust mufflers range themselves around the chief engineer. The taller two shrugged out of heavy, equipment-laden packs while the shortest one held out a tricorder for Scotty to examine.

"Take a look at station ninteen-aught-nine," he begged Scott. "Is that a valid data point?"

"Can't be. It's way off scale." Scotty punched a series of tests into the other man's tricorder, then watched the display flicker back the results. Even from inside the Bean, Sulu could see the Scotsman's craggy eyebrows jerk up in amazement. "Where the blazes is the transducer that measured that point?"

"In the Little Muddy River, just south of Bull's Eye crater." The other man peeled back his dust-filtering scarf to reveal an anxious, bearded face. "So it's valid? There really is three thousand cubic meters of water coming through per second?"

"The pressure transducer might be malfunctioning," Scotty said dubiously. "If a rock fell on top of it, or it got buried under too much olivium mud—"

"The discrepancy in vertical and horizontal pressures would have shown up in the internal system checks. That data is real." The new voice belonged to a woman, although it emerged from the most broad-shouldered and athletic of the three cloaked figures. She swung around to stare hopefully up at Sulu through the cockpit window. "You've *got* to take us with you, so we can see where the water's coming from—"

"Mr. Scott!" That was a voice Sulu did recognize, despite the hoarseness caused by too many weeks of continuous hailing. He also recognized the excitement that quivered perceptibly beneath the communications officer's poise, and scrambled out of the Bean's cockpit, heading back down the narrow passageway between the lateral antigrav generators into the crowded cargo hold. By the time he made it out the hatch, Uhura and Rand had joined the tense knot of people gathered beside the rear thruster plate. "—a ping off the shuttle's automatic responder," Uhura was saying, while she unwrapped her dust muffler. "We couldn't get much of a fix on its location, but it's transmitting the code for being powered down and intact!"

"Any voice contact?" Sulu demanded, pushing unceremoniously past the three government employees to join her.

"No," Uhura admitted. "But we were right on the

shoulder of our last frequency band and barely making contact. More intermittent signals—like voices—might have been smeared out by refractive variability." She glanced past Sulu, at yet another dust-cloaked figure moving down the hangar. This one was guiding a cargo sled full of equipment and more sacks of supplies. "Um—how much more room do we have in the Bean?"

"Not very much," Sulu said. "Not unless you want to off-load some of the emergency rations you told me to put on board."

"Well, we may have to," Uhura said. "I promised some sick and starving settlers that—"

"Commander Uhura," the bearded man said urgently. "We've got a more urgent problem than starvation to deal with here. Now that our data network's finally sorting out signal from noise, it looks like there's a potentially hazardous situation up in the headwaters of the Big Muddy—"

"A potentially *catastrophic* situation!" The female hydrologist pulled her dust filtration scarf off as well, revealing tousled blond hair and an intense frown. "Those flow rates in the Little Muddy don't make any sense, coming in the dry season like this. Not unless that water's leaking out of Bull's Eye's crater lake—"

"—at three thousand cubic meters per second—" the bearded man interjected.

"—through some of those conduit hot springs up there," the third scientist, a dark-haired and wiry man, chimed in. "All it would take would be one landslide on the crater rim—"

"—followed by rapid down-cutting and outflow—"

"—and we could have a flood wave big enough to wipe out every settlement between Southfork and Big Muddy!"

Their intertwined voices rose in a chorus of scientific passion that reminded Sulu of Leonard McCoy when faced with an imminent medical crisis. He exchanged considering glances with Scotty, Uhura, and Rand, but it was actually Neil Bartels who spoke first, from behind his loaded cargo sled. To Sulu's surprise, the technical officer sounded more irritated than upset.

"Tom, weren't your hydrologists scheduled to inspect the walls of the impact craters in Llano Verde back when you first realized they were starting to fill up with water?"

The bearded man swung around, blinking at his fellow government employee. "Yes. Yes, we were," he said after a minute, as if he had to pause to remember. "But we had to get the hardwired monitoring system up and running before the dust season started, and after that we never got the kevlar bodysuits we requisitioned for fieldwork. The last time I spoke to the governor about it, he said he thought it would just be best to wait until the dust season ended—"

"—and the rainy season started?" Bartels snorted. "You should have known better than to let a sociobiologist tell you when to do fieldwork! There's no way you're going to get Sedlak's permission to go out now, with the dust storms worse than they've ever been."

"We don't need his permission," said the female hydrologist. "We're not taking one of his shuttles or any of his precious Emergency Services team. We're just going to hitch a ride with Starfleet."

Sulu opened his mouth to object, but Uhura had already nodded agreement. "We've only got room for two of you," she warned. "And a few pieces of lightweight equipment."

"That'll be enough," McElroy said, silencing the

other two hydrologists' incipient protest with a stern look. "All we really need is a couple of maps and our scientific tricorders. I was planning to stay here in Big Muddy anyway, to monitor the hydrologic data network." He glanced over his shoulder at the hangar doors as if he could already hear the thunder of floodwaters coming toward them. "Just in case that crater gives out before you get there."

Chapter Six

THERE WASN'T MUCH Chekov could do for Reddy.

Starship security personnel received more extensive first-aid training than anyone on board except the medical division. Unfortunately, that training tended to assume a basic field medical kit, or at least some means of obtaining clean water. At worst, protocol expected that any guard tending an injured shipmate only had to hold tight until his starship beamed them to safety or sent in reinforcements. Nowhere was it acknowledged that the worst possible hell was having enough training to understand how badly a comrade was injured without being able to do a thing about it.

Whoever had bandaged Reddy had done it tight and clean. Chekov used part of the least filthy sheets in the house to add another few layers to the wrap, and in the half-hour he stayed with Reddy after that, no additional blood soaked through. He chose to take that as a sign the bleeding had abated somewhat.

"Maybe he just doesn't have anything else left to leak," Baldwin suggested when Chekov shared his cautious optimism. He decided at that point to greatly limit how much of his own thoughts he would share with Baldwin.

Reddy drifted toward consciousness without ever really surfacing. Cinnamon-brown skin had bled out to a horrid sallow, and the faintly blue tinge to his lips betrayed how little oxygen circulated through his tissues. At one point, eyes made shiny and sightless by shock found Chekov in the darkness. "It's the dust," Reddy explained in a startlingly normal tone of voice. "You can't see anything through all this dust."

Chekov got two swallows of the overfiltered water into him during that moment of near lucidity. Then he'd handed the bowl off to Baldwin and climbed stiffly to his feet. "I'm going to look for a radio, in case the dust clears enough for us to use it."

Baldwin made a skeptical noise through his nose as he took Chekov's place by the bed. "You're kidding, right?"

Chekov almost answered him, forgetting for a moment his new rule against handing Baldwin fuel for his cynicism. Instead, he closed the door on his way out and pretended not to hear when Baldwin called after him, "Hey . . . C.C.? Where are you going to look?"

He worked his way through the homestead methodically, and more quickly than he'd hoped. The place had apparently been abandoned for months. The dilithium generator tucked between the plates of the main dome would chug happily along for another thousand years, supplying the place with lights, heat, and air filtration, but there was little in the way of domestic equipment left for it to power. Even the water-recycling unit had been stripped. If there had ever been a comm hitched into the homestead's grid, there was no evidence of it now. No food or even food crumbs in the tiny kitchen, no eating utensils, no dishes. The most useful discovery was two five-liter jugs of water in the third and last bedchamber, neatly stacked near the hinges of the swinging door where they were hidden each time the room was entered. Not even the minimal decorations he'd seen in his own room, though. Just a sagging double bed, and a dusty, rumpled comforter not quite big enough to cover the entire mattress.

He carried the water back to the main chamber, then stood holding it for what seemed a terribly long time, not sure where to go from here. He didn't need the sight of Plottel's body, still framed by the lonely kitchen window overhead, to remind him of their dismal options. No matter who waited out there in the dust, no matter what finally happened to Reddy, Chekov and Baldwin had to leave. They had no food, precious little water, and absolutely no hope that rescue would find them here. The only variables under their control were which direction to set out in, and whether to take Reddy with them or wait here until he died. Chekov had a feeling Baldwin hadn't yet accepted that aspect of their situation—that some stubborn part of the colonist firmly believed they could wait prudently for rescue, save Reddy, and somehow keep themselves from either starving or having holes blown in their bodies all at the same time.

By contrast, somewhere around the time he'd had to swallow the bitterness of saving Plottel from drowning only to see him so horribly murdered, Chekov realized that none of them were going to survive without the benefit of ruthless pragmatism.

It was that pragmatism which finally drove him outside to the barn. He didn't know what he expected to find out there. Some kind of landline connection, maybe, like what the locals had been promised at the beginning of the dust season. Or signal flares. Pigeons, even. Perhaps deep down inside he'd known that he'd find precisely nothing. But he couldn't ask Baldwin to help him load Reddy onto a makeshift stretcher and drag him out into the storm unless he could look the man in the face and tell him truthfully, "Yes, I looked everywhere. No, we have no chance of surviving if we stay here. We have to leave, and we have to leave now."

Dust and screaming wind transformed the hundred or so meters from the central chamber to the barn into an impossible expanse when he viewed it from behind the safety of a window. Chekov remembered all too clearly the burn of sand whipping against his skin, dust searing his unprotected eyes. To make matters worse, he'd taken no prophylactic treatments against the olivium radiation before heading down to Belle Terre. Why should he? He was only supposed to be in Eau Claire for a few hours, with a real medical facility just around the corner. He'd be leaving the system altogether in a few more months. It had seemed a waste of medicine when McCoy offered him the antiradiation treatments a few weeks before. Now, a persistent headache and lingering nausea reminded him that even brief exposure to unstable transperiodic elements exacted a heavy price. And they no doubt had a good bit of walking yet to do.

The largest of the old comforters served well enough as a hood and muffler, shielding his eyes from the wind and keeping a majority of the dust off his face and hands. There wasn't much to be done for his lungs. Chekov managed to stave off the worst of his coughing until he'd ducked into the barn's relative safety, then ended up on hands and knees as his body fought to expel every molecule of olivium he'd just inhaled. *This is how I'm going to die,* he thought at one point when stars danced in his vision for want of a single productive breath. Not from the radiation, not from some primitive colonial weapon, but from coughing up so much dust that he finally had no lungs left to breathe with.

Once he could manage two or three breaths in a row, he let the blanket slide to the floor and climbed upright. Stalls lined one side of the narrow building, empty shelves and bins the other. Moldy straw—or hay or alfalfa, he had no idea which—filled only one small corner of the upper story, and a door on the opposite side from where he entered led to a three-sided pole structure carpeted in mummified manure. He tried to remember the name of the leggy, sweet-faced non-sheep the colonists had defaulted to when dust and radiation took its toll on their original ungulates, but could only come up with the apparently appropriate word *guano,* which he knew wasn't right. Whatever they were, the homestead's owners had apparently taken them along with everything else when they left. Or they'd been stolen by whoever drove the rightful owners away. In either case, he knew he wouldn't find a comm unit in the pens. So he turned to the tiny storage room as his last hope before convincing Baldwin they had to leave, and found the heavy oilcloth package where it had been shoved to the back of the workbench.

He'd unwrapped it expecting a cache of tools that

two desperate men might find useful. Instead, he found himself holding a contraption that wasn't good for anything except killing another human being.

The gun lay exposed atop its square of oiled fabric, its pieces carefully sorted as though it were nothing more significant than an air-filtration pump, waiting its turn for repair. Already down on one knee, Chekov sank the rest of the way to the ground and studied the dilemma he'd unfolded.

For nearly a decade now, his world had been a place where tools classified as weapons were coded, counted, and secured outside the reach of the general crew. A place where people highly trained in the respect and use of those weapons had to sign them out, return them at the end of the day, and construct detailed explanations if the charge on the power pack was reduced by even so much as a photon—it didn't matter if the phaser was used to warm a rock, send up a signal, seal a broken weld, or stun an aggressor in self-defense. On board a starship, there was nothing—absolutely *nothing*—the average crewman could get his hands on that was able to do anything as brutal and inhumane as what had been done to Plottel and Reddy. Yet here on Belle Terre, any colonist with a workbench could apparently construct his own little instrument of torture, then proceed to use it on anyone he pleased.

The weapon's mechanism was frighteningly simple—a magazine for holding projectiles, a spring-action loader assembly, and a manually triggered firing pin. Nothing apparently explosive in the weapon itself, which meant the propellant must be built into the projectiles. Wrapped with the dismantled rifle were five smooth, tapered metal cylinders. Jacketed, with a strike plate on the back of each. Chekov held one against the main workings of the firing mechanism, and nodded slowly as the details of its engineering became clear. An impact from the firing pin against the projectile's strike plate ignited an explosive propellant within the jacket, launching the projectile at some horrendous velocity down the barrel of the weapon and across whatever distance the propellant and the barrel's rifling would allow. There had to be some method for ejecting the spent jacket and chambering the next projectile, of course. He had a feeling the function of that mechanism became obvious once the weapon was reconstructed.

So this was what Pardonnet's dream of Eden had done to its people—seduced them onto the frontier with promises of freedom and opportunity, then stranded them with their own base humanity when all those promises flashed into hardship and dust. Instead of perfecting their medical supplies, developing radiation-resistant crops, or working hand-in-hand to create an olivium-proof communications network, the colonists had turned against each other, summoning an all-too-easy solution to the fears now stalking them under cover of the dust which was their real enemy. They murdered strangers, abandoned their homesteads, and left each other no option but to turn into the same kind of monsters if they wanted to save their own lives.

Hating himself, hating the prospect of mutilating a human life the way someone had already done Plottel and Reddy, Chekov carefully replaced the weapon pieces in their oilcloth wrapping. Then he gathered up the bundle with its five opportunities for murder, and carried them into the house for reassembly.

* * *

"How much time are we going to get at the *next* stop?"

Sulu didn't bother answering that question. He was in the middle of the critical upward thrust that took the overloaded Bean off the ground and up through the thickest part of Llano Verde's dust layer. With no working proximity sensors, and the high wall of the Gory Mountains looming just to the south, he needed all his concentration to keep the vertical flight vessel oriented straight up. A flicker of peripheral vision told him Uhura had shifted the experimental communicator on her lap so she could turn around and answer the more vocal of their two backseat passengers.

"Dr. Weir, we agreed to let you *observe* the river at each of the stops we made, not wade in and start measuring it." The calm patience in Uhura's voice amazed Sulu. He'd lost his own tolerance two landings ago at Windblown, when it had taken him an extra half-hour on the ground to track down the two scientists. Weir hadn't protested much then, since she didn't seem to share Dr. Greg Anthony's obsessive need to measure the olivium contamination level of every muddy rivulet he stepped in. But in Culvert, where the increased volume of the Big Muddy River had been much more noticeable, Weir had to be dragged forcibly out of the churning water when she refused to stop measuring flow rates with her tricorder. Sulu could still smell the odor of rotting mud and olivium on her boots.

"You just don't get it! I know you want to find your friend, but there are thousands of people who could be in danger down there." Weir's emphatic gesture swept the area below them, although all that could be seen through the Bean's windows was a featureless haze of gray-brown dust. "Every settlement we've stopped at along the Big Muddy is showing signs of increased outflow! When the monsoonal rains start—"

"—sometime later this month," Sulu cut in sharply, "you'll have had weeks to prepare. That shuttle crew could be dying *now.*"

Dr. Weir had the grace to snap her teeth shut on whatever she'd been going to say, although from the soft thump Sulu heard, he suspected an elbow in the ribs from her fellow scientist had something to do with her sudden tact. For a long while after that, the Bean was filled only with the hiss of dust slithering across their duranium hull as they broke through the storm into the bright glow of early-afternoon sunlight. Uhura blinked and then turned off the experimental communicator on her lap. As long as they were above the dust layer, there weren't going to be any olivium-amplified reflections for her to detect.

It had taken longer than either of them had wanted to leave the continental capital. That was mostly because Neil Bartels had to be convinced that a single data point—from an automated data network that until recently hadn't even been working—constituted a valid scientific crisis. After they'd discussed it for several minutes, it turned out that what the chief technical officer really wanted was enough justification to keep from losing his job if Governor Sedlak ever found out that he'd known about the unauthorized field excursion in advance. To get his approval, McElroy had to promise to keep Bartels updated on everything his field team discovered, which in turn meant Sulu and Uhura had to promise to allow the hydrologists to observe the condition of the Big Muddy River anytime they landed near it.

So far, unfortunately, that had been every single stop

they made. In retrospect, Sulu decided, they should have started tracking the cargo shuttle from the first settlements scheduled for supply drops, rather than the last ones along the Big Muddy. That way, they could have just dropped the hydrologists off at Bull's Eye crater and not wasted so much time.

An overload warning beeped from the Bean's antigrav controls, and, a minute later, the vertical flight vessel sank back down toward the dust layer as it passed through a strong downdraft near the mountains. Sulu gritted his teeth and kept his hands steady on the controls, knowing it was useless to try and gain altitude against the wind. The addition of two hydrologists, two tissue regenerators, and a hundred kilograms of dog food meant the antigrav thrusters were already at maximum lift capacity and could no longer compensate for changes in atmospheric pressure.

If he'd weighed just ten kilos more himself, Sulu thought, they would've only been able to take along one of the two field hydrologists McElroy wanted to send with them, and they'd have had a much greater safety buffer on the antigravs. As it was, he had to wait so long before he could pull the Bean back up to clearer air that he found himself abruptly face-to-face with the craggy slopes of the Gory Mountains when he finally got there. Sulu swung abruptly around to parallel them while he checked his compass heading. The reading he got made him frown.

"Uhura, turn on the emergency landing lights."

The communications officer obeyed him immediately. She only slanted him a questioning look when the Bean continued on its horizontal course without any further aerial gyrations. "Um—are we actually in any danger of landing?"

"No, I just wanted to see the air." The crimson and gold flash of their landing lights sparked answering reflections in what otherwise looked like clear air to their starboard, outlining a column of nearly invisible glitter. "I thought so."

"What is it?" Weir poked her head between him and Uhura to see what he'd pointed at. Anthony peered over her shoulder with equal interest, but a little more politeness.

"Olivium twister." It was one of Llano Verde's most bizarre weather phenomena—a dust devil made of almost microscopic olivium crystals, spun off into the upper atmosphere from the churning storms below. The warp it caused in the planet's magnetic field had probably been distorting his compass readings for the past fifteen minutes.

"So *that's* what they look like." Anthony scrabbled in his backpack and emerged with a tricorder. He used it to track the olivium twister for as long as it stayed visible, bumping Weir unceremoniously out of his sight line when her broad shoulders got in the way. "Wow! It was worth coming along just to see that."

Weir sat back up as he put the tricorder away. "Now we know why we keep seeing radioactive hot spots in such random places around Llano Verde," she said. "Something like that could dump enough olivium on one spot to make a compass spin."

Uhura glanced over at Sulu in sudden comprehension. "That's how you knew it was there? The compass readings were off?"

He nodded, tapping at the old-fashioned magnetic detector Scotty had added to his control panel for navigating during Gamma Night. Its needle still disagreed with the alignment of the sharp peaks on their right.

The Gory range ran east-west across Llano Verde, paralleling the Big Muddy River from Windblown all the way up to Desperation before breaking into badlands and impact craters. The haze of slightly more reddish dust that curled around their lower slopes showed how they had gotten their nickname, but their snow-topped peaks thrust far up into the layer of clear air above, forming an unmistakable landmark. That gave Sulu at least one thing to be thankful for today. With the compass inoperative and the orbital platform silenced by Gamma Night, visual reckoning was all he had left to rely on.

"Do we know where we're going now?" Uhura asked. "Or do we just have to get away from the olivium twister and reorient ourselves?"

"We should be able to spot North Scarp pretty easily from the air." From the sound of plasfilm rustling in the back, Sulu guessed Greg Anthony had unrolled one of his holographic river-drainage maps. "It's right at the junction of the Little Eau Claire River and the Stony Creek. According to the map, there should be a deep gorge through the Glory Mountains there."

"It's the Gory Mountains, and the Little Muddy River." Sulu squinted along the rocky spine of peaks, looking for the slash of sky between them that would mark their next stop. "You really should keep your maps updated."

"That would be a lot easier to do if we were allowed to field-check them," Weir retorted. "But since Sedlak thinks his computer modelers can answer all his questions without the inconvenience of actually going out and collecting data—"

"You've never actually studied the rivers out here before?" Uhura's sympathetic voice made Sulu snort beneath his breath. From now on, she was probably going to allow the two hydrologists a lot more leeway in taking their mud and water measurements.

"No, sir." Greg Anthony's automatic "sirs" and more respectful manner made Sulu suspect he'd gotten at least part of his education at a Starfleet training academy. "The governor's office doesn't give Technical Services enough funds to go around, and we're always on the bottom of the priority list. The only fieldwork we've done was setting up the automated data-collection network."

"And we only got *that* done because the order came straight from Evan Pardonnet," Weir added. "Otherwise, we'd still be sitting in a bare office, doodling on our data padds."

Sulu grunted, swinging the Bean farther north to avoid a mountain outlier that looked as if it could generate more annoying downdrafts. The compass was starting to swing back into alignment with the mountains, but he still didn't entirely trust it. "What I want to know," he said, "is how someone like Sedlak ever got elected governor of Llano Verde in the first place."

"Sulu," Uhura said reprovingly.

"Well, can you see him campaigning for votes?"

Weir surprised him with a crack of laughter. " 'Sedlak, the only natural selection.' I have to admit, I can't see it, either."

"I don't remember voting for him," Anthony said. "And we elected all the continental governors as a group back on Earth, so no single interest group could dominate a small region out here."

"Maybe one of the governors-elect got killed on the journey here," Weir suggested. "Or resigned their post. Sedlak might have been appointed as a replacement."

"Or promoted from a government bureaucracy job," Sulu said.

"Neil Bartels said Sedlak was a sociobiologist," Uhura reminded him. "Not a bureaucrat."

"Then maybe he was transferred from an academic post. That would explain all his theories about moral expendability and colony survival—" Sulu broke off, seeing the mountain range take an abrupt downward plunge into the dust layer. The snowcapped peaks reappeared a short distance away, but there was just enough open space left between the two escarpments for a river to thread its way through. "There we go. No Escape."

It was a settlement he'd visited on one of his test flights and wasn't particularly looking forward to landing at again. The original name of North Scarp had been more apt than most of the colony's romantic nomenclature, since the entire community was perched on the steep northern slopes of the Gory Mountains, overlooking the canyon carved through them by the Little Muddy River. There were almost no horizontal streets in town, much less open plazas or other places for a shuttlecraft to land. The town reminded Sulu of the steep hills of San Francisco, or some of the villages along the south Italian coast. He supposed the original intention in settling here had been to recreate that kind of hillside charm. If it had been up to him, though, he'd have plunked the whole settlement down a few miles further north, on the less scenic but more practical high plains.

Apparently, Dr. Weir agreed. "Didn't anyone back at the colony headquarters look at the survey maps of this planet before they let people decide where to put their settlements?" she demanded. Sulu heard the plasfilm map rustle in the back seat. "Look at that, Greg—it's right inside an incised meander. No wonder they call it No Escape."

"Wait until you see it." Sulu began a careful descent into the dust. He tried to center the Bean as evenly as possible over the gap between the mountains, but the double dose of downdrafts he was getting along with the usual wind-tunnel suck of the gorge itself wasn't making it easy to keep the craft steady. He glanced at the compass again, to reassure himself it really had returned to its normal orientation. Once he was in the dust, it was all he was going to be able to go by.

"Belt in," he said. "This may not be real pretty."

Since Uhura was already wearing her safety harness, she turned around to make sure the hydrologists got theirs on correctly. "Put your tricorder away in your pack, Dr. Anthony, and clip it to the floor," she advised. "Maps, too. They might not be able to hurt you if they go flying around, but they could block the pilot's view."

"And that wouldn't be good." Weir rolled up the plasfilm maps, then folded and stuffed them unceremoniously into her tunic pockets. The Bean was bouncing and swaying now as it tried to compensate for every shift of mountain wind, but the hydrologist's voice never faltered. "So, Mr. Sulu, you never told us how long we get to look at the river at this stop."

"That depends on how well this descent goes," Sulu said between his teeth. The Bean's vertical jouncing was under control, but its side-to-side swings weren't as easy to damp out with his limited antigrav maneuverability. He could feel them growing stronger as they got closer to the surface. Visibility had dropped to almost nothing now, with dust sheeting and slithering past their windows in fitful sprays. "If we hit really hard, you may be here for the rest of your life."

"However short that is," Weir said, cheerfully.

A sudden updraft destabilized the careful balance of the three antigrav thrusters, and Sulu gave up trying to make conversation. He kept his eyes fixed on the compass and the horizontal level, compensating for each change in wind speed and direction and hoping he was staying on course. If he was even a tenth of a second late on each correction, he could be creating a sidelong drift that would carry them into the side of the narrow mountain gorge. And with the amount of olivium swirling around him, he doubted his proximity alarms would go off much more than a millisecond before they hit.

"Oh, my God!"

Sulu felt Weir bump the back of his pilot's chair with her sudden swing toward the Bean's port side. He wasted a moment glancing that way, just in case she'd seen the side of a mountain looming through the dust, and was reassured to catch only a glimpse of shadowed fields and the vague silver glint of water below the thinning haze of dust. They were going to be lucky. The dust storm was getting blown away at ground level by the strong downdrafts of cold air rolling off the mountains.

"Bev?" Anthony whacked his colleague on the shoulder to get her fixed attention off the landscape. "What were you yelling about? You scared us half to death."

"You should be scared half to death," the female hydrologist said grimly. "Take a good look at that canyon, Greg."

He craned past her to study the silver glimmer of the river, growing brighter and clearer as they dropped through the last of the dust. Sulu was making a final adjustment to the antigravs, one that corrected for the strong, steady push of the winds flowing off the mountains. He could already see the housetops and chimneys of No Escape resolving out of the dull red-brown color of the mountain soil, but he couldn't seem to find the rough gravel beach along the river where he'd landed on his previous visit.

"Oh, my God." This time it was Anthony who made the comment, underlined a moment later by Uhura's wordless gasp. Sulu opened his mouth to ask what they were staring at, but before the words could even emerge, a closer look down at the rooftops told him why he couldn't find his beach anymore.

The Little Muddy River was running through the streets of No Escape.

The mayor of No Escape was not happy to see them.

The job of tracking him down had fallen to Uhura and Anthony. After fifteen minutes of looking for a landing site, Sulu had finally been forced to hover with the Bean over a convenient rooftop while the rest of them scrambled out. Weir had broken out a flotation vest from her equipment pack and headed for the main channel of the flooded river, with Sulu following her from above in the Bean. In case she needed him to drop her a lifeline, he had said to Uhura, although Uhura suspected it was also a way to keep the errant hydrologist in sight until the time came to leave. Greg Anthony, on the other hand, had become much more cooperative since Uhura had needed to track him down at their first stop. He insisted on accompanying her to the roughhewn building Sulu had identified as the town hall, only pausing once or twice to measure olivium radiation levels in the ankle-deep water they were wading through.

"Well, where've you been?" No Escape's mayor swung around from behind his desk and glared at them before they could even introduce themselves. Outside his small office, the town hall was filled with the wails of tired children and the howls of tied-up dogs. It had apparently been pressed into service as a relocation center for the homeless. "I've been sending messages down to Au Contraire for five days now! You just getting around to reading your mail? Or did you decide you had more important things to do than rescue five hundred settlers from a flood?"

Uhura heard Greg Anthony's nervously cleared throat and realized that the hydrologist's gray-green continental uniform was what had sparked this diatribe. "We're not Emergency Services," she told the mayor. "I'm Commander Uhura of the *Starship Enterprise,* and this is Dr. Greg Anthony of the Hydrologic and Meteorologic Division. I'm sorry, but we didn't even know you were flooded until we got here."

"Didn't know?" The mayor, a stocky Asian man with an anomalous mop of curly hair, gave her a startled look. "You came here from Au Contraire, didn't you?"

"Yes."

"And no one down there has heard anything about the flooding on the Little Muddy? Not even any media coverage about us having to evacuate everyone in What's the Point?" Uhura shook her head, and he turned toward Anthony. "No government dispatches about the emergency we're having up here?"

"Governor Sedlak doesn't believe in government dispatches, or a daily news bulletin," Anthony said dryly.

"We came up to field-check a strange hydrologic reading from one of our water pressure sensors. Governor Sedlak doesn't even know we're here."

The mayor let out a frustrated noise, halfway between a groan and a curse. "Of course he doesn't! He would've probably told you it wasn't efficient to bother checking out that one measurement, even if it could have saved us from having to resettle every man, woman, and child in What's the Point!"

"You lost an entire settlement to the flooding?" Uhura asked in concern. "Was anyone killed?"

"Not as far as I know." The mayor scrubbed a hand across his face, turning its olivium-burnt ruddiness a shade darker with that ruthless massage. He looked exhausted. His second-floor office was stacked high with storage crates and furniture carted up from the floor below, and Uhura wondered if he had brought it all up himself. "I'm sorry—who did you say you were again?"

"Commander Uhura of the *Enterprise,"* she said gently. "And you are—?"

"Ang Wat." He stuck out an olivium-burned hand for her and Anthony to shake. "I don't suppose you brought any medical supplies with you? We could use whatever you've got, even if it's just a first-aid kit."

"We can give you at least three crates of medical supplies plus a high-quality tissue regenerator." Uhura glanced out the window, seeing the glitter of water in the street beside the town hall. "Is it safe to drop them off here? It looks like the water is still rising."

"It is," Ang said tiredly. "It's been rising for weeks now, but for a long time we thought it would just go away. Hell, the Little Muddy just doesn't drain that much of the Gory Range. With as dry and windy as it's been the last couple of months—well, it just didn't seem like there should be that much water."

"But the Little Muddy *does* drain Bull's Eye crater," Anthony said. "We think that's where the water's coming from."

Ang Wat snorted. "You're thinking right. We found that out the hard way. After the Little Muddy took out What's the Point, we thought we'd better see for ourselves what was going on further upstream. Didn't take long. Those hot springs up near Southfork are just about roaring with water, even when the dust's blowing. We figured it had to be coming from the crater lake. And we told that to the people down in Au Contraire, too," he added sharply.

"They may not have understood how serious it was." Uhura didn't really believe that, and she could see from Ang's sour look that he didn't either. "Is there anything else you need besides medical supplies? We're in Gamma Night right now, but we can radio the orbital platform in a few hours and have them send another shuttle out with food and blankets—"

"*Another* shuttle? We never got the shipment from the *first* shuttle," Ang Wat said indignantly.

That was the response Uhura had been fishing for. She'd discovered in the other settlements they'd stopped at that the Outland settlers were less suspicious and more helpful if she let them just complain about the lack of supplies rather than making direct inquiries about them. Perhaps they thought she was checking to see if they'd gotten more than their fair share. "You're sure the packages didn't get lost in the water?" she asked, trying to sound like someone with just a brief, casual interest in the problem.

The mayor of No Escape snorted again. "I'm sure. I

had people out for hours, listening for those sonic beacons to make sure our stuff didn't get waterlogged. The only one who heard anything was me, when they came back empty-handed and cursing. So I'll pass on another delivery from the orbital platform. I'd never get another vote in this town if I made the folks stand out in that olivium-pickled water a second time. Just drop the medical supplies off on the clinic roof before you go. It's the highest building in town, way up by the water tank."

"All right. And if it looks like the flooding from the crater is going to get worse, we'll come back and let you know." Uhura turned to leave, but the expression of deep misgiving on Ang Wat's ruddy face swung her back toward him again. "Is there some other problem we should know about?"

"Not here," the mayor said. "God knows, having the lower half of my town under water is all the problem I need right now. But if you're really going up to Bull's Eye crater, there's something you need to know."

"About the lake?" Anthony asked, frowning. "Or the olivium deposits underneath it?"

Ang Wat shook his head. "I don't know anything about either of those. But I do know this—the folks we sent up to check on those springs at Southfork almost didn't make it back alive. And it wasn't the dust storms that got 'em. They got shot at up there on that damned crater."

"Shot at?" Uhura echoed in surprise. "By alien pirates?"

"No. By a bunch of antisocial militants who came here to Belle Terre just to get themselves their own private little territory. They call themselves the Carsons, and between them they've laid claim to the whole inside of that crater, never mind that it's mostly water and hot enough with olivium to fry an egg on the ground. We thought at first they were going to try getting a water monopoly up this way, but they don't seem to care about that. They just don't want anybody getting near them." Ang Wat gave her a warning look. "So when you go to check on that crater, Commander Uhura, you be real careful. Those Carsons don't bother giving you a warning. They shoot first and then let the dust bury you."

Chapter Seven

THE LITTLE MUDDY didn't look as if it had ever been much of a river, even before the Quake Moon's explosion had turned half its drainage basin into a crater lake. Its valley was mostly narrow and nestled between two close-set ranges: the taller Gory Mountains on the north, and the smaller Goosebump Mountains to the south. From previous trips, Sulu remembered the river as a thin sliver of broken mirror far below, meandering down the valley in lazy, snake-shaped loops before running north through its narrow gorge to meet the Stony Creek and then become the Big Muddy.

Now there was a sheet of water several miles wide across that same valley, so dull and thick with mud that it looked more like an enormous spill of concrete than a flood. Sulu needed most of his attention to keep the Bean steadied against the constant buffeting downdrafts sweeping down the mountain-walled valley, but he could see enough of the devastation to make him uneasy. Even if his gut didn't want to acknowledge that the flooding in Llano Verde was starting to look almost as urgent as their mission to rescue Chekov's downed shuttle, his intellect knew it. And he suspected the hydrologists knew it, too.

"Make sure you get a good shot of the gorge entrance in the background," Weir instructed Anthony as the other hydrologist slowly panned their tricorder back and forth across the floodwaters. "McElroy will want to see how much water's been impounded there, so he can calibrate the data network."

"Already got it." Anthony brought the tricorder back to the handful of engulfed roofs over which Sulu had centered the Bean. It was supposed to have been the next settlement they stopped at to track Chekov's shuttle, which meant they'd never know if any relief supplies had been dropped there. Sulu glanced down at the turbid, swirling waters and grimaced. If this was where the cargo shuttle's trail had ended, he was afraid there wasn't going to be much left to rescue. "Coordinates 93 slash 15 on map WR9," Anthony told the tricorder's audio sensor. "Former name Mineral Point, current name—Commander Uhura, what did the mayor say this place was called now?"

"What's the Point," Sulu answered, seeing that Uhura was listening so intently to the whisper of the experimental communicator on her lap that she hadn't even heard the hydrologist.

"Current name What's the Point," Anthony told his tricorder. "Status: evacuated without fatalities, floodwaters ten meters deep and rising." He set the tricorder down on his lap and tapped in the commands for condensing its visual records into a transmittable data packet. "Is that all we need to send down to Big Muddy, Bev?"

"Wait—I want to tack on the flow measurements I took in Culvert and No Escape." Sulu heard the long buzz of data being transferred from tricorder to tricorder in the backseat. "Let me look that over and make sure the olivium dust in here didn't frazzle it. I really hate to think how much radioactivity we're breathing right this minute," she added absently.

"And wearing," Anthony said. The Bean was designed to be dustproof, but they'd made too many stops and tracked in too much mud and dirt for its limited air-recirculation system to handle. "Your face is already burned, Bev."

"Yeah, well, I didn't sign on to this colony to be a pasty-faced lab technician." She handed his tricorder back. "I recondensed it for you."

"Thanks." Anthony passed the scientific instrument up between the front seats, gently nudging Uhura's shoulder with it when she didn't immediately respond. "Our report is ready to be sent in to Big Muddy now, Commander."

Uhura finally glanced up from her frequency display and removed the audio remote from her ear. "I know, Dr. Anthony. But I'm afraid it's not going be quite that easy." Her normally tranquil face held an emotion Sulu almost didn't recognize, he saw it there so seldom. After a moment, he realized it was embarrassment. "I'm getting microflashes of signal that sound like Rand calling me, but they disappear again before I even have time to identify them, much less match frequencies and reply. And the signal from the orbital shuttle is doing the same thing. I can't even get as much of a fix on it as we did back in Big Muddy."

"Is it because the Bean is moving?" Sulu asked. He'd left What's the Point behind as soon as Anthony had finished recording the destruction there, and was already several kilometers farther up the valley, heading for Desperation, the next settlement on his list. "I could hover again, or drop down to the surface somewhere away from the flood."

"I don't think that would help. I wasn't getting any signal at all while you hovered over What's the Point." Uhura frowned down at the gleaming remote in her hand, as if it was the source of the problem rather than the bulky box sitting on her lap. "It's only when we *are* moving that I get these little flickers of response, and then it's only once in a long while."

"Does the signal look weak?" Weir asked. "Maybe it's been attenuated by the dust."

Uhura shook her head. "I don't think so. When I catch a flash of it, it looks strong and clear, but then I lose it immediately. It doesn't fade out, it doesn't break up, it just vanishes as if it had never been there." She cast a sheepish look across at Sulu. "I was so sure Rand and I had finally come up with an olivium-proof system. I guess I should have known better. 'Just because something works in theory doesn't mean it works in Llano Verde.' "

"Well, there's one thing that should still work." Sulu cut all the lateral vectors on his antigrav thrusters to zero and increased power to maximum levels. With one less tissue regenerator and a lot fewer medical supplies on board, the Bean kicked upward like a balloon released from a child's hand. The maneuver got no reaction from Uhura, since she was used to Sulu's ruthlessly efficient piloting style, but he heard gasps and curses from the backseat as tricorders bounced and maps scattered. "Hang on, we're just going up to talk to the orbital platform."

"No problem," Weir said cheerfully. "Wow, what a rush!"

Anthony didn't sound quite as thrilled. "Are we sure Gamma Night is over?" He cradled his tricorder in one arm, holding his maps down with the other.

"No," Sulu said. "But with all the olivium down here, this is the only way to find out." They were already in the dust-storm layer above the mountains, and he had to raise his voice to be heard over the sleeting sound of particles hitting the hull. "We'll just have to reorient on the way back down if you want to keep recording the flood."

"If we can get in touch with Big Muddy, I won't have to," Anthony said. "Once McElroy knows what parts of our hardwired data network to look at, he can use Commander Scott's signal-noise reduction unit to determine floodwater levels for the whole valley." A cyclonic wind gust whirled the Bean into a blind sideways skid until Sulu could adjust the antigravs and break free of its grip. When he spoke again, Anthony sounded a little more breathless, but that could have been from the effort of hanging on to all his gear. "If we had enough P537 modulators in stock, we could actually map all the flooding from Big Muddy. But we've only got enough right now to watch selected nodes in the data network."

"Nodes!" Uhura jumped in her seat as if someone had kicked her from behind. "That's what those flashes of signal are!"

Sulu was too busy wrestling the Bean out of another whirling dust vortex to reply. All he could hear from Anthony was the sound of a muffled curse, but Weir said conversationally, "Wave-interference nodes, you mean? Wouldn't that give you some fade?"

"Not if they were frequency-specific." The Bean's gyrations didn't stop Uhura from tapping a data query into her experimental communicator's console, although she did have to pause occasionally to make sure she'd hit the right keys. "There are only certain electromagnetic frequencies that can refract through the crystals of olivium in the dust at the right angle to amplify themselves. But there are so many different crystal forms of olivium that when Rand and I combined her refraction system with my reflection system, we thought we had a wide enough frequency range to bounce the signal off the dust-air boundary at any possible angle."

"That sounds reasonable," Weir said. "So why are you getting interference nodes?"

"Because we forgot about the fact that each individual olivium crystal will still absorb any frequencies that *it* can't refract." Uhura's exasperation was palpable. "Only a few frequencies should match all possible crystal refraction angles. Those are the only ones that will show a net increase in signal strength over distance."

"—so only the places *those* frequencies happen to reflect to are going to see any kind of signal," Weir finished. "And those places are where you're getting your microflashes?"

"I think so." Uhura braced herself to read the console's display as the Bean lurched through the turbulent upper eddies of the dust storm. Sulu could already see the vague shoulders of the Gory Mountains appearing through the haze to the north and east. "The computer says only two of Rand's frequencies can refract through every single crystal phase of olivium. The two-theta reflectance angles are seventy-eight and ninety-five degrees, which would create circles of signal reception centered on the spaceport and spaced either twenty-one or thirty-five kilometers apart. There should be an especially strong reception circle every one hundred and five kilometers, where the two bands concatenate."

"That's nice," Anthony said between gritted teeth. "Except that we don't have any instrument capable of telling us how far we are from the spaceport right now."

Uhura glanced over at Sulu in concern. "You can't tell where we are based on your navigation program?"

He snorted. "After all the departures we just made from my flight plan to see how bad the flooding was? I'm not sure I even know what *direction* Big Muddy is—"

Sulu broke off, feeling the Bean shake off the last tearing crosswinds. The dragon's hiss of dust across the hull dropped to a whisper, then to silence. "*That's* better. See if you can raise the orbital platform, Uhura. They'll be able to give you our distance from the spaceport right down to the centimeter." He paused, but the communications officer made no move to lift the audio remote she still held in her hand. He glanced over to see her staring out her side of the Bean's cockpit, into the blood-red glow of sunset. "Uhura?"

"Greg, do you see that?" For once, Weir actually sounded intimidated. "It's not an olivium twister, is it?"

"I don't—I don't think so. It's too big."

Sulu bumped a right lateral component into every antigrav thruster, swinging the craft around in a quick semicircle so he could see what they were talking about. Tricorders skidded and fell in the backseat, but for once there was no response from the hydrologists. They were staring at the dust storm below them.

It cut down through the dust like the whirling tunnel of a tornado, spinning off subsidiary twists and eddies of wind on every side, but never diminishing in intensity itself. Dust poured into it like a whirlpool and was flung outward again, forming a thick storm wall that buttressed the clear air inside. It never moved, as if it had been captured in the tight embrace of the Gorys and the Goosebumps. Intellectually, Sulu knew it was just a cold-air downdraft on a massive scale, twisted by the rotation of the mountain winds around it. But it looked more like the eye of a hurricane, right down to the reflected red glitter of sunset off the water at its base.

"Oh, I get it now," Weir said.

Uhura threw a puzzled glance back at her. "Get what?"

"Why they call it Bull's Eye."

Sulu frowned down at the distant gleam of blood-stained water. "That's the crater lake down there?"

He heard the rustle of maps being picked up from the floor behind him. "It's in the right place for it," Anthony confirmed. Uhura had set down her remote and reached over the bulky box on her lap to activate the Bean's standard communicator panel. "According to this, the crater sits right where the Gory and Goosebump mountains come together, at the head of the Little Muddy."

"And this Southfork place you want to go, to check on where the flood is coming from—it's right on the rim of that crater?"

"Yes." Weir peered over Sulu's shoulder at the Bean's console, as if it could explain what was going on below. "Does that grim look mean we might not be able to land there?"

Sulu's frown got a little deeper when he realized she'd been checking the duranium gleam of the instruments for his reflection rather than their readings. "I won't know until we get closer to the surface, but there's a good chance—"

"Sulu, I've got the orbital platform," Uhura said abruptly. "They want to talk to you. Patching through to main speakers."

Static filled the Bean's cockpit as a wayward plume of dust drifted past them, thrown out like a waterspout from the chaos below. Sulu put all his antigrav thrusters back on vertical lift, and after a minute the static cleared. "—your mission," said a firm, familiar voice. "According to Governor Sedlak—"

"Sulu to Kirk." He wouldn't normally have interrupted his commanding officer with the higher priority of a hail, but the mention of Sedlak's name had filled him with misgiving. "Sir, we missed the first part of your message. Are you aboard the orbital platform?"

Uhura's head shake told him she knew the answer even before Kirk said, "Negative, Mr. Sulu. The *Enterprise* is still in fringe space around the Belle Terre system."

"They're piggybacking on the orbital platform's signal to get around the curve of the planet," Uhura said softly. "And to punch through the dust haze we've got even up here."

"We have at least a dozen potential pirate vessels lurking out here, and I'd rather not let them out of my sight," Captain Kirk continued. "Update me on the status of your mission."

Sulu winced, knowing Kirk wasn't going to like the first part of what he had to say. After all, it had been Kirk's orders Chekov had skirted by volunteering for that relief supply mission in the first place. "Sir, we invited Commander Chekov down to spend some time with us on the planet. He hitched a ride—"

"—on a civilian cargo shuttle," Kirk finished, somewhat impatiently. "Governor Sedlak has already told me about that, Mr. Sulu, and about the loss of the shuttle. Have you found any trace of it?"

"No, sir. We've tracked back almost half of the stops it should have made, and we haven't found any dropped cargo yet." Sulu steeled himself to deliver the news that would irrevocably change the nature of their mission. "While searching, Captain, we discovered a massive flood in progress in the mountains of Llano Verde. The people in the capital don't know about it yet. We have an urgent data packet to send to Chief McElroy of the Hydrologic and Meteorologic Division of Technical Services."

"Transmit it to the *Enterprise*." Few people could match James T. Kirk's swiftness in adapting to emergencies, but he had trained his bridge crew to be almost as fast. Uhura reached back immediately for the tricorder, making Anthony grunt in surprise. The hydrologist fumbled around, then finally found it under the maps piled on the Bean's floor and handed it to her. She had the tricorder plugged into the main communicator panel and uploading in seconds.

"Data packet received," said Spock's calm voice in the background. "Flood conditions confirmed, Captain."

"Send that information down to the continental authorities now, as well as to the main colony headquarters," Kirk told his science officer. "How bad is the flooding you've seen, Mr. Sulu?"

"Potentially catastrophic," said a loud voice from the Bean's backseat.

Sulu glared at his instrument panel, hoping Weir caught that expression, too. "One settlement has been totally evacuated and another is partly under water. We don't know how much worse it will get until we investigate the source of the flooding. That should be at our next stop."

"The problem is that we can't warn the towns downstream if they're in danger, Captain," Uhura cut in. "We still don't have a working communications system."

"Governor Sedlak told me that, too," Kirk said. "He seems to feel I wasted your time by assigning you to this mission. However, since he wouldn't be finding out about this flood if Mr. Scott hadn't developed a dust-proof shuttle, I'm not particularly inclined to agree." They could hear the thoughtful breath the captain took, even through the patched-through connection. "Sulu, best estimate. Are you going to need the *Enterprise* down there?"

Sulu opened his mouth to say yes without thinking, then closed it again. He couldn't just defer instinctively to his captain's superior ability to deal with a crisis. Kirk had a serious situation on his own hands, and he was asking Sulu to weigh the danger Llano Verde's settlers faced from flooding versus their vulnerability to alien pirate raids. In that balance, the possibility of rescuing Chekov barely tipped the scale. With any luck, Sulu thought glumly, the cargo shuttle would turn out to have gone down far away from the Little Muddy River.

"According to the scientists who've seen the data firsthand, sir, the situation could get a lot worse. If it does, we don't have the capacity to evacuate the down-river towns in time." Sulu heard Weir let out a breath of relief behind him, but he wasn't done yet. Honesty, and his long months of exposure to the independent settlers in Llano Verde, forced him to add, "On the other hand, I'm not sure the colonists would want the *Enterprise* coming to their rescue."

"Neither am I," Kirk said ruefully. "I've got Pardonnet waiting on one channel and Sedlak on another, and I suspect they're both going to tell me to do something different. I'll make my decision about whether to return to Belle Terre after I've talked to them—and after you've reported back on the source of that flooding. Understood?"

"Understood, sir." Sulu had known the search for Chekov would have to be delayed to deal with the flood crisis, but the direct order from Kirk still made his stomach twist. His commander must have heard his dismay even in that brief reply.

"Don't worry, Mr. Sulu. We're not going to give up on the missing cargo shuttle," Kirk assured him. "I'm under orders from Starfleet to deliver a first officer to the *Reliant,* and I intend to carry them out. We'll just have to trust Mr. Chekov to take care of himself until we have time to find him."

"Stop . . ." Baldwin's voice, desperate and breathless, tugged at Chekov from two meters back. "C.C., please . . . we gotta stop . . ."

Chekov nodded, not at all sure Baldwin could see the gesture through the persistent haze of blown dust and the swaddling of cloth they both wore. But he slowed cautiously, twisting his grip on the roll of sheet in his hands and veering toward the only tangle of dead brush in sight. Even that extra distance proved almost too much; he dropped to his knees as soon as he was halfway out of the wind, leaning back to lower the sheet and its occupant to the ground with as much control as possible. He heard Baldwin stumble to a stop with a weary grunt, and hoped neither of them had jolted Reddy too badly in trying to get him out of the weather.

When they'd left the homestead, the plan had been to head downslope in thirty-minute increments. Baldwin—by virtue of owning a working wrist chronometer—would signal their stops, and they would rest as long as necessary to keep themselves from succumbing to the olivium and Reddy from suffering too much from the travel. They had most of a day's sunlight in front of them, and both the five-liter bottles of water. Surely there were other homesteads between here and the base of the crater. If they paced themselves carefully, Chekov was confident they could get most of the way down Bull's Eye's slope before dark, even with Reddy suspended on a sheet between them. They would be out of the dust and back on track for Eau Claire by morning.

That original plan blew away on the first blast of radioactive wind. Even bundled in every spare blanket and sheet they could find, they hadn't managed ten meters before both were coughing up dust and stumbling with olivium-induced fatigue. Baldwin called their first stop what felt like hours after they walked out the homestead's door; Chekov suspected it was more like fifteen minutes. Any chance they had of surviving depended on their ability to creep down a hostile mountainside, fifteen minutes at a time, ahead of whoever had ambushed them on the lakeside. The lump of anxiety clenching his stomach rolled over into a more primitive fear. For the first time since landing on Belle Terre, Chekov found himself unable to imagine how any of them could come out of this alive.

After that, they focused simply on moving. Whichever of them needed to stop called for it; they'd both done so an equal number of times. They downed the water by careful mouthfuls, sat back-to-back to form a windbreak for Reddy's stretcher, and didn't even argue anymore. Chekov had a feeling this was because Baldwin was rapidly losing the motivation to keep fighting at all. Taking Reddy to help was the only thing holding the two of them together, and very likely the only thing keeping Baldwin alive. Chekov didn't let himself worry about how he was going to take care of Baldwin once Reddy finally stopped breathing. If he thought that far ahead, nausea and dizziness squeezed in too tight, and it was all he could do to pull himself up out of the sand and start walking again.

He listened to Baldwin now without turning. An artificially cheerful voice telling Reddy about things the pilot was no longer aware of, a voice Reddy might or might not have still been able to hear. It was all Baldwin could do besides hold up his end of the sheet, and Chekov saw little harm in letting him do it. Bad enough that one of them agonized over the realistic details of their situation—forcing everyone else to accept just how bad things were wouldn't bring them any closer to getting out of it.

Digging underneath the quilt wrapped about his head and shoulders, Chekov worked to loosen the knotted sheet strapping one of the water bottles across his back. It was only half-full now, but still thumped to the ground with a reassuring slosh when the knot came undone. He tucked the rifle's muzzle through the bottle's handle to weight it from rolling away in the wind—not because the rational part of him believed it could go anywhere, but because irrational precautions against devastating loss had already become second nature. Because in nightmares you could leave things unattended and they were just gone, with no possible explanation. And the boundary between reality and nightmare grew thinner every hour they were out in this hell.

He crawled around the wind-scarred bush with his face tipped down and toward one shoulder, dragging the sheet in one hand as he felt out the way. He would have held his breath, but had learned the hard way that the compensating inhalation at the end would be far worse than a series of tiny, protected pants. So he tried to keep his mouth away from the wind, tucked behind a fold of quilt, until his back was to the tempest and he could rise up on his knees. Then he let the storm's heavy hand plaster the sheet against the bush like molecule-thin reflectant against a starship's hull. He adjusted the edges with a couple of neat flicks, then crawled back around to the little bubble of relative stillness he'd created on the other side.

Baldwin had already pulled Chekov's half-empty water bottle and its accompanying rifle in out of the wind. He sat only partway in the shelter, leaving a majority of it for Reddy. Chekov settled down to form a sort of third wall, coughing into his hands and trying to stay out of the way as Baldwin opened their dwindling water and carefully unwrapped Reddy's face.

They all three looked like hell. The red glow across Baldwin's cheeks and forehead might have been from sunburn, except the dust didn't allow enough ultraviolet through the atmosphere to produce a respectable burn. The colonist's hands shook as he tipped a small portion of water into Reddy's mouth, and his breathing was audible even over the wind. Chekov felt as if he were looking into a mirror. His own face ached with inappropriate heat, and every airway all the way down to his lungs was clogged with dust, dry to the point of cracking. He'd started shivering before they even left the homestead. Not because of any chill—Belle Terre was nothing if not temperate during the day—and not just because he'd had nothing to eat for going on thirty hours. The planet was simply killing them.

He let Baldwin tend to Reddy, the way he had at every other stop, and turned his own attention toward clearing the worst of the dust out of the rifle.

The loading and firing mechanisms were as simple as he'd expected, the assembly of the components as straightforward as any weapons officer could have wished. He'd had a single primitive weapons seminar at the Security Academy—a distant lifetime ago—and retained from it only a vague memory about the inaccuracy of ballistic weapons due to the perturbations in a projectile's flight path caused by wind and gravity. Given the vagaries of the former and the persistence of the latter, he didn't know how anyone on Belle Terre could hit anything with such an artifact. But they had, which meant he had to assume they could do so again.

That awareness raised the ugly question of whether or not Chekov could protect them from another such attack. He and Baldwin had never talked about Chekov's position on the *Enterprise*—maybe Baldwin just assumed everyone in Starfleet knew how to field-dress a belly wound and assemble unfamiliar weapons—but it was clear what the colonist expected from him, and the promises Chekov had made to Plottel on the lake bottom hung over everything like an unfulfilled contract. Whoever had brought them to the homestead had done so for reasons that remained ominous as long as they were unknown. To keep them under surveillance? To send them a warning about their vulnerability on Belle Terre? To give them false hope before finally hunting them down? It wasn't Chekov's job to figure out their motives, only to keep his own team members alive. If that meant doing the unthinkable to some future aggressor, he was duty-bound to make sure he was capable.

And that was exactly what he'd done, just before they'd left the homestead's shelter. While Baldwin prepared Reddy for the journey, Chekov had quietly taken the reassembled gun and one of the heavy metal projectiles out into the barnyard's maelstrom. Loading the projectile into the rifle, he'd chambered it with a harder pump than he'd expected it to need, shouldered the smooth plas-steel stock, and taken aim across the yard at the squared-off top of one metal fencepost. At the Security Academy, they'd test-fired reed-slender rifles that discharged with a report like the delicate bursting of a balloon. The projectiles were no bigger than the tip of his finger, and the breezy gusts off Chesapeake Bay had kicked them hither and yon like so many butterflies. Chekov had been one of only two cadets to hit his assigned target, and even then hadn't managed to come anywhere near where he'd been aiming. They'd all laughed about it, congratulated themselves on being lucky enough to live in an era of line-of-sight armaments, and went back to working with their phasers with nary a backward glance.

Standing out in the dusty barnyard, he tried to remember everything about brandishing those little rifles and focusing on targets one hundred meters away. Belle Terre's angry winds tore over him from the right; his own slow, careful breathing shifted the barrel ever so slightly; his heartbeat pulsed beneath the stock where it rested against his left shoulder. This projectile was larger, heavier, the propellant load undoubtedly more explosive than the toy guns he'd used years before. He kept his eyes trained on the fence post, felt out the strength of the wind with his whole body, lifted the barrel and aligned it slightly more to the right, took a single slow, deep breath. Held it. Waited for that moment of stillness between the beatings of his heart. Depressed the trigger.

For one miraculous moment, he thought the gun had discharged without so much as a sound. Then he realized that the omnipresent wind had silenced, his breathing had grown eerily quiet, that the entire world had suddenly leapt to a cottony white distance on all sides. The bone-deep ringing in his ears wasn't noise, it was deafness. Slapped by a thunder too loud to process, his hearing had simply gone into hiding, waiting for the echoes to recede.

Across the barnyard, the top of the metal fence post was shattered. A monument to violent efficiency, frozen in a moment of supernatural silence.

Come to think of it, that was when he had first started shaking. He hadn't been able to stop in all the hours since.

"Hey, C.C. . . ."

Chekov blew down the length of the gun's barrel, then snapped it shut again. "Don't call me that." They'd argued at their first stop about whether Chekov actually needed a meaningless nickname. But the more Chekov protested, the more Baldwin persisted, and Chekov finally just defaulted to not responding unless Baldwin addressed him by his proper name.

"No, seriously, come here."

The lack of humor in Baldwin's voice erased

Chekov's irritation and brought him crawling over to Reddy's side. Baldwin had unwound the blankets from the pilot's face and rolled down the edge to fit his hand inside. As Chekov approached, Baldwin took his hand and guided it under the blankets. Chekov knew what he'd feel even before Baldwin splayed his hand against the warm tack of wet fabric. Reddy made a wordless little noise, but stirred only faintly. His face was paled to the color of stained ivory.

"We keep hauling him around like this," Baldwin whispered, "we're gonna kill him." As though stating the obvious too loudly would cause it to come true.

Chekov withdrew his hand and pulled Reddy's covers back into place. *If we don't haul him around,* he couldn't say to Baldwin, *he's going to die anyway.* The only thing that would change was their chances of dying along with him. "It's getting dark." An equally obvious statement that they still couldn't do very much about. "We should at least find somewhere protected to stay for the night." He looked around, seeing nothing but wilderness and the prospect of a hideous night spent out in the open. "Stay with him," he said at last. "I can move faster alone. I'll try to scout out an easier route."

Baldwin shouldered in and took over the task of bundling Reddy, as though Chekov couldn't be trusted to do a proper job of it. "An easier route to where?"

"Anywhere." Chekov reached back to place the rifle carefully between them, then climbed to his feet without saying anything further.

He had already tugged the quilt back around his face and turned to head out when Baldwin grabbed hold of his pantleg to stop him. The colonist lifted the gun by one finger through its trigger guard, so that the barrel lifted a few centimeters off the ground. "What am I supposed to do with this?" he asked, somewhat peevishly.

Chekov pretended not to notice the self-conscious heat that rose into his face. "Protect yourself while I'm gone."

Baldwin gave a snort that might have been a laugh and tossed the gun back on the ground. "I can't hit a bulkhead with a phaser, much less some fanatic half a klick away in a dust storm. I don't even know how to aim the thing." Catching hold of it by the barrel, he shoved it back across the dust until it bumped into Chekov's feet. "I saw you outside before we left, C.C. You take the damned thing." He looked up with eyes more serious than Chekov had ever seen on him before. "Just make sure you get 'em before they get us."

Chapter Eight

THERE WAS something familiar about Desperation.

"I feel like I've been here before," Uhura said, peering at the hazy view outside the Bean. She leaned forward to scrub at the cockpit window, but the dust was mostly on the outside, settling in the afterdraft of their landing, and there was nothing she could do about the twilight. Despite that, her memory insisted that she knew this town. Its wide central plaza, which Sulu had used as a landing site, was lined with old-fashioned ironwork benches. Matching wrought-iron gates and balconies decorated the stucco buildings on three sides of the plaza, while on the fourth rustic logs projected out from a long town hall to form a portico. Did it suggest the French Quarter of New Orleans? Some ancient piazza in Tuscany? Or maybe one of the medieval city-states of Rigel V?

"Sulu, look at this place. Where does it remind you of?"

The pilot lifted his head from where he'd rested it on his forearms after he'd cut the antigrav thrusters. The trip down to Desperation had been a nightmare of wind shears and dust devils spun off the nearby Bull's Eye crater. Only swift reflexes and years of experience had let Sulu maintain any semblance of a normal descent, and even so there'd been moments when Uhura hadn't been sure they'd reach the ground in a single piece.

"I think they built it to look like Sante Fe," he said after a moment's frowning thought. "Or maybe Taos."

"Definitely Sante Fe," Weir said from the backseat. The hydrologist still sounded cheerful, but there was enough hoarseness in her voice to make Uhura give her a concerned look. Both scientists seemed more haggard and sick than the Bean's lurching descent could entirely account for. Anthony's skin had turned dusky red from radiation exposure, and Weir was breathing with the quick, shallow rhythm of dust-induced asthma. "I did some post-grad work at Los Alamos. We went down to Sante Fe for dinner all the time."

"So did I, when I was testing shuttles at White Sands," Sulu said, yawning. The exhaustion in his voice mirrored the lines etched into his usually smooth face and the deep shadows beneath his eyes. He'd gotten up before dawn the previous day to make the trip to Mudlump, and he'd been flying through sleeting dust, violent crosswinds, and jagged mountains ever since. "Did you ever try the banana, tamarind, and mint salsa at the Sunflower Hill Inn?"

Uhura set her experimental communicator on the floor and unbuckled her safety harness with a decisive snap. "Before we start comparing Mexican restaurants,

I think we should all pay a visit to the tissue regenerator."

Anthony started to get up, then groaned and fell back into his seat. Uhura barely managed to catch his tricorder before it spilled to the floor. "I don't know why I feel so bad," the hydrologist said between his teeth. "I got my radiation booster shots right before we left."

"It's probably my driving." Sulu extricated himself from his harness and helped the other man to his feet, while Uhura turned to give a hand to Weir. "Antigrav thrusters aren't known for being easy on your stomach."

"No, I think it's the olivium." Weir swayed a little as she stood, but waved off Uhura's offer of support. She followed Sulu and Anthony gingerly down the Bean's passageway, past the cooling crackle of the antigrav generators. "It's radioactive *and* transperiodic, remember. That means you're getting a double whammy from gamma and mu-epsilon radiation."

"Whatever the problem is, the tissue regenerator will fix it," Uhura said. "Stand here, Dr. Anthony."

Anthony grimaced as he obeyed her. "Is this a good time to say that I really hate regenerators? They make me feel like I'm getting transported sideways one molecule at a—*ow!*"

Uhura straightened from having switched on the self-contained medical unit. It let out a loud buzz of alarm as it detected the hydrologist's cell damage, and the filmy glitter of tissue-repair beams played over his thin, wiry frame for a surprisingly long time, making him grimace and yelp. Sulu tugged Uhura aside after a moment, drawing her back a step behind a stack of emergency rations.

"Have you noticed they're feeling the radiation

worse than we are?" he asked, beneath the hum of the regenerator. "Is it because they keep getting themselves covered in olivium-contaminated mud?"

"I don't think so," Uhura said. "The antiradiation drugs Dr. McCoy gave us were designed in the *Enterprise*'s medical labs specifically for the radiation here in Llano Verde. But he told me the continental government refused to accept them. They insisted they could manage with the generic antiradiation drugs they had on hand." She saw his frown deepen. "What's the matter?"

"Chekov hasn't had any antiradiation shots at all," Sulu said. The hydrologists had traded places, making the tissue regenerator buzz in alarm all over again. "If the olivium can make these guys sick, what do you think it's doing to him?"

Uhura repressed a shiver. "Chekov knows about the radiation problem. He's probably safe inside the cargo shuttle." Sulu's dubious look told her he didn't believe that, either. "At least we have a hospital-grade regenerator to use on him when we find him."

"If we find him!" Sulu said in frustration. "It's been a full day now since the shuttle went down! It's going to take at least twelve more hours to get Captain Kirk the report he wants, especially since we can't fly to—"

A muffled explosion outside the Bean cut off the rest of his sentence. It was followed by the pure crystalline ring of something deflecting at high-speed off their duranium hull. Sulu cursed and turned around to dive toward the cockpit. Uhura barely managed to catch him before he left the hold.

"Stay here," she snapped. "That's an *order!*"

That brought Sulu up short. "You don't outrank me."

"Okay then, that's a *request*. You're the one who told

me that Outlanders use projectile weapons because of dust depolarization."

Weir and Anthony had been watching the confrontation between the two Starfleet officers with bewildered faces, but Uhura's words—and a second muffled explosion outside the cargo hold door—made them drop abruptly to the floor. "If they see you through the windows, they might decide to aim for you. That would definitely shatter the windows, not to mention your head."

Sulu's scowl deepened as a third detonation went off outside, followed by the now-familiar ricochet off the Bean's duranium hull. "Then how are we going to stop them? They can't hear us through the hull, and we can't hail them on any communicator frequency."

"No, but we can chase them out of shooting range before we open the doors and tell them who we are." She pointed past him at the two lateral antigrav generators, and saw his face light with understanding. "On my count of three."

Sulu nodded and disappeared up the gangway.

Uhura headed for the aft generator, pushing aside several piles of dog-food sacks to get there. She was familiar enough with Scotty's dustproof design that she could find the field-distortion controls with only a little searching. All of the Bean's nonvertical movements were made by modifying the shape and size of its antigravity field in such a way that air was sucked through its self-contained thrusters. It only took a moment for Uhura to set the vertical lifting vector to zero and aim the horizontal thrusting component outward. "One," she shouted over her shoulder, and heard the hydrologists relay the count forward to Sulu. "Two. *Three.*"

The generators came back to life with a roar, followed by the sound of several distant explosions in a row. Since none of them were followed by the clang of anything hitting the Bean's hull, Uhura suspected her strategy of startling their unknown attacker with an outward blast of dusty air had been successful. She ducked out from behind the dog food and joined the rest of the Bean's crew in the cargo hold.

"All right," she said. "Let's open the door."

"Are you sure it's safe?" Anthony asked. The scientist was still wearing the faint red afterglow of olivium poisoning on his cheeks, but he seemed to have regained much of his energy and alertness. "We don't even know why they're shooting at us."

"Maybe they think we're alien pirates who got through the *Enterprise* blockade," Weir suggested. "I've heard stories about Outlanders getting killed just for the olivium dust on their floors."

"Those are rumors," Sulu said. "The *Enterprise* hasn't allowed a single verified raider into this system."

"That you know of," she retorted.

"It doesn't matter who the settlers think we are, or why they're shooting at us," Uhura said firmly. "What matters is that they're sitting right on the edge of a crater lake that could flood them out. We have to warn them—and the longer we sit here, the more time they have to aim at us again." She swung her dust muffler around her shoulders, keeping the hood and scarf-filter down so her face remained visible, then tossed Sulu's cloak at him. "Dr. Weir, I want you and Dr. Anthony to stay in here until we tell you it's safe to come out. Sulu, open the door."

The pilot punched the controls one-handed while he fastened his muffler closed. The cargo-hold door dropped down to make an exit ramp, but the only thing they could see beyond it was a swirl of dust so thick that they all broke into spasms of coughing. The hydrologists hurriedly reached for their own mufflers, while Uhura tried to catch her breath long enough to speak. All she succeeded in doing was making a harsh rasping sound.

"Well, *there* you are." A figure in a weather-beaten canvas muffler appeared through the stirred-up dust, the long glint of some projectile weapon slung casually across one shoulder. The voice was deep and drawling and apparently immune to dust, since Uhura saw no filtering scarf draped beneath the broad-brimmed hat. Dark eyes gleamed at them from a face whose strong lines could have belonged to a marble statue, except for the reddish radiation burns on the skin. "With as long as you sat here not doing anything, I thought maybe you had all passed out from lack of air."

"Is that why you were shooting at us?" Anthony demanded. Having been the first to put on his filtering scarf, he was also the first to get his voice back. "You were trying to break the door open?"

"Sure. It's my job to do things like that." The hat was swung off, releasing a thick dark mane of hair, then dusted against a pantleg to show them the badge gleaming on the front. "I'm Carmela Serafini, mayor of Desperation and sheriff of Bull's Eye County. And you are—"

Uhura had her own voice back now, more or less. "Commanders Uhura and Sulu of the *U.S.S. Enterprise,*" she said. "And Drs. Weir and Anthony of the Hydrologic and Meteorologic Service. We're here to track a missing cargo shuttle, and to help with the flood emergency."

"Is that so?" Serafini pulled her long-barreled weapon

off her shoulder, making the hydrologists take a wary step back and Sulu a precautionary step forward. The mayor gave him a humorous look as she blew dust out of the weapon, then placed a protective cap over the open mouth. "Now, that's interesting, because I didn't know we *had* a flood emergency. Why don't you all come on over to the pub and get a drink, and tell me all about it."

The sun burned a bloody pool across the sky as it slipped behind the mountains. Olivium dust shimmered in the atmosphere like layer upon layer of gossamer, rippling the jagged horizon until everything ahead of Chekov seemed to exist under the surface of an impossibly huge lake. At the bottom of that lake, painted in premature shadow and then relit by artificial means, a homestead that might almost have been the one they abandoned huddled against the foot of a great slope. A homestead with herd animals trilling musically from inside its barn, and the silhouettes of people drifting back and forth behind its dusty windows.

Tears of relief pushed into Chekov's eyes; he blinked them impatiently away. They weren't rescued yet. Not until he'd approached these colonists, secured their help, and retraced his steps back to Reddy and Baldwin and brought them in to safety. Not until they'd eaten, burned their radiation poisoned clothes, and gotten a message through to Eau Claire. Not until he'd put his arms around Uhura and Sulu, and finally sat down for a dinner now half a lifetime overdue.

The rut he'd followed to this place could hardly be considered a trail. When he'd first stumbled across it, snaking between rocks like a tiny dried-up river, he'd been a little afraid that his desperate eyes saw a path that wasn't really there. But it had headed downward, and—if it wasn't just a figment of his imagination—it gave him something to follow back toward where he'd left Baldwin and Reddy. He stuck to the little trail as best he could while the light began to fade, finally staggering into a near run when the path widened into a clear, hoof-beaten track. It was only the awareness that sunset would illuminate him against the sky with fearful clarity that finally slowed him. No sense giving would-be snipers a better shot than they already had. Dropping to his seat, he half-climbed, half-slid down the last several meters of trail, into the homestead's farmyard.

Shadow knifed across the ground like a bolt of velvet fabric. The stone under him cooled abruptly, palpable degrees of difference where night had lain just a few minutes longer, thanks to the mountainous heights on all sides. Chekov paused at the end of his slide for a moment, and tried to hug his shivering under control. He wasn't just trembling now, but shuddering. Heavy, gut-deep spasms that were equal parts hypothermia and radiation. They couldn't stay outside in this cold. Not overnight, not even for a few hours. He was easily the most hardy of the three, even before the radiation and Reddy's wounding, but he harbored no illusions about how long he could survive unprotected in the desert night. If there was any humanity left in the Outland, these colonists wouldn't turn them away to certain death.

Cradling the rifle across his chest, its muzzle angled skyward, Chekov struggled to right himself at the bottom of the incline. Darkness all but erased the ground under his feet. He picked his way carefully up to the fence surrounding the barn, then trailed one hand along the topmost rail to orient himself as he made his way around. Inside, little hooves clattered and shuffled against the dirt floor; the herd beasts' murmuring voices stitched a delicate euphony of whistles and trills in the twilight air. He'd seen them only once before, but he could picture them clearly—charmingly russet and gold, with spry little commas for tails and ears as tall and furry as a rabbit's. He'd watched them ferried down to the planet via the orbital platform during the first months after their arrival at Belle Terre, and had been amused by their hums and grumbles, not to mention their habit of spitting loudly to express just about any opinion. Someone had told him then that they originated in the mountain areas of South America, and had been chosen for colonial transplant because they were hardy and radiation-resistant. What they most reminded him of, he realized as he turned the corner and faced the homestead complex head-on, were diminutive Asian camels.

Two members of that larger species made man-height lumps in the yard between the house and the barn, their legs tucked under them in a tangle that hardly looked comfortable. They hadn't come through the orbital platform—they'd been engineered here on the planet, after the Burn littered the atmosphere with olivium-infected dust and rendered Llano Verde impassable by more conventional means. Chekov had heard colonists complain about the camels more than praise them, faulting them for everything from their odor and seasick gait to their noisy stomachs and foul dispositions. Everyone agreed, though, that they were all that kept Llano Verde from falling into complete isolation. Able to routinely cross the dust-riddled wastes and get messages from town to town, one camel was now worth more than the entire colony's all-terrain vehicles. Indispensable. Invaluable.

Not something to be left outside overnight in a storm.

He dropped into a crouch, meaning to hide himself neatly just next to the fence line. Instead, radiation-sick muscles betrayed him, and he slewed sideways into the rails. One of the camels swiveled an ear in his direction, but neither could be bothered to open its eyes. Chekov froze for an agonizing moment, hyper-alert for any other movement in the darkened farmyard, then lowered himself shakily to his knees. The wind wailed hoarsely over them all.

If these camels hadn't been carelessly abandoned to the weather by the colonists who owned them, then they'd been ridden here recently, and left out only long enough for their riders to finish some bit of business before continuing their journey. Otherwise the camels would have been stripped of their tack and stowed in the barn alongside the herding animals, safe and warm and protected. Chekov couldn't imagine anything compelling enough to drive a human out into this storm that didn't involve a gunshot wound and fear of the invisible predators who'd originally ambushed you.

Unless, of course, you were the predator, and you were hunting down the ones you'd left alive.

The door to the house swung inward, spilling a blurry square of light onto the air in front of it, the ground below. A mass of bodies darkened the door, separated from it, split into three humanoid figures and one dog. The owner of the homestead—bareheaded, dressed only in a light tunic and trousers—paused just inside the doorway. He hunched over slightly, one hand through the dog's collar to keep it close beside him, and nodded with the terse, metronomic rhythm of someone who is agreeing just to end the conversation and not because he's really in accord. One of the goggled, mufflered figures hung back to exchange a few more words with him; the other limped out to the camels with his orange-and-green striped scarf hanging unwound about his shoulders.

Dismay churned, cold and heavy, in the pit of Chekov's stomach. He recognized the man by his scarf, by his build, by the limp Chekov himself had put in the man's knee. Unlike Chekov and his party, these two looked fit and well rested. If nothing else, they didn't have a dying companion to drag around between them, and the heavy swing of their water jugs meant they weren't having any trouble finding shelter and support among the locals.

Chekov backed awkwardly along the fence line, afraid to turn away from the scene for fear of getting a duranium projectile in the back of his skull. His rifle dragged an unsteady line in the dirt beside him. From the doorway, the dog swept a keen look in his direction and lifted its tail high over its back. He didn't wait to see if the humans noticed its eerie stare. Ducking around the edge of the barn, he broke into a run back toward the hills he'd come from while the dog exploded into a flurry of barks.

The slope fell apart under him as he scrambled up it on all fours. The rifle slipped out of his grip twice before he finally defaulted to throwing it up the hill ahead of him, meeting it on his way up while it slid back down, then pitching it uphill again. The horrified, civilized part of him insisted, *Leave it! Forget about the damned thing!* But the frightened, animal part of him answered without words, conjuring the memory of

Plottel's ruptured body, amplifying the bitter taste in his mouth as he anticipated being shot in the back while running away.

The whole of Belle Terre seemed a death trap. He regained the narrow confines of the trail, but couldn't seem to gather the strength to pull himself upright. Olivium heat bathed him in sweat, wrung the strength from his muscles. Dust clogged his nose and throat until his vision grayed from lack of oxygen. The dog's voice—lost to distance only a few moments ago—swelled everywhere now, purposeful and excited, overlaid on itself in echoes until it became a swarm. Dragging himself to his feet using a waist-high rock, Chekov rolled to plant his back against the stone and tried to remember the direction to the homestead, the direction to Baldwin and Reddy. Soft, busy hoofbeats clamored up on him from a branch in the path, and the barking solidified into a pair of distinct, interwoven voices.

I don't want to do this, he thought with startling, desperate clarity. The rifle was already braced against his shoulder, its muzzle dancing erratically in response to his trembling. *I don't want to be the man who murdered Plottel.* But he didn't want to be Plottel, either.

A wave of dusty brown beasts crested the rise, their long ears pressed flat against the dust, their tails flitting about in what might have been alarm. The first few animals hopped left and right with surprise just before they would have collided with him. The rest followed one by one until the whole group unzipped down the middle and flowed past on either side. The dog driving them—the same dog? a different dog? the only dog on Belle Terre?—flashed into view close behind them. It swept in an graceful arc, low to the ground, as though intent on circling the fragmented band and cinching it back together. Then its ice-blue eyes locked on Chekov, and it froze. A second dog appeared over the crest in a sort of shocking, 3D déjà vu. It swung leftward, crouched, glanced aside at Chekov, and struck the same pose as its twin. Staring, pricked ears angled forward, tails and heads swung low. They were the same dog, the homesteader's dog, yet different dogs, with eyes and expressions and carriage so hauntingly consistent that Chekov found himself dizzied by their keen intensity.

That, more than anything, was what made him almost miss the human who came up the trail behind them.

She slowed when he jerked the rifle toward her, but eased a good three meters closer before finally coming to a stop. On her own terms, not his. He tried to think of some way to warn her off without threatening to shoot—something he wasn't sure he was able to do.

"Nessie, Lynn, that'll do." A steady, patient voice that left little room for discussion.

The dogs whisked back to orbit her feet, finally settling into identical crouches on either side. Their eyes never left Chekov. He couldn't see the woman's eyes past the falling dusk and her dust-scarred goggles, but her silence was as good as a stare. Under its weight, he felt painfully transparent.

"Well," she said at last, no visible part of her moving. "You're not a Carson and you're not a Peacemaker. That leaves either homesteader, or guy from the missing supply shuttle." Slapping gently at her leg, she drew the dogs in close, then slowly, confidently, crossed the distance between them and put her hand on the shaking muzzle of the gun. "Welcome to Belle Terre, shuttle guy."

"Sheriff?" Weir asked in Sulu's ear, as they stood shedding their dust-mufflers just inside the pub's doors. "I didn't know Outlanders elected sheriffs."

He gave the hydrologist a warning look, aware that the incredulous tone of her voice might carry across the room despite her attempt to speak softly. The pub's mock-adobe walls were thick and its windows were covered with wool rugs to keep out drafts, resulting in an oddly hushed quiet. Or perhaps it just seemed hushed in comparison with the tumult outside. A random symphony of wind played constantly in Desperation, shrieking and hooting most of the time, sometimes accompanied by the percussive chatter of windblown gravel and sometimes by the unexpected hiss of rain swept off the crater lake. The gusts had plastered Sulu's dust-filtering scarf so tight against his face on the walk up from the plaza that he felt smothered. He understood now why Mayor Serafini and most of Desperation's other inhabitants walked through their dusty streets bare-faced.

"There's probably a lot you don't know about Outlanders," he said meaningfully, watching Serafini clear seats for them at the pseudo-mahogany bar with a wordless jerk of her chin. The men who'd been occupying those seats moved away in equal silence, as if all the town's citizens had fallen out of the habit of speaking. "It's not a good idea to make too many assumptions."

"We know that," Weir said indignantly. "We're scientists."

That statement didn't exactly reassure Sulu, but before he could make his warning any clearer, both hydrologists headed for the bar to order beer. Sulu followed them with a sense of foreboding that made him ask the bartender for water rather than alcohol. The level of stress and tension he'd seen on faces they'd passed in the street had been unusual even for Llano Verde, and the silent, weather-beaten people in this pub didn't look much happier. Living with a perpetual cyclonic storm just upslope had to be hellish. When you factored in the hostility all Outlanders seemed to feel for government bureaucrats and the mounting frustrations caused by this first bad dry season, you got a potential powderkeg. All it would take was a single thoughtless comment to ignite it.

"So, about this flood emergency." Carmela Serafini downed her mug of beer in one long swallow, then set it back on the bar with a definitive clang that got it immediately refilled. "I hear they got high water further down the Little Muddy. How bad is it?"

"What's the Point had to be totally evacuated," Uhura said. "Half of No Escape is under water, and the river's still rising."

"No kidding?" The mayor's voice sounded affable enough, but there was a glint in her dark eyes that Sulu didn't like. She tapped a finger on the slightly murky glass of water the bartender had just handed Uhura. "Think it'll come up high enough for us to get some? You can see for yourself how low our reservoir is."

"You've got three hundred meters of water just upslope from you," Weir said before Sulu could stop her. "Can't you use that?"

"Not unless I want to glow in the dark from drinking it. The olivium levels in that crater-lake water are high enough to mine." The mayor of Desperation took another long swallow of beer, her lean throat muscles rippling with the motion. As far as Sulu could tell, the alcohol seemed to have absolutely no effect on her. "The bureaucrats down in So Unfair said they'd build us a filtration plant, but we just can't seem to see it for the dust."

"*Told* you," Anthony said. Carmela Serafini gave him a quizzical glance, but the triumphant finger he pointed was at Weir. "I knew those anomalous olivium levels had to be coming right from the source."

"All right, so I owe you a doughnut." The hydrologist drained the last of her own beer, then thumped her tankard down with a decisiveness equal to Serafini's. Despite that, Sulu noted, the bartender made no move to refill it. "I still say we've got as much water coming through the porous matrix as through fractures, which means the tensile strength of the crater wall should be more than ten on the Hutchinson scale."

"Not if there's a continuous conduit system—"

"Hold it right there," Serafini said sharply. "Are you two hydros saying that the lake in Bull's Eye is where that floodwater is coming from?"

"Well, where else *could* it be coming from?" In her quest to snag the bartender's attention, Weir either didn't see or chose to ignore Sulu's warning look. Her voice lifted with scientific enthusiasm. "Our data network shows increased flow in the Little Muddy all the way up to the springs at Southfork. If our visual inspection confirms that—"

"—you're going to stick drainage pipes through the crater walls and take all our water away?" Serafini finished.

The preoccupied scientist didn't seem to hear the note of challenge in the mayor's voice, but people at several nearby tables swung around to follow the conversation. Sulu stiffened, and Uhura hurried to intervene.

"It's not a question of stealing *anyone's* water," the communications officer said, while Sulu caught Weir's attention by the simple expedient of putting a hand over her tankard when the bartender finally came to refill it. He stifled the hydrologist's protest with a look so quelling that she finally seemed to get his unspoken message. "We'd actually rather have your water stay right where it is. What we're worried about is that the lake could break through one of the crater walls and wipe out every town downstream, as far away as Big Muddy."

Serafini let out a crack of laughter as sudden and unexpected as the sound of her projectile weapon. "Miss Uhura, have you ever seen Bull's Eye crater? It's a kilometer wide across that rim wall, if not more! Technical services surveyed the whole thing before they let us build here, and they said it wouldn't break or flood out even in monsoon season."

"They also said they'd build you a filtration plant," Greg Anthony pointed out. "Everyone knows you can't trust those people down in Au Contraire."

The pause that followed the government hydrologist's remark echoed with enough startled indrawn breaths to make it clear that everyone in the pub was now following this discussion. The mayor choked on a swallow of beer, then glared at him while she caught her breath again. "What exactly do you mean by *that?*" she demanded, when she could finally speak.

The hydrologist glanced at Sulu and Uhura, as if checking to make sure he had permission to continue. Seeing that alarm and shrewd self-interest had replaced much of the hostility on Carmela Serafini's face, the pilot gave him a quick nod.

"The original studies of olivium impact craters on Llano Verde assumed they were just like impact craters anywhere else in the galaxy." Anthony's droning professorial tone lent a conviction to his words that all of Weir's passion hadn't been able to create. "What they forgot is that the olivium ore inside the fragments of the Quake Moon was still unstable, so it continued to generate heat and radiation after impact. As a result, Bull's Eye is actually more like a volcanic caldera. The heat beneath it has disrupted the regional water flow system, creating a network of underground caves, conduits and reservoirs for springs like the ones at Southfork." Anthony took a deep breath. "The more open space there is underground, the weaker the rim will get. Eventually, it won't be able to withstand the lake's water pressure anymore, and the whole side of the crater will fail."

"And you think this could happen at any minute?" Serafini demanded, looking skeptical again.

The hydrologist shook his head, looking puzzled rather than defensive. "If you'd asked me two days ago, I'd have said it wouldn't happen for another fifteen years. But the levels of olivium dissolved in the Little and Big Muddy are way higher than they should be, given local dust contamination. The only place that hot water can be coming from is here, and the only way it can be picking up so much olivium is by flowing through the buried ore and back out again. In big conduit networks."

"Damn." It was all the mayor of Desperation said, but the single word held a wealth of cynicism, anger, and pride. She finished the last of her beer, then swung

around to scowl at the group of men who'd moved away from the bar at her command. "Malin, Shaw, Banjak—start pulling together enough supplies for a one-day trip to Southfork. Take at least twelve other men with you. I want you out of here in an hour."

The abrupt volley of orders didn't seem to surprise anyone in the pub. Three men dressed alike in heavy workboots, dust mufflers, and wide-brimmed hats stood and left the bar without a word. The remaining bystanders turned back to their drinks, as if the matter had now been settled.

"Mayor Serafini," Uhura said, after a moment had passed without any further explanation. "If you're taking a party up to examine the springs at Southfork—"

"No, thank you, ma'am. That party is all yours." Serafini's even teeth showed in an expression that didn't quite seem to be a smile. "I don't expect you'll have a real good time at it, though. The winds up at Southfork can rip your skin right off your bones. Even the guanacos quit humming up there." She must have seen the exchange of considering glances between Sulu and Uhura. "Well, how else did you plan to take a look at that crater? You didn't think you were going to fly that jumping bean right up to the rim, did you?"

"No," Sulu said, answering Uhura's unspoken question as well as Serafini's. "But why do we need fifteen people to take us there?"

"Because I'd like you all to make it back down again," the mayor said. "I don't suppose you've heard about it down in We Don't Care, but we've got some militant separatists living in the high country. That Carson gang used to just take potshots at anyone who trespassed on their land, but lately they're starting to harass settlers right off their own claims. We've had to deputize a force of Peacemakers just to keep the score more or less even." Serafini finished the last of her beer and stood up without throwing down any of the plastic poker chips that Outland settlers used instead of encoded currency cards. "Of course, we haven't seen much of the Carsons around here lately. Rumor has it they're salvaging some emergency cargo drops that fell way off target, over on the north side of the crater."

Sulu caught the mayor by the arm as she turned to leave, heedless of the gleaming weapon she'd slung back over her shoulder. "Were those the cargo drops that should have come here?" he asked urgently. "From yesterday's run?"

"Afraid so." Serafini shook her sleeve free of his grasp, a real smile tugging at the corners of her mouth this time. "Don't look so worried, son. Even without the cargo drops, we've got enough smoked guanaco sausage to last us 'til the monsoons start." She twisted her hair up in one hand and slapped her hat back over it, dark eyes glinting under the brim. "Assuming Bull's Eye doesn't decide to split its guts in the meantime. If it does, then all you'll have to worry about is how to get the hell out of Desperation."

Chapter Nine

WATER. Decadent, copious, warmed to just below the point of burning. Chekov hadn't thought anywhere on Belle Terre possessed enough water to flush the fear and dust and sickness out of him, but their rescuer had said simply, "I've got a good reclamation system—use as much as you want," as though completely unaware of the miracle she'd so casually tossed toward him. Fifteen minutes of bloodstained mud swirled down the drain from his hair and face and body before he could even feel the sting of the water against his olivium-burned skin. He would have lain down on the floor of the shower stall and slept right then, drugged insensate by the hot, pounding spray. But he was still faintly afraid of drowning, and even more afraid that he'd awake somewhere in the Outland and discover that this was all only a cruel dream. So he settled instead for sinking to his knees and bowing his head almost to the tile, letting the water sheet over him and run its persistent fingers down his neck and through his hair. Every now and again, he inhaled a handful of clean liquid into his sinuses and let it flush through, imagining it washing all of the olivium out of him, down the drain, far away. If this was weakness, he welcomed it for the first time in his life that he could remember. He'd had too much of being strong these last two days.

The woman's dogs had found Baldwin and Reddy through the dust and gathering dark when Chekov proved unable to stand long enough to lead the way. He'd let the woman half-drag, half-carry him until the sheet-tangled bush came into view. At that point, he somehow found the strength to push her off, staggering ahead to rouse Baldwin and take up his end of Reddy's homemade stretcher. They loaded their meager supplies onto the back of the small pack animal—the kind whose name *wasn't* guano—then set off into the night with the woman in the lead and the dogs sweeping nervous ellipses back and forth behind them.

After that, they might have hiked for hours, they might have hiked for days. Chekov's entire awareness had distilled down to the excruciating task of placing one foot in front of the other, not dropping Reddy, not falling down. By the time they reached their rescuer's homestead, functioning had become little more than an unconscious habit. He couldn't muster the energy to feel surprise when confronted with the large dug-in structure, or its airlocked entries, or the cleanroom lab in its basement. He helped carry Reddy as far as the doors to the cleanroom, then steered Baldwin back upstairs as their host loaded the pilot into a Federation-issue stasis drawer. When she finally rejoined them upstairs, Baldwin had already collapsed in one of the two small bedrooms, and Chekov had stripped him and used a wet dishtowel from the kitchenette to swab off the worst of the dust. While he would have liked to dump the irradiated clothes in a flash-burn disposal chute, he settled for throwing them into the farthest corner of the room.

"You guys are gonna need to eat," the woman informed him as she hooked Baldwin up to a portable blood-scrubber. She fitted the tubes and medicine vials with an economy of movement that came from far too much practice. "Since you're the only one still standing, you can use the shower. I'll throw together some food, and see if I can't scare up another batch of antiradiation meds for you." When he'd only stared at her as though unable to understand even rudimentary English, she turned him to face the bathroom and gave him an encouraging little shove. "Your friends aren't going anywhere. Take your time."

Chekov was out of his clothes and stepping into the shower before the first truly suspicious thought finally surfaced in his exhausted brain. They had no real reason to trust this woman. She could turn them over to their pursuers as easily as any other homesteader, kill them herself as they bathed and slept, with no one in Eau Claire the wiser. But she could have left them for the storm to kill if that was all she wanted. Why go to this much effort just for the sake of misleading them? Then the hot water crashed over his head and washed coherent thought away.

Thought came back to him, along with a sweet, rich aroma that infiltrated the steam-filled bathroom and coiled around him on the floor of the stall. Chekov suspected the smell of any food, no matter how rancid, would have appealed to him just now. The cramping of his empty stomach pulled him upright when nothing else could have. He dragged himself reluctantly out of the shower, buried his face in the pile of warm, dry towels folded on the chair nearby, and wished he could take this feeling of safety and cleanness with him into the Outland.

He left more hair on the towels than he would have liked, but no more than he really expected. Considering how many hours he'd spent breathing and wearing this planet's olivium, he was happy not to be shedding teeth as well. He finger-combed himself into what he hoped was a half-presentable state, then stooped to check under the steam for the clothes he'd left in a jumble by the door.

A tracery of sand marked the corner where he'd shucked them, but the clothes themselves were gone.

So that's the plan, he thought, picking through the towels for the driest, least rumpled one. *She rescues us from the Outland just to kill us with embarrassment.* He tried to remember the last time he'd been forced to walk out of a bathroom and face a woman without at least a pair of underwear to his name, but couldn't bring anything immediately to mind.

He heard movement in the kitchen area, crept only as far as the doorway with the towel clutched about his waist to peek in at where she sampled her own handiwork while arranging dishes on the counter.

He cleared his throat self-consciously. "Excuse me. . . ."

She glanced over her shoulder at him, flashing a quick but unmistakably friendly smile. "Terrible, isn't it? Middle of the night, and here I am eating half your food." She tipped one of the bowls toward him, not that he could make out the contents from this distance. "I hope you like oatmeal."

Chekov nodded absently, wondered why he bothered with a response. "You took my clothes."

"Of course I did." She tucked her nut-brown hair behind one ear as she turned back to her work. "You were just a few rads short of glowing in the dark." Then, as though sensing his objection before he voiced it: "Don't worry—I know better than to throw away a Starfleet officer's uniform. It's in the decontamination unit." Drying her hands quickly on the front of her trousers, she crossed to a chair on the edge of the central dome's sitting area and scooped up a pile of clothes Chekov hadn't noticed before. "I don't know how much of this'll fit—just some spares I've got left over from other visitors. But it should hold you 'til your uniform comes out." She presented the pile on both hands as though offering a royal platter. "Take your pick."

He hesitated, not sure how to free up one arm to receive the pile without losing his grip on the towel that was his only barrier between minimal dignity and complete embarrassment. She saved him from having to agonize very long. Shoveling the clothes over to him, she left him no option but to let go of his towel with one hand and scrabble to hang on to both clothes and towel as he retraced his steps backward into the bathroom. "Um . . . thank you . . ." he managed, a little awkwardly. She was already headed back for the kitchen, tossing him an acknowledging wave over one shoulder without turning around.

Safely back in his little steam and tile chamber, he picked through the eclectic collection of shirts, trousers, and socks. It had been a long time since he'd had to make decisions about what to wear, other than dress or day uniforms. Chekov quickly settled on a loose knit pullover in the same ice-blue as the dogs' eyes. At least three sizes too big for him, it looked comfortable and warm—too attractive to pass up after a night spent in the desert chill.

None of the many pairs of trousers fit. He stepped into all the likely candidates, then finally settled for a pair apparently cut to accommodate a teen-aged boy. It was stitched of the same heavy cotton as everything else the Outlanders favored, which made it completely devoid of give. Chekov spent longer struggling into the pants than it ever took him to get dressed on board the *Enterprise.* Afterward, he couldn't bend forward far enough to pull on his socks, so he had to peel himself out of the trousers again just to insure that his feet wouldn't get cold. His only consolation was that getting fully dressed the second time didn't take nearly so long.

When he finally slipped out of the bathroom to pad back into the kitchen, he was keenly aware of the blush warming his face beneath the radiation burns, and tried to will it away. Nothing like accepting a stranger's hospitality only to reveal you barely knew how to dress yourself when presented with civilian clothing.

She was just returning to the main dome herself, towing the waist-high scrubber from Baldwin's bedroom into the well-lit kitchenette. "There you go," she commented cheerfully as she nodded him toward an open chair. "You look a good bit more presentable. Don't trip over the dogs."

He hadn't even noticed them until then. They looked up in unison as he stepped over one, then shifted and resettled as though strange men tiptoeing above them were an everyday occurrence. For all Chekov knew, it was. He eased himself into the offered chair with all the dignity he could manage in stocking feet and overtight trousers, and tried not to think about the fragrant bowls of food sitting barely an arm's length away on the counter.

The scrubber bumped against the table as its owner rolled it into place. "Right-handed or left?" She ripped open a pack of self-sterilizing pads and quickly wiped down the machine's connections.

Chekov tore his attention away from the food. "Left."

"Give me your right arm."

He obeyed with a little nod, shoving the tunic's loose sleeve as far up his arm as it would go and presenting his forearm palm-up on the table between them.

"Sorry about the Dark Ages," she said, pinning his wrist with one hand. "I've got the scrubber and plenty of radiation meds, but nothing like a medical-grade tissue regenerator. Otherwise we could have done something a little more constructive than just dumping your friend into stasis."

"That's all right." It didn't help any of them to dwell on things they couldn't change. Besides, Chekov had done this before, a long time ago, when less-than-ideal circumstances had rendered primitive blood-cleaning and intravenous medication the only options available to treat prolonged first-stage radiation exposure. He'd rather hoped to make it through the rest of his life without ever having to tolerate the uncomfortable chemical treatments again. Still, if Belle Terre didn't qualify as a less-than-ideal circumstance, few other places did.

He pretended to be distracted by something fascinating about the sleeping dogs while the woman sterilized the inside of his elbow with a few quick swipes of a pad, then slipped home the first large-bore needle. It stung, but not as badly as he'd expected. He stole his first look at her handiwork as she was taping down the length of tubing and verifying the set of her clamps.

"You're a doctor?" he guessed.

She glanced up at him with an expression equal parts surprise and amusement. "Me?" Her smile broke into a short laugh. "No. A biologist. I was supposed to manage the cloning and care of Belle Terre's livestock until the homesteads got well established." That explained the downstairs cleanroom and the portable cell-scrubber. "Instead, I crank out radiation-resistant camels and guanacos and dogs, and patch up sick homesteaders as much as I can. Gwen Thee." She thrust out her left hand as though routinely called upon to offer pleasantries backward, and he took it with a little smile.

"Guanacos," he said.

That made her eyebrows go up. "I hope you don't think that's your name, or you're sicker than I thought."

He felt his cheeks go warm again. "Sorry. I'm Lieutenant Commander Pavel Chekov. It's just—I couldn't remember *their* name."

That earned him a laugh and then a nod of what might have been approval, or at least some indication that his answer wasn't entirely unexpected. "It's good to meet you, Lieutenant Commander Pavel Chekov."

He angled his head to one side as she reached to pull down his collar. "You knew I was from the orbital shuttle when you first saw me." This time, the chemical swab along the length of his collarbone felt chilly and slick, like the inside of his stomach. "How did you know we were out there?" He didn't want to have to fear her, didn't want to try and reconcile her kindness with the brutality of Plottel's murder or their abandonment in the empty homestead. "Do you have a radio?"

"Radios don't work in Llano Verde." She tossed

aside the used pads, carefully sorted another length of tubing from the tangle exiting the machine. "Word came around the crater from some homesteaders on the other side that Eau Claire had lost an orbital shuttle with a four-man crew. Nobody said anything about Starfleet being on board, but . . ." She trailed off into a shrug, as though the Fleet's presence didn't need any further explanation.

The needle she slipped into the vein under his collarbone wasn't really four times as large as the one in his arm, but it felt that way. He clenched his opposite hand into a fist and allowed himself the luxury of a wince that was more graphic than he'd really wanted it to be. But he didn't tense or pull away, which was the important part. At least, that's what he kept reminding himself.

Thee turned the needle gently to adjust it, then paused before taping it in place. "That okay?"

He started to nod, stopped himself, and forced a smile instead. "I've had a whole lot worse." He didn't think she'd appreciate how indelicately an Orion medic could place the same intravenous lines. "So—" He took a steadying breath and changed the subject as she turned away to release the clamps and set the scrubber into action. "Does this mean that I'm receiving medical attention from a veterinarian?"

Even the cell-scrubber's heavy thrum didn't drown out her laughter. "You're getting first aid from a lab rat who knows just enough human anatomy to know where to hook up the lines." Scooping up both bowls from the nearby counter, she slid one in front of him and claimed the other for herself. "Don't take this as any kind of replacement for a serious gene rework once you get back on board your ship."

"I wouldn't dream of it. How's Mr. Baldwin?" he asked.

"Sleeping. No worse off than you." She leaned across the table to pass him a spoon, but caught hold of his hand instead and peeled it open palm-up between them. "Maybe even a little better." The frown on her face—reflecting both irritation and concern—would have looked just as appropriate on Uhura. "What the hell did you do?"

He'd almost forgotten about the burn. It seemed such a minor inconvenience compared with the rest of his problems. "I grabbed the barrel of a projectile weapon while it was fired." He answered the implied criticism in her lifted eyebrow with a defiant upward tilt of his chin. "The owner had already killed one member of my team. I was trying to keep him from killing the rest." Right now, he just wished she'd let go of him so he could attack the food while it was still warm.

"Uh-huh." She kept a firm grip on his wrist as she twisted around to rummage on one of the scrubber cart's shelves. "And running away wasn't an option?"

"At the time?" He tried to soften the irritable edge to his tone. "No, it didn't seem to be."

She scooted her chair around the small table, finally positioning herself so that their knees were nearly touching. Another expert flick of her wrist tucked her hair behind her ears again, and she switched on the small first-aid regenerator without even bothering to glance at its charge. "Lieutenant commander's kind of an elevated rank for a security lunk." The regenerator's narrow beam itched where she drew it across his palm. "Are you the chief?"

He almost pulled back in surprise, but managed to

hold his reaction down to a slight twitch of his hand. "Who said I was in security?"

"I was in Starfleet sciences for more than twenty years," she explained, smiling somewhat indulgently as she worked. "We did a lot of crazy things, but taking on armed gunmen wasn't one of them." One shoulder lifted in a shrug.

Chekov watched her play the small regenerator back and forth, not sure how bothered he should be by the security trademark stamped across his forehead now that he was supposed to be moving into command. "I was chief of *Enterprise* security for the last couple of years."

Thee took that in with a considering nod. "Past tense implies you aren't on the *Enterprise* now."

"I'm transferring to the *Reliant* as first officer."

"Congratulations!" The smile she tossed up at him was bright and sincere. He surprised himself by letting it evaporate his irritation as easily as a sunlit day. "I was first officer on board the *John Glenn* for her first two tours. She's another little Miranda-class science vessel like *Reliant.* Sturdy little ships, although a bit sparse on personal space. Start practicing folding your underwear into teeny, tiny squares now."

"Past tense implies you aren't with the *John Glenn* anymore."

Another smile. He liked how easily they came to her. "Retired. A little early," she agreed before he could ask. "What can I say?" She transferred her gaze to the dogs who had wandered into the sitting area to take up opposite corners on the long couch. "I started to want a home that didn't move around or decompress. And I missed having dogs. When I heard about the Belle Terre project, I just knew I had to be here. So I signed up as head field biologist, and the rest, as they say, is history."

"Including the Burn." Chekov expected the same flash of rancor that mention of the incident ignited in every other Belle Terre colonist. Instead, she only sighed and tossed a measuring glance up into his eyes.

"If I wanted to bump around the frontier without getting my hands dirty, I could have stayed on the *John Glenn.*" The regenerator's persistent warble ended on a complex trill, and the itch in his hand receded to a warm, pleasant tingling. Thee tipped his palm into the light. "There you go—" She patted it briskly, sealing her handiwork. "Good as new. And judging from the way you're staring at that oatmeal, your insides are doing better, too. Sorry."

She re-presented the spoon, and he took it with what he hoped was an appropriate level of decorum. Even so, he'd finished one bowl of the grain and dried fruit mixture, and two cold glasses of water, before it even occurred to him there was anything else to say.

"Do the colonists you deal with know you used to be in Starfleet?" he asked when she paused in her dishwashing to check the cell-scrubber's readings. Whatever they told her must have been encouraging; she dropped another ladleful of oatmeal into his bowl before turning to finish scraping out the pan.

"Some of them," she said over short bursts of hard running water. "It doesn't always come up." Another glassful of water joined the fresh food. "Why?"

He took two swallows to clear his mouth, then a third to wash the oatmeal out of his throat. "The colonists who know—" But he wished now he'd taken longer to consider exactly how to phrase his question.

"Does it affect your ability to work with them?" he settled on at last.

"If you mean, 'Are they so bitter you can't get a straight answer out of them?' It depends." She turned off the water again, shaking her hands half-dry over the sink before returning to the table. "One thing you've got to remember, Commander, is that willingness to take on risk isn't the same as preparedness." She sat facing the cell-scrubber, one hand on the mechanism, one hand on his knee. "These people wanted a more challenging life than they could have back on Earth, but that doesn't mean they *really* understood what it means to live without a safety net. You and I know that you can't always go back and make a bad thing right again. They've had their hands held in the most prosperous sector of the Federation since the day they were born. They're mad at God, or Fate, or Evan Pardonnet for not protecting them from what everybody in Starfleet already knows—that the frontier isn't romantic or poetic or glamorous. It's just hard. Starfleet is just the easiest place to aim that anger, since they don't want to aim it on themselves."

"The man they killed yesterday wasn't in Starfleet," Chekov reminded her grimly.

She waved that off with an impatient shake of her head. "That was the Carsons. That's different."

"Why?" he wanted to know. "Aren't the Carsons colonists, too?"

Thee thought about that for a moment, then sighed. "I suppose. Although I don't know that they think of themselves that way." She didn't sound as though she thought of them that way, either. "They talked a lot in the Conestogas on the way out about setting up their own little environmental Mecca on Belle Terre, separate from the rest of the colony, living on the planet's terms instead of forcing Belle Terre to live on ours." She made a face and turned abruptly back to the cell-scrubber, obviously trying to mask her distaste of the subject in productive activity. "After the Burn, I didn't think they had anything left on this hemisphere to protect. I expected them to hunker down with the rest of us, at least until everything got back on its feet. Instead, they were the first to disappear into the Outland."

Chekov clenched his teeth against a roil of frustrated anger. "Where they started shooting people."

"That's recent. Either they've had some sort of philosophical schism, or the olivium's made them bonkers. They've pretty much claimed the whole top rim of Bull's Eye. Most of us are happy to let them have it. It's that much less acreage we have to manage."

From what he'd experienced of the terrain inside the crater, it was acreage they were no doubt better off without. "I saw the ones who attacked us getting provisions from the homestead near where you found me. Do the other colonists always help them when they're tracking people?"

She broke open another ampule of the antiradiation meds, injected it into the scrubber's intake port. "That would have been the Rohaus place. And, no—" He could almost feel the river of fresh chemicals ice its way into his bloodstream. "—there's not much of anybody who helps out the Carsons when given a choice." She pitched the ampule into a recycling unit on the other side of the kitchen. "But a lot of homesteaders don't consider staring down the business end of a projectile rifle as having much of a choice."

At that, Chekov flexed his recently healed hand, appreciating the distinction. "Then someone took a big chance getting us to shelter. Any idea who?" When she shook her head no, Chekov said, "You should have told someone what's been going on. Your continental governor, or the colonial liaison. The *Enterprise* could have sent in teams to clear the Carsons out, or at least helped the homesteaders set up protective measures so they couldn't be taken advantage of."

"Newsflash, Commander—as traumatized and unprepared as these people may be, they're still damned independent." She didn't sound angry. Just earnest, and very sure about what she knew. "They came here to get away from hand-holding. They don't want Starfleet to waltz in and fix all their problems for them." She readjusted the scrubber's settings on her way back to her seat. "Besides, in Big Muddy—"

He interrupted her with a frown. "Big Muddy?"

"Eau Claire." She looked at him expectantly, although he couldn't begin to guess what reaction he was supposed to offer. "Eau Claire is French for 'Clear Water'?" she prodded. "But after the Burn none of the water here runs clear, much less the main river, so instead of Clear Water it's Big Muddy?" Then, somewhat more insistently. "Get it?"

He did. He just didn't see the point of invalidating every map on the colony all for the sake of a clever wordplay.

Thee rolled her eyes in laughing disappointment and made a show of rooting through the rest of the handheld tools on her cart. "I'll have to see if I've got something in here to fix your sense of humor." But she gave up before actually coming up with anything. "Anyway," she went on, settling back in her chair, "it takes weeks to get messages down to Big Muddy by camelback, and sometimes they don't get there at all. When they do, we're either told that we have to sit tight a while longer because the dryland farmers on the other side of the impact crater are in worse straits than we are, or that Governor Sedlak will take our concerns under consideration. Which is a bureaucratic way of saying no without having to actually say it."

Chekov recognized that ploy from a dozen other governments. "Don't any of the homesteads have communications lines? Or radios?"

Thee shook her head. "I told you—between Gamma Night and the dust, radios are useless. A couple of the towns have landlines—Useless Loop, Bad View, maybe Desperation. Half the time the lines are down because of weather, the other half because the Carsons tore them out. You can hike two days through the dust just to not make a call from any of those places."

"I have to get a message through to Eau Claire," he persisted. If Uhura and Sulu knew enough about the shuttle's crash to get word out among the colonists, then they knew enough to be worrying about him as much as he would have worried about them. "Can you get me to one of those towns?"

"Right now?" When he only nodded, she gave an incredulous laugh. "You're kidding, right? It's the middle of the night!"

"I don't have a sense of humor. Remember?"

She met his determined gaze with a look of surprising appreciation. "How could I forget?" Powering down the scrubber, she quickly reset the clamps before air could backwash into the lines. "I'll make a deal with you," she said, collecting a few loose squares of gauze into a little mat in her hand. "I've got a couple of dogs I need to deliver out near Useless Loop tomorrow." She slipped out the subclavian needle so neatly, he barely realized she was finished until she pressed down the gauze to stave off additional bleeding. "Be real nice to me tonight, and maybe I'll take you along."

Something about that ultimatum brought the blush back into his face. "How nice are we talking?"

She pretended to consider the question before moving to slide out the needle in his arm. "I've got fourteen dogs, ten of them under twelve weeks old," she said at last. She flashed him a wicked grin as she folded his arm over the last square of gauze. "Why don't you use your imagination?"

It was midnight, and Sulu still hadn't managed to get the hell out of Desperation. He wasn't sure whom he was more annoyed at: Uhura for leaving him here, Serafini for the way she'd delayed his departure, or Chekov for getting himself lost on Belle Terre in the first place. The only thing he *was* sure of was that he was cold, miserable, and completely in accord with the nickname that had been given to this particular Outland town.

Their plan had made so much sense when he and Uhura hatched it over a quick dinner of emergency supplies, lukewarm tea, and the local guanaco sausage, which tasted like dusty pepperoni. Why wait twenty-four hours to continue their search for Chekov when they could resume it this very night? While the hydrologists studied the springs on the crater rim and Uhura used the slow trip to find the range where her communicator worked, Sulu could fly the Bean to all the remaining settlements where the lost orbital shuttle had been scheduled to drop supplies. This way, if the danger of a catastrophic flood seemed immediate, Uhura would be able to radio a warning down to Rand in Big Muddy on the trip back down. And if Sulu managed to pinpoint the most likely site of the shuttle crash, they could go straight to Chekov's rescue after sending their flood report to Kirk. All Sulu had to do, Uhura decreed, was unload the emergency supplies Desperation needed before he left.

Sulu got his first inkling of trouble when he'd seen the unsmiling and silent group of deputized civilians who arrived to escort Uhura and the hydrologists up to the crater rim. It wasn't the warlike look of the armored and tracked vehicle they called a dust-crawler that alarmed him so much as the long-barreled projectile weapons they all carried. Just like the one Serafini had used to blast dents into the Bean's duranium hull. When he suggested a change in plans, however, Uhura had stood firm on their decision to split up. He had been tempted to pull rank on her, but he intellectually knew that was irrational. Besides, she kept reminding him of how much time had passed since Chekov's shuttle had disappeared from the orbital platform's screens. The relentless internal clock in Sulu's head—the one that kept ticking away their friend's chances for survival—did the rest.

So Sulu stayed behind, counting crates of relief supplies while Uhura heaved her experimental communicator into the dust-crawler and the hydrologists gathered up the last of their field gear. He'd watched them rumble off into the darkness, the deep growl of the crawler blending so gradually into the roar of Desperation's winds that Sulu never really knew when it was gone. After that, he'd gone to hunt for Carmela Serafini, to ask for help in unloading the supplies her settlement needed. He'd found her in the long, rustic-timbered building that contained the town hall, the town jail, a communications depot, a citizens' bank, and a continental claim-staking office. Despite the early-evening hour, the building was almost entirely deserted. That was Sulu's second indication of trouble.

"Well, now. I thought you were going up to Southfork with those friends of yours." Serafini pushed back the brim of her hat to regard him with an unexpectedly critical gaze. "What's the matter—you scared of the Carson gang?"

The gibe stung Sulu with more force than he'd expected, and he had to grit his teeth for a moment before he could reply in a manner befitting a Starfleet officer. "We still have a missing cargo shuttle to track," he said at last. "I'll be heading for Useless Loop as soon as I get your relief supplies unloaded."

"Will you?" The mayor leaned back a little farther in her chair, looking amused now. "You may not have noticed, Mr. Sulu, but folks in Desperation don't go out much after dark. For one thing, it gets colder than the back side of the Quake Moon. For another, you never know when a windstorm will come down from Bull's Eye and blow you into next week. So I don't know who's going to help unload those supplies of yours."

"You don't have any more Peacemakers here who could do it?"

Serafini shook her head. "I've got one shift out patrolling and another one guarding the jail. All the off-duty boys went upslope with your friends. You should have told them to unload the supplies before they left."

Sulu didn't bother to say what he was thinking—that the only orders he would trust the sullen-looking Peacemakers to obey were those of the mayor herself. "That's all right. I'll just wait and unload the supplies when I come back tomorrow or the day after—"

"And let those greedy guanaco herders up in Useless

Loop get first crack at our stuff? Hell, no." Serafini scrambled to her feet, just as he'd hoped she would, although Sulu hadn't foreseen the belligerence with which she grabbed up her projectile weapon once again. "I'll roust out the folks from the pub and a couple of private clubs I know. If they can stay out drinking, I guess they can stay out unloading cargo. We'll meet you in the plaza in half an hour."

It had actually been more like an hour and a half before the mayor showed up again, with a handful of recalcitrant and noticeably intoxicated "volunteers." By then, the night had turned just as cold as she'd said it would. Sulu kept forgetting that this town had originally been called Desert Station, since the longer he stayed here the more appropriate its new name became. But the cold, dry bite of the night air reminded him strongly of the winter he'd spent at the White Sands Test Range in New Mexico a few years before. Unlike those luminous nights in Alamogordo, however, in Desperation neither starshine nor streetlamps broke through the dust-hazed darkness. Only an occasional shiver of light leaked out of the town's adobe buildings when the wind blew hard enough against their rug-draped windows.

Between the cold, the dusty dark, and the inebriation of his helpers, Sulu couldn't manage to off-load more than a few crates of supplies an hour. To Serafini's credit, she never left during the operation, although she never actually helped, either. Instead she wandered back and forth between the Bean's emptying cargo hold and its cockpit, prominently displaying the weapon Sulu suspected was his helpers' primary motivation while she asked idle questions about how the antigrav generators worked. By the time the last crates were on the ground, and the last of the laborers had vanished back into their clubs, it was nearly midnight. And the wind was rising fast.

"Looks like it's going to get a little rowdy out here tonight." Serafini paused halfway down the exit ramp, squinting across the plaza at what looked like a curling gray bank of fog. Only the slither of dust and sand pelting into the Bean's hold told Sulu it was wind-driven sediment instead of mist. Occasional gusts of stronger wind curled entire sections of it up off the ground in whiplash streaks, then dropped it back into the roiling mass below. "You be careful, Mr. Sulu. However bad it is down here, I expect it's ten times worse up in the dust layer."

"Yes," Sulu said bleakly. "It is."

He watched the mayor walk back to the town hall, ramrod straight despite the battering gusts, and wondered how on earth she managed it. The wind was already rocking the Bean back and forth with gentle groans, like a giant's hand caressing a puppy. Even after Sulu closed the cargo doors, the temperature inside the little shuttle kept dropping, dragged down by the wind chill transmitted through its bare metal hull. Sulu pulled his dust muffler closer around him and headed for the cockpit, intending to turn on the antigrav generators for their waste heat, if nothing else.

The blue-green phosphorescence of the control panels threw oddly bright reflections up onto the windows, now almost completely covered with windblown sediment. The thick coating of dust turned a flash of light in the northern sky into what looked like a glowing nebula. It wasn't until Sulu heard the slow roll of thunder that he realized it had been a lightning bolt. He waited for a second one, to make sure it hadn't been a fluke of dust-sparked friction, and to estimate whether he had enough time to outfly the storm.

Before he could decide, something pale and indistinct smeared across the cockpit window in front of him. After a moment, it resolved into a gloved hand, clearing an oval porthole through the dust. The hand disappeared, replaced by a face like a desert nomad's, so completely wrapped and hooded that only a pair of goggled eyes could be seen through the folds of cloth.

"What on earth—?" Sulu leaned forward, trying to see how someone had managed to scramble so high up the side of his sleek-hulled ship. Another, brighter flash of lightning gave him a glimpse of ragged, rolling fur and beast nostrils narrowed into unhappy slits. Then his view was abruptly blocked by a piece of paper smacked against the window from the outside and held down firmly despite the tearing wind. Its hand-scrawled message was blunt.

You're going to be killed. Leave Desperation before it's too late.

Chapter Ten

"UHURA. To. Rand. Come. In. Rand."

No need to worry about communications burnout now. Uhura had to shout each word between gasps for breath, using all the force of her voice to keep the sound from getting lost in the howl of the crater winds. She'd tucked her transmitter inside the folds of her filter scarf to increase her chances of being heard, but there was nothing she could do about the way the rim's altitude stole her breath. She also had to be careful not to lose sight of the actinic glare of the crawler's work lights, hazed as they were by Southfork's steaming hot springs. Outside that diffuse glow, the night was thick with dust and erratic spurts of rain from the crater's wind-churned lake. If she went too far astray in her quest to find the right distance for her communicator to work, Uhura was afraid she might never get back.

It had taken six hours to make the lurching journey

here from Desperation, although the hydrologists swore it seemed longer. When Uhura finally hauled herself out of the metal-walled vehicle, she felt bruised and jolted enough to believe them. But she'd spent the entire trip so intensely focused on trying to hear Rand's communicator signal that she didn't notice the bumps or the slow passage of time. She'd caught occasional flares of connection during the trip, longer and more distinct than the microflashes she'd gotten from the Bean. Once, when they'd been stopped by a muddy, flooded stream, she'd even been able to make out an entire phrase: "—Commander Scott needs to know—" uttered in Rand's distinctive soprano. But before she could answer, the Peacemaker up in the driving turret had backed the dust-crawler away to find another route up the crater slope.

Even those brief breakthroughs had been useful, however. Uhura had been careful to find a seat from which she could watch the crawler's odometer turn with its tracks, despite the unwelcome looks that had gotten her from the Peacemakers on either side. She'd noted the distance between each connection node they'd crossed on their journey and, if her calculations were correct, there should be another such node within a hundred meters of the place where they'd finally ground to a stop. All she needed was enough time and voice to find it.

Most of the Peacemakers had retreated back to the crawler after turning on its work lights for the hydrologists, although a handful disappeared into the murk, presumably to patrol for outlaws. Uhura suspected the rest of them were drinking and playing cards inside their windproofed vehicle. They'd certainly made no attempt to guide or assist the hydrologists across the steaming pools and mudflats ringing the main cascade of Southfork's hot springs. The entire area smelled unpleasantly of sulfur, and a phosphorescent mist floated above the thermal waters, reflecting back more than just the glare of the work lights. Uhura had watched Greg Anthony measure the olivium content of that mist when they first arrived. She hadn't seen his results, just the bleak look he exchanged with Weir before they doggedly set to work measuring the water flow of the springs themselves. The hydrologist hadn't measured any radiation levels after that.

"Uhura. To. Rand." She took another few steps to change her position, lugging the heavy experimental communicator with one hand while the other pressed against the side of her dust muffler's hood to keep the audio remote positioned against her ear. "Come. In."

Thunder rumbled along the crater rim, almost like a reply. Uhura paused to peer up at the night sky, trying to see any flash that might be lightning through the dust. They'd rolled through two of Bull's Eye's violent cyclonic thunderstorms in the crawler, and, at least once, a lightning bolt had hit so near that Uhura could smell the ozone past the crawler's dust filters. The last thing she wanted, on this windswept high rim, was to be standing taller than anything else around with another storm on the way.

"Uhura. To. Rand. Come. In."

"Here!"

Uhura stared down at her communicator's dust-filmed display, but a hand tugged at her elbow before she could even get her hopes up. She turned and saw Bev Weir behind her, dripping muddy water from her dust muffler. The scientist must have been soaked to the skin beneath that sodden cloak, but what little

Uhura could see of her face in the distant lights looked disgruntled rather than distressed. The smell of sulfur clung to her like smoke.

"What's the matter?" Uhura demanded loudly.

Weir clapped her gloved hands together to knock off some of the crusted mud, then brought them up to cup around her mouth. "Not the right place!" she yelled back. "Not enough water!"

Uhura frowned, glancing back at what she could see of the hot springs. Steam rose thick over the series of cracks where the water emerged from the crater rim, but the wind blew enough of it away to reveal an improbably wet wedding cake of flowstone below, hundreds of layers as ornately fashioned and draped as confectioner's icing. At the foot of the springs, a necklace of muddy pools steamed and sputtered up miniature geysers before pouring their excess water down a raw gully, away into darkness.

"You're sure?" Uhura shouted.

Weir nodded so emphatically Uhura thought she was going to fall over. She reached out to steady the hydrologist and felt her spasmodic shivering through the thick cloth of her dust muffler. Weir leaned hard against that support, but it was only to get her mouth closer to Uhura's ear.

"There's not enough water coming out to flood that ditch down there, much less the Little Muddy," she insisted. "We've got to go further downhill and look for more outlets."

"Maybe there aren't any more outlets." Uhura could feel her own gloved hands getting wet and cold as she held onto the hydrologist. "I think we should get you back into the crawler."

Weir didn't bother shaking her head, she just yanked

free of Uhura's grip. "Greg says the conduits have to be there!" Her yell was barely audible past another growl of thunder. "The olivium level's off the scale. He's gone to wake up those idiots in the crawler, and tell them to follow us. Come on!"

Uhura wasn't sure if she understood the scientific logic behind this decision, but Weir's stride was reassuringly strong and decisive—and she was heading straight downhill, away from the danger of lightning strikes. Uhura hefted her communicator and went after her.

At the edge of the work lights' halo, Weir paused again, but only long enough to yank the slender stick of a dilithium flare out of her pack and ignite it. Brilliant bluish light enveloped them in a ten-meter cocoon, and Uhura felt an entirely groundless sense of safety fill her, as if the light were a defensive shield instead of just a disorganized jumble of photons. She walked more confidently inside it, leaping across runnels of hot water and steaming patches of mud, and balancing against the increasing grade of the slope. The unwieldy weight of her experimental communicator was the only thing that slowed her down. Uhura thought briefly about leaving it behind, but she had far less faith in her ability to find it again than she did in her ability to survive a fall with it into a mud puddle.

"This way." Weir veered to the left across the rocky slope, although Uhura had no idea how she knew which way to go. She couldn't see anything outside their globe of light except the constant swirl and rush of dust; couldn't hear anything except the ominous rumble of thunder. Then it occurred to her that this particular roar of thunder had gone on for much longer than it should have, and showed no signs of stopping. The smell of sulfur washed over them again, much stronger than before. Uhura felt the back of her throat prickle and turn sour from it.

Weir stopped so abruptly that Uhura nearly tripped over her, and had to drop her communicator to catch her balance. It landed with a soggy thunk that told her just how sodden the ground beneath their feet was. A moment later, Uhura knew why. An errant spray of windswept droplets fell across her just like the rain swept off the crater lake. But this "rain" was hot and burned like acid when it hit her exposed skin. She opened her mouth to ask Weir if they should move back, and let out a wordless cry of protest instead as the hydrologist flung the dilithium torch far out into the roaring darkness ahead of them.

The arc of light traced a thin bluish ribbon across a massive sheet of falling water, so wide they couldn't see the other side. The torch plunged downward with the cataract until it vanished into the billows of steam at its base, briefly lighting them from the inside like an exploding fireball before vanishing completely. The roaring sound of the falls seemed even louder when it was gone.

"Damn," muttered Weir. "I owe Greg another *doughnut.*"

"What?" Uhura reached out to catch at the hydrologist's shoulder, both to get her attention and to steady herself against the irrational fear of plunging down into the darkness along with the rushing waters. "What are you talking about?"

"All the floodwater *is* coming from a conduit system through the crater rim. You'd never get this kind of discharge just from groundwater flow." Another gust of wind spattered them with hot droplets, and this time even Weir yelped at their sting. "We better go back and tell him before those idiot Peacemakers drive their crawly thing right over the edge of the falls."

Uhura took the deepest breath she could manage inside her dust-filtering scarf. "I hope you have another dilithium flare. Otherwise, we're going to be stepping in a lot of mud puddles."

"Don't worry." Weir leaned down to pull another slender emergency stick from her field pack. She ignited it with a quick smack against her leg, then held it up to take one last look at the cataract behind them. "Wow. I thought it was going to be bad, but I never expected anything like this. It's not going to take this kind of erosion long to—"

With the sharp kick of metal hitting metal, the dilithium flare jerked abruptly out of Weir's hand. She cursed and snatched her fingers back, curling them in as if they hurt. Uhura started to take a step toward her, then heard the delayed crack of an explosion too flat and focused to be thunder. Instinct turned her step into a dive, catching Weir around the knees and bringing them both down with a sodden crash right on the muddy verge of the falls.

"What the hell—"

"Someone's shooting at us!" Uhura yelled past the water's roar. Rock exploded a few feet away from them, and a moment later she heard another belated explosion. "With projectile weapons! They're going to get our range in a minute—come on."

Weir's disbelieving look turned to terror when a third projectile smacked right through the outspread cloth of her dust muffler. She scrambled to her feet without further urging from Uhura, following her in a zigzag path downhill and along the edge of the cascading hot springs. "Where are we going?" she yelled as they ran.

"Around in a big circle, then back to the dust-crawler," Uhura yelled back. "The Peacemakers have guns, too. Maybe they can chase these people away."

"But we don't know where—" Weir paused to catch her breath. The exposure to the hot springs' olivium-rich water had put the asthmatic wheeze back in her voice again. Uhura heard her take a couple of tearing breaths, then try again to speak. "The crawler was—coming toward us."

"Then they should hear the explosions even sooner." A projectile hit the ground nearby and threw splatters of mud up into Uhura's face. She redoubled her efforts at evasive action, wondering how long it would take the Peacemakers to intervene, how the outlaws had gotten past their patrols. And wondering how long Weir could keep up the bruising pace with her breath coming sharper and more painfully each time she dragged it in.

A ravine loomed up in front of them, vaporous with steam. Uhura swung left, realizing she'd followed the course of the hot springs too far. Another explosion seemed to rise on its own from the muddy ground just behind them, followed by a crack much closer and more definite than the ones she'd heard before. She slewed to a stop, realizing she was trapped between armed outlaws, a ravine too wet and treacherous to cross, and the steaming rapids that led away from the base of the crater falls. Weir pulled up behind her, gasping.

"Only one place—to go now." The hydrologist gave her a smile so crooked Uhura thought at first it was a grimace. "You ever body-surf down a canyon—like Slide Rock in Arizona?"

"No." It was impossible to see in the dust-clogged darkness, but Uhura thought she could hear the approaching thud of several booted feet over the wind's shriek and the rumbling of real thunder. The firing of projectiles had stopped, as if whoever was after them knew they had their quarry trapped, and didn't want to use up more munitions than necessary. "What if there's another big waterfall further down?"

"I'd rather risk it than sit here and wait to get shot." Weir's shadowy figure stripped off field pack and dust muffler, then wound the heavy cloak carefully around her torso to protect her from internal injuries. Uhura bit her lip, then followed suit. She gave her experimental communicator a wistful glance as she stepped away from it, over to the side of the rushing channel. Weir was already sitting on the bank, legs dangling in the steaming water. "Feels just like a nice hot bath. See you at the bottom!"

And with that she was gone. Uhura blinked, but the dusty night had closed down over the hot springs, and she couldn't even tell if Weir had managed to keep her head above the swirling thermal waters. It was as if she had never been there at all.

The footsteps were coming closer. With a shudder, Uhura began to lower herself down on the bank, ninety-nine percent sure it would be the last thing she ever did. Her feet were already in the warm water, and she was gulping the long, deep breaths she knew would oxygenate her blood, when hands fell on her from behind, snagging her arms and hauling her backward from the verge.

Uhura swung sideways against her captor's grip, intending to use the scissors kick Chekov had taught her for breaking a hold from behind. What she faced was so unexpected, however, that she froze in mid-kick with uncertainty. Instead of the hooded outlaw she'd expected, what she saw in the darkness was the metallic sheen of an infrared face-mask and the glimmer of a sleek dark kevlar suit, complete with a life-support pack on the back and no weapon in sight. What on earth was a continental government employee doing out here in the middle of nowhere? Uhura opened her mouth to ask, but five more kevlar-clad figures materialized from the dust before she could speak. Three cradled the same kind of long-barreled weapon as the Peacemakers, while the other two carried the unmistakable—and highly illegal—humming cannister of a portable forcefield generator.

That was when Uhura realized she'd been captured by the Carsons.

Chekov had never dreamed Llano Verde could be so beautiful.

He'd awakened spontaneously when sunrise was still little more than a threat in the eastern sky, a transparent blush poured through the veil of dust. After a night that had seemed ten lifetimes in length, the sun had finally arrived to shame the darkness into retreat. Slipping into clean clothes for what felt like the first time in ages, he watched from his bedroom window as mylar shimmers of olivium dust crawled haphazardly skyward, like bubbles in a glass of champagne. In their wake, a sheer, coldly lit underlayer of fresh air separated from the morass above it. Clear as crystal and four times the height of a man, it spread like a blanket as far as each horizon, granting a glimpse of the russet and almond landscape Llano Verde kept so jealously hidden all the rest of the time. In that glimpse, Chekov saw the first possibility of hope for this ravaged planet.

The rest of the main house was silent, not even a stir

of dogs disturbing the dawn, so Chekov helped himself to a few handfuls of dry rations and another glass of water, then crept outside to follow the sounds of canine yipping.

The air tasted crisp and impossibly dry, but not so much as a molecule of dust invaded his breathing. He began to wonder if everything about the horrors of last night had been just one monstrous hallucination. Or if he was hallucinating this oasis in the Llano Verde desert, and was in reality still huddled under the naked bush with Baldwin and Reddy, dying.

Except that he didn't think he would have hallucinated a dozen urine-perfumed puppies. They greeted his arrival in the big kennel building with much wiggling and jumping, decorating his uniform trousers with smelly puppy footprints when he let himself into their enclosure, and nibbling playfully at his hands when he bent to excavate their various dishes from under their dancing feet. Thee had not exaggerated the amount of mess these little black-and-white dynamos could create. Chekov almost wished he'd kept on the borrowed clothes from last night until he'd finished here.

The puppies' large enclosure and each of the adult enclosures opened into a series of fenced runs outside. Chekov let the four adults out one at a time, inspecting each one in an effort to determine which two had been his escorts back to the homestead last night. He even tried addressing them by name—calling "Nessie" or "Lynn" when they squeezed past him—but saw no more recognition in the distrustful glances they threw his way than if he'd been speaking to them in Russian. They might all have been the tired dogs on the kitchen floor, or none of them. The uncertainty was eerie.

The puppies were more of an effort to herd out the door. He finally succeeded by pretending to dash outside with them, then quickly backpedaling and closing the door behind them before they could figure out how to curb their momentum and bumble back after him. He left them leaping and rolling and yapping at each other, ripping back and forth in the big pen as though made of ignited jet fuel. Cleanup on the inside went much more quickly after that.

Thee found him with his jacket discarded over an exposed water pipe, his tunic sleeves pushed up past his elbows, and a pathetically shivering puppy suspended over the same washtub he'd used to scrub all the dogs' dishes.

"What are you doing?" Her voice was an incredulous laugh as she nudged the door to the outside shut with one hip. The aroma of synthetic coffee, strong and hot, steamed up from the insulated cups she carried in either hand.

"You said to use my imagination," Chekov reminded her as he squeezed the last of the water out of the puppy's rat-thin tail.

Thee deposited both cups of coffee on the back of the washtub, then bent to scoop one of the last dry towels off the floor underneath it. "Well, you obviously have a better imagination than I gave you credit for." She swept the puppy into her arms, scrubbing it vigorously dry even as she dodged its frantic kisses. "Yes, I know," she exclaimed fondly, rubbing its head with her chin, "Uncle Pavel gave you a horrible bath." Then, glancing up at Chekov, "What did you use for soap?"

He toweled himself off with the edge of the puppy's wrap. "I didn't. I really just rinsed them off."

"*All* of them?"

"Just the babies. But I swept out all the floors and gave everyone fresh water." He smiled at her disbelief, reaching over her shoulder to reclaim his jacket. "Was that nice enough to earn me a trip to Useless Loop?"

Apparently it was. Thee picked out two of the puppies who had already fluffed back up from their baths, and took them into the house for tagging while Chekov finished his bitter coffee and ate another generous breakfast. Lynn and Nessie ignored everyone from their sleeping places on the couch—where Chekov guessed they'd been the whole time he'd been out tending to their sisters. Baldwin joined the activities in time to do away with what was left of the food but turn down offers of more. He was still pale and shaky, but had otherwise rebounded to his pre-crash levels of annoyance. A good sign, Chekov assumed, although in some ways he'd rather have had back the silent, defeatist Baldwin of only a few hours ago.

Thee briefed Baldwin quickly on the dogs' basic care, and showed him how to maintain the generator that powered everything in the complex, including Reddy's stasis drawer. "We'll have a medical transport team sent out from Eau Claire," Chekov promised him. "If the *Enterprise* is back in orbit, I'll bring her medics down myself."

"You better, C.C." That same frustrating grin on his face, but very little humor in his tired, dispirited eyes. "Otherwise, me and Reddy are gonna haunt you 'til the day you die."

He'd known that since they'd left Plottel all alone in that abandoned homestead. He didn't need Baldwin to threaten him with it now.

They took a single camel, plenty of water, and the best substandard antiradiation shots Belle Terre had to offer. Chekov was still feeling a little dizzy from the injections when he accepted an ochre-and-gray dust wrap and muffler from Thee. She showed him how to wrap it with just a few dramatic sweeps, then handed him a bag filled with squirming puppies and slapped him smartly on the behind to encourage him up onto the kneeling camel. He had a feeling this was going to be a long and interesting ride.

Although he tried to avoid it, the camel's seasick gait forced him to loop one arm around Thee's waist to keep from pitching off one side or the other. She didn't seem to notice, although the puppies grunted sleepy little complaints from inside their pack when Chekov's attempts to stay mounted threatened to squish them between the two riders. He loosened the neck of the bag with his free hand and peeked in at them to make sure they were all right. Identical white noses prodded at his fingers while identical ice-blue eyes reflected the dusty sun like polished silver coins. He craned his neck to study the adult dogs trotting along either side of the camel, and verified that the same narrow white blaze bisected each of their skulls.

"Do they all look the same?"

Thee cocked her head back over one shoulder. "Who?"

"The dogs. They aren't just the same color, they're identical." He understood that breeds of dogs could be startlingly similar to an uneducated observer. When he was a boy, his family had progressed through a series of bearlike white Samoyeds with cheerful black eyes and toothy smiles. He and his parents could still identify any of them from holos and pictures, even twenty years later, but no one outside his family ever could. "Are they more than just the same breed?"

"Good guess," Thee acknowledged, rewarding him with a clap on the knee. "They're all the same *dog.*"

Of course. He felt stupid for not having realized it sooner. "Clones."

Thee nodded and returned her hand to the camel's reins. "When the Burn made it impossible to use the automated herd-management equipment, we didn't know what we were going to do. I mean, you can handle stock without autobots or dogs, but it's a real pain. As it turns out, one of the pencil-pushers over at colonial headquarters had a pet border collie who generously donated her genome to the ranchers of Llano Verde. I've cranked out twenty-eight puppies so far—enough to hold most of the homesteads until we can get a variegated batch of border collie gene sets in from Earth."

Chekov watched the lean, wary dogs pacing along beside him, and tried to imagine them as anyone's pets. They seemed a thousand years away from the friendly puppies in his lap, only a few steps up from completely independent wild animals. "Can't you just engineer gene variety into the dogs you're making?" he asked. "Breed a second generation from these once they're adults?"

This time, the elbow she aimed into his ribs was clearly meant as admonishment. "Don't they teach you anything in security school?" she scolded.

Not about cloning dogs, he thought about telling her, but didn't.

"If that original pet had been a boy, I could have cloned both girls and boys off the original cells—it's just a matter of dropping the boy's Y chromosome and duplicating a second X to make a girl. But starting with a girl means I've got no Y chromosome to play with, so the only thing I can make is more girls. Which is too bad." She startled him by leaning back far enough to actually look at him, a teasing smile just showing above the edges of her muffler. "I don't really like female border collies," she whispered, as though trying to keep the dogs themselves from hearing. "Boys are much easier to manage."

Chekov caught himself blushing again, and was glad for the dust muffler to hide his expression. "I see."

He suspected she saw more in his eyes than he would have liked. Her smile widened, and she straightened again in the saddle. "That original female carried a recessive color-masking gene," she went on, "which at least gave me the option of turning out both black-and-whites and blue merles. Between that, piddling with eye color and ear sets, and punching up their radiation resistance, we've already got a little variation to work with once the new genomes arrive. But it would sure be nice to have more than just this one flavor of girl to work with."

"You've been working with dogs a long time," Chekov guessed. "Haven't you?"

Thee nodded. "My whole life, before Starfleet. I've owned them and trained them since I was a kid. I think it had a lot to do with why I went into biology." She patted the camel beneath her, perhaps thinking fondly of all her animals, or perhaps just letting it serve as a substitute for the dogs. "Who could have known I'd end up six months out from the Federation border, helping splice together a new kind of collie for the frontier?"

"Belle Terre's lucky that you were here."

"Other way around. I'm the one who's lucky to be here."

He looked out across the blasted landscape, at the

wind-scarred rock and naked bedrock, at the rare and brittle silhouettes of trees that punctuated an otherwise empty horizon like snubbed-out matchsticks. "You really think that? Even after the Burn?"

The camel labored up a crumbling rise, the dogs darting ahead to disappear over the hilltop. "Is the glass half-empty or half-full?" Thee stood forward in the saddle to lift some of her weight off the camel's back. "Sure, things are harder than we hoped for when we set out for Belle Terre. But Llano Verde is also a kind of blank slate, just waiting for us to write a new future on her face. How many other places . . . can you . . . ?"

Distracted by a tussle of movement in the puppy pack, Chekov didn't realize at first that she had trailed away into silence. The Outland had that effect on things—disruptive, combative, always dashing off in unexpected directions that required a repositioning of your thoughts before you could find your footing again. When he looked up from the pack, he fully expected to see some new chasm blocking an otherwise well-trodden path, or an avalanche, or the reappearance of by now familiar dust storms.

Instead, he saw the remnants of a shattered homestead spread across the narrow valley, its split power source wafting rivulets of superheated plasma into the air above a carpet of slaughtered and partially disemboweled guanacos.

Chapter Eleven

"COMMANDER? Can you get up now? There's someone here we think you should see."

Startled out of uneasy sleep, Sulu tried to sit up to see who was talking to him. The muscles of his back and shoulders, knotted from long hours of piloting, then bruised by almost as many hours on the lurching back of a camel, cramped in protest. He groaned and dropped back into his tangle of dusty blankets, narrowing his eyes against the glare of light. Something snuffled at his shoulder, then whined. A moment later, he felt a wet warmth slop across his cheek.

"All right, I'm awake!" He used his elbows to lever himself up this time, but it still didn't put him out of range of that enthusiastic licking. "You can call your dog off now."

"Kinney, down." The backlit figure in the doorway sounded a little breathless, but his voice still carried enough snap to drop the big, husky dog to the floor. A much smaller dog ran a circle around it, plumed tail frisking eagerly, but the big one never took its dark eyes from Sulu. "Sorry. She's usually not that friendly with strangers."

"I probably smell like dog food. The shuttle's full of it." Sulu scrubbed at his eyes, feeling the familiar day-after muzziness of having slept too little after too long a period of wakefulness. He glanced around the bare plas-steel walls of the prefabricated bedroom, trying to find a window so he could tell if it was day or night. All he saw were sacks that looked as if they had once held food or seed grain, tacked up in the places where windows should have been. Outside, a muffled wind hooted and moaned. "Is the storm over?"

"It's never over." The red-haired man put a foot out to sweep Kinney out of the way as Sulu got unsteadily to his feet. When his face caught the light, Sulu could see that it had once been handsome, but the blistered scars of too much radiation exposure had turned it into an expressionless mask around his pale eyes. "We'd better get you to the emergency med unit."

"No, it's all right. I'm just a little sore." Sulu's response was unthinking, born more of the assumption that his radiation shots were still protecting him than an actual assessment of his health. Now that he thought about it, he could feel an uncomfortable tightness across his own cheeks, as if he'd gotten sunburned during the long night journey to this homestead. There was a hollow not-quite-nausea in his stomach that he hoped was merely hunger. Between the long camel ride and the sleep he'd tumbled into as soon as they'd arrived, Sulu had no idea how many meals he'd missed since last night's makeshift dinner in the Bean.

He still regretted having left the experimental shuttle behind in Desperation, but there hadn't been any other alternative. Peals of thunder had chased him from the cockpit back to the cargo hold, and when he'd opened the loading-ramp door, a close bolt of lightning had thrown the three camels and two riders waiting outside into stark black-and-white relief. Wind blasted into the Bean hard enough to steal Sulu's breath even through the filtering scarf he'd donned as a precaution against dust. He knew there was no way he could take the shuttle up in this weather. But he also couldn't ignore the warning that had been slapped against his cockpit window. When neither of the turbaned riders moved or made a threatening gesture toward him, Sulu had pulled his dust muffler close around him and walked out into the shriek of the storm.

As if that had been the sign he'd waited for, the nearer rider drummed his boots against his camel's sides until it grunted and sank reluctantly to its knees. Its rider slid off with more efficiency than grace, then handed his reins to the second mounted figure and came to meet Sulu at the bottom of the Bean's loading ramp. Even the closest buildings around the plaza were hidden by the thick fog of flying dust and sand that surrounded them. No settler sane enough to stay inside in this weather would ever see this midnight meeting.

"Who are you?" Sulu shouted over the storm's roar.

"Outland Station Six!" The man cocked his head for a moment, as if the words should mean something to Sulu, then went on. "We got word that you were here. We came to tell you it's too dangerous to stay."

Sulu felt his mouth twist wryly against the strangling cloth of his dust filter. The wind was hammering at him so hard that he probably looked as drunk as the men who'd helped him unload the shuttle. "No kidding!" he yelled back, staggering and lurching against its fickle push.

The camel rider took another step forward, shaking his head. "Not the storm! We waited for the storm so the Peacemakers wouldn't see us. They're going to kill you!"

Sulu sucked in an incautious breath and nearly gagged on his filter scarf. He spit it out again with a cough and a curse. "The *Peacemakers?* Not the Carsons?"

"Whoever. You're not going to get out of here alive." The man glanced over his shoulder, not at the unseen town but at the camels now snorting and stamping their broad feet into the dust. They had turned their sloping rumps into the wind, eyes and nostrils both squeezed shut. "We gotta go before they decide to bed down. Come on!"

He headed for his camel, slapping at its chest with one gloved hand until it sank to its knees again. Instead of mounting, the rider moved to the other unmounted beast and got it to kneel, too. Then he looked a wordless question back at Sulu.

There was only the space of a breath in which to choose, and Sulu suspected that his life rode on his decision. Common sense told him that he didn't know these men, couldn't guess what their agenda was, had no reason to believe that the threats against his life were real. Duty argued for staying with the Bean, guarding it, and continuing his mission. But intuition contradicted all of that. Like a thundercloud rising through dust-hazed skies, the worry and misgivings Sulu had felt in his months of traveling the Outland were coming back now to clamor at him. There was something wrong deep in the dusty heart of Llano Verde, a threat so formidable that it could drive men out into a radioactive storm just to contact a stranger. Sulu couldn't ignore that sign.

So he'd left the Bean behind, with a silent apology to Commander Scott for abandoning his brainchild, and scrambled awkwardly up onto a camel's back instead, wedging himself into a harness frame clearly meant to carry cargo rather than a human being. The storm wrapped them in a cloak almost as good as a Romulan ship could have generated, so thick that Sulu never did know when they'd left the town behind. All his attention during the trip had focused on the struggle to stay aboard his swaying mount, fighting the unruly wind gusts that threatened to slap him off and the more treacherous ambush of long-delayed sleep. When they'd finally arrived at a far-flung Outland homestead, Sulu had barely stayed awake long enough for a long swallow of water before his constant yawns got him sent to a spare bedroom.

Now, as the red-haired settler guided him down a modular connecting hall to the homestead's kitchen hub, the two mismatched dogs trotting at their heels, Sulu realized he didn't know his rescuers' names. If he'd been told them at any point on the late-night journey, he must have forgotten.

"I'm Hikaru Sulu," he said by way of introduction as he was ushered into the warmth and surprising bustle of the kitchen. "Lieutenant commander, *U.S.S. Enterprise.*"

"Yes, I know."

"Andrew, I think that was your cue to introduce yourself." Sulu recognized that voice as the one that had shouted at him through the storm in Desperation.

Its owner was seated at the kitchen table, stirring large amounts of synthesized sugar into a mug of tea. He had a sturdy build and dark hair, and looked as if the radiation didn't bother him quite so much as his fair-skinned partner. "I'm Joe Agee, Commander, and your friendly tour guide there is Andrew Bertke. Welcome to our hundred hectares. Hope you like how the dust tastes around here."

Sulu wasn't sure if that was a new Outland greeting, or just a private joke between the two settlers. Either way, it didn't seem to require a response. "Mr. Bertke said there was someone you wanted me to see."

"Yes, but there's no big rush. Get yourself some breakfast first." Agee waved his spoon in the direction of the stove, where covered bamboo racks were steaming in several big woks. On the griddle beside them, fragrant smoke rose from mung-bean and egg pancakes being flipped by a serious young Asian girl. She handed Sulu a plate full of dumplings, steamed buns, and pancakes, while an older sister poured him a cup of tea, smoky and dark as the lapsang souchang he used to buy in San Francisco's Chinatown. Sulu thanked them both, then lifted an inquiring eyebrow at Agee and Bertke as he sat at the table.

"Neighbors' daughters," Agee said in answer to the look. "We asked the Wongs to keep an eye on things yesterday while we came to get you. They decided to stay on and help with all the cooking this morning." His smile was a little crooked, but looked real enough. "Trust me, you don't normally get fed this well around here."

Sulu bit into a bun filled with sweet corn and what he hoped was barbecued guanaco. "Something special's happening today?"

"Well, you're here, aren't you?" Bertke said.

Agee snorted and threw the last pieces of his steamed bun to the waiting dogs. "Don't pay any attention to Andrew, Commander. He's grumpy because we didn't bring a spare camel for that fancy tissue regenerator of yours." His smile got a little more crooked. "We didn't really believe your friend Uhura when she said she'd bring it."

"You're the settlers who talked to Uhura in Big Muddy?"

"Outland Station Six," Bertke said. "I have to admit, I never really thought you Starfleet geeks would come up with a communicator that worked out here."

"Is it still working?" Sulu demanded, dropping his fork abruptly. This must be one of the nodes that Uhura had talked about, where her olivium-amplified signal reflected perfectly off the top of the dust layer. "Have you heard someone named Rand hailing us?"

That made both men burst into laughter, contagious enough to draw quiet giggles from their neighbors' daughters. The two dogs, who had been orbiting around a tug toy like growling binary stars, dropped it and barked in solidarity. "Have we *heard* her?" Agee said at last, while Bertke was still chortling. "Mr. Sulu, we haven't heard anything *but* her for the past twenty-four hours. Just 'Rand to Sulu, Rand to Uhura' for hours on end . . . we thought she must have loop-recorded it, except that if we talked back, she was always really there."

"You've talked to Rand, too?"

Agee lifted an eyebrow at him. "Who do you think told us you were in Desperation?"

"Can we hail her now?" Sulu was already on his feet, leaving half his breakfast untouched on his plate.

"We've got to make sure Big Muddy knows about the flooding—"

"—in No Escape and What's the Point?" Bertke speared a dumpling with a fork and popped it whole into his mouth, wincing as his scars stretched with the movement. "Rand said they knew about it. The news got sent down by camel express, then confirmed by a subspace message from your starship."

Sulu sat back down to his breakfast, frowning. "Have they started to evacuate the cities downstream?"

"No, of course not," Agee said. "Those idiots in Emergency Services are telling everyone there's only a little water in the streets, and everything else they hear is just a rumor."

"That's why Rand keeps hailing you," Bertke added. "She says Commander Scott and some guy named McElroy are watching some kind of hydraulic network and they think their pressure calibration must be off, because the numbers are coming in a lot higher than they should be."

"It's a hydrologic network, and the numbers are probably exactly right," Sulu said. "No Escape is half under water by now, and What's the Point's been completely destroyed."

"See." Bertke pointed a fork across the table at his partner. "I told you we should have just said we knew Emergency Services was lying."

"And why should she believe *us?"* Agee demanded. "We also told her that our fields glowed in the dark, and that Gabby got blown onto the roof by a windstorm."

"Well, she *was* on the roof of her doghouse."

Sulu swallowed one last dumpling and stood again. "Where's your communicator? Rand will believe what

I tell her, and maybe Commander Scott can convince the governor to issue an evacuation order."

"Maybe cows can graze on dust and squirt out purified olivium," Bertke said gloomily, but Agee was already up and heading for another hallway. Sulu followed, with Bertke and the dogs trailing behind.

They passed one storeroom where an Asian couple and two younger women were sorting through emergency rations, and another where a dark-haired woman in kevlar chaps and vest was cleaning out dust filters with an industrial-strength vacuum. She turned it off when she saw them long enough to say, "She's still not awake. I left Keith there so I could get the horses' dust gear ready to go."

"Thanks, Heather." Agee led Sulu farther down the hall, shaking his head as he heard the vacuum turn back on. "Everyone else put their horses in stasis and cloned camels from the DNA bank after the Burn. But the Putirkas came here specifically to raise Arabians. I never thought they'd get them to breathe through a dust mask."

"Good thing they did," his partner said. "They'll be a lot faster at getting the word out about the flood."

The dogs, trotting ahead now, led them to the end of the modular corridor and into what must have been the homestead's office. Computers and automated farming controls were stacked against the walls, imprisoned in dustproof cases, and old-fashioned account books and scraps of paper covered the two big desks in their place. But the communicator that sat on one corner was alive with lights and the hissing crackle of an open connection. In fact, that was the only sound coming from it.

"That's odd," said Bertke. "Usually you can hear her hailing even out in the hall."

Sulu told himself that the grinding in his stomach was the result of a hastily gulped breakfast. He took a deep breath and pressed the communicator's transmission key. "Sulu to Rand. Come in, Rand."

Silence was all that answered him.

Instinct pulled Chekov off the camel more quickly than he thought he could dismount. He swept the rifle clear of its bindings at the back of the saddle and glanced to see that it was ready to fire as he reached up to pull on Thee's cloak.

"Bob? Jan?" Her voice ricocheted off the banks of the little valley, frightened and desperate. A dozen meters farther down the slope ahead of them, the dogs turned and stared back at her in alarm.

Chekov clenched his fist in her wrap, suddenly desperate to drag her down out of harm's way. *"Quiet!"*

She wrenched herself loose with both hands. "Don't start ordering me around, mister!" she snarled. "I didn't—!"

But he had her off the camel and pinned against its bulk before she could do more than swing at him in impotent anger. "You said it yourself—" He leaned in close, the rifle aimed off to one side and his free hand wound in her collar. "This is what I do! I trusted you with the medicine, you have to trust me with this." He gave her a little shake to make her look straight at him. "Agreed?"

Thee's dark eyes burned with frustration. But she nodded grudgingly, and he felt her resistence leach away. He let go of her cloak and took a measured step toward the homestead. "We're going to find out what happened," he promised, "but you have to stay close to me and be quiet."

She grabbed at his arm when he would have turned away, pointing at the saddle above him. "If you won't let *me* ride up there, don't leave the puppies up there either."

Chekov swept the squirming bag over one shoulder, then tucked Thee behind him and took hold of the camel's reins. He didn't know how effectively the big creature could shield them from rifle fire, and hoped they wouldn't have to find out.

They half-slid, half-walked down the incline into the farmyard, braking their momentum to match the camel's slower gait as much as possible. Wind, already warm and tasting of olivium, finger-painted the air with the stench of aging blood. Chekov swallowed hard against the metallic bitterness it brought into his own mouth, but had no real illusions about clearing it away. He kept his eyes on the ruined homestead as they picked their way through the carcasses, their feet making soft, wet noises in the dirt. The rest of his senses stretched in all directions, straining to split him into pieces in his effort to hear every footstep, smell every windshift, feel the beating of any heart not accounted for within his small group. Whoever had done this hadn't been gone very long—if they were gone at all. Only the faintest tracery of dust lay over the carcasses, and the blood had barely begun to thicken in the sand. Chekov tried to follow the confusion of human and animal footprints in that ochre mud, but could tell nothing about where the attackers had come from, or where they might have gone, only that enough riders had stormed these grounds to keep the guanacos fairly well confined while they were slaughtered. Or perhaps the raiders had the help of herding dogs. He didn't mention that possibility to Thee.

Less than ten meters from the blasted homestead, the camel scissored its ears flat against its skull and settled stubbornly onto its knees. Alarm riding up into his throat, Chekov tugged hard on its reins to try and stop it from lying down completely. It rolled him a sinister glower, but otherwise ignored him. Thee took hold of his wrist with a shake of her head. "You're not going to muscle him into going anywhere," she whispered. "He won't fit inside the house anyway. Leave him."

Those ten completely exposed steps until they reached the door of the homestead took an eternity.

Chekov flattened himself against the frame just to one side of the broken door, carefully balancing the strap on the puppies' sack across his shoulder so he could hold Thee back with one arm. "You know the people who own this place?" He mouthed the question more than spoke it, but felt her nod against his shoulder. "Call them. Quietly."

"Jan? Bob?" He could tell from the shuddering breath she heaved that she'd been crying, but he heard no sign of it in her voice. "It's Gwen."

Wind moaned through the open door, then turned itself away again. The silence afterward made his teeth hurt.

"Again." Chekov stepped through to the unlit interior with the rifle leading. Dust lingered on every surface, glittering faintly in the cool inside air. Thee clung close against his back, making the puppies squirm and grunt with discomfort, and called over his shoulder more loudly than before. He waited patiently for an answer he suspected would never come.

Only two rooms let off the central chamber. Every

container from the kitchen to the tiny storage hold was smashed and its contents scattered like shrapnel from a bomb blast. Dry rations slithered like ball bearings under their feet, and something pale and powdery stenciled ghostly footprints down the halls, across trampled bedding, on broken doorways and dented bulkheads. Whatever personal items these people owned lay jumbled into a heap, like the foundations of a bonfire, and splashed with what Chekov could only hope was more guanaco blood.

He stopped Thee in the front room, before she could follow him back out into the sun. "Stay in the house—"

"Like hell." She jerked away from him when he moved to take hold of her elbow. "I'm not letting you leave me in here."

He gritted his teeth against a frustrated sigh, but backed away with hands clearly making no attempt to restrain her. "Gwen, I'm not going to leave you. But I can't promise that I can protect you and myself at the same time—"

"Then let me take care of myself." Fear and grief brightened her eyes to feverish spots in the house's dimness. "Starfleet taught me how to defend myself."

But against these kinds of awful weapons? he wondered, acutely aware of the heavy rifle in his hand. Against these kinds of people, who terrorized their fellow colonists and slaughtered defenseless animals just to prove they were able?

As if she could read his thoughts, she tried to explain, more evenly, "The people who live here weren't your friends, they were mine. Don't try to shield me from what happened to them. You don't have that right."

Chekov could have argued that point—security's entire reason for existence was to protect fellow officers from harm, emotional as well as physical. The fact that she was no longer Starfleet and he was no longer a member of security didn't lessen that obligation in his mind. Still, if it had been Uhura and Sulu who were missing among all this carnage, he wouldn't have let anyone, not even Captain Kirk, tell him to sit tight while someone else searched for their bodies. Nodding grimly, he shifted the puppies higher on his shoulder and ushered Thee along with him out into the yard.

With air temperature rising as morning wore on, the ceiling of dust was beginning to crumble, sinking back downward like blood in water. Chekov led them across the open distance to the barn as quickly as possible without slipping in the carpet of gore. It couldn't have been fast enough. By the time they reached the big double doors, his eyes stung with the stench and his stomach had cramped into a knot of nausea. He didn't know whether to hope they found nothing inside the barn, or found an answer—no matter how horrible—to their quest, so they could leave this bloodbath and not look back.

He motioned Thee to drag the door aside, and positioned himself to slip through the instant it cracked wide enough. It felt like stepping into a cooler. Sunlight hadn't touched this darkness since the day before, and it folded in around him like a smothering cloak. He shushed the puppies still hanging down his back, and paused when he felt Thee's shadow fall over him from behind. "Call them again," he told her.

Pain smashed through his skull before she said anything, bright as a lightning flash, and he was facedown in the dirt with the rifle skittering away from him. He lunged after it, tangling with himself and the bundle of puppies. Someone cried out, "Bob! Stop it!" even as an awkward kick caught him in the side, and he rolled to avoid another blow with only partial success. Puppies yelped from underneath him, and a more substantial blow to his already bruised breastbone sent him sprawling and gasping for air.

"Stop it!" the woman's voice shouted again, very near this time. "You'll hurt the puppies!" Chekov wasn't sure if she was yelling at him or his attacker.

It was a woman's hands, though, which pushed him aside and yanked the wailing puppies out from under him. She thumped to the dirt right beside him, her curly blond hair catching what little light spilled in through the open doors as she scooped both puppies out into her lap. She didn't look like what Chekov expected in a homestead raider.

The rifle barrel that prodded him hard in the chest, however, fit his image perfectly. He froze, still coughing, and glared up at the stocky man on the other end of that gun. It wasn't the cocked firing hammer that dried his mouth and shocked him into silence, or even the knowledge that Chekov himself had made sure the gun had one of its four remaining projectiles already chambered before starting into the farmyard. It was the naked desperation in the other man's eyes, the helpless anger that had him crying and contemplating violence all at the same time.

"It's okay!" Thee dragged at the man's arm, trying to pull him off to one side. "It's okay! He's with me!" Her voice sounded muzzy, distant, no doubt a side effect of whatever had impacted with the back of his head.

"I don't care who he's with!" Bob Mayr used the rifle barrel to ruck Chekov's cloak higher up on his hip, exposing the flash of Starfleet red underneath. "He's cost me twenty head of guanacos," he raged, jabbing at the swatch of jacket hard enough to make Chekov wince, "not to mention every supply contact I had in Useless Loop."

Chekov tried to push himself up on his elbows, was stopped by the rifle's muzzle and his own fiercely pounding head. "I never did anything to you."

"You're here, aren't you?" Mayr snarled.

"Bob, don't be stupid." His wife hugged both puppies to her with one arm, then rocked up on her knees and offered Chekov her hand. "He's got no more control over what the Carsons do than we have." Chekov took her arm gingerly, staggering upright alongside her with half an eye still on her husband, his loaded rifle, and the discarded shovel Mayr had left behind him on the floor. The thought of that metal blade slamming into the back of his head made him feel even more sick and dizzy.

"I'm Jan Mayr," the woman introduced herself as she dusted him off and straightened his wrap. It was a strangely considerate gesture, made only a little frightening by the tears on her face and the glossy blankness of shock in her eyes. "This is my husband, Bob." As polite as though he wasn't holding Chekov at the end of a gun. "Thank you so much for bringing the beautiful puppies."

Thee reached again for Mayr's arm as Jan fell into silent weeping. "Bob," she asked softly, "what happened?"

He didn't take his eyes off Chekov, though his face softened somewhat at the sound of his wife's tears. "The Carsons have pretty much set up a base in Useless Loop. I'd heard they were going house to house, asking after some Starfleet guy who'd gotten himself lost in the Outland. Word was he was worth a thousand liters of water, and they didn't care whether or not he was alive." Chekov felt a horrified twitch deep in his stomach, but said nothing to interrupt. "When they got here and asked if I knew anything, I told them it was none of their business what I knew." The gun sank as he turned toward Thee, its barrel shaking slightly. "I'm tired of getting pushed around, Gwen. Water rights and comm access are one thing. I'm not going to let some gang of Outland bullies tell me who to help and who to hate."

Thee nodded her understanding, then gently took the rifle out of his hands. Chekov's heart thumped hard with relief.

Mayr looked impossibly tired. "What're we going to do?"

"We'll clone you new guanacos," Thee reassured him. She held the rifle out toward Chekov without taking her attention away from Mayr. "I've even got some better gene sets now."

Chekov stepped forward to take it from her, carefully settling the hammer back down against the strike-plate. Even that little bit of movement made his head sing, but not as much as the uncomfortable rage Mayr's words awoke in him.

"And when they kill those?" Mayr gathered his wife up in his arms, holding her and the puppies so hard his fingers whitened. "And the ones after that? What are we supposed to do then?"

"They're not going to kill any more of your animals," Chekov promised him. "Or anyone else's." He looked at Thee, still standing where Mayr had left her near the fallen shovel. He wished for a moment that they were alone, that he could vent some of this horrible anger to a sympathetic fellow officer instead of forcing himself to maintain his composure in front of civilians. "Independent doesn't mean abandoned," he said in place of all the other things boiling up inside him. "The *Enterprise* can't stand by and let people be terrorized like this. Not and call herself a starship." He stopped himself when he heard his voice roughen, took a steadying breath, and asked more evenly, "What's the closest town with a communications line after Useless Loop?"

Jan Mayr looked up from her husband's embrace, scrubbing at her eyes with the back of one hand. "That would be Desperation."

Chekov nodded a curt, silent acknowledgment. What an appropriate name.

"Is this normal?" Sulu swung away from the silent communicator toward an equally silent Agee and Bertke. The settlers' uneasy expressions told him it wasn't, but Sulu pressed ahead anyway. "Are there times when the connection to Big Muddy goes out? Maybe because of Gamma Night?"

"I don't know," Agee said. "It never did before."

Sulu didn't even try to stifle his frustrated groan. He could feel the curse of Llano Verde settling down on him like a strangling blanket of dust. "Something must be wrong down at her end."

"Maybe the power's out," Agee suggested. "Or . . . or maybe they decided to evacuate after all."

"Or maybe," said Bertke slowly, "this damned Peacemaker conspiracy runs a lot deeper than we thought."

Sulu swung around to stare at the two men. "Tell me

what's going on out here. Or, at least, what you think is going on."

Bertke's scarred face seemed to stiffen even further. "What we *know* is going on," he said flatly, "is that most of the settlers around here are getting substandard medical care, inadequate food supplies, and a whole lot of excuses for why nothing can be done to help them. The only ones who are making out are government officials and the guys who wear Peacemaker badges. And both of them claim to be fighting some outlaws that nobody else has actually seen."

Sulu frowned. "You're saying the Carsons don't exist?"

"They might exist," Agee said. "But if they didn't, I think the Peacemakers would still have made them up. It's just another thing, like the radiation and the dust and the water problems, to keep us occupied while the Peacemakers do something behind our backs."

"What are they doing behind your backs?"

"We don't know!" Bertke's and Agee's voices joined in mutual exasperation. "We've been too busy being sick and tired and afraid of outlaws to notice," the red-haired settler continued. "All we're sure of is that Desperation is their headquarters."

"That's why you came to meet me there?"

Agee nodded. "The word got put out through the grapevine last week that any strangers who went to Desperation might not be heard from again. We figured that whatever the Peacemakers were up to, it must be coming to a head, and they didn't want any witnesses they couldn't keep under control."

"Like me." Sulu felt his stomach clench with sudden realization. "And like the rest of my shuttle crew. Oh, my God. Mayor Serafini sent them out to Southfork in a dust-crawler full of Peacemakers! Is there any way we can get up there?"

Bertke and Agee exchanged somber looks, then shook their heads simultaneously. "We don't have time," the darker-haired settler said. "And if we understood what she said before she passed out, Southfork is the last place anyone should be going right now."

"She?" Sulu glanced from one of them to the other, and his brain made a belated connection. "Is this the person you thought I should see?"

In answer, Bertke swung out of the office and headed back down the hall. The dogs waited for Sulu to join him before frisking ahead. Behind, Sulu could hear Agee press the transmission key and say, "Outland Station Six to Rand. Come in, Rand." His deep, patient voice sounded as if it could continue that hail for quite a while.

In the kitchen, the Asian girls were now serving breakfast to an entire cluster of neighbors, talking softly and worriedly amongst themselves as they milled and waited. They fell silent when Bertke and Sulu came through, but it was an expectant silence rather than a hostile one. Bertke shook his head at them, and said, "We're going to wake her up and have Mr. Sulu talk to her. Then we'll make a decision."

The gathered people in the kitchen heaved a collection of sighs: some wistful, some impatient, some resigned. Sulu glanced back over his shoulder at them as they went back down the hallway that led to the homestead's bedrooms.

"What decision do you need to make?" he asked.

"Whether or not to evacuate ourselves." Bertke knocked gently on a bedroom door, then pushed it open without waiting for an answer. Inside, a light burned low beside an occupied bed, and a slender young man in a rocking chair looked up from a book.

"She's still sleeping," he said quietly.

"I know, Keith. But we need to wake her so we can decide what to do." Bertke leaned over the bed and gently touched the person lying in it. She woke with a desperate gasp, like a person starving for air after a long time underwater. "What?" she said thickly. "Where—"

Sulu recognized the asthmatic wheeze, much worse now than it had been even when they arrived in Desperation. "Dr. Weir?" He moved around to the other side of the bed, and saw her head turn blindly to follow his footsteps. Radiation blisters had ravaged her usually cheerful expression, her eyelids so badly swollen that she couldn't squeeze them open. Sulu heard his voice gentle with regret. "Bev? This is Sulu. What happened to you?"

The hydrologist ran a tongue across her blistered lips and winced, then drank from the water glass that her attendant held for her. "Idiot Peacemakers," she said with a ghost of her old intensity. "Took us to the wrong hot spring. Commander Uhura and I went on foot to find the big one. Someone shot at us, I never saw who. I jumped in the hot spring to get away." She reached up to touch her face, then hissed and pulled her equally blistered fingers away. "Not too smart, huh? I guess it was full of olivium."

"Keith and Heather Putirka found her out in their horse pasture when they went to round up the stock," Bertke said to Sulu. "We've treated her with our emergency medkit, but it's not much good at surface damage." He touched his own scarred face ruefully. "As you see. We did get most of her internal injuries fixed, though."

"Commander Sulu!" Weir's head turned blindly against her pillow again, and she was breathing hard, as if she could locate him by scent. "Commander Sulu!"

"I'm here." He didn't dare touch her blistered hand, but he sat on the side of the bed so she could feel the mattress sag with his weight. "What's the matter?"

"We saw a waterfall, before we got shot at—bigger than Yellowstone! Too much water for the crater rim to handle. It's going to erode and erode until there's a landslide. Then all at once, the whole lake will go!"

Sulu took a deep breath. "When will that happen, Bev?"

"Anytime," Weir said, gasping. "Anytime now. You have to tell Big Muddy, and all the towns below. And all the settlers, like the ones who found me—"

Sulu dared a gentle touch on the least blistered part of her wrist. "You already told them. They're ready to get the evacuation orders out now." From the corner of his eye, he saw Bertke nod at Keith Putirka, then head back down the hall toward the kitchen. The clamor of questions that echoed back to them didn't last long, and was immediately followed by a bustle of departure. "Bev, do you know what happened to Greg Anthony and Uhura?"

She started to shake her head, then groaned and shuddered for a moment until the spasm of nausea passed. "Never saw Greg," she managed to gasp. "Don't know if he got shot or was with the Peacemakers." Sulu decided not to burden her with the knowledge that those two possibilities weren't mutually exclusive. "Commander Uhura was right behind me, getting ready to jump in."

Sulu frowned across the rumpled bed at the young colonist. "You didn't find a second—" He didn't finish the question, and it wasn't because Putirka was already shaking his head. The word "person" seemed far too cold a way to refer to one of his two closest friends in the world, and he couldn't bear to say the word "body."

Even without seeing the gesture, Weir must have guessed Putirka's answer from the quality of the silence that followed Sulu's question. "Maybe the commander didn't jump in after all," she said to Sulu, consolingly. "Maybe the Peacemakers showed up in time to stop her."

"Yes," Sulu said grimly. "That's what I'm afraid of."

Chapter Twelve

A SHARP JAB in the ribs catapulted him awake, back into the helmet of pain he'd been wearing all day. Chekov squinted against the swarming dust—which had completed its recapture of the planet's surface by midday—and thanked God for the dust muffler which had kept him from choking to death while he slept.

Although death might have been an improvement over the way his head felt right now.

"You awake?" Thee tossed the question back at him without turning. A chill gust of wind almost tore it away before he heard it.

Chekov forced himself to straighten despite the sting of sand and half-frozen mist against his face. "I am now." He couldn't see the dogs to either side, but he heard their rhythmic panting underneath the saddle's creak and the camel's sighs, and he knew Thee would never have lost track of them, even in this darkness.

Dusk had settled heavily over the desert, dragging with it wet downdrafts off the summit of Bull's Eye and the rumble of distant thunder. They'd crossed more than forty kilometers on camelback since mounting up this morning. Chekov could feel every step of the trip.

Thee reached back to clap him on the knee in what he at first took to be good humor at his expense. Yet she sounded sincerely concerned when she said, "Sorry, sweets, but you're the one who ran into the shovel. You know the drill."

He did. Which didn't make being startled out of exhausted sleep every sixty minutes any more pleasant.

"How's the head?"

"Hurts." An honest answer that didn't even begin to describe how much he wished he had taken that shovel to Bob Mayr instead of the other way around. Blinking over her shoulder, he pointed at a blurry smear of light coalescing out of the dust ahead of them. "Is that Desperation?"

"It better be. Otherwise, Alison Gebauer's map isn't worth the padd she drew it on."

Before setting out for Desperation, they had headed first for the Gebauer homestead, led by the Mayrs and carrying what little of the homestead's possessions had been deemed salvageable. Chekov had ridden the camel behind Jan Mayr and the puppies, despite his protests that he could walk the ten-kilometer distance as well as any of them and didn't need to be coddled. Even so, Bob Mayr must have apologized twice for every klick they traveled. Chekov finally gave up and accepted the ride as part of that apology. When he found he couldn't dismount without help when they finally reached the Gebauers', he even acknowledged that perhaps he wasn't as unscathed by the shovel attack as he would have liked to believe.

Ed Gebauer had proved a surprisingly talented cook, throwing together a quick, delicious meal while Bob Mayr and Gebauer's wife, Alison, pieced together a map of the most direct route to Desperation. Thee hovered over their shoulders as they sketched and argued, while Chekov did his best to remain upright as Jan Mayr performed earnest introductions to each of the Gebauers' half-dozen identical dogs. He hadn't been able to decide if this was important to her because it distracted her from thinking about the life and animals she'd already lost, or if she'd simply decided it must be important to him because he'd been the one carrying the puppies. Whichever, he accepted each introduction with equal grace, and petted the dogs in turn so that none of them would feel left out.

When he and Thee finally set out again, they left armed with a warm packet of leftovers, two full jugs of water, and nowhere near enough daylight hours in which to make it to Desperation. So the Gebauers also fitted Chekov with a pair of Ed's old trousers, heavier than his uniform and designed to stave off the chill of Belle Terre's night, and a good pair of tread boots built for navigating the sands. "You'll be there in no time," Alison had promised. "Just go wide of Useless Loop, and don't let the Carsons see you."

The first was easy, the second less certain. Between trying to scan the horizon for any sign of human life, drifting in and out of confused, headachy dreams about dogs and dust and loaded rifles, and Thee elbowing him awake every hour or so to check on his concussion, Alison's "no time" had swelled into the longest trip of Chekov's life. He welcomed the town's appearance now with a leaden relief far outweighing what Desperation's empty streets and silent buildings deserved.

A few lonely footprints crisscrossed the big central plaza, insignificant dimples in a sea of damp sand. Their camel cut an unhurried arc through the middle, obliterating lesser trails with its long strides and platter-like feet, aloof to the wisps of music drifting out of the one or two still-lighted buildings nearby. Thee brought them to a halt beside a line of wrought-iron benches and hopped down as lightly as though she'd mounted only a moment before. "Now let's hope somebody's up and around to let us in."

Chekov dragged himself off the camel with considerably less aplomb. "And that there really is a landline we can use to call Eau Claire."

"Yeah, that, too."

He managed to land on his feet, although his legs felt so loose and exhausted that he wouldn't have been surprised if he'd sprawled to the ground upon landing and had to be left there until morning. He'd never thought before about the details of what it meant to be saddle-sore. Now he understood why all the men in the old American western video plays walked as if they were bowlegged. Leaning forward to rest his forehead against the camel's smelly flank, he listened to Thee trot up the short flight of stairs and pound on the municipal building's wooden doors. Her knocking boomed flatly throughout the plaza, dying away as quickly as it sounded. He didn't bother to lift his head until she rejoined him at the foot of the stairs. "No one home?" he asked wearily.

"No. But not every place is closed." She nodded toward one of the lit windows on the other side of the square. "Let's see if we can find somebody to let us in over there."

She scooped up the camel's reins on her way past,

leading it across the plaza slowly enough that Chekov could steady himself on the girth as he walked alongside.

Desperate Measures looked and smelled like a drinking club, but without the voices and laughter. Music flirted with the nighttime mist, prerecorded and cheerfully inappropriate, and one or two shadowy figures drifted sluggishly past inside the olivium-frosted windows. Thee tied their camel to one of the wrought-iron benches, then called the dogs tight to her side while Chekov reached to open the old-fashioned hinged door. She caught his arm before he even touched the doorknob. "Aren't we forgetting something?"

He blinked at her, trying to recall all the items on their agenda. The only thing his brain kept circling back to was the land communications line.

Plucking his jacket sleeve into view from underneath his dust wrap, she gave it a meaningful shake. "Rumor has it these dryland farmers aren't the most neighborly types to begin with. Considering what we both know about Belle Terre's relationship with Starfleet right now, maybe we'd be better off leaving this outside?"

He pulled his arm back under his cloak, stung by her suggestion. "I'm not going to lie—"

"You don't have to lie," she insisted. "Just don't rub their faces in it." When he only set his jaw in stubborn resistance, she sighed and crossed her arms. "Pavel, look, do you want to make this comm call? Or do you want to mount up for No Escape just because the locals don't see any reason to make life easier for Starfleet?"

Teeth still clenched at the unfairness of it all, Chekov managed to squirm out of his jacket without actually taking off the outer wrap. What would it take to make these people see that Starfleet was not their enemy?

The heavy uniform balled up almost small enough to fit into a saddlebag, but not really, leaving a wistful glimpse of burgundy to soak up the occasional cold scatters of rain, even after he fought to tie the cover flaps back down.

It took Chekov both hands to push the drinking establishment's warped door inward. Sand gritted under the door's lower edge, dragged between floor and portal like so much broken glass, and light slashed out to stab at Chekov's night-adapted eyes. The pain in his head soared up another octave. A half-dozen patrons scattered down the length of the long, narrow room looked up with bored curiosity, as though daring anyone's arrival to be worthy of their interest.

"What the hell—?" Just inside the door, a slim, dark man with a coil of hair that brushed the back of his seat pushed angrily away from his table. "Get those filthy beasts out of here! This isn't a guanaco pen!"

Chekov jerked a look behind him, not sure what he expected to see. A flock of guanacos trying to avoid being made into sausage? A stampede of camels seeking shelter from the wind? Instead, he nearly bumped into Thee as she stooped to snatch reflexively at the dogs' collars.

"It's all right." Neither one of the dust-laden sheepdogs had made any attempt to move forward, but she gave them a sharp tug back anyway, keeping them tight to her knees. "We're only here to—"

The stranger produced a weapon from seemingly nowhere. A smaller, stockier version of the projectile rifle Chekov had left out on their camel, with handle and barrel shortened until it could be wielded in only one hand. "Take the damned things back outside," the colonist said with deliberate slowness, brandishing the gun more than really aiming it, "before I shoot them."

Chekov stepped more directly in front of Thee and the dogs, capturing the man's gaze with his own. "If you so much as point that weapon in this direction," he said evenly, "I will break your arm when I take it away from you."

He felt Thee's hand knot in the back of his wrap, but didn't turn to look when he reached back to pry her fingers loose. He didn't care if he was overreacting, didn't care that every face in the bar turned toward them in the heavy silence following his threat. After fourteen hours on a camel, swallowing God only knew how many kilos of olivium dust, he was in no mood for incivility from disaffected colonists.

"We just need to get in touch with Big Muddy." Thee grabbed hold of him again from behind, much more firmly this time. "Point us in the direction of whoever can get us into the comm office and we'll be out of here."

"Why would I want to do anything to help out a guanaco herder?" The man looked less certain than he sounded, but his gun was still up and ready to fire.

"Because I've had a very long day," Chekov told him, "and I have a very short temper."

This time, Thee twisted the collar of his wrap hard enough to make him put a hand up and tug for breathing room. "Because we're all on this planet together, and all any of us wants to do is survive." She leaned around Chekov to rake her eyes across every local in the room. "I'm not asking for your first grain harvest, for God's sake. Just tell us who's in charge of your communications office."

One of the men closer to the bar went back to his

reading as though no longer interested in the discussion now that violence wasn't likely. Another spoke up grudgingly. "He's not in charge, but the guy you want to see is Zander Nyrond. He owns the Seldom Inn, the ugly place on the other side of the quad."

Thee waited until they were back outside to smack him. The blow, clearly intended for the side of Chekov's head, swerved at the last second and hit his shoulder, as if she'd just remembered his concussion.

"Ow!" Even that distant impact renewed the echoes of pain that sloshed inside Chekov's skull. "What was that for?"

"Was that your idea of keeping a low profile?" Thee dropped her voice an octave and adopted a fairly unconvincing Russian accent. " 'Shoot the dogs and I'll break your arm'?"

He fell into step beside her and the camel, still rubbing his shoulder to hide the sting to his pride. "That was my idea of defending you and the dogs."

Her snort sounded decidedly underwhelmed. "I should have just let you wear the jacket."

Despite their informant's description, the Seldom Inn was markedly more attractive than Desperate Measures, not to mention any other building in sight. Dust-tarnished brass trimmed the door and windows in dismal khaki, whorling into intricate feet beneath the bellies of empty planters, flattening into handplates for the door's operational controls. There might once have been clever designs painted on the stucco walls. They were faded now to little more than pastel outlines, hinting at a lost grandeur that made the hotel's current state seem that much more pitiful. For a building not even a year old, it could have been three hundred. Belle Terre seemed to have that effect on everything.

Chekov pulled Thee to a stop just outside the door. "Let me go in alone this time."

"So you can get into another testosterone-oozing contest without me there to stop you?"

He decided not to comment on her characterization of their last encounter. "Remember what you said about my uniform? Do I need to make the same speech about the dogs?"

He didn't. She settled to the steps with one dog draped across her lap and the other seated patiently beside her.

The Seldom Inn's entry turned out to be a surprisingly high-quality airlock, with a strong but not unpleasant atmosphere cycle that blasted dust off his clothes in a great whirling cloud. While Chekov didn't particularly feel cleaner when the process was done, the warmth of the fresh air was a welcome contrast to the dank, dirty weather outside.

The inside door drifted open with a sigh, a stark contrast to the grinding manual entrance at Desperate Measures, and the smell of hot tea and jasmine rolled over him. Unlike its dilapidated exterior, the lobby of the Seldom Inn was tidy and well lit, draped with more greenery than all the rest of Llano Verde combined. Brightly colored ottomans and throws punctuated the room, while artfully placed display cabinets and laser sculptures granted it the illusion of being larger than it probably was. Half a lobby away, three men looked up from their table, then reached calmly but distinctly for the wide-brimmed hats sitting nearby. Chekov paused just inside the doorway and eyed those locals warily. Thee might not give him credit for it, but he really had learned something from the encounter at Desperate Measures.

"Oh, my God! Rupert!" The voice was loud, excited, and distinctly British. "What on Earth are you doing here?"

Chekov turned, not even sure the Englishman was addressing him, and found himself enveloped in a hug that knocked him nearly breathless. His attempt to push away earned him an even tighter squeeze and the disconcerting brush of a beard against his cheek. The voice in his ear was as cheerful as it was quiet.

"Unless you want to get your head blown off, give me a kiss and act like you're glad to see me."

The requested kiss was the hardest part.

After that, Chekov discovered that he was Zander Nyrond's younger brother, Rupert, when Nyrond enthusiastically introduced him to the three men still eyeing him suspiciously. Once they were convinced, based on additional hugs and hair-rufflings, that he really was their host's beloved sibling and therefore no one of any consequence, they grunted and went back to their beer. It was certainly an improvement over the hostile welcome they'd received just a few doors away.

"So, how the hell're you doing?" Nyrond enthused, dragging Chekov back toward the front of the room. "How's the wife and kids?" He stole a glance out the airlock, waved to attract Thee's attention, and gave a little squeak. "Oh, you've brought 'em with you! Hello, Ethel! The girls look lovely! Come on inside!"

Whether or not she could hear Nyrond through the portal, Thee could obviously tell that his gesticulations were directed at her. She met Chekov's gaze through the cloudy portal, eyebrows raised in query. All he could offer was a helpless shrug.

Nyrond kept up his animated monologue all through

the airlock's cycle, Thee's uncertain embrace, and a whirlwind trip up the ornate spiral stairs to the second floor. It wasn't until he'd filled them in on Aunt Pauline's trip to Vulcan, Uncle Mort's success at the anthropology symposium, and Mother's latest bout with olivium-induced bronchitis that he ushered them into their own private suite and pulled the door shut behind him with a flourish.

"Well." The moment of silence during which Nyrond took a noisy breath and ran both hands through his wavy dark hair reminded Chekov of an actor's pause backstage before his next big scene. "What a good sport you are. If my brother were actually as pleasant, I might invite him over from Bad View more often." He flashed a blinding and well-practiced smile as he extended his hand. "Zander Nyrond, sole proprietor of this fine hotel. And your host for the evening, since you're not going anywhere until we find a way to smuggle you out of town safely."

Thee recovered first, giving the man's hand a single quick pump. "Gwen Thee."

"Pavel Chekov." He took Nyrond's hand as an afterthought, and only because it was left hanging in the air until he did so. "And what do you mean, smuggle us out of town?"

Nyrond cocked his head, eyes dancing puckishly. "What? No rank? I thought you Starfleet fellows used your ranks like your first names."

Chekov's heart leapt up into his throat in surprise.

"He's a lieutenant commander," Thee offered, apparently unconcerned to discover that even discarding his Starfleet jacket could not confer anonymity on Chekov.

"There, you see? I was betting lieutenant."

"It's a recent promotion."

"You knew I was Starfleet?" Chekov finally blurted. He still hadn't gotten past the psychic nature of Nyrond's comment. "I'm not even wearing my uniform!"

"It's not the uniform that makes the man, you know," Nyrond explained, somewhat sympathetically. "You fellows just all have a look about you."

"You're saying that it wouldn't matter how I dressed, you'd recognize in an instant that I was Starfleet?"

The innkeeper bobbed forward to give him an amiable slap on the shoulder. The same one Thee had smacked, Chekov discovered with a wince. "Don't feel bad, mate. It's not your fault. It's the haircut."

Somehow, Chekov didn't find that observation particularly reassuring. "I'll keep that in mind on my next undercover mission," he said glumly. "While I'm being tortured to death by Klingons."

Thee snorted and patted the comforter to entice both dogs up on the bed, then began the careful task of stripping out of her dust wrap without showering sand all over the carpet. "Do you enjoy making strangers into extended family?" she asked Nyrond. "Or is there something more to this little charade?"

That much, at least, Chekov had figured out. "The men downstairs in the bar. They're Carsons, aren't they?"

Thee looked impressed, but Nyrond rolled his eyes in theatrical disbelief. "Carsons? Not by a long shot, they're not. *Those* blokes are what you call Peacemakers." He darted neatly forward to accept Thee's wrap across his arms, then retreated back into the suite's tiled foyer where the dust would be easier to sweep up. "They're here to protect us from the Carsons, although personally I can't say I feel very protected. They either work for our fine mayor or the other way around—it isn't always easy to tell."

"And I take it they don't like Starfleet." Chekov stayed next to Nyrond as he shrugged out of his own wrap.

"There's been no particular mission statement, but . . ." Nyrond trailed off into a shrug as he bundled Chekov's wrap up with Thee's. "We had some Starfleet people show up yesterday. The Peacemakers took them off in a dust-crawler last night and came back without them this morning. And our dear mayor—who may or may not be the one giving the Peacemakers their orders—hasn't been seen since then, either." He ducked into the room's small closet, produced a cleaning bag with a neat flourish, then stuffed both dust wraps inside. "Draw your own conclusions."

Chekov already had. The image his mind conjured wasn't pleasant. "Did you see these Starfleet people?"

"A couple of line officers and two of Big Muddy's geologists—or biologists, or phrenologists, some kind of 'ologists." The distinction was obviously unimportant to him. "I was rather hoping they'd spend the night. This hotel could stand the business."

Chekov turned to where Thee sat on the bed, tugging off her boots. The dogs had curled up like commas around her, already half-asleep. "They must have been looking for me."

"Why would they need geologists to look for you?"

He fought down a swell of irritation. "I don't know why they need geologists," he conceded, waving the question aside. "But the friends who invited me down here must know by now that I'm lost. They would look for me." Then, because it seemed as compelling an argument as any: "Why else would anyone come to Desperation?"

Nyrond nodded. "He's got a point there."

Thee frowned, stripping off her socks to stuff them deep inside her boots. "Where did they take these Starfleet officers in the dust-crawler?" she asked Nyrond.

The heavy plastic bag in his arms crackled under his shrug. "Haven't a clue. Sorry, but the Peacemakers don't let me read their diaries."

A little bit of the hotel keeper's dramatics went a long way. Chekov found himself beginning to miss Baldwin's more forthright provocations. "We have to go out and find them," he told Thee.

"There's a lot of territory between here and nowhere." Thee levered to her feet carefully between her sleeping dogs, cutting off his interruption with a frank shake of her head. "I'm tired, Pavel. The dogs are tired and the camel's tired. And whether you want to admit it or not, so are you. I'm not going back out into the desert tonight just to get us both lost in the dust storm."

The clatter of wind-whipped sand splashed loudly against the suite's transparent aluminum windows, chased around the backside of the hotel by a ghostly moan. Chekov swallowed his protest with an effort. "Then we at least have to call Eau Claire and report them missing," he insisted. "Someone needs to know what's happening out here." He swung to face Nyrond. "The person we need to contact is Commander Montgomery Scott, at the Continental Technical Services Lab."

The Englishman's brilliant smile never wavered. "How nice. And you expect me to do what? Hop on a camel and go chat with him while you sleep?" The razor's edge of sarcasm all but sliced the words off his tongue.

"You don't have to go there," Chekov said irritably. "Just get a message through on your landline."

Nyrond gave a little laugh. "I don't have a landline. All I have is the local franchise for the camel express mail service." He looked from Chekov to Thee as though amazed by the surprise on their faces. "Oh, come! With everything else you've already seen? Surely you've guessed how the communications hierarchy works here." When Chekov only shook his head, the innkeeper leaned close with an air of delicious conspiracy. "Here's the inside scoop, my dears. The only landline in Desperation belongs to the Peacemakers."

The Bean was missing.

Even at night, from half a kilometer away and through a haze of windblown dust, Sulu could see that Desperation's central plaza was empty. Leaning a little further out from the shelter of the iron-stained rock formation that Agee said marked the limit of Peacemaker patrols, he adjusted the infrared filter on his goggles and scanned the rest of the town. A number of people in hooded dust mufflers walked the dark streets, all with the long glint of a weapon in their hands or hoisted across a shoulder. There was no sign of the experimental flight vessel.

Cursing beneath his breath, Sulu swung around and skidded back down the slope to where Agee waited with the camels. There were seven of them this time, four loaded with food and personal possessions, and one strapped with two air-filtered crates that occasionally let out a muffled bark. Sulu and Agee had done the packing earlier that afternoon, while Andrew Bertke, Heather Putirka, and a few other settlers who could handle Putirka's prancing Arabian mares rode out to spread evacuation warnings to every homestead within fifty kilometers of Southfork. The remaining settlers had gone back to their own homes to pack up their children and possessions while Keith Putirka hauled the still-mending Weir to high ground in the Gory Mountains, safely cushioned in the straw of a robotic farm hauler converted into a covered wagon. Pulled by two huge Belgian geldings, with an indignant Arabian stallion tethered alongside, the wagon held the five Belle Terre-born foals that were all the Putirkas bothered to save of their own homestead.

Sulu and Agee had taken a different and more dangerous route, one that detoured south to Desperation. They hadn't been able to raise a signal from Rand or Scott in Big Muddy all afternoon at the homestead, despite frequent attempts and the constant crackle of an open connection. With the weather back to what passed for normal in Llano Verde—a windblown haze of dust—Sulu hoped he could sneak into town, take the Bean, and carry Weir's warning about the imminent catastrophe directly to the continental capital. Agee hadn't been sanguine about his chances of success, but the one thing neither of them had foreseen was that the vertical flight vessel simply wouldn't be there.

"They couldn't fly it themselves, could they?" Agee shouted through the wind's howl when Sulu relayed the bad news. Being overheard by the enemy was the one thing they didn't have to worry about on this particular reconnaissance mission. "Isn't it experimental?"

"Yes, but the antigravs are standard issue. Someone looking at the controls might have thought they knew how to fly it." Sulu spat out the filter cloth that a sudden gust of gale-force wind had jammed into his mouth. He was dressed like Agee in desert nomad garb today, but no matter how tightly he tried to wrap the folds of cloth across his face, he still kept getting gagged. He turned sideways to the gusting wind before he tried to speak again. "Which means there's probably a billion pieces of Bean lying around here somewhere."

It was hard to see Agee's expression past his goggles and scarf, but his voice sounded thoughtful. "Why would they need to go anywhere in it? Does it look like they're evacuating the town?"

"No," Sulu admitted. "I can see lights in most of the buildings. And there are Peacemakers on patrol."

"Three or four?"

"More like a couple of dozen."

"Then they're expecting trouble," Agee said. "That must be why they moved it."

"You think they wanted to cover up the fact that we were ever in town?"

Agee must have made a scornful noise. Although the sound itself was lost in the wind, Sulu could see the outward bulge of the cloth over his face. "Wouldn't you? If you'd led one Starfleet officer into an ambush and lost track of the other? Everyone on Belle Terre knows by now that your captain doesn't take his losses lightly."

"But where could you hide a shuttle that size?"

"If it were me?" The settler gave him a serious glance. "I'd drag it out into the desert and push it over a cliff, so it looked like it crashed there. But the Peacemakers would never do that much work unless they had to. I'm betting they just hauled the damned thing into the stable and covered it with straw."

Sulu took as deep a breath as he could manage, considering his options. There weren't many, and none were promising, but he couldn't just run for the hills and hope for the best, like the settlers had. "Wait here for an hour," he told Agee. "If you don't see me—or the shuttle flying off—by then, you'll know I got caught. Leave for the Gories to meet Andrew."

"Just *leave* you? After all the trouble I took to rescue you from the Peacemakers in the first place?" the settler asked in exasperation. "Why don't I come with you instead and make sure you don't get caught?"

"This is my job—"

"And it's *my* colony." Agee was already ground-tying the camels, all except for the two they had ridden and the one that carried the dogs' crates. "These Peacemakers are Belle Terre citizens. That means Belle Terre citizens should take some responsibility for getting rid of them." He slapped their two camels on the chest, making them grunt and drop to their knees. "Anyway, you don't even know where the stable is."

That effectively settled the argument. Sulu mounted up with a grunt of his own as his leg muscles protested all the unaccustomed riding, and followed Agee through the iron-stained tumble of impact debris and down the long slope to Desperation. They spent most of the trip discussing, at the top of their lungs, the various strategies and maneuvers that might get them into the stable. It turned out all they needed to do was ride into town on obviously tired and droop-necked camels.

"Stable's that way," said the first Peacemaker to see them, brusquely. "Pub closes at eight."

And that was it. Sulu and Joe Agee exchanged puzzled glances. Not to be challenged, or at least asked for some identification, in a town as heavily guarded as

Desperation seemed a little suspicious. Sulu considered riding right back again in case this was a trap, but the camels really were tired and in need of food and water. So he followed Agee through the dusty, ill-lit streets to a big, arched building that must have been intended to serve as the shuttle hangar for some future regional spaceport. It looked like a gull stretching its wings above the buildings around it: the pub, a hotel, a supply store, and several drinking clubs. The two-story door in its side had a much smaller door cut into it, appropriate for camels, horses, and wagons to pass through. But the larger door was almost as wide as that on the *Enterprise*'s main shuttle bay. Sulu suddenly understood why Agee had thought this would make a good hiding place for the Bean.

But when they ducked inside the echoing dimness of the building, they found it mostly empty. Although one corner was covered in straw, it was scattered so stingily that Sulu could see the plasteel floorboards through it. Several camels had bedded down there anyway, lying with their knees folded in the awkward way that looked as if it couldn't possibly be comfortable, eyes closed and heads swaying gracefully as they chewed over their ruminated food. One in particular looked almost as tired as their own camels, and was covered with even more dust. It kept its eyes open as it chewed, as if its surroundings weren't entirely familiar and trusted, but it wasn't that or the unusually well made saddle on the ground beside it that snagged Sulu's disbelieving eye.

It was the unmistakable gleam of Starfleet burgundy on the sleeve that flopped out from one overstuffed saddle pack.

* * *

Uhura woke up with no memory of having gone to sleep.

She blinked up at the darkness, awareness seeping back slowly enough to make her wonder if she'd been stunned or drugged into submission by her captors. But what she felt wasn't a sick chemical hangover or the muzzy aftermath of a phaser impact. It was a tingling, ghost-fine vibration deep in her muscles and bones. Uhura would have put it down to olivium poisoning and exhaustion, but she actually felt surprisingly alert, without a trace of heat across her cheekbones. She sat up, putting a hand down on either side of her narrow cot to see if the vibration was coming from outside. It wasn't; it was definitely and somewhat disconcertingly inside herself. But at least her upright position gave her a glimpse of a shadowed doorway on the far side of her room. Or her cell.

Uhura managed to swing her feet to the floor and haul herself to her feet with the kind of silence that she thought Chekov would approve of. Unfortunately, her third step barked her shin against something large and heavy on the floor, making her yelp in sudden, smarting pain. Nothing moved outside the door, and after a minute Uhura unfroze herself and reached down to pat at the obstacle she'd hit.

Cold duranium casing met her questing fingers, its shape so familiar and yet so unexpected that Uhura froze again. What kind of outlaws would capture someone, then considerately place their communications device inside their cell with them? For all they knew, Uhura could have used it to get in touch with the continental authorities.

For all she knew, she still could.

She bent down, her fingers searching for the transmission key. Pressing it automatically woke up the communicator from power-saving mode, and showered the dark cell with minute reflections of light from the colored diodes on its panel. Uhura sank to the floor beside it, absently rubbing at the sore spot on her shin. As softly as she could, she said, "Uhura to Rand."

"I believe your communicator is broken," said a voice from the other side of the cell. "We already tried calling, and got no response."

Uhura shot to her feet and swung around in the direction of that ashy shadow across the room. It widened, as if a door already ajar had been swung a little farther open. The voice on the other side was quiet, measured, and distinctly female—not what she'd expected from an outlaw. Even though Uhura knew that those of her own gender were just as likely to break the law, and could be capable of just as much outrage when they did it, her mental image of the militantly antisocial Carsons somehow had never included any women.

"It's not a very well designed system," Uhura said into the patient silence. She wasn't sure why she was answering so truthfully, except that some quality in that voice seemed to demand it. "It's supposed to use olivium to amplify its signal and the atmospheric dust layer to reflect it, but that restricts the places where it can work to a spot every twenty or thirty kilometers."

"Too bad." A slender shadow stepped around the door without needing to push it wider and lifted a hand to the old-fashioned wall controls. Light blossomed inside the "cell," and Uhura saw that it was actually a small and spartan bedchamber, much like the dorm room she'd lived in as a Starfleet cadet. Its walls were austerely blank, and the few belongings on top of the narrow chest of drawers were arranged with delicate neatness.

"Your hydrologist was quite insistent about sending a flood warning to Big Muddy," the woman continued.

"My hydrologist?" Uhura stepped forward, torn between relief and suspicion. "You brought Bev Weir here, too?"

Her captor shook her head, looking somber. "We searched as long as we were able, but I am afraid we couldn't find her. It was brave of your friend to jump in the river to get away from us, but not very sensible. Only a complete regeneration could have counteracted the olivium poisoning she received."

The comment made Uhura realize what her internal ghost vibration was: the cellular backlash of being healed by a low-grade tissue regenerator. "Is that what you did to me?"

"Of course. We never withhold medical treatment, even for non-native species like you and me." The woman's voice held an ironic note that Uhura wasn't quite sure she understood. "Your radiation shots had reached their limit of effectiveness, but at least you were spared the kind of multiple projectile wounds Dr. Anthony had. I am afraid he'll retain visible scars, at least until you get him back to the hospital in Big Muddy."

"You brought Greg Anthony here, too?" Uhura took another step forward, almost within contact distance. Her captor—if that was what she was—didn't make the slightest effort to retreat out of range. "And you're going to let us both go back?"

"Of course." The woman's level, dark gaze never wavered. "If we can't use your communicator, the only other option is for you to carry the flood warning yourselves."

"It's not an option for you to warn Big Muddy?"

The dark-haired woman shook her head. "Our policy has always been to refrain from interference in both natural and human processes. And, to be truthful, many of us thought the rupture of the crater lake might actually benefit Llano Verde, by reducing the number of colonists trying to make this Burned land support them. We never considered how much worse the olivium contamination would be after such a flood until we spoke with Dr. Anthony. It was," she added wryly, "something of a wake-up call."

They regarded each other in thoughtful silence for a moment. "Lieutenant Commander Uhura, Communications Officer, *U.S.S. Enterprise,*" Uhura said at last.

"Brittany Linville, desert vegetation specialist, Belle Terre chapter of the N.R.C.S.," her companion responded.

"N.R.C.S.?"

"The New Rachel Carson Society," Linville said. "We're here on a long-term volunteer mission to make sure the colonization process doesn't destroy Belle Terre's native ecology. You've heard of us?"

"Yes and no." Uhura took a deep breath, remembering the warnings and rumors repeated as far away as No Escape. Not a single one had mentioned that the "Carson outlaws" were a group of dedicated ecologists intent on saving Belle Terre's wildlife. "Let me guess. You're *not* the ones who've been shooting at people around the rim of Bull's Eye crater, are you?"

Linville's voice turned ironic again. "Not unless we're shot at first. Even then, we would rather use our forcefield to protect ourselves from projectiles while we move out of range, just as we did after we found you at Southfork."

"Then who *was* shooting at us back there?"

"The Peacemakers," Linville said, with a calm distaste much more convincing than any flare of emotion could have been. "The same people who pushed us off our nature reserve, terrorized our neighbors into leaving their homesteads along the crater rim, and shot down the missing orbital shuttle—"

"*What?*" Without thinking, Uhura reached out to grab at the woman's arms. She felt more than saw Linville's surprise at that invasive touch and quickly let go again, but her voice still shook with urgency. "You know that for sure? You saw it?"

"No," Linville said. "We found the survivors afterward, unconscious near the crater lake. We didn't know who they were, but we could tell the Peacemakers had tried to kill them, and that alone made them worth saving. One was too hurt to be carried any great distance, so we left them at an abandoned homestead while we went to get our medical equipment. When we got back, they were gone."

"How many of them were there?" Uhura demanded.

"Three. Two colonists and a Starfleet officer."

It was the oddest feeling. Uhura hadn't realized just how sure she'd been that Chekov was dead, not until she felt the shock and incredulous relief that Linville's words provoked. Just as quickly as the feeling swept through her, however, it was washed away again by an ominous thought. "Do you think the Peacemakers found them there while you were gone?"

"At first, we did," Linville admitted. "But it seems more reasonable now to assume they escaped. In the past two days, the Peacemakers have burned several homesteads, and now we hear that they have taken over the entire town of Useless Loop. They appear to be looking for a specific person from the orbital shuttle, one who injured some of their own men. Those they speak to say they would be happier to find him dead than alive."

"That would probably be Chekov." Uhura took a deep breath, trying to realign herself to this new state of affairs. "We'll have to find him before the Peacemakers do, but the first thing we have to do is warn Big Muddy about this flood." She glanced down at her duranium-hulled communicator, brightly lit but ominously silent at her feet. "If you can give me a map, and some idea of where we are on it, I think I can find a spot where this will work. It may take a little walking to get there."

Linville inclined her head politely. "You'll have to take our guides with you—it's hard to navigate this area even in daylight, and all but impossible in the dark. I would also suggest you take time to eat something before you leave."

"Is there time?" Uhura wasn't sure she could even remember the last meal she'd had, but the urgent need to get the flood warning out transcended any possibility of hunger. "Does Dr. Anthony know how much longer we have until the crater bursts?"

"No," said Linville. "But we do. The shafts create small discrepancies in the gravitation field. From those, we calculated that the first one was only a hundred meters away from the rim when it broke through to the springs at Southfork. The other two were five hundred meters from the rim when we measured them last night, right before we found you. They're advancing at approximately twenty-five meters an hour."

Uhura still hadn't managed to fully absorb the first part of that comprehensive answer. *"Shafts?"*

"From the olivium mine inside the crater wall."

Linville's lifted eyebrow conveyed a degree of irony even Mr. Spock would be hard pressed to match. "Surely, you're not surprised, Commander Uhura. You must have realized by now that illegal olivium mining is the only reasonable explanation for what's going on here in Llano Verde."

Chapter Thirteen

"PAVEL, for the millionth time, come to bed."

Chekov glanced away from the impenetrable midnight outside their hotel room's window. A tiny bedside lamp splashed precious little illumination across the suite's only bed, but it was enough to highlight the dogs sprawled across half of it, and Thee buried under all the pillows somewhere in between. "I'm not tired." With the storm's dusty fist occasionally rattling off the hotel's walls, his stomach churning from too many worried thoughts, and his head still throbbing despite a handful of the best analgesics Zander Nyrond could dig up, the half-truth fell out of him easily enough.

"You're not a very good liar," said Thee's muffled voice. Just in case he didn't already know.

He turned back to the window with an acknowledging tilt of his head. "I can't sleep," he said, more accurately and more reluctantly.

"Want to talk about it?" Bedding rustled and one of the dogs gave a sleepy groan as Thee discarded enough pillows to work herself into a sitting position.

Chekov looked away from the window again, caught off guard by that suggestion. "No." He didn't even talk to Sulu and Uhura when things bothered him unless he absolutely couldn't avoid it. It seemed somehow unfaithful to breach that moratorium with someone his friends didn't even know.

Thee snorted and smacked her fist deep into one of the discarded pillows. Perhaps as another substitute for his head, Chekov thought wryly. "Okay, let me explain how this works. If you're going keep me up all night, pacing around like a border collie after a fly, then I get to chat about what's worrying you. And you're not allowed to answer in words of one syllable." She looped her arms around her knees and settled back against the headboard. "Talk or sleep, it's your choice."

"It's just . . ." He wasn't even sure which part of her proposition he was responding to. "I hardly know you."

"So I can't possibly understand?" She sounded irritated, maybe even a little hurt. It struck him as strange that exclusion from his emotional turmoil should bother her. "Am I supposed to be stupid enough to believe this is all about your head still hurting, or the dogs on the bed, or some archaic sense of chivalry, and not about you tearing yourself apart because you're worried about your friends?"

Saying it seemed to grant Chekov's fears a life of their own. He shivered convulsively, feeling again the frigid wind and the bitter bite of olivium dust against his skin. "I've been out in that," he tried to explain. It came out very quietly, too much like a child's explanation of a nightmare.

Thee's response held no trace of judgment or ridicule. "I know you have."

"If you hadn't found us when you did . . ." He shook off the rest of that thought, suddenly superstitious about where pursuing it might lead. "And now we're just sitting here, doing *nothing* because we're afraid of a few civilian bullies with guns . . ." Or maybe just afraid of the guns. Anger tightened Chekov's throat, followed quickly by a sick, leaching sense of self-hatred. Bad enough that he was the reason Sulu and Uhura had braved Llano Verde's Outland to begin with; he couldn't bear to accept that his squeamishness about the colonists' primitive weapons might be the only thing that kept him from saving his friends in their own crisis. Especially if what they needed to be saved from was the same kind of fate Dave Plottel had met . . .

"We're up here doing nothing, Pavel, because there is *nothing* we can do." Thee raised her voice to talk over what must have been an expected protest, although he made no move to interrupt her. "I know that's hard for you security types to accept, but there really are times when the best course of action is to rest, *preserve yourself,* and use all that energy where it can do some good." She shifted among the pillows, facing him more directly. "It's dark out there, with wall-to-wall dust and thunderstorms. Even if we could sneak out past the Peacemakers, we wouldn't be able to see a damned thing, and we'd be just as likely to get killed as to save your friends."

Chekov couldn't argue with that. He hadn't fared too well on any of his journeys through Llano Verde's dust, not even when all he had to worry about was getting Baldwin and Reddy down off the slopes of Bull's Eye crater. "There's the landline in the Peacemakers' office." He couldn't quite let go of the conviction that he was being cowardly and disloyal as long as there was something—anything—he could do to rescue his friends. "We could contact Eau Claire, have them punch a message through to Captain Kirk."

"You could also get shot trying to break in and spend the next three hours dying."

A flash memory of Reddy, bleeding out and nearly dead. Of Plottel with a hole the size of a fist in his back. Chekov clenched his jaw and swung back to the window, trying to convince himself that those were good enough reasons not to try and help his friends.

Thee sighed again, almost as if she could hear what he was thinking. "Do you ever take no for an answer?"

He watched a dark curtain of dust sweep up the side of the building and crash into his window. "Not often."

"You must be a pain in the ass to live with."

Chekov thought about Sulu, haranguing him for his stubbornness, and managed a faint smile. "So I've been told."

Thee stirred again, pushing one of the dogs off onto the floor. When he turned to look, she reached out her hand toward him through the half-darkness. "Pavel, come to bed."

He opened his mouth to answer her, even took a step into the room. Then a shadow blacker than the nighttime outside fell against the windowpane, and his attention snapped back over his shoulder. A humanoid silhouette, as distinct as a paper cutout, solidified out of the storm winds and craned up to peer into their window.

Chekov ducked to one side, out of the blanket of light, and hissed at Thee to switch off the bedside lamp. She was already there, stretching across a startled dog to snap the room into darkness. Chekov snatched up the rifle from where he'd left it against the wall. He had his hand on the window latch, the rifle hefted over one shoulder like a club, before their visitor had even finished his surveillance. Chekov whipped the window open, toppling the intruder inward and onto the floor amid a flurry of alarmed barking. He straddled him in a single step and raised the rifle high—

"Pavel! Pavel, don't shoot! It's me!"

Chekov froze, shocked into immobility by that familiar voice. "Hikaru?"

Sulu lowered his hands and tugged the masking folds of cloth away from his face. "I don't know how to break this to you," he remarked, his voice a good bit less frantic, "but the other end of the gun is the one all the colonists use."

Chekov caught the helmsman by the front of his dust muffler and heaved him to his feet. He almost couldn't believe he was real until his friend's hug tightened painfully around him. "We thought the Peacemakers had killed you," he said, between gasps and volleys of barking. He heard Thee give a single, sharp command and the dogs fell silent again.

"Not for lack of trying." Sulu blinked in the sudden light of the bedside lamp, pushing away from Chekov to steal a look toward the bed, Thee, and the watchful dogs whose collars she was holding. "Um . . . should I come back later?"

Thee made an odd noise, half laugh and half exasperated sigh. "It probably wouldn't matter if you did." She released the dogs with a quick hand signal that kept them on the bed. "I'm Gwen Thee, attached to the Belle Terre biology division. You must be one of the two friends he's been fretting about ever since we got to Desperation."

Sulu returned her smile with a readiness Chekov found himself a little irritated by. "Lieutenant Commander Hikaru Sulu, from the *Enterprise.*" The pilot moved to close the still-open window, shutting out both the chill and whoever else might be within earshot on the street. "Uhura and I brought the Bean out to track your supply drops as soon as we realized your shuttle had gone down," he told Chekov over his shoulder. "We got as far as here, then Uhura had to take Weir and Anthony—" Chekov frowned a question, and Sulu quickly sidestepped to explain, "—two of the hydrologists from the colony's Hydrologic and Meteorologic Services—"

Which raised the other question that had been plaguing Chekov. "Why did you need hydrologists to come looking for me?"

Sulu sighed. "Trust me, we didn't. But the continental governor in Eau Claire won't let anybody set foot in the Outland without an overwhelming probability of coming home again. That's why there weren't any regular search-and-rescue teams out looking for your shuttle. The hydrologists needed to come up here to study the river, and we were the only ride they could get. Uhura felt sorry for them and gave them permission to come along."

"Where are they now?"

"I don't know!" The helmsman paced a few steps, seemed to realize what he was doing, and came back again. "The Peacemakers took Uhura and the hydrologists upslope to check water flow rates through the crater wall—"

"—and then came back without them," Chekov finished for him.

Sulu nodded. "I've been hiding with some farmers near here since then. They managed to find Dr. Weir, although she was in pretty bad shape, but there's been no sign of Uhura or Dr. Anthony. Weir says they were attacked by Carsons."

"Or maybe by Peacemakers?" Thee asked cynically.

Sulu gave her a quick nod. "That's what I'm afraid of. The farmers who rescued me said there's some kind of conspiracy going on around here, and that the Peacemakers are a big part of it . . . but that's not the *real* problem."

"It's not?" Chekov frowned at him again. "Then what is?"

The pilot took a deep breath, as if he hated what he had to say. "The Big Muddy's going to flood."

Before Chekov could ask, Thee volunteered sweetly, "That would be the Eau Claire River to you, Pavel."

He angled an unamused look in her direction. She responded with a thoroughly aggravating smile.

"Water levels are already way too high all along the Little Muddy," Sulu continued, either not noticing their byplay or choosing to ignore it. "A couple of the smaller towns are completely flooded out. Once the crater wall lets loose, it's going to make a flood wave that'll take out everything from here down to the capital."

Chekov didn't know for sure how long a stretch of river that was, or how many towns and homesteads and guanaco barns it encompassed, but even a handful of lives lost on this fledgling colony would constitute a disaster. The loss of the whole riverside population could be a planetary catastrophe.

With a resigned groan, Thee hauled herself out of bed and reached for the dusty trousers she'd left draped on a nearby chair. "Our first priority is to get a warning out to the rest of the valley, right?" she asked pragmatically. It occurred to Chekov that a haircut wasn't the only way you could know a Starfleet officer, active or retired. "How long do we have?"

"According to Dr. Weir, the flood could start at any minute. The farmers we were able to reach have already started evacuating, but there's no way word of mouth can travel the length of the river in time. Not in this weather. I came back to Desperation to get the Bean and head straight for Big Muddy."

Tentative hope leapt in Chekov. "The Bean is here?"

Wincing at Chekov's optimism, Sulu shook his head. "Not anymore. I thought maybe they'd hidden it in the stables, but all I found there was somebody's tossed-off Starfleet jacket." It was a transparent attempt at his usual humor, and somehow made the situation seem even more grim. "Which means the Bean is probably in a million pieces over the side of a cliff somewhere."

Taking all their hopes for an easy trip to Eau Claire along with it.

"How did you figure out we were here?" Now fully clothed, Thee sent the dogs to sit by the door and extracted their freshly cleaned dust mufflers from the closet.

"This is the only hotel in town." Sulu took one of the cloaks and passed it along to Chekov. "And this was the only lighted window that wasn't covered by a sack. I figured it had to be you. Desperation doesn't seem to get many tourists."

Chekov nodded absently, accepting the dust gear with one hand and collecting up his rifle with the other. Going out into the darkness was no longer an abstract prospect. Whatever danger they might encounter at the hands of the Peacemakers was minuscule compared with the greater danger that thousands of unwitting colonists were in. Even the search for Uhura would have to be deferred until the evacuation orders had been delivered. Chekov grimaced, knowing now why Sulu hadn't liked telling them about the flood. Chekov would just have to hope that Uhura had fared as well as they had, finding refuge with someone as kind as Sulu's farmers, as strong and reliable as Gwen Thee.

"Pavel . . ." Sulu took hold of his elbow and made him turn. "If she's out there, we'll find her." His gaze was sympathetic yet stern in a way only years of friendship could convey. "But you know she'll kill us if we let Big Muddy get flooded because we went looking for her before we sent a warning down."

She would. Chekov knew she would. Just as surely as he would hate himself if anything happened to her in the time it took them to warn Eau Claire.

Taking a deep breath, he disengaged from Sulu's grip and shook out his dust wrap to swing it on. "There's a landline to Eau Claire in the main Peacemaker office."

"No." Thee snapped Chekov a glare that was clearly meant to remind him of their conversation a few minutes ago. "It's too dangerous—"

"And too unreliable," Sulu added firmly. "Whatever conspiracy these Peacemakers are involved in reaches all the way down to Big Muddy. Even if we can secure our end of the line, there's no guarantee that the person we're talking to will pass the warning along. I think we have to deliver this message in person or not at all. If we could find the Bean, or even some mothballed colony air transport . . . I just need something I can *fly!*"

"I know where there's something." The answer was suddenly clear to Chekov—as clear as the air above the churning crater lake. He blinked his mind back to the moment and found Sulu staring at him quizzically. "If you're a good enough pilot to get it above the dust layer," he said, donning his dust muffler with a practiced flick of his hand, "there's a slightly waterlogged cargo shuttle we could salvage right at the top of this crater."

Every new world is a new chance to learn.

The old motto was running through Uhura's head again as she followed three shadowy figures through the dark maze of boulders in which the New Rachel Carson Society's camouflaged headquarters were hidden from attack. The night was thick with dust, and even their dilithium torches barely carved out the next few steps ahead of them. In the hours they'd been out here looking for a communications node, Uhura's borrowed kevlar dust suit had scraped her knees and elbows raw, and trapped her body heat so efficiently that sweat stung against every centimeter of chafed skin. Each step was a battle fought against blasting wind, shifting rocks, and treacherous drifts of dust, a search for that invisible place in the darkness where olivium crystal refraction and atmospheric reflection combined to form a perfect but elusive partnership.

So far, what Uhura had learned from Belle Terre was to never again take open communication channels for granted.

She had always supported the idea of developing an olivium-proof communications system for the Burned regions of this planet, but that was mostly because it was the kind of professional challenge she loved to rise to. Even the long, frustrating weeks of trying to hail Sulu, and the random silences of Gamma Night, had only taught her how much personal annoyance could be caused by a lack of communications. But this olivium mining conspiracy that had spread like an undetected cancer across the heart of Llano Verde, with its miasma of misleading rumors and the potentially catastrophic flood that no one could be warned about—none of those would have happened if there'd been a working communications system in place here from the beginning. Outland settlers could have talked to each other, put two and two together, sent reports and warnings into Big Muddy . . .

She didn't notice that the kevlar-clad figure in front of her had stopped until she bumped into her. "We're four meters north-northeast of our last checkpoint, Commander," said Linville's suit-amplified voice. The heavy experimental communicator swung as lightly as a tricorder on her shoulder, and she wasn't even out of breath. "Should we try calling Big Muddy again?"

"Yes." Uhura reached out to steady the communicator while the woman lowered it to the ground. She would have preferred to carry it herself, but her new Carson allies had strict rules governing their excursions into the outside world. Their policy was to stay out only as long as their defensive forcefield's power cell lasted—one of the reasons they hadn't been exterminated by the Peacemakers a long time ago. Even though Uhura's calculations suggested that the nearest communications node lay just west of Carson headquarters, the jumbled impact debris blanketing the area made it impossible for her to lug the communicator herself. She'd been forced to entrust it to Linville's stronger but far more cavalier hands, wincing every time it slammed into a rock surface or thudded carelessly down into a drift of olivium dust. She just hoped its inner circuits could withstand as much stress as its duranium shell.

She crouched down to wipe off the thick coating of dust that the output screen had collected and wake the communicator up from power-saving sleep. The rainbow glow of its diodes refracted through the blowing dust and sparked an answering glitter off the silver cannister of the illegal forcefield generator. It had been set down by the other two members of their group, one of whom squatted to fiddle with its adjustments while the other hauled herself up to a convenient sheltered ledge on the boulder that towered over them.

Uhura unsealed one edge of her infrared faceplate, wincing at the immediate influx of dust and wind. Her night vision, formerly enhanced by the cloudy glow of infrared augmentation, dimmed down to black nothingness. She had to fumble to find the communicator's output panel so she could put her ear against it and listen to the feedback from her signal. It sounded as if the connection might be open, or at least getting close to a node. There was a peculiar crystalline hum that the communicator made when its signal was being entirely absorbed by olivium interference. She couldn't hear any of that here.

"Uhura to Rand," she said, coughing as she resealed her faceplate. The suit's air-cleaning unit was far better than the loose filter scarf of her dust muffler, but it hadn't been designed for someone who kept unsealing her suit. "Come in, Rand. Uhura to Rand. Come in, Rand."

"Any luck?"

The amplified snap of that voice told Uhura it didn't

belong to either Linville or Karen Roth, the young technician who kept their forcefield calibrated. She peered up through the cold bouldery darkness at the red glow of human warmth that was kicking its heels on the rock ledge. When Linville had announced to her fellow Carson scientists that Uhura needed escorts to help find her communications node, Lori Tamasy had been the first to volunteer. She'd introduced herself as an aquatic ecologist, but from the easy way she held her projectile weapon cradled in the crook of one arm, Uhura suspected she'd had at least some private security training at some point in her past. In fact, she seemed to be the nearest thing the Carsons had to a field commander. That must have been why she'd offered to come along, since from the beginning she'd been asking Uhura that same question with exactly that tone of doubt and impatience.

"Not yet." Uhura pushed the communications box a half-meter to the right in an attempt to punch up the signal she thought she could see dancing in the noise. "But I'm getting closer."

"Better be," said Tamasy. "We've got to head home soon."

"Do we?" From the quizzical sound of Linville's voice, Uhura was sure the woman had lifted at least one eyebrow. "It's been less than two hours since we left."

"However many hours is still more than we'd planned on being out tonight," Tamasy said. "You know we can't drain the power cell. We've got to leave first thing in the morning."

"Uhura to Rand," Uhura said into the communicator. "Come in, Rand. Uhura to Rand." She paused, listening to the crackle of the channel. When no reply came, she began shoving the box even further to the right, joined after a moment by Linville.

"Where do you have to go tomorrow?" she asked the woman, whose warmer shadow was even more intensely red than Tamasy's. "Are there other people who need to be rescued from the flood?"

"No, but there's an entire river ecosystem that does," Tamasy said, before the woman could reply. "If we want to save it, we've got to stop those other mine shafts before they break through the crater wall."

"You're going to take on the miners in their own territory?" The communicator plowed through a drift and threw a dark mantle of heat-absorbing olivium dust across all their shadows before the night wind blew it away. "How does your society's noninterference policy justify *that?*"

Tamasy didn't answer her, leaving it to Linville to finally reply. "There are many who think it doesn't," she admitted. "They will carry our native DNA banks to higher ground in the Gory Mountains, in the event the rest of us fail to stop the flood from coming. That will ensure that at least some native life survives, whether or not the colony does."

There was nothing Uhura could think of to say to that, so instead she yanked the communicator back around to face her. "Uhura to Rand," she said. "Come in, Rand."

The signal response meter stayed so flat that, for a moment, Uhura feared the olivium dust had finally done its circuits in. She frowned and cracked open her faceplate again. Even past the rising wind, she could hear the unmistakable hum of olivium interference across the channel. She gritted her teeth and resealed her infrared mask, then began to drag the communicator back to its original location. She hoped all that dust inside her hood would keep her embarrassed expression from showing.

"I thought Dr. Anthony said the mine conduits had already weakened the crater rim to the point where it could go at any moment," she said, before anyone could comment on her course reversal. "Even if you stop the mining, there's no guarantee you'll stop the flood."

"That doesn't mean we shouldn't try," Tamasy said. "Once we're inside, we might be able to collapse some of the conduits and keep the flood from being quite so catastrophic."

The Carson biologist's voice was so matter-of-fact that it took Uhura a moment to realize she was talking about a suicide mission. She gave the communicator a fierce yank to drag it past its original position, then smacked the transmission key with unnecessary force. "Uhura to Rand," she snapped. "Come in, Rand."

The signal monitor spiked upward as if her vehemence had kicked it into cooperating. This time, Uhura was careful to turn the communicator in a slow arc so she could see in which direction the signal was getting stronger. She ended up facing Tamasy, who was watching her with the impatient glare of a tethered hawk.

"I'm just about ready to leave," the Carson leader said.

"We're close to the node," Uhura said. "Just give me another five minutes to find it."

"You know I was one of those who voted with you to stop the mine," Linville said to Tamasy. "But I fail to see the point of leaving here before we warn the settlements downstream. Even with our intervention, the probability of a flood remains high—"

"And it's getting higher with every minute we spend walking in circles out here!"

"We're not walking in any more circles." Uhura dragged the communicator another half-meter to the left and found her way blocked by rock. She looked over her shoulder, intending to ask Linville for help, but a long arm reached down from above and yanked the communicator away from her before she could say a word. She went up after it, her kevlar boots scrabbling for purchase on the dusty rock until Tamasy caught her by the arm and hauled her in like a floundering fish. Uhura found herself plopped unceremoniously down on the ledge beside her communicator. The strong peak on its signal readout was all she needed to see to make up for that indignity.

"We're at the node," she said, and knelt to press the transmission key. "Uhura to Rand. Come in, Rand."

The communicator responded with a crackle she could hear even through her sealed faceplate. Uhura felt her heart pound up into her throat. That, she knew, was the olivium-augmented equivalent of a hailing frequency opening up.

"Commander Uhura? Is that you?"

"Yes!" Uhura stared down at the unrevealing readouts on her display panel. That thin voice was almost as hoarse and exhausted as her own, but she knew it didn't belong to either Scotty or Rand. "Who's this?"

"It's me. Neil Bartels." The colony's chief technical officer sounded surprised, as if he'd thought she would recognize him. Perhaps he didn't realize just how strained his voice had become. "When we didn't hear anything else after you left No Escape, we were afraid something really bad had happened. Where are you?"

Even in the dusty darkness, Uhura could see the warning scowl Tamasy gave her. She amended what she'd been going to say. "In the middle of nowhere. We had to hike out here to find a place where the communicator would work. Where are Commander Scott and Lieutenant Rand?"

"Out helping direct the evacuation effort," Bartels said. "Along with every other person in the building. You're lucky I came back in to make another public announcement over the landlines, or no one would have been here to hear you calling."

Uhura's sigh of relief was so deep that it made her filter hiss with the effort of cleaning so much air so quickly. "Then you got the flood warnings from No Escape?"

"And from the orbital platform and from the *Enterprise,*" Bartels said wryly. "All the civilians have been evacuated, and we're letting the civil servants go now. Is it really true that the crater is about to burst? None of my engineers can believe it, but I didn't want to take any chances."

"The reason your engineers can't believe it is that it wouldn't be happening if it weren't for an illegal olivium mine that's been cut through the crater rim."

"What?"

"The mining is being done by a group of settlers from Desperation who wear badges and call themselves Peacemakers," Uhura told him. She'd used the previous hours of walking to condense all of her information into a terse, efficient package for transmittal. "They've terrorized or chased out all the settlers around Bull's Eye to keep them from noticing the mining activity. They tried to kill us to keep us from finding out how badly the crater is already leaking. Greg Anthony nearly died, and I still don't know where Sulu and Bev Weir are."

"Oh, my God." She wouldn't have thought Bartels could sound worse than he had at the beginning of their conversation, but the exhaustion in his voice had turned to horror. "How close is the crater to collapsing because of this—this illegal mine?"

"It could go at any moment," Uhura said. "We're going to try and—"

A hand swept out before she could finish that sentence, ruthlessly slapping Uhura's hand away from the transmission key. She gasped, off-balance and flailing from the blow, but the same hand caught her by the scruff of her kevlar hood and pulled her back onto the rock ledge again.

"Sorry," Tamasy said. "But you don't know who else might have been listening to your conversation."

"Neil said he was alone."

"Maybe he was," the Carson biologist said, although she didn't sound too convinced of that. "But even so, there are other places where this communication system of yours works, aren't there? How do you know the olivium mine isn't one of them?"

Uhura opened her mouth, then closed it again. "You're right," she said. "Sorry. I should have known better than to discuss strategy over an open channel."

She could see a quick, humorless smile glint behind Tamasy's faceplate. "Yes, Commander, you should have. Just for that, you don't get to go to the olivium mine with us."

"Oh, yes, I do," Uhura said flatly. "You're going to need a communications officer there."

"Why?" Tamasy demanded. "If all the cities down to Big Muddy are already being evacuated—"

"That still doesn't save Llano Verde's environment, does it?" Uhura glanced upward to check her intuition. The dust storm hung thick overhead, turned a dull red by the infrared glow of its own internal friction, but high on the western horizon, a thin slice of true night darkness appeared over the crater rim. It was what she'd hoped to see: the clear column at the center of Bulls Eye's permanent cyclonic storm, free of olivium interference from the crater lake to outer space. "If we can haul this communicator up to the mine, the *Enterprise* can use its signal as a pinpoint focus for its phaser banks. They can collapse the mine conduits and seal the rim better than anything you could do from the inside."

Tamasy eyed her for a long moment, then gave her a quick approving slap on the shoulder, hard enough to rock but not unbalance her. "Not a bad plan," she said. "Assuming the *Enterprise* is actually anywhere in the vicinity of Belle Terre."

"Don't worry," Uhura said, rubbing at her kevlar-scraped shoulder. "If I know Captain Kirk, it will be."

Chapter Fourteen

"YOU'RE NOT going to believe this," Greg Anthony said. "But I'm starting to miss that dust-crawler we were in yesterday."

Uhura threw the hydrologist a concerned glance. He claimed that the Carsons had run him through their tissue regenerator enough times to make his teeth chatter, but there were still faint red radiation burns on his face and an odd stiffness to his torso where the blunt metal projectiles of the Peacemakers' weapons had torn through bone and skin and cartilage, leaving uncomfortable scars. They'd shot him point-blank when he'd gone back to ask them to move their crawler, he'd told Uhura when she'd asked him about it. She could still hear the ring of disbelief in his voice, see it in the way his hands moved across his chest as if to catch the sudden spurts of blood. One of the Peacemakers had asked if he was ready to leave. When Anthony told them that he and Weir were sure there was more floodwater coming out farther down the slope, the man had calmly swung his weapon toward him and said, "Yep, you're ready to leave."

That was when the firing started. Anthony said he couldn't remember it ending, probably because he was in shock by then, but he did remember clutching his scientific tricorder to his chest the entire time. Its duranium casing had saved him, deflecting the projectiles meant for heart and lungs into shoulder muscles and rib cage. Weir's flung dilithium torch had helped, too—first by attracting the Peacemakers' attention and turning their fusillade toward her and Uhura, and then a second time by floating past the Carson scientists who were running a gravity scan on the mining conduits below the rim. They'd managed to snatch Uhura out from under the Peacemakers' noses, but didn't find Anthony until much later, passed out from shock and blood loss. If the Carsons hadn't brought along their emergency medical stabilizer, the hydrologist would undoubtedly be dead.

"Are you feeling sick?" she asked now.

"Yes. Motion-sick." Anthony took several deep breaths in quick succession, making the airfilter on his kevlar dust suit hiss. Even behind the translucent mask, Uhura could see how his face had tightened into a grimace.

"Sorry," Tamasy said without looking over her shoulder. A thick haze of dust made it hard to see the terrain across which they were driving, and the Carson biologist occasionally had to slam to a halt to avoid the sudden steaming gashes of hot springs. "I'm trying to get us to the mine as fast as I can."

"I know. That's the problem."

The Carsons referred to their dust-proofed exploration vehicle as a roller, but it actually bounced across the rugged landscape on six oversize and oversprung wheels. Its agility and speed explained how the scientists could so easily evade their enemies as they moved around the crater rim, but the price they paid was a never-ending series of lurches and jolts that rattled teeth and wrenched stomachs. Uhura opened her mouth to ask if their emergency medical supplies included anti-nausea shots, but before she could, Karen Roth leaned around the steel cannister of the forcefield generator and did something to the controls of Anthony's dust suit. Uhura could hear his relieved sigh even over the drone of the roller's gyromagnetic motors.

"I increased the oxygen augment," the young technician said. "The suit adjusts it automatically for elevation, but you can cheat a little if you have to. Do you need more, Commander?"

"Not right now," Uhura said. She was wedged in securely enough between Anthony and her bulky experimental communicator to weather most of the exaggerated bumps. And she'd spent enough time flying with Sulu in the Bean to have gotten used to this kind of motion. "How much farther have we got to go?"

"Another ten kilometers," Tamasy said. "I'm staying low and outside the crater until we come to the mine shafts. The Peacemakers mostly patrol high and inside the rim."

That explained why the haze of dust outside their roller hadn't cleared since they'd left the Carson headquarters earlier that morning. Uhura craned her head to peer out the roller's side window, at what looked like a bizarre portico of thick white columns looming through the dust. It took her a moment to realize that each column was the steam geyser of an active hot spring, and then another moment to see that each spring was linked to the next in a continuous cascade of boiling water. Before she could say anything, Tamasy had gunned the roller's gyromagnetic motor in an attempt to vault the thermal runoff. The vehicle leaped obediently from the rocks at the water's edge, but the two back wheels splashed down on the far side with a jolt that made even Uhura's hardened stomach lurch. Muddy hot water splattered across the back of the roller and then slowly sizzled off again, leaving slightly scorched marks on the windows where it had been.

"I don't even want to *think* about how much olivium was in there," said Greg Anthony.

Uhura frowned. "There seem to be an awful lot of hot springs down here. Is it because we're so low on the slope?"

"No," Tamasy said grimly. "This is the way we always come around to this side of the crater. Most of those springs weren't here two days ago."

A somber silence fell inside the vehicle. The six environmentalists who'd chosen to confront the olivium miners cradled their weapons in steady hands, their faces impassive behind the infrared faceplates they'd worn to see inside the mine. They were mostly young and mostly female—the New Rachel Carson Society seemed to appeal more to women than to men—but Uhura wouldn't have wanted to face them in a battle. Or Greg Anthony, whose pleasant face had turned hard and cold when he'd heard what happened to Bev Weir. With scrupulous honesty, Linville had informed the government hydrologist about the slim probabilities she'd calculated for overcoming the Peacemakers and collapsing the mine from inside, and the even smaller possibility that they could contact the *Enterprise* and have the crater rim sealed from outer space. All Anthony had said in response was "Can I have one of those weapons?"

Now, minutes away from their goal, Uhura could only hope that Sulu had managed to call Captain Kirk from the Bean and let him know how bad the situation in Llano Verde had become. If he had, she knew she could depend on the *Enterprise*'s commander coming to their rescue. But if he hadn't, she was afraid that between the Carsons, the Peacemakers, and the doomed crater lake, no one was going to get out of Bull's Eye alive.

"Are you sure you left it underwater?"

Chekov might have found Sulu's question insulting under any other circumstances—after all, one didn't just imagine a hundred nightmarish meters in leaking environmental suits. But given Orbital Shuttle Six's perch on one of the more level stretches of Bull's Eye's inner rim, not to mention the unmistakably dry supply cargo now disgorged onto the sand all around it, Chekov had to admit that a moment of clarification might be in order.

"I'm not only certain about where we left it," he shouted over the booming wind, "I'm also certain it couldn't fly." Had the weather really been this ruthless when they first made the hike out of Bull's Eye? How in God's name had they ever managed to survive? "I can't believe they were able to get it off the bottom."

"Maybe they didn't." Thee, flat to the ground on the lip of the crater, just like him and Sulu, reached across one of her crouching dogs to point down toward the water's edge. A dark, distinct fringe of wetness discolored the ground from several meters below the shuttle to the lap of the lake itself. "Mud that deep didn't just wash up. I think the water level's dropping."

Sulu rose up on his elbows to squint toward the other side of the thirty-kilometer-wide crater. Chekov doubted he could see a dozen feet past his own nose. "The beginning of our flood?" he wondered aloud.

Chekov couldn't let himself believe that they'd arrived too late to accomplish what they had to. Not after traveling without sleep all the way from Desperation, and sucking in enough olivium and dust to mummify their own lungs along the way. Although the logical part of him knew it had been hours ago that they traded camels with Joe Agee in Desperation's stables and sent him on to meet up with his partner, it felt like it had only just happened. Even the diffuse brightness of encroaching dawn couldn't convince his internal time sense that enough time had passed to allow all those innocent people to die. "The shuttle's above the mud line," he pointed out with stubborn certainty. "It's been moved."

Sulu looked over at him keenly. "And that bothers you."

Everything about this colony and what was going on here bothered him. The complete absence of people guarding the raised shuttle bothered him. The callous discarding of the precious supply cargo, and the humanitarian help it represented, bothered him. Chekov contented himself, however, with saying, "It bothers me that I don't know why they moved it." He found the rifle under his wrap, pulled it loose as he crawled a short distance away from Sulu and Thee. A symbolic separation that would also tacitly prepare them for his decision. "Let me scout around the rim. When I've got a better view of the terrain and can cover you, I'll wave you down." Because he wasn't sending anyone down this slope until he was positive there was no one waiting to repeat what had already been done to Plottel.

"You've just got to get in one last hurrah as chief of security, don't you?" Sulu squeezed his shoulder briefly, tightly, then let him move away. "Don't dawdle."

Chekov hadn't intended to.

Mist torn off the surface of the lake sheeted rocks and slope alike, turning the talc-fine olivium dust into a sticky, slimy coating on every surface. Chekov clutched at spars of upthrust stone as he picked a trail away from the others, the rifle tucked under one elbow and angled down toward the uneven ground. Sunrise hadn't worked the same magic at these elevations that it had several kilometers farther down—there was no lifting of the dusty shroud, no hopeful stillness in the lashing wind. If anything, the arrival of sunlight only made matters worse. It was hard not to fixate on all the things that could go wrong when even the rocks behind which you hid looked so much like jagged teeth in the dawn's light, the lake far below as hungry and churning as a monster's maw.

He slipped to his bottom, slid between a narrow cut in the stones, and came out a little lower on the slope. Chill mist lashed against his cheek, and wind whistled through the tight space he'd just traversed like an impatient ghost. Swallowing hard to clear the dryness from his mouth, Chekov pressed himself as flat as possible into the next break in the rocks, and stared downslope at each angle, each depression. Somewhere in the surreal shadows and misleading light, images teetered on the thin line between what instinct feared and logic looked for. He'd seen art in a spaceport's gallery once that made a game of hiding faces and creatures in what otherwise appeared to be innocuous landscapes. Uhura had been charmed by the paintings, proclaiming them clever and creative. Chekov had found them unbearably disturbing. They'd been a security officer's nightmare made manifest, where the threat looked like anything, hid anywhere.

He felt as if he were trapped in one of those paintings now.

Logic said all the rocks and sand and blowing dust were of the same material, and so essentially the same color. But distance and moisture and the uneven handprint of shade and sun created a chaos of shapes, textures, and movements. When his glance first skated over a pool of black and dusty gray, his eye identified the composition as a collage of rock and shadow a dozen meters clockwise and farther down the slope.

Instinct snapped his attention into sharper focus. Maybe it was a subtle movement, or a shift in the pall of dust that let a finger of sunlight suddenly reach down and clarify things with its touch. But he blinked down the grade at the confusion of shadows not once but twice before the wide-brimmed black hat and rain-soaked dust muffler separated from the background and solidified into the form of a man.

Chekov's heart slammed fiercely against the rock beneath him. The Peacemaker faced across the slope, toward a spot high on the rim above the water and the waiting shuttle. Was this the same way the sniper had been positioned when Dave Plottel stumbled wearily out of the lake? A ready view, and a rifle balanced casually in a notch between two rocks where even the most vicious gust of wind couldn't knock it to one side.

Twisting to follow the Peacemaker's gaze, Chekov searched the direction from which he'd come with redoubled intensity. Maybe the man had seen him before he slipped out of sight and now didn't realize that Chekov had circled around behind and above him. Or maybe the camels they'd abandoned just shy of the crater's rim had developed a sense of curiosity, and made their own way over the lip to strike a noticeable target against the lightening sky. Instead, Chekov's eyes were drawn inexorably to the Starfleet officer crouched and waiting to make his way down to the shuttle. Little more than Sulu's head was visible above the knot of boulders sheltering him, but it was enough.

"Sulu! Get down!"

Wind stole the words almost before they left his throat. He could barely hear the shout himself, knew it had no hope of traveling the torturous distance to his friend. Chekov lunged to his feet, saw Sulu's expression change, and dropped his own rifle to wave the helmsman *down!* with both arms. *"Get down!"* he screamed again. Not because he thought Sulu might hear him this time, but because he had to do something, anything to appease the accusing ghost of Dave Plottel.

Sulu turned away to begin his climb down to the shuttle.

"No!"

Chekov threw himself down the slope, sliding and scrambling to intercept the lone Peacemaker, or at least grab his attention long enough to let Sulu regain cover. The planet separated them the way it did everyone—with wind, and rock, and dust, and distances too great to cover on foot before disaster. He called out again when he saw the Peacemaker notice Sulu's movement, rise into a crouch, and draw his gun up off the rock.

Sulu still didn't seem to hear. Chekov grabbed a rock, meaning to throw it, but couldn't jerk it loose from the hillside. Instead, he stumbled to his knees in the slippery mud and slammed up against a shelf of stone still too far away from anyone to do any good.

I don't want to do this I don't want to do this—!

He struggled with his conscience until the Peacemaker settled his rifle against his shoulder and swung it to track Sulu's progress. Then he shut down the horrified voice in his head, drew back his own rifle's hammer with his thumb, and took aim at the wide-brimmed hat so far below him.

A single shot was all it took.

Uhura had thought the wind gusts were bad up on the crater rim, where they'd battered the Carsons' roller to a grinding halt and sent it into a sidelong skid across the barren rock slopes. But once they crossed over the top and began descending the other side, the sound of the wind increased to a hurricane roar. The roller didn't just stop and skid now, it actually got most of its wheels lifted completely off the ground. Only its heavy suspension, and Tamasy's firm hands on the wheel, saved it from overturning when it was bounced back down again.

Anthony leaned closer to Uhura, but even so she only caught part of his comment. "—why the Peacemakers use crawlers!"

She nodded, gritting her teeth against the roller's next lift and drop. The sky above them was slowly turning blue as they cut through the inner fringes of the dust-walled cyclone around Bull's Eye. The glare of sunlight pouring down through that rupture wrapped everything in a thermal halo of infrared, throwing strange dancing auras off the sunward side of rocks. Farther down the slope, Uhura could see the platinum gleam of the crater lake, heaving and churning with the swells kicked up by the maelstrom around it. It looked as if it were boiling, too.

"Uhura to *Enterprise.*" She had to shout just to get the communicator to register the sound of her voice over the wind's howl. Instead of listening for a reply, which she probably wouldn't have heard between the wind and the muffling kevlar of her dust suit, Uhura kept her gaze pinned on the signal readout. Back in Big Muddy, she and Rand had tuned the transmitter output to the range of normal electromagnetic frequencies that could be amplified by the olivium crystals in Llano Verde's dust. That meant her hail had traveled to the *Enterprise* at normal light speed, not with the instantaneous touch of subspace. Still, unless the starship was too far away to help, it should only take several seconds for a reply to come back again.

So far, nothing had spiked on the signal response meter.

"Almost there!" That was Linville's voice, rising above the storm's fury in a belly-wrenching shout. "Prepare for mine entry!"

The wind's roar muffled the sound of weapons being loaded and extra projectiles being transferred from belts to pockets, but it couldn't drown out the thin shriek of the forcefield generator warming up, at least until it disappeared up into the ultrasonic. Uhura pulled the carrying strap of her communicator over her shoulder, then put her mouth down closer to the transmitter. "Uhura to *Enterprise!*" she called again, but still got no reply.

The roller slewed to a stop, in a protective jumble of

rock debris thrown up from the crater floor. Uhura could see the mouth of the mine just beyond it—not the civilized barred and gated opening she'd expected, just a raw gaping wound in the crater's flank with a jumble of debris spilling out of its mouth. There was no sign of Peacemakers nearby, but Uhura didn't let that lull her into a false sense of security. She knew they could be hiding just around the bend of the mine.

"Is this the only entrance?" she demanded over the fading drone of the roller's gyromagnetic motors.

Tamasy was already opening the door of the roller, and either didn't hear or didn't bother to answer her. But Linville looked around and nodded. "It splits three ways inside to follow the ore," she said. "But we've got to stay together, within five meters of the forcefield generator for safety."

Uhura opened her mouth to say that she had to stay near the entrance to call the *Enterprise,* but the woman was already out in the blasting wind of the crater. Anthony and Roth were next to go, carrying the heavy silver cannister of the forcefield generator between them. Uhura took a deep breath, then dragged the communicator across the seat and out after them. The wind met her with a slap that nearly sent her back inside the roller, followed by just as hard a gust in the opposite direction. Weighted down by her gear, Uhura fought in vain to catch her balance. She ended up on her knees, crouched under the gale-force winds while sunlight paradoxically streamed its bright infrared glitter all around her. She had to find the communicator's transmission key by touch rather than by sight.

"Uhura to *Enterprise!*" she shouted. "Come in, *Enterprise!*"

"Come on!" She could barely hear Linville's shout,

but there was no mistaking the woman's intention—she caught Uhura under the shoulders and swept her into motion, communicator and all. She never even had a chance to see if her hail got a reply before they were all running up the slope, in zigzag paths that were more a result of wind direction than any evasive maneuvers on their part. By the time Uhura made it up to the mine mouth, she was gasping so hard from the fierce exertion of the run that she wasn't sure she could have heard shots even if they'd been fired at them.

After the gale blowing outside, the quiet inside the mine entrance seemed almost cathedral. Uhura saw Roth and Anthony set down the forcefield generator and fell to her knees within its shelter, fumbling the communicator box around in front of her to see the signal output. There was still no flicker of response from the *Enterprise*. Uhura looked up to meet Tamasy's inquiring glance and shook her head.

"Nothing," she said. "Were we getting shot at out there?"

"No. There was no sign of anyone outside." The Carson biologist scowled into the darkness behind them, as if its silence bothered her. "Or in here. There's usually automated crawlers coming in and out of here loaded with ore—you can hear them a kilometer away. I don't hear them."

"Perhaps they've abandoned the mine," Linville said. "It would be logical, if they knew how close the crater is to collapsing—"

"If they knew that, then why the *hell* did they keep mining for so long?" Tamasy demanded in sudden, fierce anger. She thumped a gloved hand into the wall of the mine, hard enough to make Uhura wince. "We kept waiting for them to stop before the mine weakened the crater! We were all so sure that's what they were going to do, that we wouldn't even have to interfere—and now when they *have* stopped, it's a day too late and two hundred meters too close to the edge! *Why?"*

"Because they wanted the crater to collapse," Uhura said.

Silence fell inside the mine again, and the Carsons turned to stare at her as if she'd suddenly sprouted horns and hooves. "*Wanted* it to?" Linville said at last. "Why?"

"To wipe out any evidence of illegal mining. And to cause so much destruction that no one, not even the *Enterprise,* would have time to track them and the missing olivium." She saw the confusion in Greg Anthony's eyes change to understanding, but the Carsons still looked puzzled. "You've been assuming the miners planned to stay here on the colony with their profits, and wouldn't want to destroy it. But the Peacemakers could have cut a deal with the Kauld or some other alien pirates—"

"—in order to be evacuated from this living hell."

The voice that finished that sentence was so familiar that Uhura nearly fell over her communicator when she jerked toward it. A light had flared to life farther down the mine shaft, silhouetting a handful of men in distinctive Peacemaker dust mufflers. She opened her mouth to say "Neil?" but before she could even make a sound, the Carsons had lifted their rifles, aimed, and fired.

Chekov's hands shook as he pulled another handful of projectiles out of his pocket and fitted them, one by one, into the body of his rifle. He'd never had the weapon fully loaded before. He hadn't known it would hold so much ammunition.

"Now all we have to do is hope there are no Peacemakers hiding in the hills, waiting to jump out and shoot us." Thee pulled shut the hatch to the shuttle's outside airlock, shoving it once with her shoulder as though verifying that the seals would still hold. She stripped out of her dust muffler and threw it toward the bench where Plottel and Baldwin had once shared a container of orbital platform water, about a million years ago. When Chekov didn't look up at her passage, she paused and bent to peek over his shoulder. "Where'd you'd get all the ammunition?"

No condemnation in her question, yet he felt a shameful flush in his cheeks that wasn't caused by the hours he'd spent in olivium-tainted dust. "I found it outside." *On the body of a man I killed because this planet wouldn't let me leave without taking at least one human life.* That was the curse of Belle Terre, he thought. It either killed you with its radiation and dust and flooding, or you fed it someone else's blood to make it grant you a reprieve.

He felt Thee's uncertain pause, her half-drawn breath as she tried to decide whether to push for something more than a too-easy answer to her question. Then Sulu joined them from the cargo shuttle's cockpit, and the opportunity was past.

"What do you want first?" the pilot asked. Chekov was never certain if Sulu truly never noticed the tension when he walked into such tableaus, or if he was just too thoroughly a gentleman to let on. "The good news or the bad news?"

Thee straightened. "There's good news?"

"There's always good news." Ever the optimist, Sulu came to stand where Chekov could see him without getting up from the deck. "Whoever pulled this old girl out of the lake not only cleared the engine intakes, they've installed filters that ought to at least let us fly long enough to get above the dust."

They could always worry about making a controlled crash-landing at Eau Claire, once they dropped below the dust mantle again. Chekov snapped the rifle closed and climbed to his feet. "What's the bad news?"

"We're still not going anywhere."

Sulu led the way back into the cockpit, waving Chekov into the copilot's chair as he retook the helm. "I've run through two start-up sequences so far. Diagnostics say that everything's a go, but I'm not getting ignition. It's like my start-up command just isn't being heard."

They should have known it wouldn't be this easy. "In addition to the clogged intakes, we also lost sensors and inertial control."

Sulu shook his head. "Olivium radiation messes up the readings but doesn't necessarily kill the equipment. It's the dust in the mechanisms that does that." Lean hands flew through another start-up sequence on the helm panel. Chekov watched the progression of readings, looking for some sense in the sequence as the shuttle's systems locked up, aborted, and fell quiet.

He was still frowning over the incomplete start-up when Sulu reached in front of him to tap at one of the console's controls. "Is this something the colonists installed up on the orbital platform?"

A keypad and a blank readout screen, wedged between the controls for monitoring cargo bay atmosphere. Chekov hesitated a moment, trying to recall the board's configuration during the few minutes he spent in the cockpit on the way down. "No." Saying it made him even more certain. "No, it was a standard shuttle control board. This was added after we abandoned it."

Laying his rifle carefully across the console at the base of the front window, Chekov slid out of the copilot's seat to pry off the main maintenance panel. The spiderweb of new wiring seemed to engulf the entire board.

"They must have installed some kind of governor." He slipped his finger behind a programmable monitor chip, tried to pop it loose without success.

"Do you need something to cut the connection?" Thee asked from the cockpit's doorway.

He shook his head, then realized that neither she nor Sulu could see him clearly while he was half-underneath the copilot's seat. "Not here. This is just some sort of monitor . . . or interface . . ." He squirmed backward out of the crawlspace to sit back on his heels and look at Sulu. "I can't disconnect this until I find out where it's actually tied in."

"Then get going." Sulu nudged the maintenance panel closed with his foot. "You track it down, and I'll see if I can't initiate a manual start-up sequence that bypasses the damned thing."

Thee followed Chekov back into the main compartment, hanging back only long enough to order her dogs out of the way when Chekov pulled loose another panel halfway up the starboard bulkhead.

"Anything I can do to help?" she asked.

Chekov identified the new connections easily enough, following the main cable between two fingers until he couldn't stretch his arm any further behind the plating. "Just take things as I hand them to you." He angled a look down the bulkhead, toward where he guessed his hand had ended up. "And bring me a cutting torch from that equipment locker."

He could sense the shuttle trembling as he peeled back section after section of bulkhead to trace the new wires. He wanted to believe it was the heavy hand of the wind that rocked the heavy ship, or some success on Sulu's part in waking up the quiescent engines. In reality, he knew it was erosion in the crater walls themselves, shaking Bull's Eye like an earthquake. He hoped the crater's protests meant they still had time before the flood began, but he had an ominous feeling that just the opposite was true.

Thee interrupted his brooding as she accepted yet another still-warm piece of bulkhead and threw it out of the way behind them. "Do you think they know about the flood?"

Another tangle of wires, heading off in a dozen distracting directions. "Who?"

"Whoever pulled the shuttle out of the lake."

"I don't know. Maybe." But even as he separated out the branch of wires he wanted, Chekov remembered the broad-rimmed hat of a Peacemaker on the man he'd killed outside the shuttle, and the crawler full of Peacemakers who had taken the hydrologists up to check on water levels only to turn around and kill them. "Probably. Why else would they want to keep anyone from investigating the water levels up here?"

Thee spun open the lock on the hatch leading to the rear cargo hold while Chekov made a burn on the wall to mark the direction of their wiring. "I really hate people sometimes." She sounded bitter for the first time since he'd met her. "I hate knowing that we can go from civilized Federation citizens to selfish barbarians within six months of setting foot on a new planet."

Chekov stopped her from slinging the door open and turning away from him. "Aren't you the one who told me that willingness to take on risk isn't the same as preparedness?" He lifted her chin and made her look at him. "No one came to Belle Terre intending to become a barbarian."

"So that makes it all right to shoot each other with primitive weapons and sentence everyone downriver to die?"

Guilt squeezed his heart in an unforgiving fist. "No," he admitted, very quietly. "That doesn't make it all right." *But I understand a little better than I used to how easily barbarism can sneak up on you when you feel like you've lost all other options.* He reached around her to drag open the cargo bay door. "But maybe it explains how people like the Peacemakers could be so desperate to get away from Belle Terre that they'd do something stupid like hijack a cargo shuttle."

A throb of familiar heat swelled out at them as the door rolled into its pocket, and Chekov took an involuntary step backward as though transperiodic radiation could be ducked or otherwise avoided. Thee bumped him from behind, rising up on tiptoe to steal a look into the crowded cargo bay.

Her dyspeptic snort sounded right next to his ear. "Of course, this could also explain why someone would be desperate to get away from Belle Terre."

The hold was stuffed nearly to bursting with the eerie glow of pure olivium.

Chapter Fifteen

THE SECOND-WORST nightmare of a communications officer's life was not to be able to hear. The worst nightmare was not to be able to hear when you knew someone was trying to contact you.

The thunder of projectile weapons had exploded inside the confined space of the mine like a photon torpedo blast. Uhura felt the impact without actually ever registering it as a sound. She fell to her knees and clapped her hands over her ears, but the damage had already been done. She had been slammed into a deafness so complete that it pounded deep inside her skull, preventing her from hearing either the return fire from the Peacemakers or any commands from her Carson allies. It also kept her from hearing any sound that might have accompanied the distinct spike that had just appeared on the signal detection monitor of her communicator. The inquiry soared into a full-blown peak of response, paused as if waiting for a reply, and then sank again until it disappeared back into flat-line noise.

Uhura watched the panel for another minute, but no further hailing signal came. She reached for the transmission button, intending to respond even if she couldn't hear the words she made, but a body fell across her before she could complete the gesture and slammed her to the ground. Gasping for breath, Uhura struggled free of the frighteningly dead weight, keeping her own profile as low to the ground as possible. Had their forcefield generator stopped working? Or had deafness prevented her from hearing a command to move, so that she was no longer inside its protection?

A quick glance through the faceplate told her the body beside her belonged to Linville. Despite its limpness, Uhura felt no breaks in the kevlar bodysuit, saw no patches of wetness with the bright infrared glow of fresh blood. She glanced up from the woman in bewilderment and saw another Carson fall, this time only a meter away from the forcefield generator. Most of the rest were still firing, but their deafening fusillade of shots made no impact on the silhouette of the Peacemakers. Uhura saw the tallest kevlar-suited figure drop her projectile weapon and swing around, hands slashing the universal "down" signal at the rest of them. The glitter of the phaser beam that caught her was unmistakable inside the dimness of the mine. She crumpled before she had a chance to follow her own command, and although a few Carsons managed to hit the ground before the phaser beams caught them, it didn't save them from being targeted. Uhura gritted her teeth, watching the pale fire of the light weapons flick from body to body, and grimly waited her turn to be shot.

But the glittering stopped while she was still aware and

breathing. Thinking that perhaps the Peacemakers had mistaken her stillness for a phaser-induced collapse, Uhura kept her head low and forced herself to close her eyes. The silent pounding inside her skull had beaten itself into a whispering froth, through which she was beginning to discern the thin edges of sounds. The faint raindrop sound she heard must be the echo of booted footsteps coming down the mine, and that leaf-like rustling was probably the sound of voices. Uhura couldn't distinguish any words, but she could hear how calm and unhurried the conversation was. How could people who'd just been shot at be so composed, she wondered? An instant later she knew the answer—for the same reason that she'd been composed herself during most of that battle. Until she'd seen the unexpected glitter of phaser beams, she'd been certain the Carsons' forcefield would protect her from any harm. The Peacemakers must have finally obtained a forcefield of their own.

One set of footsteps resolved out of the muffled raindrop patter, growing louder and more distinct as they approached her. They came to a stop less than a meter away, and Uhura felt her eyelashes flutter with the effort not to look up. She heard the ghost bark of a laugh; then a hand reached out and shook her roughly. She couldn't tell what was said, but the unrelenting tone of that voice told her there was no point in any more playacting.

She opened her eyes and saw what she'd expected but still couldn't quite believe. Neil Bartels, the chief technical officer of Llano Verde, squatted on his heels beside her, an oversize dust muffler puddling around him on the mine floor. His mild face, with its pale city skin and puffy technician's eyes, looked utterly incongruous under the flat-brimmed Outlander's hat he wore. Beyond him, Uhura could see the tall figures of several

Peacemakers aiming their phasers at her. Not at him, at her. The significance of that support was quite clear, even before a gloved hand fell lightly on Bartels's shoulder. Uhura looked up to see Carmela Serafini's strong, radiation-burned face appear behind the government technician.

"Kick that Starfleet idiot awake," the mayor of Desperation said, in a voice sharp and cold enough for Uhura to make out every word. "We've got to get out of here before the crater collapses."

"No, we don't." The solid centers of sounds were reaching Uhura now, and she could hear the disturbing ring of self-congratulation in Bartels's voice. "Trust me, Carm. I engineered this mine so that the far end was where the crater would break, not up here where the ore was stored. We have plenty of time to get to the orbital shuttle."

That earned him a snort from Serafini, along with a smack hard enough to rock him back on his heels. "And what if those *other* Starfleet idiots figure out how to use your fancy olivium-proof antimatter drive and take off while we're diddling here? Come on, Bart! If we don't get your sweet little girlfriend down there in time to stop them, you're going to find yourself floating facedown in the Big Muddy along with her."

Uhura scrambled to her feet so abruptly that Neil Bartels scuttled back out of her way and even Serafini took a startled step back. "You're not going to use me as a hostage to get my friends killed!" she said, and dove directly between the two of them. She was trusting that the Peacemakers wouldn't dare fire their weapons at their own leaders. The five steps she got away with told her she was right, but the diving tackle by Serafini that brought her down was more brutal than

Uhura had gambled on. She landed on the mine floor half-twisted beneath the other woman's hard-muscled weight, and heard the sickening inward punch as a rib cracked beneath the impact.

Uhura gasped for breath, then cried out with the pain of taking it. The pain blossomed into a dizzying roar as Serafini hauled her ruthlessly to her feet, dimming her vision and fogging her hearing once again. By the time her senses had returned, Uhura found herself being half-dragged and half-carried by two silent Peacemakers, back out toward Bull's Eye crater. A painful twist gained her one last glance back into the olivium mine. The scattered bodies of the Carsons lay where they'd fallen, near the dark gleam of Uhura's experimental communicator. She could hear its patient hailing chirp fade behind her as they stepped out into the howl of the crater winds.

It wasn't the sound of that automated hail that had sparked Uhura's attention-grabbing break for freedom, nor was it her very real reluctance to be used as a hostage to stymie whatever Sulu—and maybe Chekov?—were trying to do. It was the unmistakably conscious lift of breath that she'd felt in Linville's chest, and the consequent flash of understanding that whatever Bartels had done to make the phasers work inside that olivium mine, the results hadn't been entirely fatal. All she had to do was distract the Peacemakers from noticing that the Carsons were alive, and then Linville would be free to contact the *Enterprise.*

The only question after that was whether Captain Kirk could arrive in time to save them as well as the colonists of Llano Verde.

"Stop gasping," Carmela Serafini said irritably. "I know how to fly this thing."

That was debatable, but Uhura knew better than to argue with her captor. Even if she'd wanted to, she wasn't sure she had the fortitude. The last thing she'd expected after getting hauled through the jumble of impact debris outside the olivium mine was to see the familiar smooth contours of Sulu's vertical flight vessel concealed among the boulders and guarded by yet another of the ubiquitous Peacemakers. Uhura had been so sure that the pilot had escaped the conspiracy's reach and gotten in touch with Captain Kirk that the sight of the Bean hit her harder than the throbbing ache of her cracked rib.

A muzzy exhaustion was seeping into her now, leaching away her ability to think of what else she could do. It didn't help to know that her fatigue was probably a blend of shock and radiation exposure, or that there was a tissue regenerator in the cargo hold of this very vessel that could erase it all in a few moments. With her hands bound behind her, and a silent armed Peacemaker wedged beside her in the cockpit's passenger seat, all Uhura could manage to do was hold her breath in anticipation of the painful bounces and spills that Serafini seemed to think were the Bean's normal cruising style.

"Too bad you didn't think to grab that pilot before he snuck out of town," Bartels said from the other side of the Bean's front seat. The baleful look Serafini shot at him made Uhura shiver, but the chief technical officer didn't seem to notice. "If he steals my shuttle, Carm, I'm never going to forgive you," he added querulously.

"Your shuttle?" Serafini sent the Bean over a ridge on the crater wall with less than a meter of clearance. "All you had to do was fake an emergency request for supplies up to the orbital platform. That's hardly what I call a major effort."

"If it weren't for me," Bartels snapped, "you and your Peacemakers would never have found your way off Belle Terre."

Serafini was wrestling the Bean through a wild corkscrew turn against the wind, but the cold note in her voice had deepened noticeably. "Don't be so sure of that, little man."

Bartels made a scornful noise. *"Please.* The only thing I give you to do is keep the hydrologists away from the hot springs and take care of the supply shuttle's crew. Look how well *that's* worked out." He slanted his ally a belligerent look. "You think it was easy to sabotage all of Starfleet's efforts to get a working communications system up and running? Or simple to feed Sedlak enough false data to make him disregard all those flood warnings? If I hadn't falsified his signature on those arrest warrants, the Starfleet personnel still left in Big Muddy would be out running through the streets telling people to evacuate!"

Even through Uhura's tiredness, that callous comment sparked a flicker of indignation. "You locked up Rand and Scott? Did you *lie* to me about evacuating the city?"

Bartels gave her a half-careless, half-uneasy look. "Well, I had to. You don't know that damned governor the way I do. He's easy enough to fool, if you feed him enough fake data to make the colony look like it's fulfilling all his favorite sociobiological theories about communities evolving and adapting to new environments. But once I'm gone and Sedlak realizes he's been tricked, nothing will stop him from making sure we get caught and punished by Starfleet. Flooding the city's the only thing we could do."

Uhura's exhaustion retreated a little more beneath the hot flare of her anger. "You're going to kill thousands of people and destroy most of this colony just to distract Sedlak from your trail?"

"Oh, no," said Carmela Serafini. "We're hoping to actually kill the bastard."

"You Starfleet types never understood," Bartels said, and Uhura could hear the passionate self-justification in his voice. "I came to this colony on a contract that specified everything—work hours, benefits, bonuses, even an option to retire here if I wanted. But it was never meant to apply to a place like Llano Verde! The overtime and the extra technical problems, the malcontent settlers and the damned unbearable weather—"

"—and the worthless olivium deposits that would make you a fortune if you just took them somewhere else in the sector," Serafini finished cynically. "That possibility wasn't in the contract either, was it, Bart?"

The technician surprised Uhura with the vehemence of his head-shake. "That's why you're here, Carm, and how you talked all your boys into working for you. But I just want what's rightfully mine. I did all the extra work they wanted, I even figured out ways to get around their olivium problems—tuning up phasers to olivium's crystal resonance frequencies, retrofitting antimatter drives with olivium feedback cycles. But when I asked for one-tenth—just *one-tenth*—of what those inventions would have been worth anywhere else in the sector, do you know what Sedlak said? 'You're trapped here just like the rest of us. If you want this colony to succeed, self-preservation will eventually force you to give your inventions freely to Llano Verde.' "

"So you decided to show him how wrong he was, by cutting a deal with the Kauld," Uhura guessed. "And you sabotaged everything that might have made life easier on Llano Verde after that." Bartels said nothing, but the guilty hunch of his stooped shoulders told her she had guessed correctly. She exhaled as much of a sigh as she could manage past the fierce ache of her ribs. "Neil, didn't it ever occur to you just to request a transfer to another part of Belle Terre?"

Before he could reply, Serafini dropped the Bean into a more precipitous downward bounce than any Sulu had ever tried. Uhura heard Bartels and the Peacemaker cursing, and even her own hardened stomach lurched. The ground loomed up below them much faster than seemed safe. "Reverse power to all thrusters!" she told Serafini urgently. *"Now!"*

The mayor's hands shot out to adjust the antigrav controls, but even with that last-minute upsurge, the Bean's momentum brought it to earth with a crash and skid that sent rocks flying ahead of it down the crater slope. Uhura cried out as her ribs were jarred, her eyes watering so badly with the pain that she could barely see. By the time she caught her breath and blinked her vision clear again, the Bean had stopped its downward slide only a few tens of meters above the heaving gray lid of the crater lake.

"How about that," said Carmela Serafini in calm amusement. More than ever, the mayor of Desperation sounded to Uhura like a total sociopath. "A perfect landing."

Bartels spat out a mouthful of what could have been either blood or vomit, then gave her a seething look. "What was so damned perfect about it?" he demanded.

"Where we ended up." Serafini pointed straight out the Bean's cockpit window. Even from the backseat, Uhura could see the outline of a grounded orbital shuttle dwarfing their smaller craft. A face appeared in the cockpit window facing theirs, a face with familiar dark Asian eyes and an incredulous expression. "Now that they know we're here, let's see if they want to do a little horse-trading."

"I can't believe this," Sulu said, staring out the shuttle's cockpit window. Canted, rock-scuffed, and covered in dust, the Bean could almost have been mistaken for another chunk of impact debris, if it hadn't been for the thin flags of steam rising from its overheated antigravs. "Someone actually got it to fly."

"I wouldn't call that flying," Gwen Thee said, emerging from the gangway. Sulu could hear her dogs barking in identical agitation back in the cargo hold, although he wasn't sure if they were protesting her absence or just responding to the thunderous arrival of the Bean. "It looked more like a controlled crash to me."

"Better than we managed, the first time we came down here," Chekov said gruffly. He shouldered past Thee, and dropped into the copilot's seat, his pockets jangling with spare ammunition. Unlike Sulu, he didn't waste any time staring across at the Bean to see who in God's name could be flying it. Instead, the former security officer ran his hands across the control panel to make sure their shields were still fully powered up, then pulled his weapon onto his lap and started loading more projectiles into it. Sulu watched his friend for a long moment, not liking the harsh lines that had carved themselves into his haggard face. When Chekov snapped the weapon shut and wordlessly started sealing the flaps of his jacket, Sulu frowned and reached for the shuttle's communicator.

"It won't work," Chekov said flatly. "Not with all the olivium we have on board, not to mention what's still left out in the crater."

The screech of radiation-generated static that spilled out from the open hailing channel would have told Sulu that even if Chekov hadn't. Instead of turning the communicator off again, however, he began fiddling with the signal modulation, dialing the volume up to a banshee shriek that made Chekov grimace and Thee yelp in protest. Sulu paid no attention to either of them, merely adjusting the output frequency filters until the noise subsided to a more tolerable prickly throb.

"What was the point of that?" Chekov demanded, when his exasperated voice could be heard again.

"Negotiation," Sulu said simply. "We have their olivium. They have a shuttle with a communicator that can reach up to the orbital platform."

The Russian snorted. "And you think they're just going to let us run over there and call for help? If Captain Kirk is anywhere nearby, they've got to know they're going to be captured."

"Not if we guarantee them safe passage out of the system." Sulu glanced over at the security officer and saw the fierce disagreement he'd expected in his scowl. "What's more important, Pavel? Shooting a few Peacemakers to punish them for what they've done, or saving thousands of lives?"

The blunt words had more effect than he'd expected.

A darker color stained Chekov's face beneath the painful red of his radiation burns, and he snapped his teeth shut on whatever objection he'd been going to make. "Call them" was all he said.

"Too late," Thee said, leaning between them to get a better view of the Bean. "It looks like negotiations have already started."

Sulu turned to follow the direction of her gaze. The cargo hold door of the Bean had swung down while they were arguing, and two figures were picking their way down that steeply tilted ramp. One was tall and broad-shouldered under a Peacemaker dust muffler and wide-brimmed hat, armed with a projectile weapon that was unmistakably pointed at the other. The hostage wore a strange kevlar dust suit and walked with an unfamiliar painful stiffness, but the faceplate of her suit had been opened so they could see the well-known coffee color of her skin.

Sulu's and Chekov's curses were simultaneous, but with his long-barreled weapon blocking his exit, the security officer took a few seconds longer to extricate himself from his seat. Despite that, he still managed to catch Sulu before he could enter the gangway to the cargo hold. "You're not going out there!"

Sulu tried and failed to shake him off. "Of course I am. I can't shoot that thing to cover *you.*"

"Nobody has to go out there," Thee advised them. "The Peacemakers are hailing us."

Chekov pivoted to catch Thee before she could touch the communicator, yanking her back despite her scowl. "I don't want them to know how many of us there are."

It was all he needed to say to the former Starfleet officer. She stepped with him into the shadows at the rear of the orbital shuttle's cockpit, clearing the way for Sulu to scramble back into his seat.

The sound coming from the communicator was an indistinct mumble until Sulu pushed the frequency output up closer to its normal levels. "—make a trade," he heard through the banshee howl of olivium radiation. "Your shuttle for ours."

He recognized the voice he heard. He just didn't believe that he had heard it.

"What are you waiting for?" Chekov hissed from behind. "Answer him!"

Sulu swallowed, tasting the acrid tang of olivium in his throat. It was one thing to find an illegal olivium-mining operation hidden out in the middle of the Outland. But to discover that the corruption caused by the ultra-rare metal extended all the way to the continental capitol made him feel a little sick. "We hear you, Bartels," he said into the communicator, without ever taking his eyes from the weapon aimed at Uhura. "Tell your man outside that we're willing to make the trade."

If Llano Verde's chief technical officer minded being recognized, his irritable voice didn't show it. "For God's sake, get rid of that noise!" he shouted back at Sulu. "Narrow down your subspace reception frequency to the band between 1.5 and 1.7 millikumars!"

Sulu reached out and found the appropriate control. The shriek of subspace interference faded to a serpentine hiss, soft enough to let him hear Bartels's contemptuous snort. "Good thing *we* had the communications officer," the technical officer said. "Otherwise, you might've already figured out how to call the *Enterprise.*"

Sulu gritted his teeth on an urge to cut the connection with the Bean and do exactly that. But Uhura had been marched halfway between the two vessels by then, close enough for him to see the grimace of pain on her face whenever the blasting crater winds caught her. Sulu also recognized the strong-boned face of her captor. He'd last seen her in much the same stance, keeping her weapon aimed at the drunks of Desperation as they unloaded supplies from the Bean. Despite the fierce cyclonic gusts, then and now, Serafini's aim never wavered.

"How do you want to do this trade, Bartels?" Sulu asked.

"Fast," said the technical officer bluntly. "Serafini wanted me to leave a few Peacemakers on board here until we had the orbital shuttle under our control, but I don't like the looks of that lake and I want to get out of here before the whole damn crater wall goes."

Surprised, Sulu glanced to the right through his cockpit windows at the heaving gray surface of Bull's Eye lake. It looked distinctly foamy now, as if it were being whipped to a frenzy somewhere deep beneath the surface. He couldn't tell for sure if the level had dropped further, since all the rocks around the shoreline had been wetted down by spray and rain, but he thought it had.

"All right, let's make it fast," Sulu agreed. "I'll come over to the Bean while you get all the Peacemakers out of it. Serafini can keep Uhura covered. When I give the signal that the Bean is clear, my friend Chekov will drop the shields and you can let Uhura go—"

"No good," said Bartels. "Serafini was supposed to pilot us up to our rendezvous, but after this landing, I don't want her anywhere near the cockpit. There's enough olivium loaded on that orbital shuttle to power up a starship, and the feedback circuit we're using to keep the subspace radiation from messing up the antimatter drive might not be stable at high speeds. Flying out of Bull's Eye is going to be about as safe as driving a wagon loaded with nitroglycerin through a tornado. I want a Starfleet pilot."

Sulu frowned and closed the communicator channel before he twisted around to meet Chekov's dark gaze. "We have to get the Bean up high enough to bounce a flood warning off the orbital platform to Big Muddy," he said.

"And I'm not good enough with antigrav thrusters to do it." The Russian finished his thought with the ease of shipmates who'd served together for more than a decade. "But I *can* fly a standard-issue Federation shuttle like this one."

"You can?" Thee glanced over at him, one wry eyebrow lifting. "Even more talented than I thought . . . So we get to take Bartels and his Peacemakers up to their rendezvous with alien pirates. That should be fun."

Chekov gave her the half-irritated, half-embarrassed glance that Thee seemed able to draw out of him at will. "You have a strange idea of fun."

"I know. That's why I'm still hanging around with you."

Sulu toggled the communicator channel open again. "Bartels, my friend Chekov is also a Starfleet pilot. He's agreed to take you off planet so I can try to salvage what's left of the Bean."

He half-expected the continental official to reject that offer, but instead heard him take a thoughtful breath. "Is this your friend from the orbital platform that you and Uhura were so worried about?"

"Yes."

"The same one that Serafini's Peacemakers kept losing track of after the shuttle went down?"

"Yes."

Bartels grunted. "Then he's not an idiot. And you wouldn't let him do something suicidal, like fly a shuttle he's not qualified for. Right?"

"Right," Sulu said. "Is it a deal?"

"Almost. I want to hear your friend Chekov promise not to call Captain Kirk on that shuttle communicator before he drops his shields."

Chekov startled Sulu by leaning forward immediately into the range of the communicator's voice detector. "You have my word of honor as a Starfleet officer, Mr. Bartels. No one will call Captain Kirk on this communicator."

"Good. Then send Sulu over to Serafini. I'll have the Peacemakers out of here by the time she lets Uhura go. Bartels out."

Sulu cut the communicator off again, then gave Chekov a questioning glance. "Why did you tell him that?"

"Because it's true. *You're* the one who's going to call the captain and you'll be using the Bean's communicator to do it." Chekov hauled him out of the pilot's seat and sat down there himself to examine the control panel. "Anything special I should know about taking this up?"

"Don't try to fight the cyclonic winds. Circle with them until you're up at the top of the dust storm." Sulu glanced out worriedly at the too-stiff figure standing under guard out in that perpetual storm. Other figures in dark dust mufflers were starting to emerge from the tilted cargo hatch of the Bean. "I'm going to head over now, before Serafini gets too impatient. I'll pulse the antigravs three times to let you know we're clear to go. That way, if they point a weapon at my head and make me give you a false report over the communicator, you'll know to keep the shields up."

"Good idea," Chekov said. "I'll try to delay them here for a while after you've taken off. That should give you a head start for calling the ship."

"I don't think you're going to be able to wait too long," Thee said somberly. "Look at that water."

Both men glanced out at the crater lake. It had begun to swirl and suck downward in a spot just inside the rim, like water draining down a bathtub. The mine conduits draining the lake must have begun opening even wider underground, Sulu realized. The big flood was beginning.

"I'm going," Sulu said, and scrambled to his feet. He paused only long enough to drop a hand on Chekov's shoulder, although his words were ostensibly aimed at Thee. "Don't let him do anything stupid and heroic once he's up in the air with those Peacemakers, will you?"

"I'll try not to," she said dryly. "But you know how hard it is to break old dogs of bad habits."

Whirring with alarm, the tissue regenerator poured its healing glitter over her from wind-burned face to aching ribs to kevlar-scraped ankles. Uhura shuddered violently in response, as if the filmy glow were ice-cold water instead of an intangible beam of healing photons. At first she thought her shaking must be a delayed reaction to having spent so long on the wrong end of Carmela Serafini's projectile weapon, or perhaps a side effect of the molecular rearrangement that was fusing her ribs and mending her skin. But after the noise of the regenerator had faded down to silence, leaving a familiar ghost vibration deep in her bones, Uhura could still feel that violent shaking. It took her another minute to realize that it was the shuttle itself that was quivering around her, as its antigrav thrusters roared up to full strength. Sulu must be pulsing them outward to signal Chekov that they were clear to go.

Uhura disentangled herself from the emergency medical device that Sulu had dumped her into as soon as they'd boarded the Bean. Despite her protests, he'd turned it on even before he searched the ship for any sign of lurking Peacemakers. So far, it seemed as if Neil Bartels had kept his word, but unless she'd been in the regenerator for longer than it had seemed, the pilot couldn't possibly have had long enough to look for any booby traps that her former captors might have planted before they left. Uhura scrambled through the tilted corridor that led to the cockpit, hearing the uneven throb of the two generators on either side. She hoped that was only because one had been more deeply buried by the crash than the others.

"No sign of tampering?" she demanded, as she slid down into the canted copilot's seat. The smell of leather and smoke that she associated with the Peacemakers still lingered strongly in the confined space, but Sulu's head-shake was emphatic enough to reassure her.

"Commander Scott still has about a million test circuits hooked up to monitor the Bean's system performance during flight," the pilot said. He made an adjustment to the control panel and the Bean heaved itself into a more normal landing position. The uneven pulse of the antigravs smoothed back into a more normal growl. "Everything reads nominal, except for the alignment on that left antigrav thruster. I think it'll generate enough of a field to get us out of here, but I'm going to go slow just in case."

"We can't go too slow," Uhura said. Through the dust-sluiced window, she could see the tremendous gyre that was building out in Bull's Eye's crater lake, as more and more of the water was sucked through the crater wall below. She didn't want to think about what the steaming falls at Southfork looked like now. "We've got to get a warning down to Big Muddy."

Sulu increased power to the thrusters obediently, but he also nodded at the Bean's standard-issue communicator inset into its control panel. "Why don't you call from here? The *Enterprise* might hear you even if the orbital platform didn't."

"They already did," Uhura said, remembering the inquiring peak of response that she had seen, not heard, back inside the olivium mine. "But I never got a chance to call them back." She switched on the Bean's control panel, then froze with her fingers on the transmission key. A random crackle of interference filled the cockpit, probably from the olivium-rich rocks around them. "Will the other shuttle overhear us?"

"Not if you cut out the subspace range from 1.5 and 1.7 milli-kumars," Sulu said. The Bean was off the ground now and penduluming slowly up into the fierce crosswinds of Bull's Eye. "That's the only frequency that can make it through the olivium radiation aboard that shuttle."

"Is that another thing Bartels knew and didn't tell us?" Uhura shook her head in aggravation. "If we'd managed to discover *half* of what he did about olivium, we wouldn't be in this fix now. Uhura to *Enterprise*. Come in, *Enterprise*."

Given the background haze of olivium radiation, the voice that answered her was remarkably clear. And remarkably calm. "The *Enterprise* has already been contacted, Commander Uhura," said Linville. "She is on her way to Llano Verde at maximum warp speed, with an estimated time of arrival forty-five minutes from now."

"Do they know about the flood?" Uhura demanded. "Did they send a warning down to Big Muddy through the orbital platform?"

"Yes. Captain Kirk said he would use his Starfleet override authority to make the evacuation mandatory." There was a pause, and what sounded like a murmur of voices in the background. "No one has managed to get a warning to the smaller towns along the Big Muddy, though. Dr. Anthony and Dr. Tamasy have been trying to use the hydrology data network to contact them, but the landline seems to have broken in the last few minutes."

Uhura began to reply, but the Bean hit a tearing sideways gust and was yanked abruptly out of the clear air of the crater, into the chaos of the storm wall around it. Sulu's curse was barely audible over the sudden shriek of the winds, but Uhura could hear the laboring growl as the pilot jammed the antigrav thrusters up to maximum lift. The faint imbalance between the engine noise of the two lateral generators turned into a painfully loud stutter. Uhura opened her mouth to ask Sulu if he wanted her to go back and check on the left engine, when the experimental shuttle jerked upward as abruptly as a puppet yanked on its string, then fell back again toward clearer air. She saw a ragged ridge of rocks pass beneath them with only meters to spare; then they were skating down beneath the dust storm once again, this time down the outer flank of Bull's Eye crater. It looked much darker than Uhura remembered from their last journey, its jumbled rocks glistening in the sun like dark molten glass. Uhura followed that dark gleam downward and watched it turn into a kilometer-wide sheet of flowing water, cascading down from somewhere up higher in the dust storm.

"Linville," she called into the transmitter. "Can you still hear me?"

"Affirm—" The reply was thinned down almost to a whisper by the intervening wall of olivium dust, but when Uhura dialed the 1.5 to 1.7 milli-kumar frequencies back up to their normal level, the signal strengthened. She augmented that same subspace range on her own transmission frequency, recognizing it as one of the bands she and Rand had originally programmed into her prototype communicator.

"Forget about that landline, and get to higher ground!" she told the Carsons. "The entire south side of the crater is covered with water."

"Is it steaming?" That was Greg Anthony's voice, sounding more distant than Linville's and a lot more shaky. "Does it look like what we saw coming out of the mine conduits at Southfork?"

"No," Uhura said. "I can't see any steam at all."

She thought she heard a groan at those words, but the growing squeal of interference might have misled her. There was no mistaking Anthony's next words, however, even through the dust-attenuated connection. "Get to No Escape as fast as you can!" the hydrologist said. "That water's not coming out of the mine conduits, and that means the crater wall has started to collapse. With the weight of all that water behind it, it won't be long before it bursts."

"How long will the people in No Escape have to evacuate after that?" Uhura asked.

"As long as it takes for the first floodwaters to get there," Anthony said grimly. "This is going to be like the Johnstown flood four centuries ago—the water will travel in a giant shock wave, hundreds of feet high and full of all the debris it picks up along the way. And after it hits No Escape, there won't be anything left."

Chapter Sixteen

"So, you're our pilot."

The woman was taller than Chekov, taller than most of the men who followed her through the airlock hatch. She slapped dust off her trousers with the same wide-brimmed hat Chekov had grown to hate in the last few days, but never took her eyes off him. Not even when she flashed a crooked smile and spat onto the deck between them. Chekov suspected she would claim she only meant to clear the dust from her mouth, but she wouldn't expect him to believe it. He didn't. It was all he could do not to spit back at her.

A quick visual tally of the phasers and projectile weapons scattered among the Peacemakers erased any half-formed ideas about overpowering them, or somehow tricking them out of their weapons. Chekov's rifle and the handful of ammunition still heavy in his pocket made for a pitiful defense against the kind of menace they represented. He was glad he'd hidden Thee and her dogs in the empty environmental suit locker, gladder still that the dogs would stay silent just because she told them to.

"Yes," he said after what seemed like too long a silence. "I can fly this shuttle."

Serafini's smile widened, although it came no closer to being sincere. A quick jerk of her chin peeled one of the five black-hatted Peacemakers away from the others. "I hope you don't mind," she said sweetly as the man stepped forward and closed his hand around the barrel of Chekov's rifle. "These projectile weapons just make such a mess when you shoot 'em indoors." Chekov released the gun without resisting, but his teeth gritted together so hard he thought they'd crack. "That's a good boy."

He wondered if she'd ever noticed how much mess they made of people, whenever and wherever they were fired.

"Come on, Carm, we need to get going."

The small, red-haired man who pushed to the front looked surprisingly comfortable with the phaser in his hand despite his neat civilian suit and bland face. Chekov recognized his voice as that of the man Sulu had called Bartels, and made a mental note not to underestimate someone who had so callously orchestrated the disaster they were all now scrambling to avert.

"Why don't you all head back to the cargo hold and get strapped in for the trip," Bartels suggested. "We don't need you to get the liftoff started."

"Don't you?" Serafini tossed Bartels a glance the way someone else might toss a dog a bone. Then she sailed her hat toward one of the empty supply crates, and turned toward the rear, but not before Chekov saw the raw flash of disgust in her eyes. "Come on, boys." The Peacemakers trailed behind her like dust in a comet's tail, shucking various wraps, hats, and coats as they went. The shuttle's ventilation system labored to clear the air in their wake.

Bartels waited until the hatch had closed behind the last one before heaving an aggrieved sigh. "If brains were olivium, not one of them would have enough to blow his nose." He used the phaser to motion Chekov toward the cockpit, although his voice remained as congenial as only a professional bureaucrat's could. "I don't imagine that thinking two steps ahead of them for the past few days has been a herculean task for you. No offense."

"None taken." Chekov took his time moving into the cockpit, adjusting the pilot's seat, strapping himself in. He'd promised Sulu he'd delay Bartels on the ground as long as possible, and it was one of the few promises he'd made since coming to Belle Terre that he was confident he could keep. Glancing up from the console, he looked across the dusty distance between the two craft, at the barely visible image of Sulu behind the Bean's windscreen. It looked as if the pilot was already strapped in, but he saw no sign yet of Uhura.

"They're only in this for the money," Bartels said with another sigh. "Even Carmela."

Chekov powered the engines down to full shutoff, letting them cool while he ran an unnecessary diagnostic on the board. "You, of course, are endangering thousands of lives for purely altruistic reasons." He flashed the landing lights on-off, on-off to let Sulu know everything inside was okay.

"Hey, the colonists knew when they came to Belle Terre that death was a possibility." If Bartels noticed or understood anything Chekov did with the helm console, he didn't comment on it. Settling into the copilot's chair, he kept the phaser trained on Chekov while he made himself comfortable. "We may have speeded up the time line a little, but that crater wall would have given way eventually. They can't build their homes on a floodplain and then complain about the water in their basements."

Chekov wondered if he truly saw no difference between a natural disaster and a man-made flood designed to kill as many colonists as possible. Outside, three quick, fierce clouds of dust enveloped the Bean as Sulu pulsed the idling antigravs, and Chekov closed his eyes briefly in silent relief. Whatever else happened now, he could take comfort in knowing that Sulu and Uhura were safe. Probably safer than anyone else on Belle Terre, at least once they were airborne. "You said there was a feedback circuit that let this shuttle fly?"

"Yes." Bartels leaned forward to glance under the console at the maintenance panel Chekov had left open. "Did you disconnect any of this?"

"No." Although he wished now that he had.

Bartels keyed a long string of code into the pad that had been added to the console, glancing aside at Chekov after every few numbers as though checking to make sure he was paying attention. Then, apparently reading something that disturbed him in Chekov's impassive silence, he paused with his hand poised above the keypad. "In case it matters to you," he said with a casualness that made Chekov want to hit him, "what happened when you first got here—the Peacemakers killing everyone on board your shuttle. That was just business. It wasn't personal."

It told Chekov a great deal about the level of trust

among the members of this conspiracy that no one had bothered to inform Bartels that only one of the shuttle crew had died. "It doesn't matter," he said grimly. Just as it wouldn't matter to a jury, if he could only manage to drag Bartels and the rest of them in front of one. Instead, they were escaping with a shuttle full of olivium that they'd mined at the expense of the people they were supposed to be serving. He turned his attention pointedly back toward the helm, unable to stand looking at this particular traitor any longer. It made him feel only a little better to see that the dusty shadow of the Bean was long gone. "Let's get this shuttle started and get out of here."

It had taken the titanic impact of an olivium-rich fragment from the Quake Moon to form Bull's Eye crater. All it took to destroy it was a cascade of flowing water no more than a few feet deep, pouring relentlessly over a sag in its southern side.

Sulu watched the collapsed section of rim widen as they approached, allowing more of the crater lake access to the unprotected lowlands below. He was flying as fast as the Bean's two good antigrav thrusters could push them through the drag of downslope winds, but he was afraid it still wasn't going to be fast enough. The left generator's misalignment meant the Bean had to fly at an awkward angle, slamming shoulder-first into Llano Verde's turbulent winds rather than piercing them sleekly with its nose. It also meant they didn't have enough lift to get above the dust storm, in order to get a navigational fix from the orbital station. Sulu never thought he'd be grateful for Gamma Night, but at least it had taught him how to use landmarks on the ground to steer by. Right now, he was hugging the flank of Bull's Eye, using the crater's downslope winds to give them a dust-free view out into the adjacent valley. Somewhere out there was the muddy expanse of river that would lead them to No Escape.

"Is that the Little Muddy?"

Uhura had a better view from her side of the slewed cockpit, but far less experience than Sulu at judging the size of the river channels that were forming beneath their shuttle. He craned around to check the one at which she pointed, then shook his head.

"No. Too narrow."

The communications officer drummed her fingers nervously on the Bean's communicator, rendered useless now by dust. Sulu could hear the frustration in her voice. "Shouldn't the Little Muddy start where all the water is coming out? Weir and Anthony said the springs at Southfork were its headwaters."

"They were. But that's not necessarily where the mines are making the rim collapse." Sulu banked the Bean outward to skirt an upthrust ridge of stronger rock that confined the pouring rush of water. "If the shafts cut obliquely across the rim—"

"—then Southfork could be further west of here," Uhura finished. "But it can't be too far—"

The break in her voice didn't alarm Sulu at first. He was used to her attention being dragged away anytime they rounded a curve of the crater and got a new view of the landscape ahead. But this time there was some quality in Uhura's silence—perhaps her sudden intake of breath, perhaps his peripheral awareness of how still she was—that warned Sulu to look up from his flight controls.

The sheet of water pouring over the crater rim behind them had just been the beginning, he realized. The resistant ridge of rock was not a shoreline but an island, separating the shallow falls from the roar and rising mist of a much larger cataract. Sulu watched the gleaming lake plunge over the rim and explode into bursts of spray and immense splashes as it cascaded down the crater's eroding slope. The waterfall had already carved a canyon several tens of meters deep into the crater wall. Even as they watched, the rupture gouged itself deeper and deeper, until it hit what must have been the last remnants of the vein of olivium the Peacemakers had been mining.

The entire south rim of the crater erupted into a wall of billowing steam, flung debris, and angry water. Sulu never got to see what happened after that, because the shock wave from the explosion sent the Bean tumbling helplessly out of control.

Chekov lifted the shuttle just as Sulu had suggested—banking with the cyclonic sweep of the wind instead of trying to bull straight into it. Even so, the force of the hard gusts tilted the whole craft, rocking it like a sailboat on rough seas. Chekov rotated them to put the wind at their stern, steadying the shuttle's trajectory around the bowl of the crater without actually increasing their altitude. He wasn't sure how long he could get away with making minimal progress in maximum time. Even if Bartels never noticed how far they weren't getting, the planet itself wouldn't tolerate the shuttle plying its turbulent atmosphere for long. Whether from dust impaction or olivium-radiation overload, Chekov understood that he flew a precarious balance between killing time and killing them all.

Flashes of green-gold light flecked the shuttle's screens, like a malfunctioning transporter wave that never quite took hold. Chekov watched the readings for the shield generator spike with each microscopic olivium ignition. He wondered how long it would be before the radioactive backwash from those tiny impacts finally overloaded the shields and left them vulnerable to every punishment Belle Terre could fling their way.

A monstrous updraft kicked the shuttle in its belly, jolting them briefly upward before dropping them into partial free fall. Bartels clutched at the console with both hands. "Watch your wind shear!" He recovered enough to thrust the phaser menacingly in Chekov's direction, as though that might improve his attention to piloting. "I thought you knew how to fly this thing!"

"Just because I can doesn't mean I have to." Chekov dropped them intentionally this time, and heard Bartels bark a cry of protest.

"I can only guarantee that feedback circuit up to mach three in atmosphere," the technician shouted. "After that, the electrostatic buildup from the dust against the screens gets strong enough to disrupt the loop." Chekov brought them steady again, sobered at least a little by the prospect of yet another crash-landing. "Doesn't this tub have inertial dampeners?"

"It has them. They just don't work anymore. You should have thought of that when you designed your olivium-proof engines." He angled the nose downward just enough to get a visual on the ground. It seemed to swim below them, glossed over with a gossamer veil of dust that peeled aside just ahead of their passage. "What about once we're out of the atmosphere?" he asked. "What's our top speed once we're in vacuum?"

Bartels leaned forward to peer out the window, as if to see what Chekov could possibly be seeking. "Warp one point five. Assuming the engines are properly calibrated and balanced. Why aren't we gaining altitude?"

The slump in the crater wall might have been lovely in other circumstances. Water cascaded over the crumbling edge in lacy billows, reaching fingers of foam hundreds of meters high. "How long will we have to maintain that speed?"

Bartels said nothing for a long moment, staring down at the wall of water. But it wasn't horror on his face, or even surprise. Just a self-absorbed curiosity, as though he found the process fascinating but not particularly upsetting.

It wasn't until Chekov dipped down to follow the course of the flood that Bartels jerked a look in his direction. "What are you doing?"

"Exactly what you think I'm doing." The lake itself boiled like a witch's cauldron, surging to dump its innards through that ever-widening notch. Wind dragged the shuttle halfway around the crater before Chekov could break free. Once he did, the shuttle wrenched over nearly onto its side in overcompensation. They tumbled down into the dust like a rock thrown into muddy water.

Bartels threw himself back into his seat, his face drained of all color but the radiation red on his cheeks. "Commander—"

"Chekov." It seemed only fair to remind Bartels of his name, considering he was about to ruin the man's life to the best of his ability.

"Commander Chekov . . . I don't think you appreciate how very badly I need to get off this planet."

"Mr. Bartels, I don't think you appreciate how little I care." Finding a slipstream, he released the shuttle into a steep dive along the crumbling crater wall. The speed indicator didn't quite reach mach two, but it pushed up against it from below.

The phaser shook visibly when Bartels lifted it to Chekov's temple. "Please—" He sounded frightened and angry at the same time, just like a spoiled little boy. "—just do as you promised and take us into orbit."

The floodwaters seemed to clear the clouds from above them, dragging roils of dust behind them like a cape, pushing a pressure front of air in front of them like a battering ram. Chekov couldn't tell if the roaring he felt in his bones was the voice of the waves or the shuttle's engines laboring against the wind.

"Commander, if you don't take this shuttle into orbit, I will kill you where you sit. I'm serious."

Chekov threw him a glance of pure disdain. "Am I supposed to believe that you and your friend didn't already plan to kill me as soon as we reached your rendezvous?" The dumbfounded glaze of Bartels's expression almost made Chekov smile. "Or was it even sooner?" he continued, bringing the shuttle into line with the swath of clearer air carved out by the flood. "Getting out of the atmosphere is the difficult part of the trip, after all. I'm sure Serafini could pilot a shuttle through open space."

Bartels didn't respond. Chekov hadn't really expected him to produce a convincing argument, but it did surprise him a little to discover Bartels had been startled speechless.

"I'm dead no matter what happens." Chekov rapped a finger against the speed indicator, just to get Bartels thinking. "Shoot me while we're traveling at twice the speed of sound, and you'll be dead, too."

Something jolted the shuttle hard from behind, knocking them both back into their seats. Chekov grabbed the panel and pulled himself forward, trying to orient himself using the view out the window even as he pored over the console in search of some alarm.

"What happened?" Bartels nearly shouldered him aside trying to get to the speed indicator. "What's our airspeed?"

Chekov elbowed him back into his seat. "Your feedback circuit is fine. It's not our speed." He found the reading he was looking for in front of Bartels, hidden away on the uppermost corner of the copilot's board. He switched the screen view aft and downward. "Someone blew the rear airlock."

Bodies—human bodies—tumbling into the ravenous dust. Chekov counted five before they were lost to the storm. He couldn't tell if any of them were alive. For their sakes, honestly hoped not. While the dust storms at ground level hadn't proved nearly powerful enough to strip a person's flesh from their bones, he wouldn't have wanted to meet these upper-level wind blasts unprotected and awake to realize it.

"Oh, my God!" Bartels threw off his seat restraint, standing to splay his hands against the viewscreen as though a closer proximity to this horror might clarify his view. "What happened? Where's Carmela?"

Chekov didn't bother to answer. He punched in a command that made the shuttle take up a safer holding pattern above the dust, then unlatched his own seat restraint with one hand and punched Bartels across the face with the other.

"Pull up!" Uhura braced herself against the downward rush of free fall, grateful for the shock webbing that automatically leaped out from the seat and laced itself around her. She could see the dark desert landscape hurtling toward them on Sulu's side of the cockpit. "Pull up—we're falling too fast!"

"I'm trying!" Sulu had slammed the controls for his two working antigravs as far to one side as possible, trying to compensate for their weakened left thruster. Unfortunately, that was the side toward which they were falling. Uhura felt her heartbeat hammer up into her throat as the ground loomed closer and closer, then g-forces slammed her backward into her seat as the scenery abruptly rolled sideways. The pilot had finally managed to convert the Bean's downward momentum into an equally high lateral velocity. Before Uhura could suck in even one relieved breath, however, the experimental shuttle tore through the last few meters of clear air and plowed deep into the haze of Llano Verde's perennial dust storms.

"Can you see the ground?" she shouted at Sulu.

"No, but I know it's there."

A rising spiral of wind caught the Bean and tossed it upward before Uhura even had time to be surprised by the pilot's response. Sulu grunted and wrestled the shuttle back down again, using the friction of the rising air mass to reduce their speed to more reasonable levels.

"The problem with flying near the Gory Mountains usually isn't hitting the ground," he explained to Uhura. "It's staying close enough to the ground to see where we're going."

"Oh." The shuttle bounced through another turbulent updraft, and she had to grit her teeth against the uneasy protest of her stomach. "Did you see the Little Muddy before the crater wall blew out?"

"No. Did you?"

"Yes." She'd known as soon as she'd seen the broad glimmer of water in the distance why Sulu had been sure none of the other rivers they crossed could be the trunk stream. "It was further off to the southwest, about twenty-five degrees to the crater wall where the falls came over."

"Twenty-five degrees?" Sulu cast a thoughtful glance out through the cockpit window. Uhura tried to follow his line of sight, but the only thing she could see in any direction was a roiling gray sea of dust. She heard the pilot take a deep breath; then the Bean veered abruptly to the right. "I'm just guessing," Sulu said, before she could ask. "For all I know, I'm flying us right back to Bull's Eye."

"I don't think you are," she said. "Can you feel the downslope winds?"

"No." Sulu paused a moment, then smiled at her. "Which means we must be riding on them. Thank you, Uhura."

"You're the one who guessed right," she reminded him. "Can we get any closer to the ground?"

His answer was a series of controlled downward swoops, each canted only slightly by their malfunctioning antigrav. The final drop took them through a filmy underbelly of dust and back into the relatively clear air of a broad valley. Uhura glanced down, eager to see if they had finally located the Little Muddy, then felt her breath evaporate out of her as if she had been punched.

The river below them had gone from the contained shimmer of high water she had originally glimpsed to a churning black chaos of mud, water, and debris filling the entire river valley from side to side. It was easy to see the break and crash of wave crests hurtling downstream with that deluge, but Uhura didn't realize until Sulu swooped downward one more time that some of them were taller than the *Enterprise.*

"Oh, my God," she said. "The flood wave's already going down the Little Muddy."

Bartels reacted instinctively, lashing out with the phaser in his hand instead of firing it. Chekov ducked back away from his swing, caught it, and twisted the gun out of the technician's fist before he had a chance to recover. A glare of brilliant sunlight washed through the cockpit as the shuttle broke through the grimy clouds to freedom. Whether that blinded Bartels or simply shocked him into submission, Chekov couldn't tell. But he struck the technician one last time before dragging him out of his seat, just to make sure there would be no further unpleasant surprises.

"Gwen!" Chekov could hear the banging rattle of her fight with the suit locker door, but didn't dare turn away from Bartels long enough to check on her progress. "Get the aft doors!" he shouted when he heard the door finally slam aside. "Lock them! Now!"

Dogs swept to circle him from behind, darting in to steal sniffs of Bartels's prostrate body while Chekov quickly checked the charge on the phaser and lowered the setting to heavy stun. Trading his purloined rifle for this more familiar weapon lifted a heavy burden from his heart.

"Who's driving?" Thee asked as she slid to a stop by the cargo bay doors.

"The computer." Chekov glanced at her over his shoulder, only to have Bartels stir groggily and recapture his attention. "Have you got those doors?"

A frustrated bang prefaced her answer. "There's no lock." He realized she must have kicked at the door.

"Then jam them. Destroy the controls." He danced away from Bartels only long enough to grab a handful of the restraining straps bolted into the starboard wall. "She'll have to open them manually. That should buy us some time." An adjustment to the phaser's settings and a quick burst of fire severed the connections.

On the other end of the compartment, Thee swept up the cutting torch they'd left on the floor outside the cargo bay and began attacking the door controls. "Who are we locking in?"

"Her name's Serafini. She's his only surviving accomplice." Chekov flipped Bartels onto his stomach and planted a knee between his shoulders. "Don't move!"

The pressure of a phaser against the back of his neck was all the threat Bartels needed.

"How can you do this?" Bartels hurriedly tucked his other arm behind his back once Chekov had twisted the first one. "There's been . . . a hull breach, or an explosion . . ." He squirmed a little against the straps, but didn't really try to pull away. "We've got to find out what happened back there!"

Chekov couldn't contain a single snort of morbid amusement. "What happened back there, Mr. Bartels, is that your girlfriend used the cargo airlock to dispose of your foot soldiers. Without bothering to consult you." Giving the bindings one last yank to make sure they were tight, he quickly looped the second strap and slipped it over Bartels's feet. "Apparently I wasn't the only one who wasn't scheduled to see the rendezvous."

"She wouldn't do that to *me.*" But the feverish shake of his head said he was more shocked than certain.

Handiwork done, Chekov stepped back and tucked the phaser into his belt. "It would serve you right if I left you here to find out if that was true." But even felons deserved better than frontier justice. Grabbing the back of Bartels's coverall in both hands, he heaved him to his knees and dragged him toward the nearest cargo crate.

Thee paused with the laser cutter still glowing in her hands. "If he's not staying here, where is he going?"

"He's going to stand trial." Chekov threw open the lid, then leaned down to clear a space in the tangle of shock webbing inside. "He was willing to murder thousands of people under his care. That's not something I can let him get away with."

She turned off the torch and came forward a step. "But you promised—"

Bartels landed inside the crate with a thump. "Sulu promised," Chekov pointed out as he snapped the shock webbing tight around his unwilling cargo. "I only promised not to call the ship." He kicked the side of the crate to silence Bartels's protests. "Shut up. At least you're going out the lock alive." Then he slammed the lid on the technician's horrified expression.

Thee joined him in shoving the crate across the deck. The dogs darted back and forth in front of them, herding the crate toward the lock. "Other than a certain visceral gratification, throwing him out the airlock accomplishes what?" Her voice was calm despite the fearful paleness of her face.

Chekov reached up to cycle the airlock door. "It keeps him alive after the shuttle goes down."

When the hatch slid aside, he bent to shoulder the heavy crate into the lock, this time without Thee's assistance. She stood watching him, hands at her sides.

"Pavel . . ." She crossed behind him and bent to look him squarely in the face. "Why don't we just take him up to the orbital platform?"

Chekov backed out of the lock, closed the door. "Because Sulu and Uhura can't evacuate everyone between Bull's Eye and Eau Claire."

"Neither can we."

"No . . ." The outside door whisked open on a sky so bright and clear, it seemed to belong somewhere else. Bartels's crate tumbled free, the timer for its breaking chute and sonic beacon activated the moment it began its fall. "But if we can divert the flood itself, evacuations won't be necessary."

Thee followed him into the cockpit, her gaze intent on his face as he slid back into the pilot's chair. "I'm assuming you have an idea," she finally prodded.

Oddly enough, the fact that he knew she was going to be angry with him made him more uncomfortable than any other part of his plan. He busied himself plotting the new course into the shuttle's console.

"Pavel, answer my question."

He glanced aside at her, couldn't bear the fury building up in her dark eyes, and looked down at his controls again. "We have a cargo hold filled with olivium, and a shuttle we can aim." He started the perilous dip back into the dust storm. "We should be able to create an impact crater at least the size of Bull's Eye, big enough to catch the flood."

Her voice was almost as cold as her eyes. "Do I get a vote in this?"

"Gwen . . ."

"I'm not an idiot, Pavel. I know what you mean by 'aiming.' Was I supposed to just sit here and not notice where you were headed until we hit the ground?"

The black scar of water resolved through the floor of dust, rampaging down a river valley now boiling with mud and debris. "No, you're supposed to get into a cargo crate and follow Bartels down. The shock webbing will protect you and the dogs, and the crates are air permeable—you'll be fine until help arrives." He felt more than heard her intake of breath, and pushed on before she could interrupt. "The crates all have sonic beacons, to help the colonists find them in the dust. It's your best chance."

"And you?" When he didn't answer, she pressed, "What's supposed to happen to you?"

Chekov brought them low enough to feel the flood-churned air vibrate against the belly of the shuttle. He didn't know where the cities lay along this swollen river, and prayed his best guess would take him far enough down the span to accomplish what he intended.

"Damn you!" Thee punched him hard on the shoulder, hard enough to make him turn away from the console and face her at last. *"Damn you!* You don't have the right to endanger yourself anymore! Don't you understand that? You're first officer on board a starship! You have to think of your captain, your crew!"

"I have to think of these people, too. You know that's what being a Starfleet officer means!" He captured her hands in both of his, astonished by the depth of her anger as well as strangely touched by it. "Gwen, I'm sorry. But we don't have time to talk about this now."

She tried to jerk herself free, couldn't. "If you get your way, you bastard, we won't get a chance to talk about it later, either." Her eyes, luminescent with rage, tore a hole straight through his heart. "And what about Serafini?"

"Yes . . ." That voice, as calm and smooth as a sheet of ice, whipped Chekov out of his seat and into the cockpit doorway. "What about Serafini?"

* * *

Sulu had flown a lot of aircraft at speeds he knew other pilots would never reach. Sometimes it was a deliberate test to find the upper limits of flight, other times an urgent mission that he had to use his piloting skills to carry out. But never before had he felt as if he was racing with death itself, in the form of a giant battering flood wave released by human greed and malice.

"There!" Uhura's voice had grown so raw with exhaustion and pent-up emotion that he barely recognized it. "Sulu, is that the wave front?"

He pulsed the back antigrav again, a risky maneuver while in flight but one which gave the Bean an added spurt of forward momentum. The two working generators had long since reached the red line Scotty had installed on their power monitors as a warning against overload. Sulu was praying that the *Enterprise*'s cautious chief engineer had built in his usual generous safety margin. The only thing working in their favor was the ancient twists and turns of the Little Muddy Valley. Carved deep into the resistant bedrock of the Gory Mountains, those incised meanders were forcing the floodwater to take a less direct and slower path than the Bean. That advantage was finally paying off.

"That's it," he said, and pulsed the back thruster once again. The Bean spurted through the choppy backwash of wind and dust rising off the thundering wave front, then passed directly over the immense wall of rolling water. It moved more like an avalanche than a flood wave, toppling hundreds of meters down from its crest onto the unsuspecting valley below. The landscape it drowned was already devastated, destroyed by the bomb blast of compressed air that the flood wave pushed ahead of it. Sulu winced as he saw forests explode like matchsticks and entire buildings shatter to bits. His only hope was that earlier floodwaters had chased most of the animals and humans away from this part of the valley.

"How much farther to No Escape?" Uhura shouted over the constant booming of the flood. They were putting it behind them with excruciating slowness, but each second they gained was another second in which to evacuate the river town.

"At least another fifty kilometers." Through the usual haze of dust, Sulu could just see the deep notch that the river had carved through the wall of the Gory Mountains. He altered the Bean's course to head there more directly, abandoning the doomed curves of the Little Muddy to their inevitable fate. "It's just on the other side of that canyon."

Uhura fell silent, watching the Little Muddy's gorge loom from a shadowy gap between the mountains to a deep-walled rock chasm as they got closer. "Do you think that will act like a safety valve, and hold back some of the flood?" she asked at last.

Unfortunately, Sulu had been forced to suffer through enough fluid hydraulics classes back at the academy to know the bleak answer to that question. "No," he said grimly. "As the water rushes into a narrower space, it'll go even faster. And get even higher. By the time it finally hits No Escape, there might not be anywhere left to evacuate to."

The blue glint of Serafini's rifle guarded the shoved-open hatch, but it was the steel in her eyes that halted Chekov. That, and the gut-deep realization that if he tried to reach for the phaser on his belt, she would kill him.

"You've really screwed up everything, haven't you?"

Her eyes were narrow and cold in her radiation-burned face. "Now I've gotta choose between getting blown to bits with you or staying alive just so I can spend the rest of my life in jail."

Chekov made an effort to seem relaxed, to drop his hands so that he was closer to his weapon. "Surrender peacefully and testify against Bartels. The authorities might deal with you more leniently."

"I suppose I could do that. But . . ." Serafini reached out for her hat, letting its wide brim shade the intentions lurking in her eyes. "You know what my biggest character flaw is?"

Chekov didn't even want to venture a guess.

"I'm spiteful."

He flashed into motion before she'd finished speaking, dodging aside and down, bringing the phaser up between them in both hands. He felt the heat of its lightning, and was fairly certain he'd brought his weapon to bear and fired. But he couldn't hear it over the rifle's more thunderous report.

Chapter Seventeen

ALL THE WAY through the Little Muddy gorge, Sulu had been praying that they would find No Escape already evacuated, its citizens forewarned by the flood that had wiped out the lower half of town. Perhaps some had left, but it looked like even more had elected to stay behind, camping out on roofs and second-story porches to watch the waters rise around them. Sulu made one frustrated spiral above the town, battling the downdrafts off the mountain scarp while he looked for a good place to land. He didn't have any better luck than the first time they'd come here. No Escape's charming pseudo-Mediterranean design hadn't included any large squares or public parks, and from the air Sulu couldn't tell whether the silver gleam of water in the streets represented puddles or neck-deep streams. He finally ended up hovering over the faded red cross of the medical clinic, the same roof where he'd unloaded emergency medical supplies two days before. It was large enough for the downdraft from his antigravs to push the crowd of flood-watchers out to the building's rim, making space for him to land in their midst. The Bean settled at an awkward angle, its lame left thruster bumping down hard on the roof while the other two settled on softer cushions of idling air.

Uhura had her shock webbing torn off before the Bean had even finished landing. "How much time do we have?"

"Twenty minutes, more or less." Sulu triggered the cargo hatch open, hoping the colonists would be restrained enough not to trample each other in their rush to embark. "Don't try to prioritize the evacuation, just pack them in as fast as you can. Start with the ones on the roof."

He swung around to watch the shuttle's weight sensors, to make sure they didn't get overloaded by the rush. To his surprise, the digital readings never flickered. Frowning, Sulu lowered the cockpit's side window and stuck his head out into the dust to see if the cargo door had been damaged by Serafini's crash. The ramp had lowered itself perfectly, but the only person he could see standing on it was Uhura. Her voice rose in desperation, audible even above the banshee howl of Llano Verde's winds.

"—seen it coming! It's going to be like a tidal wave when it gets here, *hundreds* of feet high!"

"Where was it when you saw it?" That male shout of reply was equally loud, but the emotion driving it was an anger scorching enough to make Sulu search for its source. A stocky, balding Asian man had shouldered his way to the front of the crowd, staring at Uhura in a belligerent way that Sulu didn't like.

The communications officer didn't seem to notice his hostility. "Almost to the far end of the gorge," she said urgently. "We've only got about twenty minutes—"

"And you waited until *now* to come get us?" His voice towered upward in near-hysterical rage. "I've been begging for help from Big Muddy for the last *six days!* Why did you damned bureaucrats wait until the last *possible* minute to show up and evacuate us?"

If she had been the bureaucrat he'd accused her of being, Sulu thought, Uhura would have retreated from him. Instead, she glared up into his radiation-burned face. "We're not bureaucrats from Big Muddy! We're the Starfleet officers who were here two days ago, looking for the source of the floodwater. And we would have come back sooner, if it hadn't been for the illegal olivium miners we ran into up at Bull's Eye crater. The same ones who deliberately caused this flood to cover their escape from Belle Terre!"

There must have been enough impassioned vehemence in her voice to finally make an impact on the crowd. Sulu heard the colonists murmur and glance at the open hatch, but still no one made a move toward it. His stomach began to twist, a visceral reaction to the time being wasted in argument that could have been spent evacuating colonists.

"Half of us here have relatives in town, or working downstairs in the clinic," the Asian man protested. He still sounded angry, but the dangerous edge of hysteria had vanished from his voice. "You can't expect us to—"

"Listen!" Sulu shouted out the window. "You can hear the water coming!" He cut all power to the Bean's antigravs, to get rid of the whine of the generators and the rush of propelled air. He wasn't sure if that made enough silence to hear the roar of the approaching flood beneath the dust storm's shriek, but he was counting on the colonists' stressed imaginations to supply the noise even if it wasn't there.

"Load up the people whose families are here and let's evacuate them," Uhura urged the Asian man. "While we're doing that, you can send for the others' relatives. And turn on all the alarms this building has in it to alert the rest of town. We can do at least two evacuation runs, maybe three if we hurry."

That finally triggered the rush into the cargo hold that Sulu had expected. He heard Uhura directing the flow, packing the colonists in efficiently between the stacks of cargo. She continued to let them on even after the weight alarm had sounded and Sulu shouted at her to stop. He finally heard her footsteps coming toward the cockpit, but she only entered long enough to deposit two children in her copilot's seat and wrap the shock webbing back around them. Their parents slid into the passenger seats, one carrying an infant and the other a mewing cat in a plasteel carrier box.

"What do you think you're doing?" Sulu demanded.

"I only overloaded you by fifteen percent," Uhura assured him. "That's well inside Scotty's usual safety margin—"

"Not that." He jerked his chin toward the silent, wide-eyed children in the copilot's seat, even as he turned the antigravs back on. "You're staying here?"

"I can get them better organized for the next couple of runs." She was already ducking back out into the gangway. "I'll tell this set of passengers to take some of the cargo with them when they leave, so you'll have more room on the next run. See you!"

She vanished before he could object, her footsteps echoing down the gangway. Sulu listened to her giving calm instructions to the evacuees as she passed through the cargo hold, and had to grit his teeth on an impulse to close the hatch door before she could leave. He had an ominous feeling he might never see Uhura again, but at fifteen percent over their cargo loading limit, he knew that even her slight weight would add too much risk to their journey. There was one thing Uhura hadn't remembered when she was loading the colonists, and it was the thing Sulu was trying hardest not to think about right now.

The original weight limit that Chief Engineer Scott had programmed into the Bean's cargo hold sensors assumed that the shuttle had three working antigravs.

I didn't kill her, Chekov thought. Staring down at Serafini's stunned body, trying hard to remember how to drag in even a single unlabored breath, he found a numbing peace in that awareness. Whatever else this planet had done to him, it hadn't turned him into the kind of man who chose killing as long as he had some other option.

"Oh, my God . . . !"

Fatigue crashed over him, heavy and smelling pungently of blood. Letting the phaser slip from his hand, he sank to his knees as it clattered to the deck beside him. Even two days of swallowing airborne olivium hadn't made him feel this tired, this sick. He suspected what was wrong when Thee clutched at the shoulder of his jacket and awkwardly interposed herself between him and the compartment floor. Then his next abortive gasp for air filled his mouth with a sour, coppery slime, and he recognized the crushing weight boring into his chest for what it was. He couldn't tell which blasted through him first, the terror or the pain.

"Sit up!" Thee heaved him half-upright against the bulkhead, tearing at his uniform's shoulder strap with trembling fingers. "You're gonna have to help me here—they teach you guys more about this stuff." He felt the front of his jacket rip away, the clammy slap of outside air chilling the blood on the breast of his tunic. "Does this tub have a medkit?"

". . . I don't know . . ." The fluid in his voice frightened him, almost more than the pain that slammed him with every hitching breath. ". . . try under the helm console . . ." Sulu had said it was the same model cargo shuttle they'd had on the *Enterprise.*

She left him, disappeared from his sight, from the narrowing cone of his attention. Squeezing his eyes closed, Chekov tried to will away his panic, steady his heartbeat so he could breathe around the pain. But all he could see in that darkness was Reddy's blood-soaked linens, and Plottel's pallid, lifeless body.

He forced his eyes open when he felt her hand against the side of his face. "Gwen . . . we don't have time . . ." The flood waited for none of this. Serafini had known that, and Chekov knew it, too.

A glimpse of naked terror flashed across Thee's face, only to vanish again behind an iron-hard wall of resolve. "Don't tell me what we have time for." She threw open the medkit on the floor by her hip. "If you have time to get shot, I have time to patch you together."

Two hypos in quick succession. At least one was a painkiller, powerful enough to shroud his whole body in cotton. While pain suffused the blurry picture, it had lifted clear of his emotions. He knew he was hurt, he knew he was frightened, but he couldn't really feel it anymore.

A scanner's tooth-splitting warble danced through the chemical fog, and he felt her bear down on his chest as though from a thousand light-years' distance. His body must have arched gently in protest, because he was aware of aimless movement a moment before she murmured, "I'm sorry . . . I really am . . ." He wanted to tell her that it was all right, but couldn't climb back down into his body in time. She continued in an artificially cheerful voice, "The good news is: It's not as bad as it looks."

Chekov opened his eyes, blinked without being able to focus. She was spattered with blood clear to the elbows. "How much worse could it look?"

Thee tried on a smile. "How much do you know about human anatomy?"

"Enough to know that it's bad to make extra holes in it."

"Look at that—" She stroked his cheek, her head tilted fondly to one side. "His sense of humor comes out under stress."

He would have laughed for her, but was faintly afraid it would kill him.

"Missed everything important but the lung," she went on, more seriously. "And it's not bleeding bad enough to kill you anytime soon."

He wasn't sure he believed that last part. He watched her load another hypo, tried to guess how many doses she had before he drained the entire kit. "I knew this was going to happen."

Thee sorted sterile compresses off the bottom of the kit. "Don't be a defeatist."

"There was a Peacemaker . . . when we first found the shuttle . . ." He gripped her wrist, made her look at him. "Gwen, I killed him."

"You did what you had to. You took care of us." Thee pressed a clean compress into place. "That doesn't make you a murderer, Pavel."

Swallowing hard to drown the bloody taste in his mouth, Chekov let his head fall back against the bulkhead. "I didn't want to die like this," he admitted, very softly.

She pulled his jacket over the wad of compresses, sealing it so tightly he could feel his heart pound against the inside of his ribs. "I'm not going to let that happen."

When she stood, Chekov thought at first she'd gone to seek another medical kit. Then he heard the familiar rumble of a supply crate across the uneven decking, and remembered that Serafini still needed to be dealt with. It wasn't until she bumped the crate to a stop beside him that it occurred to him she had other things in mind. "What are you doing?"

She threw back the lid, unwound the mat of shock webbing inside. "What do you think?"

"Gwen . . . no!" He struggled to draw his knees up and roll to all fours away from her. Whether from pain or the drugs, he couldn't fight off the uprush of nausea and weakness that swallowed him. He collapsed in on himself, choking from the effort. "Don't . . . ! I need to pilot the shuttle . . ."

"Don't be a chauvinist." She maneuvered behind him to lock her arms around his waist and lift. "You think you're the only one who can crash a shuttle?"

The anguish that he didn't think could reach him anymore laid him open. If he could have breathed, he would have screamed in protest. But if he could have breathed, he also could have stopped her.

"Don't do this . . . !" The crate might have been kilometers deep. He felt suddenly thrust away from the rest of the world, abandoned for dead in the abyss. "Gwen, please!"

"Why?" Her face appeared over the side of the crate, and she lowered a squirming border collie in beside him. The other jumped in without having to be told. "I took an officer's oath once, too. Why is it okay for you to play hero and not okay for me?"

He didn't know how to explain. "Because . . ."

"Because why?"

—because the thought of a world without you is too desperate too dark too alone—

"Because you like me?"

The mischievous sparkle in her eyes brought tears into his own. "Yes."

She smiled with touching gentleness. "I love a man who's slow on the uptake." Then she kissed him, quickly enough to catch his drug-fogged brain by surprise, long enough to silence any other protest he might have thought to make. "Take good care of my dogs."

He saw her face for a very long time after she slammed the lid and pushed him out the airlock door.

For once, Llano Verde's wicked mountain winds were going to be a help and not a hindrance.

Sulu spiraled the Bean around into another rising afternoon thermal, using the wind's upward buoyancy to balance the experimental shuttle's unwieldy weight. Boyhood memories of wind-gliding with his great-great-grandfather told him that he ran the risk of the thermal giving out before he reached the top of the Gory Mountains and found a place he could off-load his passengers, but with time ticking inexorably away, that was a risk Sulu had no choice but to take. By the time the shuttle could have lumbered up to this height on its two remaining antigravs, No Escape would have been obliterated and the flood would be well on its way to demolishing other towns farther down the river.

The rising thermal bucked and kicked beneath them, and Sulu heard the infant in the backseat start to cry. He slid a quick glance over at the two children in Uhura's seat, and found their solemn dark eyes fixed on him rather than the scenery. If they were afraid of the shuttle's erratic movements, it didn't show.

"We're almost there," Sulu said, as much to their parents as to them. "We're going to find a place way up high in the mountains for you to wait while the flood goes past—"

"I see it!" That was the father, leaning over to peer out the cockpit's side window. "Look, here it comes—"

The thermal fluttered and sank beneath them before Sulu could manage to catch a glance. Cursing beneath his breath, he wrestled the overburdened Bean up through a layer of stiff mountain downdrafts and found another rising column of heat to ride on. This one swirled him around close enough to the steep slopes of the Little Muddy gorge that he didn't have to peer through the shuttle's side window to see the river below. The main cockpit window now framed a view directly up the narrow, incised canyon—right toward the towering wall of water crashing down over itself like a funneled tsunami. The roar hit them a moment later, so deep and bone-shaking that it sounded more like the thundering boom of an earthquake than a cataract's watery crash.

"It's already inside the gorge," said the young wife in the backseat. Her baby let out a fiercer wail, as if she'd tightened her grip without realizing it. "Oh, my God, look how fast it's moving! Are you sure you can get back in time? My parents are still there, at the clinic . . ."

"Take your children and get back into the cargo hold," Sulu said grimly. "Tell the other people back there not to worry about off-loading any cargo, because I'm not going to take the time to land. They're going to have to jump."

The parents grabbed up their children and skidded down the canted gangway for the cargo hold, while Sulu sent the Bean bouncing across the thermal. He was scanning the dust-hazed hillside ahead of him for a slice of flat space. The only good thing about seeing the flood wave roaring down the gorge was that he now knew just how high he needed to go to make sure the refugees would be safe. He found the spot he wanted at the top of a triangular black cliff, one that protruded from the steeply slanted sides of the gorge like a battleship's prow cutting through fog. The resistant rock made a triangular ledge at the top, large enough to land a shuttle on and high enough to be well out of the flood's destructive path. Sulu sent the Bean angling toward it, his stomach churning with the time it took to climb those last few meters. It seemed like an eternity before the Bean was hovering on its two good thrusters over that rock platform, its cargo hatch door lowered to within a few feet of the ground.

"Everyone out!" Sulu yelled back at the cargo hold. At first, he wasn't sure how he would know when his order had been obeyed, but the flicker of his digital cargo-weight readout caught his eye and reassured him.

Sulu watched the number there dwindle until it was almost—but not quite—back to where it had been. He scowled, wondering if someone had left some luggage behind or if, worse yet, some child had been forgotten in the mad rush to off-load. Before he could decide what to do about the discrepancy, however, a piteous mewling from the cockpit's passenger seats told him what it was. Sulu triggered the hatch door shut again, before his former passengers could jump back aboard to get the family cat.

"If we're lucky, I'll get you back to your people again," he told the feline. "If we're not, it probably won't matter anyway."

Sulu lifted the suddenly responsive Bean up above the milling crowd of refugees, then swooped over the edge of the cliff and hurtled into a steep, efficient dive down the slope of the gorge. The abandoned cat's mew became a howl of protest as its plasteel carrier went airborne with inertia, and even Sulu's hardened stomach lurched. The Bean shook so hard when he pulled it out of that dive that Sulu knew he had finally found the ragged edge of the little shuttle's performance curve. He only hoped he'd live long enough to tell Commander Scott that it had taken the loss of an antigrav to push the Bean to its aerodynamic limits.

The cat howled again as its carrier thumped back to the floor, but the sound was lost in the larger howl of wind that was sweeping over them, stronger and more sustained than any dust storm gust could be. Sulu recognized it as the leading edge of the compressed air mass being chased down the gorge by the flood wave. He realized in sudden terror that everything was wrong—the time estimate he'd given to Uhura, the elevation where he'd left the refugees from No Escape, even the steep dive he'd instinctively sent the Bean into as the quickest route back to the town. In all three cases, he'd forgotten to take into account the deadly blast of air that came before the water, destroying everything below and above with its explosions and debris.

Sulu pulsed the shuttle's antigravs up to their highest power setting, ignoring the blare of warning alarms that ignited across his control panel. His only hope now was to get above that hammering blast of wind and let it propel him from behind, but he'd lost too much altitude in that first dive and the Bean wasn't going to get it back in time. Sulu clenched his teeth and waited for the final killing blow.

It came with an unexpected burst of light, fire-white as a photon torpedo blast and with a shock wave just as powerful. Sulu felt the Bean unexpectedly lifted *up* by that impact, hurled skyward like a fragment of debris along with rocks, trees, and huge twisting spouts of water. The upward motion went on and on, taking him higher than Sulu had thought any blast of flood-compressed air could possibly have flung him. It wasn't until he saw the tops of the Gory Mountains pass below his wings that he realized he couldn't possibly still be feeling the effects of the flood wave. His scattered wits finally came back, and he began to work at the Bean's controls, finding he could once again maneuver his little shuttle despite the surprisingly turbulent air around him. Sulu swung into a wide circle and noticed the unexpected glow of sunshine across his cockpit window. The entire sky had opened up above him, almost as if a hole had been blasted into it.

A hole *had* been blasted into it.

It had also been blasted into the ground below—a new crater that split the Little Muddy's narrow gorge in half, crumbling the walls on both sides and gouging deep into its bottom. The crater walls were still avalanching and falling with enormous splashes into the water-filled interior, but already Sulu could see that it would be an even deeper and more enormous lake than Bull's Eye. The flood wave must have crashed into it just as it formed. Some of water had splashed skyward, some had vaporized in a steam blast whose remnants were still rising like smoke above the valley. But most of it had been diverted into an enormous whirlpool, circling around the edges of its new imprisoning crater rim. Farther downstream, Sulu could see the Little Muddy river already beginning to drain back to its normal levels.

Sulu felt himself shudder with sudden disbelief. Had he died and dreamed himself an afterlife in which the final problem he'd confronted in his lifetime had magically been fixed? How else could you explain the dumbfounding coincidence of a new impact crater forming just where it was most needed to contain the flood, an impact crater so wide and deep it had to have been formed by an even larger bolide than the one that had fallen from the Quake Moon?

Sulu's gut knew the answer to that question before his mind did, and knotted with fierce anguish. There was another way to make a crater that big, a deliberate alternative to the random violence of gravity and space debris. All it needed was a shuttle loaded full of ultrapowerful pure olivium.

And a suicidal pilot.

* * *

Uhura didn't think she'd ever forget the sound of the flood wave crashing down the Little Muddy gorge toward No Escape.

She hadn't really believed it was close enough to hear when Sulu first turned his antigrav thrusters off, despite the frightened couple who swore they did and begged her to take their children on her lap even after the shuttle hold was full. Uhura had put their hysteria down to Sulu's previous use of the power of suggestion, an assumption that made it easy for her to give up her seat in the cockpit and allow the entire young family to leave. But a few minutes later, while she helped carry the last of No Escape's radiation-poisoned flood victims up to the medical clinic's roof, she heard a distinct rumble in the distance. It sounded like a growl of summer thunder, except that it never really died away again. It seemed to retreat into the background for a while, while Mayor Ang Wat set off all the medical building's emergency alarms to alert the rest of No Escape's citizens about the evacuation. But it didn't take long for the subdued growl to rise into a roar, and then into a crashing thunder that made the sirens entirely unnecessary.

Uhura turned toward the gorge, drawn like the remaining settlers to stare at her oncoming destruction. The flood wave itself couldn't be seen beyond the screen of tossing trees that fringed the mouth of the gorge, but Uhura could see a churning mass of upthrown trees, rocks, and debris exploding far above the mountain's shoulder. It was the flood wave's deadly harbinger, she realized, the explosive rolling wave of compressed air blasting its way down the valley ahead of the towering wave itself. Uhura wasn't sure if it was terrifying or reassuring to know that she'd most likely be dead long before the flood wave cascaded over No Escape. The only thing she was sure of was that Sulu couldn't possibly make it back to town ahead of that swift annihilation.

Then the horizon exploded in a pure, silent shock of light.

"Get back down!" Uhura whirled around, pushing and dragging at every person she could reach. "Back into the building! *Now!*"

Some were already headed that way, perhaps hoping the walls of the medical clinic could protect them from the flood's imminent destruction. The rest must have heard the snap of Starfleet experience in Uhura's urgent voice. They turned their backs on the rising aurora that was burning upward through the sky, and rushed instead for the roof's double doors. There was a brief jam and jostle of bodies, until Uhura and Ang Wat took up positions on either side of that portal and held the settlers back until the stairs had cleared, then rationed them through two by two. They were just shoving the last handful down to safety when the sound of the detonation hit them. Uhura never heard it—she just felt the slam inside her ears and the resulting spike of piercing pain. In the utter deafness that followed, all she could do was drag her half of the roof door shut and pray that Ang Wat had the sense to follow her silent lead.

He must have—his burly body slammed against hers as he threw down the locking bar across both doors. The shock wave hit an instant later, a powerful hammering blow that promptly burst the doors inward and flung both of them backward down the stairs. The only thing that saved them was the evacuating queue of people still jammed into the lower part of the stairwell.

That mass of humanity cushioned their fall with its own swaying, jostling flow, then ebbed away beneath them and left them stranded on a landing.

Uhura hauled herself painfully up to her elbows, feeling the warmth of blood seeping from one scraped cheek and trickling from both ears. Across from her, the mayor of No Escape didn't look much healthier. His shoulder hunched at an angle suggesting dislocation, and he wore identical stripes of blood beneath his own ears. But the fierce, almost hysterical anger he'd been suppressing since she'd first seen him seemed to have been punched out by the explosion's hammer blow. The only expression she could read on his broad, radiation-burned face now was bewilderment.

Time passed, and nothing else happened. Ang Wat's puzzled dark eyes went from Uhura's face to the opening left by the burst-in doors at the top of the clinic's stairwell. The only thing pouring in through that gap was a cascade of bright, anomalous sunlight. His gaze came back again, and his mouth moved in a silent question. Like all good communicators, Uhura was trained to read lips in case visual communications were all that was available. Even if she hadn't been, however, she would have known what the mayor was asking.

"It was an explosion," she said, exaggerating the motions of her own lips in the hope he could make out her answer. She couldn't even hear her own voice, although she felt the familiar vibration of her breath through her vocal cords. "It stopped the flood."

Ang Wat frowned and pointed upward, lips silently forming another question. "From the *Enterprise?"*

"I hope so," Uhura said grimly. But deep within her

heart, she was afraid she knew that the real answer to that question was "No."

Five atomospheric shuttles from the *Enterprise* arrived a half-hour after the explosion, swooping down through the wide clear space above the brand-new crater and fanning out across the landscape. Three of them landed in No Escape, disgorging a small army of doctors, nurses, and medical technicians armed with medical scanners and tissue regenerators. Uhura, in the midst of a silent but determined search for victims of the blast wave, found herself forcibly swept up and hauled back to the medical center along with No Escape's vigorously cursing mayor. Judging by the shocked expressions on the Starfleet medical corpsmen, Uhura guessed that Ang Wat was regaling their rescuers with some of Llano Verde's most colorful new idioms and metaphors.

As colorful as those curses undoubtedly were, they didn't seem to have much effect on Leonard McCoy. As soon as they'd been settled into his newly established medical center, the doctor clapped a portable tissue regenerator over Uhura's ears first, then scolded her nonstop for risking permanent hearing loss by walking around with punctured eardrums while he worked on repairing the rest of the blast damage.

"There were other people in worse shape than me," she protested, while he did the same thing to Ang Wat.

"Not very many." McCoy sounded both surprised and impressed. "Aside from the radiation victims you already had, of course, there's not much work here for us to do. So far, we've found five folks with broken arms or ribs, one with a collapsed lung, and a couple with concussions. The rest of 'em said they heard some kind of siren and figured that meant go inside, so they did." The doctor gave her a quizzical look. "How did you know that explosion was going to happen?"

Uhura took a deep breath, reveling in the simple fact that she could once again hear the faint rustle of that sound. "We didn't," she said. "We set the sirens off when we were trying to evacuate." The word "we" reminded her abruptly of Sulu, missing since before the blast. "Has any of the other shuttles located the Bean?"

The slang term made McCoy's mobile eyebrow levitate again. "The *Bean?*"

"That's an antigravity-assisted vertical flight vessel to you, Bones." The amused ring of that familiar voice swung Uhura around toward the medical clinic doorway, her breath catching again in sudden hope. Captain James T. Kirk would never have sounded that lighthearted if he still had *Enterprise* crewmen missing and possibly dead. The *Enterprise*'s commander came over to face Uhura and held out the communicator he carried. "I believe someone's hailing you, Commander."

Uhura flipped the communicator open, blessing the sunlit, olivium-cleared sky for allowing normal hailing frequencies to function again. "Uhura here," she said.

"I found him." It was Sulu's voice, exhausted but exultant. "I remembered that the crates had whistles, so I opened the cockpit window and flew real low."

"*What?*" Uhura tucked her communicator closer to her ear, as if that could somehow help her hear better despite the noisy channel. It wasn't olivium static that was muffling the pilot's voice, but an incongruous feline howling accompanied by a flurry of canine yips and barks. Occasionally, a female voice shouted something and the barking subsided, but then another howl from the cat would start it all over again. "Sulu, did you find Chekov?"

"Chekov, and his girlfriend, and her dogs," the pilot informed her. "They threw themselves out of the orbital shuttle in those big crates we were using to send relief supplies down to the colony, the ones that whistle so you can find them in the dust. I heard the first one while I was trying to spot any wreckage in the crater lake—it was right on the rim. Once I knew what to look for, I just worked my way back up along the flight path they took from Bull's Eye to the new crater."

McCoy was unabashedly listening over Uhura's shoulder. "Did they survive the impact of the crates?" he wanted to know. "They were never designed for living cargo."

"They were both pretty banged up," Sulu said. "Thee got a heavy dose of olivium poisoning from landing so close to the explosion, and Chekov has a nasty projectile hole through his chest. They're back in the cargo hold, still arguing over who's going in the tissue regenerator first. Both the dogs seem to have survived just fine," he added wryly. "But I'm not sure if the cat will hold out until we get it back to its family. Speaking of which, I should probably stop—"

Kirk took the communicator back from Uhura for a moment. "Come straight back to No Escape, Commander," he ordered. "We've already found the settlers you evacuated, and they're on their way here for medical treatment. I'm already sending messages through the orbital platform to all the other Llano Verde towns we can contact, telling them the emergency is over. And

I'm ordering Governor Sedlak to schedule an emergency meeting first thing tomorrow, so we can discuss his policies regarding colony safety and survival procedures."

"Good" was all Sulu said, but there was a wealth of satisfaction in the word. "Is Uhura still there?"

She reached out to take the communicator back, smiling. "I'm here. What do you need?"

"Nothing," said the pilot. "I just thought you'd like to finally get to say it."

It took her tired brain a moment to realize what he meant, but then her smile widened. "Uhura to Sulu," she said. The familiar words felt like a balm to her bruised throat. "Come in, Sulu."

"Sulu here," he said. "I'm in sight of No Escape and getting ready to land."

"Acknowledged," Uhura said, and took a deep, fulfilled breath. "Uhura out."

Chapter Eighteen

SIX WEEKS LATER, Uhura barely recognized the valley of the river that the irreverent colonists of Llano Verde now called the Little Messy.

She glanced down from the side window of the Bean as Sulu swung it around in an unusually exuberant arc. After four weeks of monsoonal rains, Llano Verde's skies were nearly clear of windblown sediment, with only a faint icy glitter of olivium left high in the stratosphere to catch the glow of sunrise and sunset and make them spectacularly beautiful. Aside from the occasional quiver of their instrument readings and the faint background crackle of remnant olivium on most communicator channels, there was almost nothing left to remind them of the island continent's first excruciating winter.

Except for the pale cerulean glimmer of water Uhura could see just ahead of them.

The Little Messy's floodplain, judiciously seeded with native Belle Terre wild grasses by the New Rachel Carson Society, had bloomed into a model spring prairie, nearly Earth-like in its lush and verdant green. Unseen among those grasses were native hunting cats and lagomorphs, shy ungulates and graceful walking birds, all painstakingly restored from DNA scans of pre-Burn specimens. What wasn't there, much to the Federation's surprise and the Carsons' delight, were any settlers.

Uhura shook her head, remembering the uproar over that. Governor Sedlak might be a man of very narrow vision, to whom theories were more powerful than unseen proof, but his decisions were utterly logical. When James T. Kirk had dragged him on a tour of Llano Verde's devastated river towns, intending to show him the need for rebuilding, he'd responded by turning every flood-prone river bottom into an inviolate provincial park. His colonists might grumble and complain at the loss of prime farming land, but none of them would ever again lose a house or homestead to the rush of floodwaters.

The Bean turned again, settling down in a spiral that was more artful than necessary. Uhura dragged her gaze from the shimmering landscape to Sulu's bland profile. "Who are you showing off for?" she inquired. "I thought the hydrologists were working on the northern side of the Gory Mountains today."

Sulu slanted her an amused look. "Bev said she might drop by to check on the olivium levels in the lake, if she got a chance. How's Ang Wat doing these days?"

"A lot better since we got the new emergency alert channel up and running for the Gory Mountain sector,"

Uhura said tranquilly. "He wants to know when No Escape is going to get their own medical transport Bean from Emergency Services."

"As soon as we get to the N part of the alphabet," said the interim head of Emergency Services. "And tell him that no amount of smoked guanaco sausage is going to make that change."

"I think he's just trying to make sure he's one of the citizens you select for the pilot training."

Uhura watched the silky blue glimmer of Crash Lake widen until it stretched from wall to gouged-out wall of the Little Messy gorge. The rims of this crater were green and growing, not poisoned and dusty. Most of the olivium that had been mined from Bull's Eye had transformed itself into pure energy on impact, obeying the laws of Einstein and Cochrane. The rest had been buried so deeply that neither radiation nor heat had yet escaped.

Greg Anthony theorized that in a few more decades, minor hot springs might appear on the crater's flanks. But so far, all of his and Weir's measurements showed that the water in the crater was pure and drinkable. As a result, Montgomery Scott had spent the last few weeks happily designing a hydroelectric plant and irrigation system for all the farmers who'd been resettled on the fertile but dry lower slopes of the Gory Mountains. The upper slopes had proved more hospitable to sheep and guanaco herders, forcing the two groups of settlers to mix and intermingle along the mountainside instead of separating into isolated communities. Uhura also suspected a certain Starfleet officer who'd volunteered the remainder of his reassignment leave to help organize an effective rural police patrol for Llano Verde might also have had something to do with that.

"Do you see them yet?"

"No." Sulu circled the Bean lower, while Uhura peered out at the shores of the lake. She could see colorful splashes of wildflowers resolving along the shoreline, russet and teal and gold. The russet ones seemed to be drifting along the shore. After a minute, she realized she was looking down on the fuzzy backs of a herd of guanacos. Familiar streaks of black and white circled the grazing flock in ceaseless, instinctive motion.

"There they are." She pointed, and Sulu brought the Bean down to the surface with a less pretty but more efficient swoop. Through the opened side window, Uhura could hear the alarmed hums and trills of the animals, and the responsive whistles of their herder. A dog flashed past the Bean even as it settled, oblivious of all but its task of keeping the flock together. It circled around to catch the frightened surge of guanacos, then slowly walked them back toward its handler. Sulu craned his head out the window and whistled in amazement.

"Not too bad," he called out of the cockpit window. "All you have to do is work a little harder on that Scottish accent."

"That'll do," said an embarrassed and distinctly Russian-accented voice. "Xander, Jackson, here to me."

Uhura laughed and unclipped her safety harness, then headed back to the cargo hold. By the time the ramp descended, the guanacos were back to grazing peacefully along the shore, and Gwen Thee was scolding Chekov about his whistle commands while a handful of black and merle dogs orbited around them. Uhura smiled and lifted the picnic basket Sulu had packed for them, glad that she'd thought to remind the pilot to include some dog treats.

"Hey there." Thee paused in her instructions long enough to smile at both of them, as happily as if she wasn't giving up one of her last few days with Chekov to share a meal with his old friends. "I hope you guys brought something better than native herb salad and fruit kabobs this time. I'm starving."

"Don't worry," Sulu assured her, lugging a portable grill down the ramp after Uhura. "I got something that'll really stick to your ribs. And I know Chekov's been wanting to try it."

"I have?" The Russian looked a little dubious about that, but Uhura could see that the old lines of anxiety and regret had finally vanished from his suntanned face. The combination of hard work setting up his police force and time spent outdoors with Thee and her dogs seemed to have finally brought him the rest and relaxation he hadn't found up on the orbital platform. Or maybe that was just because of Thee. "I don't remember asking for anything special."

"Sure you do." Sulu finished setting up the grill beside the lake and lit it with a flourish that made all the dogs prick up their ears. "It was a couple weeks back, when you came to Big Muddy to testify at Serafini and Bartels's sentencing hearing. I distinctly remember you saying that you never had gotten to eat any real Llano Verde barbecue."

Thee exchanged laughing glances with Uhura, as she helped set out the plates and picnic cloth. "As I recall, those words were prefaced by something along the lines of 'Thank God.' "

"No, that was when he heard the sentence," Sulu insisted.

Chekov's tanned skin darkened a little. "A lifetime on a desert penal colony just seemed like an appropriate punishment for wiping out What's the Point and Desperation . . ."

"It was," Thee agreed. "I'm actually surprised Sedlak got so creative."

Uhura sat cross-legged on the picnic cloth, enjoying the view of the Gory Mountains across the ice-blue expanse of water. "I think Captain Kirk and Evan Pardonnet had a little something to do with that . . . You know, you guys sure know how to make a nice lake."

Thee roared with laughter, and even Chekov relaxed into an appreciative smile. "We do, don't we?" he said, and reached out a surreptitious hand to clasp Thee's. "I may have to come back and retire here, too, after a couple of tours on the *Reliant.*"

"Feel free," said the former Starfleet officer, smiling. "I'll always have a dog for you to play with."

"So you're still planning to go?" Uhura had begun to wonder during the last few weeks. As uncertain as Chekov had been about leaving the *Enterprise,* even for such a prestigious assignment, his confidence had grown visibly since starting the work of reorganizing Llano Verde's police force. He'd seemed to come into himself, grown into responsibilities even greater than those he'd had as chief of security. While Uhura thought the change suited him well, she wasn't sure if he recognized the improvement as something that would serve him well as an executive officer, or as something he could only have on Belle Terre.

Chekov leaned back on his elbows, frowning thoughtfully. "Let me see. Spend the rest of my career on a state-of-the-art starship, with a comfortably controlled climate, a full set of radiation shields, and a well-stocked medical bay—or wander around the Outland on camelback, shoveling guanaco guano." He made a show of collapsing under Thee's elbow jab, then fought her off, laughing, as he sat up again. "Yes," he said in answer to Uhura's question, "I'm going." Then, more to the point, "I'm ready to go."

Uhura couldn't agree more.

"There." With the grill finally flaming to his satisfaction, Sulu opened his insulated basket and pulled out a slab of what looked like ribs. "Ladies and gentlemen, you are about to be treated to authentic Llano Verde guanaco barbecue." He extracted a bottle of something that glittered suspiciously when he shook it. "Complete with extra-spicy olivium sauce."

"What?" Chekov's fierce scowl made both Uhura and Thee break into laughter again. "Sulu, you're not really going to put olivium in our lunch, are you?"

"The recipe calls for it," protested the pilot. "And it's not as if you can't get a quick tissue regeneration down in No Escape later on today—"

"No," Chekov said. He glanced at Thee meaningfully, then scrambled to his feet. "After all of the guano I've shoveled the last few weeks, I don't mind eating a guanaco or two. But I draw the line at eating olivium!"

"On purpose," Thee added, and stood up beside him. The dog trainer gave a quick whistle, and then the two of them flanked Sulu as neatly as a pair of border collies.

The helmsman yelped as they hoisted him up between them, but he was already laughing too hard to resist. By the time he saw where they were headed, it was too late to stop the momentum. "Uhura! Tell them to stop!" he pleaded over his shoulder.

"I don't think I have the authority to order Belle Terre citizens around," she said judiciously. "Of course, we could always establish a cooperative venture between Starfleet and the colony. How does this sound? Five, four, three, two—"

The splash that ended her countdown was big enough to quench the fire on the grill. By a vote of three to one, they decided that was probably just as well.

Captain Kirk was in his quarters when the Kauld ship attacked. It was late in the evening—past eleven—and he had been trying for the last hour to put down the twenty-first-century potboiler he had picked up for a little mindless entertainment before bedtime, but Ryan Hughes's tale of piracy and romance in the early Lunar colonies had proven more engaging than he'd expected. He was three-quarters of the way into it when the intercom whistled for his attention.

He pressed the reply button on the wall panel beside his bed. "Kirk here."

"Captain," Spock said. "Sensors have picked up a Kauld warship approaching the planet. It is a single vessel traveling through normal space under half-impulse power. It does not respond to our hails."

For a moment Kirk couldn't make sense of it. Kauld ships on Luna? In the twenty-first century? But then his own reality reasserted itself, and he remembered where he was. This was the Belle Terre system, and the Kauld had been harassing the Federation colonists ever since they had arrived here, nearly a year ago.

"Go to yellow alert," Kirk said. "Move to intercept. I'll be right there."

"Acknowledged."

Kirk looked for a bookmark, but there was nothing within reach that would work. He fingered the pages—real paper, printed especially for the colony library—

then dog-eared page 248 and set the book on his bed. He would probably hear no end of grief about that from the librarian, but it was either that or lay the book facedown and risk breaking the spine. That would probably lose him his library card, one of the few pleasures this colony world, far beyond the edge of civilization, had to offer.

He was alone in the turbolift on the way to the bridge. This time of night, most of the crew were in their quarters or at their graveyard-shift duty stations. He wondered if the Kauld knew that, and if they expected it to affect the *Enterprise*'s ability to respond. If so, they would get a rude surprise. The same people who worked the day shift rotated through night duty as well; there wasn't an inexperienced crew member on board.

And few of them would regret kicking some Kauld butt in the name of defense. It wasn't professional, it wasn't Starfleet, but there it was. These sapphire-skinned, bad-tempered, antagonistic aliens had been a thorn in the *Enterprise*'s side ever since the colony convoy had entered the Sagittarian sector. What had originally been intended as a simple escort mission while on her way into deeper space had instead become an extended peacekeeping job—in part because of these alien troublemakers.

The turbolift doors opened and Kirk stepped onto the bridge. Normally at this hour, the lights would have been at half-intensity to simulate a diurnal schedule, but during a yellow alert everything went back to full operational status. He noted that Sulu was at the helm and Thomsen was at the navigation console. Thomsen was less experienced than Sulu, but she was a good navigator, and she had been gaining much more experience since Chekov had left to join the *Reliant*.

Spock was seated in the captain's chair, but he vacated it as Kirk stepped forward.

"Report," Kirk said.

Spock stepped through the gap in the railing around the captain's chair and stood by his science station. "No change. The Kauld ship is continuing on course toward the planet and refuses to respond to our warnings." He studied one of his displays for a moment, then added, "Deep-space scans do not reveal any other supporting ships. It appears that they are acting alone."

Kirk looked past the helmsman and navigator to the main viewscreen, which showed the boxy, utilitarian Kauld fighter as it sped toward its goal: the Federation colony planet Belle Terre. Was this some kind of renegade attack? Surely the Kauld crew knew they were outgunned. Besides the *Enterprise,* there were a couple of dozen other starships orbiting the planet; mostly colony freighters, but the Kauld had learned before that those ships were far from helpless.

"They usually gang up five to one," Kirk said. "This doesn't feel right."

"It is most illogical, even for Kauld," Spock agreed.

"Helm, fire a warning shot across their bow," Kirk ordered. "Let's see if that gets their attention."

"Aye, sir," said Sulu. His fingers danced on the control console, and a bright red phaser beam lanced out just kilometers ahead of the warship.

Kirk didn't have to ask his crew for the information he needed. They reported without prompting.

"No change in velocity or trajectory, Captain," said Thomsen.

"The Kauld have activated their weapons," Spock said.

"No response to our hails, sir," said Jolley, the relief communications officer.

"They can hear us. Open a channel," Kirk ordered.

"Channel open."

"This is Captain Kirk of the *Starship Enterprise.* You are intruding in Federation space. Turn back now, or we'll be forced to interpret your actions as aggressive and act accordingly."

Cold silence answered back.

"The Kauld ship is 28,500 kilometers from the planet's atmosphere and closing rapidly," Spock said. "And there is a further anomaly in their attack strategy: I read only a skeleton crew on board."

"You think it's a kamikaze ship?" Kirk asked.

"That seems likely."

If that was the aliens' game, Kirk felt sorry for them. He didn't like the idea of firing on a poorly defended ship, but he would do it if he had to. There were sixty thousand colonists on Belle Terre who depended on him for their safety; he wouldn't risk their lives to spare a hostile intruder just because it wasn't sporting.

There was also the quasar olivium mine to consider. That, not the planet, was what the Kauld wanted so badly, and it was a prize worth fighting for. There was enough quasimatter in the core of Belle Terre's largest moon to power the entire Federation for decades. It could also power the Kauld, their rivals the Blood, the Klingon Empire, the Romulan Empire, and half a dozen other enemies as well. Kirk wasn't going to risk that out of misguided sympathy for a suicide crew. Several shipments of olivium had been intercepted by pirates on the long trip back to Federation space; if the Kauld had been behind the pirates—as Kirk suspected they were—then they already had enough to put a doomsday-type bomb on board that ship.

But since it was just one ship, there might be a chance to stop them without bloodshed. "Get a tractor beam on them," he said.

Sulu complied, but the moment the Kauld felt the effect, they fired on the *Enterprise.* Shields flared as the disruptor beam struck, and the bridge shook as the inertial dampers fought to counteract the impact.

Another disruptor shot pounded the same spot.

"Tractor beam is off-line," Sulu called out.

"Shields down to sixty percent," Thomsen said.

The Kauld had signed their own death warrant. "Lock phasers on target," Kirk said.

"Locked and ready," Sulu replied.

"Fire."

The bright red beam lanced out again, this time striking the warship directly in the port flank. Its shields flared bright as they radiated the energy, but Sulu kept the beam centered until it burned through and sliced deep into the ship's interior. Bright flame shot out of the gash, dissipating immediately in the vacuum of space . . . then an explosion ripped the ship in half and sent the two pieces tumbling in opposite directions, spewing debris from their interiors as they spun.

"Survivors?" Kirk asked.

"No life-forms register," said Spock.

"What about anomalous energy signatures? Is there a bomb on board?"

"None in evidence, but at this distance they could shield it from our sensors."

"That's what I thought. Sulu, Thomsen, target both halves. Carve them into pieces."

"Aye, sir."

The bridge crew watched as the helmsman and navigator each took a target and proceeded to reduce them to debris. They only had a few seconds before the pieces hit atmosphere, but they crisscrossed the halves of the hull with phaser fire until they fell open like blossoming flowers, then played the phasers over the exposed interiors. Power sources erupted in bright red explosions, contributing yet more destruction, but they triggered nothing resembling a true bomb.

"Cease fire," Kirk said when the first of the pieces began to strike atmosphere. They hit near the twilight band and left bright streaks of ionized air in their wakes. That would be a great light show from the ground. Some of the pieces skipped off the atmosphere and burned again farther into the daylight side of the planet.

He sat in his chair, still staring at the screen long after the last of the pieces had burned out. This had been too easy.

"Any life pods launched?" he asked.

"Negative," said Spock.

"Signals? Did they send any messages or beam anything out before we hit them?"

"No, sir," said Jolley.

"Then what exactly were they trying to accomplish here?"

Nobody spoke.

Kirk looked at the screen again, which still showed the planet turning serenely below as the *Enterprise* slid from the night side into day. "They didn't just throw a warship away for nothing. What did they get out of it? They already know our weapons capabilities. They knew we would fire on them. What did they gain just now?"

"Allies?" suggested Thomsen.

"How so?"

"Maybe they wanted to show someone how ruthless we are."

Kirk rubbed his chin, thinking. The scratchy day's growth of whiskers felt good on his hand, which he only now realized he'd been holding clenched since he entered the bridge.

"Are there any Kauld observers in evidence?" he asked.

"Nothing within the planetary system," Spock said. "I detect faint energy signatures in deep space nearly five light-days out, but even they are not conclusively Kauld or Blood."

"They wouldn't want to wait five days to find out how things came down here," said Kirk. "Keep a continual scan going for warp signatures along the wave front as the light from this heads through the solar system. And listen for subspace signals from spies on the ground—or on the moons or the outer planets. They might already have put observers in place."

He leaned back in his command chair and looked out at the planet again. White clouds over blue ocean and green-brown land; it was an oasis in a vast desert of empty space far, far away from the rest of the Federation. It had taken the colonists over nine months at warp speed just to get here. They hadn't come for the olivium, but once it was discovered they had had no choice but to protect it from the aliens who wanted it for themselves. It was too powerful to allow it to fall into the wrong hands. So now the colonists were caught in a struggle for survival in a star system so far away they couldn't even see Earth's sun with a telescope. They had enough raw power to destroy every planet between here and there—but without the technical infrastructure to harness it, it was useless to them.

Still, they had become custodians of the most sought-after element in the Alpha Quadrant. Belle Terre was already becoming a crossroads, and by the time the olivium was mined out, it would be a commercial hub for light-years around.

Provided it didn't fall to the Kauld first. And the only thing preventing that was the *Enterprise.*

What if Thomsen was right? If the Kauld had finally admitted that they couldn't win this battle by themselves, then they might be trying to win allies. That might be harder to do than it sounded, though. Before the human colonists had entered their midst, they had been busy trying to conquer every other race in their sector. Kirk doubted if anyone would join them without major concessions ahead of time, and after decades of war the Kauld had nothing to give.

Their only bargaining chip would be the promise of a share in the olivium if they won, but Kirk couldn't imagine anyone stupid enough to believe that the Kauld would actually keep that promise.

No, gaining allies wasn't their way. They were up to something else. But what was it?

Continues in
Star Trek: New Earth #4
The Flaming Arrow
Now on sale

OUR FIRST SERIAL NOVEL!

The Final Chapter . . .

The very beginning of the Starfleet Adventure . . .

STAR TREK®
STARFLEET: YEAR ONE

A Novel in Twelve Parts®

by
Michael Jan Friedman

Chapter Twelve

As soon as Hiro Matsura reached the *Yellowjacket*'s bridge, he took stock of its viewscreen.

He could see what his first officer had described to him via communicator minutes earlier—a formation of fourteen alien ships, each one a deadly dark triangle. And without a doubt, they were bearing down on the colony world from which Matsura's pod had just returned.

The last time he had seen the aggressors, they had all but crippled his ship—a setback from which the crew of the *Yellowjacket* was still trying desperately to recover. The ship's shields, lasers, and atomic weapon launchers had yet to be brought back online, and her impulse engines were too sluggish to be effective.

In short, the *Yellowjacket* wasn't fit to engage the enemy. If she entered the field of battle, she would be nothing more than a target—and therefore a liability to her sister ships.

The odds against Matsura's comrades were considerable. It galled the captain to have to hang back at a safe distance and watch the aliens tear chunks out of their Christophers.

But it didn't seem like he had much of a choice.

Aaron Stiles glared at his viewscreen, which showed him so many enemy ships that they seemed to blot out the stars.

It would have been a daunting sight even if three of his fellow captains weren't butterfly catchers. As it was, only he and Hagedorn could point to any real combat experience—a deficit which prevented the five of them from executing maneuvers as a group.

Stiles would have much preferred to fly alongside his old wingmates—veteran space fighters like Andre Beschta and Amanda McTigue and his brother Jake. Then they would have *had* something.

Of course, Shumar, Dane, and Cobaryn had plenty of former Earth Command officers on their bridges. If they paid them some mind, they might have a chance to come through this.

Yeah, right, Stiles thought. *And I'm the King of Tennessee.* If he and Hagedorn couldn't beat *four* of the triangle ships, how was their little fleet supposed to beat *fourteen?*

He scowled and began barking out orders. "Raise shields. Power to all batteries. Mr. Bagdasarian, target atomics."

Weeks, the better weapons officer, was still in sickbay. But with the aliens packed into such a tight formation, Bagdasarian wouldn't need a marksman's eye to hit something.

"Atomics targeted," came Bagdasarian's reply. And a moment later, he added, "Range, sir."

"Fire!" bellowed Stiles.

A black-and-gold missile erupted from the *Gibraltar* and shot through the void in the enemy's direction. For a fraction of a second, it was on its own. Then four other missiles came hurtling after it.

Apparently, the captain's colleagues were all thinking along the same lines he was. It was more than he had expected.

As his missile found a target, it vanished in a burst of blinding white light. The other missiles struck the enemy in quick succession, each one swallowed up in a light show of its own.

But when the alien armada became visible again, it wasn't clear if the atomics had done any damage. The enemy vessels looked every bit as dangerous as they had before.

A voice came through the comm grate in Stiles's armrest. "Stay outside them," Hagedorn advised the group. "The longer they remain bunched that way, the better our chances."

The man was right, of course. Stiles regarded his weapons officer. "Fire again!" he snapped.

The *Gibraltar* sent a second black-and-gold missile hurtling toward the alien formation. Over the next couple of heartbeats, the other captains followed Stiles's example.

Unfortunately, their second barrage wasn't any more productive than the first. It lit up the void for a moment, but the enemy shook off its impact and kept coming.

And by then it was too late to launch a third barrage anyway. They were too close to the aliens to risk atomics.

"Target lasers!" Stiles roared.

As if the enemy had read his mind, the triangle ships abandoned their formation and went twisting off in pairs. Suddenly, they weren't such easy targets anymore.

"Fire at will!" the captain told Bagdasarian.

The weapons officer unleashed the fury of their laser batteries on the nearest pair of enemy vessels. At the last possible moment, the triangles peeled off and eluded the beams.

Then they came after the *Gibraltar.*

Stiles glowered at them. "Evade!" he urged his helm officer.

Urbina did her best to slip the aliens' knot, but it tightened altogether too quickly. The *Gibraltar* was wracked by one blinding-white assault after another, each barrage like a giant fist punishing the vessel to the limits of her endurance.

A console exploded directly behind the captain, singeing the hairs on the back of his neck. As sparks hissed and smoke billowed darkly, his deck lurched one way and then the other like a skiff on a stormy sea.

But Stiles held on. They all did.

By the time the enemy shot past them, the *Gibraltar* was in a bad way. The captain knew that even before he was told that their shields were down eighty-five percent, or that they had lost power to the starboard nacelle.

"They're coming about for another shot at us!" Rosten called out abruptly, her voice hoarse and thin with smoke.

Stiles swore beneath his breath. "Shake them!" he told Urbina.

The helm officer sent them twisting through space, even without any help from their damaged nacelle. And somehow, she did what the captain had demanded of her. She shook the triangles from their tail.

It looked as if they were safe, at least for a moment. Then Stiles saw the two alien vessels sliding into view from another quarter, setting their sights on the poorly shielded *Gibraltar.*

"Enemy to port!" Rosten called out.

The captain felt his throat constrict. This must have been how his brother Jake felt before the Romulans blew him to pieces.

"Target and fire!" he thundered.

If they were going to go down, it wouldn't be without a fight. Stiles promised himself that.

But before the aliens could get a barrage off, a metallic shadow swept between the *Gibraltar* and her antagonists. It took Stiles a second to realize that it was one of the other Christophers, trying to shield him and his crew from the enemy.

He couldn't see the triangles' weapons ports as they fired, but he saw the ruddy flare of light beyond the curve of the other Christopher's hull and the way the Starfleet vessel shuddered under the impact.

The captain didn't know for certain which of his colleagues was risking his life to save the *Gibraltar.* However, he guessed that it was Hagedorn. It was the kind of chance only a soldier would take.

The aliens pounded the interceding ship a second time and a third, but Stiles wouldn't let his comrade protect him any longer. Glancing at Urbina, he said, "Get us a clear shot, Lieutenant."

"Aye, sir," came the reply.

"Ready lasers," the captain told Bagdasarian.

"Ready, sir."

"Fire as soon as you've got a target," Stiles told him.

As Urbina dropped them below the level of the other Christopher, Bagdasarian didn't hesitate for even a fraction of second. He unleashed a couple of devastating blue laser volleys that struck the enemy vessels from below, forcing them to give ground—at least for the time being.

Stiles turned to Rosten, taking advantage of the respite. "Raise Captain Hagedorn," he said. "See how badly he's damaged."

But when the navigator bent to her task, she seemed to find something that surprised her. "It's not the *Horatio,*" she reported crisply. "It's the *Maverick,* sir."

Stiles looked at her. *Dane?*

A moment later, the Cochrane jockey's voice came crackling over the *Gibraltar*'s comm system. He sounded as if he were talking about a barroom brawl instead of a dogfight.

"Looks like I bit off more than I could chew," said Dane. "Everything's down . . . shields, weapons, you name it. I'm not going to be much help from here on in."

"I'll do what I can to protect you," Stiles assured him.

There was a pause, as Dane seemed to realize whom he was talking to. "You just want to make sure nothing happens to that pistol I won."

"Damned right," said Stiles.

But, of course, the pistol was the farthest thing from his mind. He was trying to figure out how he was going to repay Dane's favor without getting his ship carved up in the process.

* * *

Hiro Matsura had never felt so helpless in his life.

The other captains were fighting valiantly, dodging energy volley after energy volley, but it wasn't getting them anywhere. With one of their ships disabled—perhaps as badly as the *Yellowjacket*—the tide of battle was slowly but inexorably turning against them. In time, the aliens would blow them out of space.

But Matsura couldn't do anything about it—not with his ship in its current state of disrepair. With his weapons down and his shield generators mangled, he would only be offering himself up as cannon fodder.

He wished he could speak to the aliens. Then he would let them know that he understood the reason for their hostility. He would make them see that it was all a misunderstanding.

But he *couldn't* speak to them—not without programming their language into his ship's computer. And if he knew their language, he wouldn't require the computer's help in the first place.

As Matsura looked on, Hagedorn's ship absorbed another blinding, bludgeoning barrage. Then the same thing happened to Shumar's ship, and Cobaryn's. Their deflector grids had to be failing. Pretty soon, they would all be as helpless as the *Yellowjacket.*

The captain's fists clenched. *Dammit,* he thought bitterly, *there's got to be* something *I can do.*

His excavation of the mound on Oreias Eight had put the key to the problem in his hands. He just had to figure out what to unlock with it.

Unlock? he repeated inwardly.

And then it came to him.

There might be a way to help the other ships after all. It was a long shot, but he had taken long shots before.

Swinging himself out of his center seat, Matsura said, "Jezzelis, you're with me." Then he grabbed the Vobilite's arm and pulled him in the direction of the lift.

"Sir?" said Jezzelis, doing his best to keep up.

The captain punched the bulkhead pad, summoning the lift. "I need help with something," he told his exec.

"With what?" asked Jezzelis.

Just then, the lift doors hissed open. Moving inside, Matsura tapped in their destination. By the time he was finished, his first officer had entered the compartment too.

"Captain," said Jezzelis, "I would—"

Matsura held up a hand for silence. Then he pressed the stud that activated the ship's intercom. "Spencer, Naulty, Brosius, Jimenez . . . this is the captain. Meet me on deck six."

A string of affirmative responses followed his command. All four of the security officers would be there, Matsura assured himself.

His exec looked at him askance, no doubt trying to figure out what could be so pressing about deck six. After all, there was nothing there except cargo space and equipment lockers.

"Mr. McDonald," the captain went on, "report to the transporter room and stand by."

"The transporter . . . ?" Jezzelis wondered out loud.

Then they reached deck six and the doors opened. Spencer, Naulty, Brosius, and Jimenez were just arriving.

"Follow me," said Matsura, swinging out of the lift compartment and darting down the corridor.

He could hear the others pelting along after him, matching him stride for stride. No doubt, the four security officers were every bit as curious as Jezzelis. Unfortunately, there was no time for an explanation.

If his plan was going to stand a chance, he had to move quickly.

The captain negotiated a couple of turns in the passage. Then he came to a door and pounded on the bulkhead controls beside it. A moment later, the titanium panel slid aside, revealing two facing rows of gold lockers in a long, narrow cabin.

Matsura knew exactly what each locker contained—a fully charged palm-sized flashlight, a small black packet of barely edible rations, and an Earth Command emergency containment suit.

There were two dozen of the gold-and-black suits in all, each one boasting a hood with an airtight visor. As bulky as they were, a normal man wouldn't be able to carry more than four of them at once—which was why Matsura had brought help along.

As Jezzelis and the others caught up with him, the captain tapped a three-digit security code into a pad on one of the lockers. When the door swung open, he grabbed the suit inside the locker and gestured for his assistants to do the same.

"Take them to the transporter room," he barked.

Invading one locker after the other, Matsura dragged out three more suits. They weighed his arms down as if they were full of lead. Satisfied that he couldn't carry any more, he made his way back to the lift.

Jezzelis was right behind him. With his powerful Vobilite musculature, the first officer didn't seem half as encumbered as his captain did. As Matsura struck the bulkhead panel and got the doors to open for them, Jezzelis helped the human with his ungainly burden.

"Thanks," Matsura breathed, making his way to a wall of the compartment and leaning against it for support.

The Vobilite took advantage of the respite to pin the captain down. "If I may ask, sir . . . exactly what are we doing?"

Matsura told him.

Then the others piled into the turbolift with them, and the captain programmed in a destination—the transporter room. As luck would have it, it was only a deck below them.

The ride down took only a few seconds. Jimenez was the first one to bolt into the corridor with his armful of containment suits. Matsura was last—but not by much.

As they spilled into the room, McDonald was waiting for them at the control console. He looked confused when he saw what the captain and his helpers were bringing in.

"Sir . . . ?" said the transporter operator, staring at Matsura as if he was afraid the man had lost his mind.

"Don't ask," the captain told him, dumping his suits on the raised transporter platform. "Just drop what's left of our shields and beam these out into space—say, a hundred meters from the ship."

McDonald hesitated for a fraction of a second, as if he thought he might have been the butt of a very bizarre joke. Then he activated the transporter system, overrode shield control, and did as Matsura had ordered.

The captain pointed to Jezzelis. "Yours next."

His first officer deposited his load on the platform. At a nod from Matsura, McDonald beamed that into space as well.

It seemed to take forever, but the captain saw every one of their two dozen Earth Command–issue containment garments dispatched to the void. Only then did he take a deep breath, wipe the sweat from his forehead with the back of his hand, and start back in the direction of the turbolift.

He had to get back to the bridge. It was there that he would find out if his idea had been as crazy as it seemed.

Connor Dane didn't like the idea of being protected by Aaron Stiles. For that matter, he didn't like the idea of being protected by *anybody.*

Unfortunately, he wasn't in much of a position to complain about it. It wasn't just *his* life on the line—it was his crew's lives as well. And he had no one to blame but himself.

If he hadn't risked the *Maverick* to keep the aliens from destroying the *Gibraltar,* his ship wouldn't be a useless piece of junk now. He would still be trading punches with the enemy instead of cringing every time a dark triangle veered his way.

Of course, the enemy had all but ignored him since the moment his ship was disabled. Obviously, they had more viable fish to fry. But eventually, they would finish frying them—and then Dane's ship would be slagged with a few good energy bursts.

Not a pleasant thought, he mused. He looked around his bridge at his officers, whose expressions told him they were thinking the same thing.

They deserved a lot better than the fate he had obtained for them. But then, so did everyone else in the fleet. There were brave, dedicated people serving under every one of Dane's colleagues.

And it looked like their only legacy would be a few odd scraps of charred space debris.

"Sir," said his navigator, "something seems to be happening in the vicinity of the *Yellowjacket.*"

Dane turned to her. "Are they being attacked?"

Ideko shook her black-and-white-striped head from side to side. "No, sir. It's something else. I—"

"Yes?" said the captain.

Ideko frowned and called up additional information. Then she frowned even more. "Sensors say they're containment suits, sir."

Dane looked at her. Then he turned to his screen, daring it to show him what his navigator had described. "Give me a view of the *Yellowjacket,* Lieutenant. I'd like to see this for myself."

A moment later, an image of Matsura's ship filled the screen. And just as Ideko had reported, there was a swarm of black-and-gold containment suits floating outside the vessel.

"I'll be deep fried," the captain muttered. He leaned forward in his chair and studied the *Yellowjacket* more closely. "There's no sign of a hull breach," he concluded.

"None," agreed Nasir, who had taken up a position on Dane's flank.

"So what are they doing out there?" Dane wondered.

No one answered him.

The captain was still trying to figure it out when one of the triangles separated itself from the thick of the battle and headed in the direction of the *Yellowjacket.*

Like the *Maverick,* the *Yellowjacket* was defenseless. It had no weapons, no shields . . . no threat to keep the enemy at bay.

Damn, thought Dane, feeling a pang of sympathy for his colleague. *This is it for Matsura.*

Of course, he expected Matsura to give the aliens a run for their money—to buy as much time as possible for his crew, or maybe even try to maneuver the enemy into the sights of another Christopher.

But the captain of the *Yellowjacket* didn't do a thing. He just sat there, as if resigned to the fact of his doom.

Dane was surprised. Matsura had seemed like the type to fight to the end, no matter how small the chances of his succeeding. *Apparently,* he thought, *I was wrong about him.*

As the alien ship bore down on the *Yellowjacket,* Dane grimaced in anticipation. But the deadly energy burst never came. Instead, the triangle slowed down, came to a stop in front of the toothless Christopher . . .

And just sat there.

Nasir muttered a curse.

"You can say that again," Dane told him.

The triangle reminded him of a dog sniffing something new in the neighborhood. But what was new about the *Yellowjacket?* Hadn't the aliens run into Starfleet vessels twice before?

Then it came to him. But before the captain could make mention of it, his comm grate came alive with Matsura's voice.

"Don't ask questions," said the captain of the *Yellowjacket.* "Just transport all your containment suits into space. I'll explain later."

Dane looked at his first officer. "You heard the man, Mr. Nasir. We've got work to do."

Before Nasir could utter a protest, Dane swung out of his chair and headed for the turbolift.

Alonis Cobaryn was stunned.

A scant few minutes earlier, he had been entangled in the fight of his life, battered by an implacable enemy at every turn. Now he was watching that same enemy withdraw peacefully from the field of battle, its weapons obligingly powered down.

Except for one triangle-shaped ship . . . and that one was hanging nose to nose with the *Yellowjacket* in the midst of nearly a hundred and fifty black-and-gold containment suits, looking as patient and deliberate as a Vulcan.

Clearly, it wanted something. Cobaryn just wished he knew *what.*

Tapping the stud on his intercom, he opened a channel to the *Yellowjacket.* "Captain Matsura," he said, "you offered to provide an explanation. This might be a propitious time."

"Damned right," said Dane, joining their conversation. "Exactly what did we just do?"

"And," added Cobaryn, "how did you know it would work?"

"Believe me," said Matsura. "I didn't. I was wishing I could speak to the aliens, tell them somehow that we weren't trying to dishonor their burial mounds . . . and it occurred to me that what we needed was some kind of peace offering. But it had to be an offering they understood—something they would immediately recognize as precious."

"Something like . . . a year's supply of containment suits?" Dane asked, clearly still in the dark.

"Remember," said Matsura, "the aliens had never seen a human being—or, for that matter, a member of any other Federation species. I was hoping they would identify the suits as our *shells*—or at least what passes for shells in our society."

Cobaryn was beginning to understand. "And if we were anything like them, these so-called shells would have great spiritual value."

"Exactly," said Matsura. "And anyone who's generous enough to present offerings of great spiritual value can't be all bad."

Dane grunted in appreciation. "Nice one."

"Indeed," remarked Cobaryn. "However, now that we have achieved a stalemate, we must capitalize on it. We must build a basis for mutual understanding with the aliens."

"As I understand it," said Matsura, "a couple of our colleagues are gearing up to do just that."

"Hagedorn here," said a voice, as if on cue. "Stand by. Captain Shumar and I are going to attempt to make first contact."

"Who died and left *him* boss?" asked Dane.

But Cobaryn could tell from the Cochrane jockey's tone that he didn't really have any objection. It was simply impossible for Dane to cope with authority without making a fuss.

As the Rigelian watched, a pod escaped from the belly of the *Horatio* and made its way toward the waiting triangle ship. No doubt, both Shumar and Hagedorn were aboard.

"Good luck," Cobaryn told them.

A hundred meters shy of the alien vessel, Daniel Hagedorn grazed the last of the Christophers' seemingly ubiquitous containment suits.

The protective garment seemed to want to latch onto the escape pod, desiring rescue, but Hagedorn urged his vehicle past it. Then there was nothing but empty space between him and the triangle ship.

Twenty meters from it, Hagedorn applied the pod's braking thrusters. Then he sat back and waited.

"What do you think they're going to do?" wondered Shumar, who was ensconced next to him in the copilot's seat.

Hagedorn shook his head. "You're the scientist. You tell me."

"I'm not an ambassador," said Shumar. "I'm a surveyor. I've never made contact with anything smarter than a snail."

"And the only contact I've made has been with a laser cannon. Apparently, we're at something of a disadvantage."

For a moment, silence reigned in the pod's tiny cabin. Hagedorn took advantage of it to study the alien ship. For all its speed and power, it didn't appear to be based on a very efficient design.

"It must be gratifying," he said, using the part of his mind that wasn't focused on the triangle.

Shumar looked at him. "What do you mean?"

"Your work on Oreias Eight . . . it gave us this opportunity. You can be proud of that."

"You mean . . . if we don't make it?"

Even Hagedorn had to smile at that. "Yes."

Shumar looked at him. "Either way, Captain, it's been a pleasure working with you."

"You don't have to say that," Hagedorn told him.

His colleague nodded. "I know."

Suddenly, something began to move underneath the triangle ship. Hagedorn could feel his pulse begin to race. He willed it to slow down, knowing they would need to be sharp to pull this off.

"Is that a door opening?" asked Shumar, craning his neck to get a view of the alien's underside.

It certainly looked like a door. Hagedorn said so.

"Then let's accept their invitation," Shumar suggested.

It was why they had come, after all—in the hope that they might obtain face-to-face contact with the aliens. Carefully, Hagedorn eased the pod down and under the triangle, all the while gaining a better view of what awaited them within.

The first thing Hagedorn saw was a smaller version of the alien vessel, sitting alongside the open bay door. Then he spotted some of the aliens themselves, standing back from the opening behind what must have been a transparent force field.

They were tall, angular, and dark-skinned, with minimal, vividly colored clothing, and white hair drawn back into thick, elaborate braids. Their pale, wideset eyes followed the pod as it came up through the open doorway into an unexpectedly large chamber.

Hagedorn landed his vehicle and the door closed behind him. He took a moment to scan the aliens more closely. He noticed that all four of them had hand weapons hanging at their hips.

"They're armed," he observed.

"Wouldn't you be?" asked Shumar.

It was a good point.

Of course, neither of them had figured out yet how they were going to communicate with their hosts. But then, it wouldn't be the first time Hagedorn had been forced to improvise.

He flipped the visor of his containment suit down over his face, grateful that he had had the foresight to hold a couple of the garments back when he received Matsura's instructions.

Then, his fingers crawling across his control console, he cracked the pod's hatch and went out to meet the aliens.

Lydia Littlejohn paced the carpeted floor of her office, remembering with crystal clarity the last time she had felt compelled to do so.

It was during the last push of the war, when Dan Hagedorn led the assault on the Romulan supply depot at Cheron. The president of Earth had paced well into the night, unable to lie down, unable even to sit . . . until she finally received a message from her communications specialist that the enemy's depot had been destroyed.

And even then, she had been incapable of sleep. She had remained awake thinking about the brave men and women who had given their lives to see the Romulans defeated.

At the time, some people had predicted that Earth had seen the last of war. Littlejohn hadn't been one of them. However, she had hoped for a respite, at least—a couple of years without an armed conflict.

Surely, her people had earned it.

But mere months after the creation of the Romulan Neutral Zone, Earth colonies were again being attacked by an unknown aggressor, and the Federation had been forced to send its fleet out to address the situation.

Officially, it wasn't Earth's problem. But the endangered colonies were Earth colonies, and the ships they sent out were Earth ships, and the largest part of their crews were Earth men and women . . . and Littlejohn couldn't help feeling as if her world were at war all over again.

"President Littlejohn?" came a voice.

She looked up. "Yes, Mr. Stuckey?"

"We've received a communication from Starfleet Headquarters. Apparently, the mission to the Oreias system was a success. The fleet has made contact with the raiders and achieved a peaceful resolution."

Littlejohn felt a wave of relief wash over her. Thank God, she thought. "Were there many casualties?" she asked.

"None, ma'am."

She couldn't believe it. "None at all?"

"I made sure of it, ma'am. I knew you would want to know."

Littlejohn smiled. "Thank you, Mr. Stuckey."

"Have a pleasant evening, ma'am."

She glanced out her window, where she could see the first stars emerging in a darkening and more serene-looking sky. *I'll do that,* she answered silently. *I most definitely will do that.*

Aaron Stiles was feeling pretty good about himself as he felt his ship go to warp speed and saw the stars on his viewscreen go from points of light to long streaks.

After all, Hagedorn and Shumar had patched things up with the aliens—a species who called themselves the Nisaaren—and engineered an agreement under which Earth's colonists could remain in the system without fear of attack. It was a far better outcome than any Stiles would have predicted.

And he and his colleagues had secured it by working together—as a unified fleet, instead of two irreconcilable factions. Sure, they'd had their differences. No doubt, they always would. But they had made compromises on both sides, and found a way to construct a whole that was a little more than the sum of its parts.

Dane had surprised Stiles most of all. The Cochrane jockey had struck him as a misfit, a waste of time. But when push came to shove, he had shoved as hard as any of them. And though Stiles would never have admitted it in public, Dane had risked his life to save the *Gibraltar.*

That was the kind of action he would have expected from a wingmate in Earth Command, not a man whom he had shown nothing but hostility and disdain. Clearly, he had misjudged Connor Dane.

In fact, he conceded, he had misjudged all *three* of the butterfly catchers. It was a mistake he wouldn't make again.

"Captain Stiles?" said his navigator, interrupting his thoughts.

He turned to Rosten. "Yes, Lieutenant?"

"There's a message coming in from Earth, sir. Eyes only."

The captain smiled, believing he knew what the message was about. It was high time Abute had called to offer congratulations. But why had the man declined to address the crew as a whole?

"I'll take it in my quarters," said Stiles, and pushed himself up out of his center seat.

It wasn't until he reached his anteroom and activated his terminal that he realized why Abute had chosen to be secretive. According to the director, the board of review had made its decision . . . and selected the captain of the spanking-new *Daedalus.*

Abute had spent a lot of time overseeing, discussing, and inspecting the construction of the Federation starship *Daedalus.* In fact, he probably knew the vessel as well as the men and women who had assembled her.

So it was a special thrill for the fleet director to be the first to beam aboard the new ship, bypassing her transporter room and appearing instead on her handsome, well-appointed bridge.

He took a look around, enjoying every last detail—down to the subtle hum of the *Daedalus*'s impulse engines and the smell of her newly installed blue carpeting. He even ran his hand over the silver rail that enclosed her spacious command center.

However, Abute wasn't alone there for very long. He was soon joined by a host of dignitaries, human and otherwise, including Admiral Walker of Earth Command, Clarisse Dumont, and the highly regarded Sammak of Vulcan.

Both Walker and Dumont looked a little fidgety. But then, they had been campaigning for a long time to secure the *Daedalus* for their respective political factions—and to that very moment, neither of them knew who had been given command of the ship.

Of course, Abute knew. And for that matter, so did the fleet's six captains. But they had been ordered not to tell anyone else, so as to minimize the potential for injunctive protests and debates.

Even so, the director had expected at least a little feedback . . . if only from the captains themselves. After all, at least half of them couldn't have been thrilled with the board's decision, and Abute had expected them to tell him so.

But they hadn't. They hadn't uttered a word. In fact, in view of what had gone before, their silence had begun to seem a little eerie to him.

The director wished all six of them could have been given command of the *Daedalus.* Certainly, they deserved it. The job they did in the Oreias system, both collectively and as individuals, had exceeded everyone's expectations—including his own.

It was unfortunate that only one of them could win the prize.

Just then, he heard the beep of his communicator. Withdrawing the device from its place inside his uniform, he said, "Abute here."

"Director," said the transporter technician on a nearby Christopher, "we're ready to begin transport."

"Do so," the administrator told him. "Abute out."

He turned to the bridge's sleek silver captain's chair and waited. A moment later, Abute saw a vertical gleam of light grace the air in front of the center seat. As the gleam lengthened, the outline of a man in a blue Starfleet uniform began to form around it.

After a few seconds, the director mused, many people there would have a good idea of who the officer was. Nonetheless, they would have to wait until the fellow had completely solidified before any of them could be certain. Finally, the materialization process was complete. . . .

And Hiro Matsura took a step forward.

The man cut a gallant figure in his freshly laundered uniform, his bearing confident, his gaze steady and alert. If appearance meant anything, he was precisely what Starfleet had been looking for.

But it wasn't just Matsura's appearance that had won him the *Daedalus*. It was the uncanny resourcefulness he had displayed in the encounter with the Nisaaren, which had saved the Oreias colonies from destruction and invited the possibility of peace.

Of all the qualities the review board had considered, ingenuity was the one they had valued most—the one they believed would prove most critical to the fleet's success as the Federation moved into the future.

And Hiro Matsura had demonstrated that he had this quality in spades.

The assembled officials exchanged glances and even a few muffled remarks—some of them tinged with disapproval. But then, the director mused, it was an understandable reaction. The research faction had been made to swallow a rather bitter pill.

The military, on the other hand, had won a great victory. If anyone doubted that, he had but to observe the ear-to-ear grin of Admiral Walker, who was gazing at Matsura with unabashed pride.

Of course, neither the admiral nor anyone else had any inkling how narrow Matsura's victory had been. Right to the end, Abute had learned, the board had been vacillating between two and even three of the candidates—though no one had revealed to him the identity of the other choices.

But that was all water under the bridge, the director told himself. Captain Matsura would sit in the *Daedalus*'s center seat. The decision had been made and no one could change it.

"Ladies and gentlemen," said Abute, "I give you the commanding officer of the *U.S.S. Daedalus* . . . Captain Hiro Matsura."

The announcement was met with applause from all present—with varying degrees of enthusiasm, naturally. In the director's estimate, it was to the credit of the research people that they applauded at all.

"Congratulations," Walker told his protégé, stepping forward to offer the younger man his hand.

Matsura shook it, a bit of a smile on his face. "Thank you, sir," he responded in crisp military fashion.

Clarisse Dumont came forward as well, albeit with a good deal more reluctance. She too extended her hand to the captain of the *Daedalus*.

"I wish you all the luck in the world," she told Matsura. "And despite the disdain *some* have displayed toward the advancement of science, I hope you will see fit to—"

Unfortunately, Dumont never got to finish her statement. Before she could accomplish that, another gleam of light appeared in front of the center seat. Abute looked wonderingly at the admiral and then at Dumont, but neither of them seemed to know what was going on.

As the newcomer gained definition, the director could see that it was Captain Hagedorn. When he had finished coming together, the fellow moved forward to stand alongside Matsura.

Abute shook his head. "I don't understand," he said.

Neither Matsura nor Hagedorn provided an answer. However, another glint of light appeared in front of the captain's chair.

This time, it was Aaron Stiles who appeared there. Without

looking at Admiral Walker or anyone else, he came forward and joined his colleagues.

Walker's eyes narrowed warily beneath his thick gray brows. "What's the meaning of this?" he demanded of his former officers.

They didn't respond. But the director noticed that there was yet another gleam of light in front of the center seat, and someone else taking shape around it.

To his surprise, that someone turned out to be Bryce Shumar. And to his further surprise, Shumar took his place beside the others.

Now Abute *really* didn't get it. What did Shumar have to do with the military contingent? Hadn't he been at odds with Matsura and the others right from the start?

But Shumar wasn't the last surprise. Thirty seconds later, Cobaryn appeared as well. And after him came Dane, completing the set.

Starfleet's captains stood shoulder to shoulder, enduring the stares of everyone present. And for the first time, the director mused, the six of them looked as if they might be able to stand one another's company.

The admiral glowered at them. "Blast it," he said, "exactly what are you men trying to pull?"

"I'd like to know myself," Dumont chimed in.

Matsura turned to her. "It's simple, really. You tried to make us your pawns. You tried to pit us against one another."

"But we had a little talk after Oreias," Shumar continued, "and we realized this isn't about individual agendas. It's too important."

"Damned right," said Stiles. "My fellow captains and I have come too far to let bureaucrats of *any* stripe tell us what to do."

Dane glanced at Walker. "Or whom we should respect. After all, we're not just a bunch of space jockeys anymore."

"We're a fleet," Hagedorn noted. "A *Star*fleet."

"And in spirit, at least," Cobaryn told them, "we are here to assume command of the *Daedalus together.*"

The admiral went red in the face. "The *hell* you are! I'll see the lot of you stripped of your ranks!"

"Perhaps you would," Abute told him, "if you were in charge of this fleet. But at the risk of being rude, I must remind you that *I* am the one in charge." He glanced at the six captains. "And frankly, I am quite impressed by what I see in front of me."

Walker's eyes looked as if they were going to pop out of their sockets. "Are you out of your mind?" he growled. "This is rank insubordination!"

The director shrugged. "One might call it that, I suppose. But I prefer to think of it as courage, Admiral—and even you must admit that courage is a trait greatly to be admired."

Dumont sighed. "This *is* unexpected. But if that's the way these men feel, I certainly won't stand in their way."

Abute chuckled. "Spoken like someone who has nothing to lose and everything to gain, Ms. Dumont. I wonder . . . had it been Captain Shumar or Captain Cobaryn who was granted command of the *Daedalus,* would your reaction have been quite so forgiving?"

Dumont stiffened, but didn't seem to have an answer.

The director nodded. "I thought not."

He glanced at his fleet captains, who remained unmoved by the onlookers' reaction to their decision. He had hoped the six of them might work together efficiently someday, maybe even learn to tolerate one another as people. But this . . .

This was something Abute had never imagined in his wildest dreams.

Turning to the officials who had been invited to this occasion, he assumed a more military posture—for the sake of those who cared about such things. "I hereby turn over command of this proud new vessel, the *U.S.S. Daedalus* . . . to the brave and capable *captains* of Starfleet. May they always bring glory to their ships and to their crews."

Everyone present nodded to show their approval. That is, with the notable exception of Big Ed Walker. But that, Abute reflected, was a battle they would fight another day.

Look for STAR TREK fiction from Pocket Books

Star Trek®: The Original Series

Enterprise: The First Adventure • Vonda N. McIntyre
Final Frontier • Diane Carey
Strangers from the Sky • Margaret Wander Bonanno
Spock's World • Diane Duane
The Lost Years • J.M. Dillard
Probe • Margaret Wander Bonanno
Prime Directive • Judith and Garfield Reeves-Stevens
Best Destiny • Diane Carey
Shadows on the Sun • Michael Jan Friedman
Sarek • A.C. Crispin
Federation • Judith and Garfield Reeves-Stevens
Vulcan's Forge • Josepha Sherman & Susan Shwartz
Mission to Horatius • Mack Reynolds
Vulcan's Heart • Josepha Sherman & Susan Shwartz

Novelizations

Star Trek: The Motion Picture • Gene Roddenberry
Star Trek II: The Wrath of Khan • Vonda N. McIntyre
Star Trek III: The Search for Spock • Vonda N. McIntyre
Star Trek IV: The Voyage Home • Vonda N. McIntyre
Star Trek V: The Final Frontier • J.M. Dillard
Star Trek VI: The Undiscovered Country • J.M. Dillard
Star Trek Generations • J.M. Dillard
Starfleet Academy • Diane Carey

Star Trek books by William Shatner with Judith and Garfield Reeves-Stevens

The Ashes of Eden
The Return
Avenger
Star Trek: Odyssey (contains *The Ashes of Eden*, *The Return*, and *Avenger)*
Spectre
Dark Victory
Preserver

#1 • *Star Trek: The Motion Picture* • Gene Roddenberry
#2 • *The Entropy Effect* • Vonda N. McIntyre
#3 • *The Klingon Gambit* • Robert E. Vardeman
#4 • *The Covenant of the Crown* • Howard Weinstein

#5 • *The Prometheus Design* • Sondra Marshak & Myrna Culbreath
#6 • *The Abode of Life* • Lee Correy
#7 • *Star Trek II: The Wrath of Khan* • Vonda N. McIntyre
#8 • *Black Fire* • Sonni Cooper
#9 • *Triangle* • Sondra Marshak & Myrna Culbreath
#10 • *Web of the Romulans* • M.S. Murdock
#11 • *Yesterday's Son* • A.C. Crispin
#12 • *Mutiny on the Enterprise* • Robert E. Vardeman
#13 • *The Wounded Sky* • Diane Duane
#14 • *The Trellisane Confrontation* • David Dvorkin
#15 • *Corona* • Greg Bear
#16 • *The Final Reflection* • John M. Ford
#17 • *Star Trek III: The Search for Spock* • Vonda N. McIntyre
#18 • *My Enemy, My Ally* • Diane Duane
#19 • *The Tears of the Singers* • Melinda Snodgrass
#20 • *The Vulcan Academy Murders* • Jean Lorrah
#21 • *Uhura's Song* • Janet Kagan
#22 • *Shadow Land* • Laurence Yep
#23 • *Ishmael* • Barbara Hambly
#24 • *Killing Time* • Della Van Hise
#25 • *Dwellers in the Crucible* • Margaret Wander Bonanno
#26 • *Pawns and Symbols* • Majiliss Larson
#27 • *Mindshadow* • J.M. Dillard
#28 • *Crisis on Centaurus* • Brad Ferguson
#29 • *Dreadnought!* • Diane Carey
#30 • *Demons* • J.M. Dillard
#31 • *Battlestations!* • Diane Carey
#32 • *Chain of Attack* • Gene DeWeese
#33 • *Deep Domain* • Howard Weinstein
#34 • *Dreams of the Raven* • Carmen Carter
#35 • *The Romulan Way* • Diane Duane & Peter Morwood
#36 • *How Much for Just the Planet?* • John M. Ford
#37 • *Bloodthirst* • J.M. Dillard
#38 • *The IDIC Epidemic* • Jean Lorrah
#39 • *Time for Yesterday* • A.C. Crispin
#40 • *Timetrap* • David Dvorkin
#41 • *The Three-Minute Universe* • Barbara Paul
#42 • *Memory Prime* • Judith and Garfield Reeves-Stevens
#43 • *The Final Nexus* • Gene DeWeese
#44 • *Vulcan's Glory* • D.C. Fontana
#45 • *Double, Double* • Michael Jan Friedman
#46 • *The Cry of the Onlies* • Judy Klass

#47 • *The Kobayashi Maru* • Julia Ecklar
#48 • *Rules of Engagement* • Peter Morwood
#49 • *The Pandora Principle* • Carolyn Clowes
#50 • *Doctor's Orders* • Diane Duane
#51 • *Unseen Enemy* • V.E. Mitchell
#52 • *Home Is the Hunter* • Dana Kramer Rolls
#53 • *Ghost-Walker* • Barbara Hambly
#54 • *A Flag Full of Stars* • Brad Ferguson
#55 • *Renegade* • Gene DeWeese
#56 • *Legacy* • Michael Jan Friedman
#57 • *The Rift* • Peter David
#58 • *Face of Fire* • Michael Jan Friedman
#59 • *The Disinherited* • Peter David
#60 • *Ice Trap* • L.A. Graf
#61 • *Sanctuary* • John Vornholt
#62 • *Death Count* • L.A. Graf
#63 • *Shell Game* • Melissa Crandall
#64 • *The Starship Trap* • Mel Gilden
#65 • *Windows on a Lost World* • V.E. Mitchell
#66 • *From the Depths* • Victor Milan
#67 • *The Great Starship Race* • Diane Carey
#68 • *Firestorm* • L.A. Graf
#69 • *The Patrian Transgression* • Simon Hawke
#70 • *Traitor Winds* • L.A. Graf
#71 • *Crossroad* • Barbara Hambly
#72 • *The Better Man* • Howard Weinstein
#73 • *Recovery* • J.M. Dillard
#74 • *The Fearful Summons* • Denny Martin Flynn
#75 • *First Frontier* • Diane Carey & Dr. James I. Kirkland
#76 • *The Captain's Daughter* • Peter David
#77 • *Twilight's End* • Jerry Oltion
#78 • *The Rings of Tautee* • Dean Wesley Smith & Kristine Kathryn Rusch
#79 • *Invasion!* #1: *First Strike* • Diane Carey
#80 • *The Joy Machine* • James Gunn
#81 • *Mudd in Your Eye* • Jerry Oltion
#82 • *Mind Meld* • John Vornholt
#83 • *Heart of the Sun* • Pamela Sargent & George Zebrowski
#84 • *Assignment: Eternity* • Greg Cox
#85-87 • *My Brother's Keeper* • Michael Jan Friedman
#85 • *Republic*
#86 • *Constitution*
#87 • *Enterprise*

#88 • *Across the Universe* • Pamela Sargent & George Zebrowski
#89-94 • *New Earth*
#89 • *Wagon Train to the Stars* • Diane Carey
#90 • *Belle Terre* • Dean Wesley Smith with Diane Carey
#91 • *Rough Trails* • L.A. Graf
#92 • *The Flaming Arrow* • Kathy and Jerry Oltion

Star Trek: The Next Generation®

Metamorphosis • Jean Lorrah
Vendetta • Peter David
Reunion • Michael Jan Friedman
Imzadi • Peter David
The Devil's Heart • Carmen Carter
Dark Mirror • Diane Duane
Q-Squared • Peter David
Crossover • Michael Jan Friedman
Kahless • Michael Jan Friedman
Ship of the Line • Diane Carey
The Best and the Brightest • Susan Wright
Planet X • Michael Jan Friedman
Imzadi II: Triangle • Peter David
I, Q • Peter David & John de Lancie
The Valiant • Michael Jan Friedman
Novelizations
Encounter at Farpoint • David Gerrold
Unification • Jeri Taylor
Relics • Michael Jan Friedman
Descent • Diane Carey
All Good Things... • Michael Jan Friedman
Star Trek: Klingon • Dean Wesley Smith & Kristine Kathryn Rusch
Star Trek Generations • J.M. Dillard
Star Trek: First Contact • J.M. Dillard
Star Trek: Insurrection • J.M. Dillard

#1 • *Ghost Ship* • Diane Carey
#2 • *The Peacekeepers* • Gene DeWeese
#3 • *The Children of Hamlin* • Carmen Carter
#4 • *Survivors* • Jean Lorrah
#5 • *Strike Zone* • Peter David
#6 • *Power Hungry* • Howard Weinstein
#7 • *Masks* • John Vornholt

#8 • *The Captain's Honor* • David and Daniel Dvorkin
#9 • *A Call to Darkness* • Michael Jan Friedman
#10 • *A Rock and a Hard Place* • Peter David
#11 • *Gulliver's Fugitives* • Keith Sharee
#12 • *Doomsday World* • David, Carter, Friedman & Greenberger
#13 • *The Eyes of the Beholders* • A.C. Crispin
#14 • *Exiles* • Howard Weinstein
#15 • *Fortune's Light* • Michael Jan Friedman
#16 • *Contamination* • John Vornholt
#17 • *Boogeymen* • Mel Gilden
#18 • *Q-in-Law* • Peter David
#19 • *Perchance to Dream* • Howard Weinstein
#20 • *Spartacus* • T.L. Mancour
#21 • *Chains of Command* • W.A. McCoy & E.L. Flood
#22 • *Imbalance* • V.E. Mitchell
#23 • *War Drums* • John Vornholt
#24 • *Nightshade* • Laurell K. Hamilton
#25 • *Grounded* • David Bischoff
#26 • *The Romulan Prize* • Simon Hawke
#27 • *Guises of the Mind* • Rebecca Neason
#28 • *Here There Be Dragons* • John Peel
#29 • *Sins of Commission* • Susan Wright
#30 • *Debtor's Planet* • W.R. Thompson
#31 • *Foreign Foes* • Dave Galanter & Greg Brodeur
#32 • *Requiem* • Michael Jan Friedman & Kevin Ryan
#33 • *Balance of Power* • Dafydd ab Hugh
#34 • *Blaze of Glory* • Simon Hawke
#35 • *The Romulan Stratagem* • Robert Greenberger
#36 • *Into the Nebula* • Gene DeWeese
#37 • *The Last Stand* • Brad Ferguson
#38 • *Dragon's Honor* • Kij Johnson & Greg Cox
#39 • *Rogue Saucer* • John Vornholt
#40 • *Possession* • J.M. Dillard & Kathleen O'Malley
#41 • *Invasion! #2: The Soldiers of Fear* • Dean Wesley Smith & Kristine Kathryn Rusch
#42 • *Infiltrator* • W.R. Thompson
#43 • *A Fury Scorned* • Pamela Sargent & George Zebrowski
#44 • *The Death of Princes* • John Peel
#45 • *Intellivore* • Diane Duane
#46 • *To Storm Heaven* • Esther Friesner
#47-49 • *The Q Continuum* • Greg Cox
#47 • *Q-Space*

#48 • *Q-Zone*
#49 • *Q-Strike*
#50 • *Dyson Sphere* • Charles Pellegrino & George Zebrowski
#51-56 • *Double Helix*
#51 • *Infection* • John Gregory Betancourt
#52 • *Vectors* • Dean Wesley Smith & Kristine Kathryn Rusch
#53 • *Red Sector* • Diane Carey
#54 • *Quarantine* • John Vornholt
#55 • *Double or Nothing* • Peter David
#56 • *The First Virtue* • Michael Jan Friedman & Christie Golden
#57 • *The Forgotten War* • William Fortschen
#58-59 • *Gemworld* • John Vornholt
#58 • *Gemworld #1*
#59 • *Gemworld #2*

Star Trek: Deep Space Nine®

Warped • K.W. Jeter
Legends of the Ferengi • Ira Steven Behr & Robert Hewitt Wolfe
The Lives of Dax • Marco Palmieri, ed.
Novelizations
Emissary • J.M. Dillard
The Search • Diane Carey
The Way of the Warrior • Diane Carey
Star Trek: Klingon • Dean Wesley Smith & Kristine Kathryn Rusch
Trials and Tribble-ations • Diane Carey
Far Beyond the Stars • Steve Barnes
What You Leave Behind • Diane Carey

#1 • *Emissary* • J.M. Dillard
#2 • *The Siege* • Peter David
#3 • *Bloodletter* • K.W. Jeter
#4 • *The Big Game* • Sandy Schofield
#5 • *Fallen Heroes* • Dafydd ab Hugh
#6 • *Betrayal* • Lois Tilton
#7 • *Warchild* • Esther Friesner
#8 • *Antimatter* • John Vornholt
#9 • *Proud Helios* • Melissa Scott
#10 • *Valhalla* • Nathan Archer
#11 • *Devil in the Sky* • Greg Cox & John Gregory Betancourt
#12 • *The Laertian Gamble* • Robert Sheckley

#13 • *Station Rage* • Diane Carey
#14 • *The Long Night* • Dean Wesley Smith & Kristine Kathryn Rusch
#15 • *Objective: Bajor* • John Peel
#16 • *Invasion! #3: Time's Enemy* • L.A. Graf
#17 • *The Heart of the Warrior* • John Gregory Betancourt
#18 • *Saratoga* • Michael Jan Friedman
#19 • *The Tempest* • Susan Wright
#20 • *Wrath of the Prophets* • David, Friedman & Greenberger
#21 • *Trial by Error* • Mark Garland
#22 • *Vengeance* • Dafydd ab Hugh
#23 • *The 34th Rule* • Armin Shimerman & David R. George III
#24-26 • *Rebels* • Dafydd ab Hugh
    #24 • *The Conquered*
    #25 • *The Courageous*
    #26 • *The Liberated*
#27 • *A Stitch in Time* • Andrew J. Robinson

Star Trek: Voyager®

Mosaic • Jeri Taylor
Pathways • Jeri Taylor
Captain Proton! • Dean Wesley Smith

Novelizations

Caretaker • L.A. Graf
Flashback • Diane Carey
Day of Honor • Michael Jan Friedman
Equinox • Diane Carey

#1 • *Caretaker* • L.A. Graf
#2 • *The Escape* • Dean Wesley Smith & Kristine Kathryn Rusch
#3 • *Ragnarok* • Nathan Archer
#4 • *Violations* • Susan Wright
#5 • *Incident at Arbuk* • John Gregory Betancourt
#6 • *The Murdered Sun* • Christie Golden
#7 • *Ghost of a Chance* • Mark A. Garland & Charles G. McGraw
#8 • *Cybersong* • S.N. Lewitt
#9 • *Invasion! #4: Final Fury* • Dafydd ab Hugh
#10 • *Bless the Beasts* • Karen Haber
#11 • *The Garden* • Melissa Scott
#12 • *Chrysalis* • David Niall Wilson
#13 • *The Black Shore* • Greg Cox

#14 • *Marooned* • Christie Golden
#15 • *Echoes* • Dean Wesley Smith, Kristine Kathryn Rusch & Nina Kiriki Hoffman
#16 • *Seven of Nine* • Christie Golden
#17 • *Death of a Neutron Star* • Eric Kotani
#18 • *Battle Lines* • Dave Galanter & Greg Brodeur

Star Trek®: New Frontier

New Frontier #1-4 Collector's Edition • Peter David
 #1 • *House of Cards* • Peter David
 #2 • *Into the Void* • Peter David
 #3 • *The Two-Front War* • Peter David
 #4 • *End Game* • Peter David
#5 • *Martyr* • Peter David
#6 • *Fire on High* • Peter David
The Captain's Table #5 • *Once Burned* • Peter David
Double Helix #5 • *Double or Nothing* • Peter David
#7 • *The Quiet Place* • Peter David
#8 • *Dark Allies* • Peter David

Star Trek®: Invasion!

#1 • *First Strike* • Diane Carey
#2 • *The Soldiers of Fear* • Dean Wesley Smith & Kristine Kathryn Rusch
#3 • *Time's Enemy* • L.A. Graf
#4 • *Final Fury* • Dafydd ab Hugh
Invasion! Omnibus • various

Star Trek®: Day of Honor

#1 • *Ancient Blood* • Diane Carey
#2 • *Armageddon Sky* • L.A. Graf
#3 • *Her Klingon Soul* • Michael Jan Friedman
#4 • *Treaty's Law* • Dean Wesley Smith & Kristine Kathryn Rusch
The Television Episode • Michael Jan Friedman
Day of Honor Omnibus • various

Star Trek®: The Captain's Table

#1 • *War Dragons* • L.A. Graf
#2 • *Dujonian's Hoard* • Michael Jan Friedman
#3 • *The Mist* • Dean Wesley Smith & Kristine Kathryn Rusch
#4 • *Fire Ship* • Diane Carey
#5 • *Once Burned* • Peter David
#6 • *Where Sea Meets Sky* • Jerry Oltion
The Captain's Table Omnibus • various

Star Trek®: The Dominion War

#1 • *Behind Enemy Lines* • John Vornholt
#2 • *Call to Arms...* • Diane Carey
#3 • *Tunnel Through the Stars* • John Vornholt
#4 • *...Sacrifice of Angels* • Diane Carey

Star Trek® Books available in Trade Paperback

Omnibus Editions
Invasion! Omnibus • various
Day of Honor Omnibus • various
The Captain's Table Omnibus • various
Star Trek: Odyssey • William Shatner with Judith and Garfield Reeves-Stevens

Other Books
Legends of the Ferengi • Ira Steven Behr & Robert Hewitt Wolfe
Strange New Worlds, vols. I and II • Dean Wesley Smith, ed.
Adventures in Time and Space • Mary Taylor
The Lives of Dax • Marco Palmieri, ed.
Captain Proton! • Dean Wesley Smith
The Klingon Hamlet • Wil'yam Shex'pir
New Worlds, New Civilizations • Michael Jan Friedman
Enterprise Logs • Carol Greenburg, ed.